WHITEGIRL
Kate Manning

"One of the many virtues of this remarkable novel is its effort to unravel the complicated relationship that many Americans have with female beauty." —Carolyn See, *The Washington Post*

"A literary and emotional tour de force that also manages to address a real issue: race in America."
—Amy Wilentz, author of *Martyrs' Crossing*

"[A] compelling debut . . . an engagingly provocative page-turner."
—*Kirkus Reviews*

"[Manning] delicately handle[s] the intimacies of an interracial relationship." —*Entertainment Weekly*

"Manning poses tantalizing questions about race, identity and beauty."
—*The Arizona Republic*

"How marriage can become a casualty of fame and celebrity, to say nothing of racial tensions, is an explosive and timely topic, and Manning makes a riveting story out of it." —*Toronto Sun*

Whitegirl

Kate Manning

Delta Trade Paperbacks

WHITEGIRL
A Delta Book

PUBLISHING HISTORY
Dial Press hardcover edition published February 2002
Delta trade paperback edition / June 2003

Published by
Bantam Dell
A Division of Random House, Inc.
New York, New York

Book design by Virginia Norey

Library of Congress Catalog Card Number: 2001053781

ISBN 0-385-33721-3

Manufactured in the United States of America
Published simultaneously in Canada

BVG   10 9 8 7 6 5 4 3 2 1

For my parents, Joan and Jim
And for my husband, Carey

People are trapped in history,
and history is trapped in them.

—*James Baldwin*

1.

was not always a white girl. I used to be just Charlotte. A person named Charlotte Halsey. But when I met Milo, when I fell in love with him, I became White, like a lit lightbulb is white. In the mirror there is my skin the color of sand, hair the color of butter, eyes blue as seawater. Just so bleachy white I am practically clear. In a heavy snowfall you'd have trouble picking me out. Even in the photographs from my so-called glamour-puss career it's hard to tell which blond is me. There I am, with what they called my "trademark smile," square teeth like Chiclets, my "fresh" look; there's my "peaches-and-cream" complexion, more cream than peach, all of them talking about me as if I were food.

Milo is black, what they call "Black," only not to me. Brown skin, a shade the newer catalogues would call *cinnamon stick* or *cocoa*. The palms of his hands are pink as the lining of seashells, and his eyes are green like beer-bottle glass. You in your sunny kitchen, or your office cubicle, or your local shopping mall may not mind that the word *black* means "soiled and dirty," means "characterized by the absence of light" or "evil or wicked or gloomy." God knows, I could have cared less myself, before.

Look it up, Milo says, it's what you hear of black: blackmail, black magic, black sheep, black mark, black-hearted, et cetera. You see what I'm saying? When I argue about this, somebody white always says: "Get over it. It's a word. It describes a group. Why be technical about it?" *It's not a word*, I think now. *It's sticks and stones.*

My daughter is called black but I am called white, which has a different bag of definitions altogether.

Why we can't call everybody by their names—*Milo and Charlotte Robicheaux and their daughter, Hallie*—I don't know. I'm sick of it, the language of it. Names will never hurt you. Ha. Names like Black, like White, will break your heart, crack it open like a melon dropped on the pavement.

Milo is always preceded by Black, and trailed by it. He wakes up in the morning to "the first black Olympic skier," "the black athlete who . . ." and goes to bed at night with it, "the blond wife of black Olympian Milo Robicheaux." His skin, my hair. Our little piano key relationship.

To me he has mostly been just Milo. I stopped seeing skin a long time ago with him. They say lovers can find each other just by using the sense of smell; that we are all really animals in that way, no different from dogs or deer. I know it's true. I could find Milo blind in a room of men, would know him by the keloid lump of a vaccination scar on his left upper arm, would know by touch the large knees knotted from surgery, the smell of him like pine trees in a snowy wind. I could pick him out just by the slow rising of his breath while he slept. So no, until this happened, up to the time of the assault, he was not black, not to me. He was Milo. He was my husband; a man—famous, okay—who liked parties and dancing, fast music, high speed of any kind. We had fights that made me cry. And him, too, he cried, too. We had long weeks without talking. We had days of just fucking, all day in bed, eating and drinking and never getting dressed. He made me smile.

He cut a smile, they said, in my neck.

Tried to kill me with broken glass, a smashed wine bottle, one of a couple I emptied that night. But he botched it, mostly hitting the silver necklace, missing the important arteries and veins, which saved my life, but not my voice. Left me mute and bleeding on the marble tiles of our kitchen floor.

Or maybe he didn't. I don't know. Jesus, I just really don't know if he did, so get away from me please. Leave me alone with your questions.

Milo loves me, I believe this. He loved me, he always said, more than he loved himself, more than he loved screwing, or skiing deep powder, or drinking dark cognac. Loved *me*. Despite *her*. I believe that. In his jail cell where he is now he writes to me: "Charlotte, please, please." He wants me to come see him, says if I'll only come, he knows I'll see the truth. Will *see*, goddammit. But if I go—if I could go, if I would—would I find out anything new? Who would my eyes discover? Milo of my dreams, of my whole early life and up till now? My Milo? Or the man who cut me up? At this point, I don't know if I've ever really been able to see him plain, underneath that skin on him, the man there, or for that matter, if he's ever seen me. Perhaps it is true what they said all along, what Darryl Haynes said: that Milo saw my hair, period. For him I was just some fever dream of hair. Some ornament, like another statuette to put on the shelf next to his medals and his loving cups. And if that's true, then was his friend Darryl right about me, too? That Milo was some kind of a taste, as he called it, of the forbidden fruit? "Just your Chocolate Fantasy," Darryl told me, laughing. "Just you on your Black Booty Quest."

"We don't see color, we see each other," I said back, and believed smugly that we had gotten past that, blind to it, besotted as sweethearts no matter what, mad for him, and he just always needing me, Charlotte. Until he didn't. Until he tried to kill me. They say he did it.

They say. It's certainly possible. It's certainly something he might have resorted to, what with all those green algae blooms of jealousy between us, the he-said, she-said of it, not to mention living through all our fucked-up, zebra-stripe, history-book history played out right here in the spotlight of our breakneck lives.

The police say: no question. They run down the evidence: My blood on his hands. Cuts on his hands. Glass on his shoes. The fact that he resisted arrest. Punched a cop. They found him leaning over me where I lay bleeding.

He says: He was trying to save me, breathe some air back into my lungs, kiss of life, mouth to mouth. So did he try to kill me? I don't know. Maybe. If he didn't, though, who did? It was dark when it happened, and I was out of it, messed up, messed up.

"You clean up this mess!" my mother would say to me, and I would try, and never get it right, crumbs all over the couch, smears of jelly on the linoleum. I'd have to go get the hairbrush, have to stand commanded to be still while she whacked my backside with the brush. She hated a mess. We had plastic covers on all our furniture. We had plastic lining the walls of the staircase, vinyl sheets of it, protecting the paint job from our hands. "There now," she'd say, smack smack smack. "Now you'll remember."

I wish I did remember. They come and ask me questions. I meet with the detectives, mouthing words, forcing whispers through my smashed larynx, or writing notes. I meet with the prosecutors, telling them what I know, going back to the beginning, over and over. They lay it out on the table, in a time line, all their evidence, pictures, stains, things the neighbors heard in the night: Mrs. Deraney across the street said there was loud music. But there was always loud music. John Cipriani, making out with his girlfriend in the parked car, heard shouting. Nothing new there, either. Not lately anyway. Blood, music, shouting, mouth to mouth, et cetera. Fill in the blanks. Find the missing clue.

Piece by piece, my daddy used to say, putting together the weekly jigsaw puzzle on our glass coffee table. *Piece by piece, Sunshine*, he said, coming home from work, snapping a male piece into a female, lifting a section into place after church. My sister and I peeled off our white gloves to help him, the boys rolled up their shirt cuffs, and we all took off our painful shoes. We did a big round one once, called "Little Red Riding Hood's Hood." It was a solid red circle, nearly impossible to put together. *Find the edges first, Sunshine*, my daddy would tell me, *start there*. While we worked he started telling us about how puzzles are made, some jigsaw technique to it, when my little sister Diana said she had to go to the bathroom. "Don't you interrupt me!" he shouted at her out of nowhere. He dumped the whole puzzle on the ground, swept it right off the table in a big dramatic brush of his big arm. "I was talking," he said through his teeth, and his arm flew in one fell swoop. The puzzle was broken on the floor. I think of it any time I hear the words *one fell swoop*. We four had to pick it up and finish the whole thing before we could go to bed. We cried and he said, "Go ahead, cry." He said, "On your knees, then, and pray to be sorry." We got down and prayed. Prayed to figure it out, put it together. We picked up the red pieces and our tears dripped on them. We finished past midnight, all our fingers red from the wet red cardboard.

It was all one color, all the pieces of Red Riding Hood's Hood were red. Whereas, I don't need to be told now, this puzzle, mine, is two noncolors, black and white. Negro and Caucasian. Much trickier, more treacherous.

Looking down now at the threadline of waves breaking below our window, by habit I search for Milo's wetsuit shape on his surfboard out there, riding fast, standing in a crouch, finding the wild ride in. He likes so much to go fast, the drug of unchecked speed. It must be hard for him in that small cell, holding still. I think he thinks about me, and I miss him, who I thought he was, and I hate him, my fingers wandering up, tracing the pink itchy ridges of scar necklacing my throat. I would like just to push him off a high building, except that he would drop so fast, and death by flying would of course be his choice of death, and why would I give him even that pleasure now? Better just to let him sit with no windows in the tiny, tiny cell, caged up like a beast. Although, you know, you're not supposed to compare a black man to an animal. Not if you're me, anyway, you can't. It's racist. Everything is, you know, for me. All this trying to talk about race; it's like being in a leghold trap, where the caught creature has to gnaw off her own leg to get out of it.

2.

I met Milo in the middle of the night. He woke me up out of a beery sleep, out of my hard and narrow college-dorm bed. I was lying there with my hands folded across my heart. Freshman Repose: 1974. My best friend of nine weeks, my unhappy roommate, Claire, slept in an identical bed across from mine, blotto, a curl of knees and sheets and clothing. The air of our room was close and hot, the breath of cigarettes and beer rising up from us drunken girls, mingling with the scent of our shampoo and our lotions and wet winter socks drying. Outside our door, the corridors of the big granite dormitory were quiet, but in certain rooms there were lights burning, gusts of wild laughter, the throb of music, husky whispers.

I woke to shouting, pounding on doors, our door.

"Let me in!" a guy was hollering, drunk. "Angela, open up, you hear?" He was hammering his fists, maybe kicking his boots, so the slim mirror on the back of our door rattled. I staggered up half sleeping, with my nightgown trailing behind like a ghost costume. "Who are you looking for?" I whispered.

"Angela Williams, goddammit," said the man outside.

The square-headed frat boys with their hard muscles and their hyena laughter were having a school-night party in one of the houses across the quadrangle. This would be a drunken pledge, I thought, looking for his date.

"This is not her room," I said, resting my head on the back of the door. "She doesn't live here."

"Excuse me. I'm sorry. Pardon me," said the voice. "Sorry, sorry, excuse me, please, my sincere apologies."

"It's okay," I said, and watched my reflection talking in close-up, breath misting on the mirror. "You've got the wrong room."

"Again, my regrets," he said. "What's your name, so I may apologize properly?" His face must have been close up to the doorjamb, right opposite mine. He was whispering now, through the crack, so I put my lips there.

"Charlotte," I said, "I'm Charlotte Halsey."

"Well, well," he said. "Call me Embarrassed. Call me Chagrined to disturb you. Call me Mortified."

"Hey, Mortified." The word made me laugh. "Mortified who?"

"Mortified Milo Robicheaux," he said, with a husk of flirtation or possibly humor in his tone, it was hard to tell. His voice made me picture an elegant, white-tied, English gent, tipping a top hat. "Forgive me for disturbing you."

"Good night then," I said, but stayed with my lips by the door crack, curious, woozy from beer.

"Sweet dreams, Charlotte Halsey."

I heard him clomp down the hall, whistling. Back in bed, I dreamed somebody was gliding on runners into the valley, sliding through the leafless woods and climbing up the fire escape outside, creeping like Spider-Man along the window ledge to shatter the cold glass over my head. I cried out and opened my eyes and it was late morning. Claire laughed at me and ice cracked off the branches, tinkling to the ground with the sound of fairy bells.

This college, Cabot College, sits among the Green Mountains of Vermont, and is always in a state of heartbreaking and extreme beauty: the bulk of hills rounding up into skies the color of swimming pools; the fur of snow trimming the black tree branches; a glare of sun off the white landscape that gilds the buildings and people at the same time it blinds you.

I loved it. It terrified me. I walked the paths of the campus with my lungs full of sharp air, wondering was I far enough away now, for happiness to be possible? I did not miss my Napa County hometown of Conestoga, California, where anyone looking at me saw Beauty Pageant

Charlotte, or Christian Charlotte, or Drunk-Driving Charlotte; where my parents saw the thread hanging from my hem, the smudge on my term paper, the blot on my reputation, the mud on the back of my sweater from lying down in the grass with Dave Mueller.

Now I was on my own. I was not the daughter who had to dust the figurines on Saturday. I could stay up late. I could say fuck. I could decide not to pray. *Fuck praying!*

And of course as soon as I thought that, my guilty fear came swinging out and kicked me like the lower leg hit by a doctor's hammer. I would go to hell for thinking such a thing. No I wouldn't. *Yes you will,* there was my father's voice again, *You will not be raptured.* Ha. *Fuck that.* As I walked along I made myself think it again, practicing the courage of my conviction. It was a beautiful morning. Way too cold to fear the fiery furnaces of hell. I filled my lungs with frozen air and watched the students passing me, watching to see how they saw me, what they thought when they looked.

I was terribly worried about how I looked, how everyone else looked. Beauty was most of the seven virtues in our household. Skin and nail beauty, hair and clothing beauty, leg and figure beauty, and what my mother claimed was most precious: Beauty inside. *In here,* she would say, and place her open hand on the flat part of her chest. *If your thoughts are beautiful, you will be, too.*

As far as I could tell, about 85 percent of my thoughts were hideous: *My teacher's mean, my stomach hurts, my sister's annoying.* Obviously, *in here* I was not beautiful, never would be, despite my mother's tutelage.

My gorgeous mother, Barbara, sold Avon products, going door-to-door in her heels and her suit just like Jackie's. Diana and I went with her once in a while, never the boys. She drove to a neighborhood and we listened in the backseat as she practiced her lines, her pitch. We waited in the car, and when she finished in one house and went to try the next one, she waved to us as if she was sitting on a float wearing white gloves up to her elbows. She carried this enormous, thrilling case that opened up into a display of cremes and shadows and glosses. The pots and samples looked like licks of candy, whipped frostings, and jellies. The eye shadow came in cakes. At our mother's knee my sister and I contoured our cheeks and made our eyes look big as bodies of water. We pushed back our cuticles and applied coats of polish to our nails. She tucked soft puffs of cotton between our wet painted toes. We held still. We held our breaths, loving her, loving the polish smells and all the equipment and the touch of her light hands on our feet, our cheeks. She was girlish, clapping and cooing when we paraded around. Her eyes went bright with pleasure at the sight of us. She was the prettiest mother, the one whose dress was admired at church, the one with the longest nails, the smoothest skin. With her we studied the fashion tips and the makeover pictures like a catechism. The homily was: "Anything for beauty." For gifts, we were given leg waxes at twelve, new blond hairs peeled up from their roots on our shins. We were in all the pageants, tap-dancing with pink tulle poufing out from our bony waists like a nightmare of cotton candy, ringlets bouncing. I was Little Miss Artichoke once, when I was eight. Then, at thirteen, I won Miss Junior Organic Produce. My mother jumped up and down, shrieking She Won She Won She Won like her horse had come in, like it was the rhinestones on her own head, the bouquet of hydroponically grown lettuces in her own arms.

"Charlotte looks just like you," said the head judge, when he met my mother.

"Does she?" she asked. "Thank you." Her eyes glittered when she smiled up at him, and she swallowed hard with some feeling I couldn't recognize exactly. She had won pageants, too, in her day.

"I'm so happy," she said, driving home. "It makes me so happy when you win."

But that was the day, in the car, when I quietly told her I didn't really want to be in any more contests, not beauty, not talent. I said I was shy. The contests made my stomach ache, made me throw up behind the reviewing stand.

Oh, that made her mad. I was just being *stupid*. What was *wrong* with me!? I had won, *for goodness sake*. I tried not to cry when she said that, and when she saw my throat working up and down, my head turned to the window, she softened up a little. "Your beauty is a gift from God, angel," she said, reaching across the front seat to push my hair off my face. "God wants us to use our gifts."

"You're the one who wants me to use them," I whispered.

"What did you say?"

I had to tell her. I couldn't stand the pressure, the eyes of the judges, the way they all watched me, inspecting me for flaws. I had to say it. *You're the one who wants me to use them.*

She looked over at me, crushed and livid. She nearly drove the car off the road. "The choice is not yours," she said. "I've paid the entry fee."

My father was my savior that time. "Fine," he said, when my mother reported on me. "No more pageants." He thought it was time for me to be in a Bible study group anyway. I started Kids for Christ that fall. I was fourteen. My mother focused on my sister's pageants now, and while she still talked to both us girls about how we would grow up to be wives with husbands for our heads, *For the husband is the head of the wife, as Christ is the head of the Church*, quoting to us regularly from the little Bible Promise Book she kept in her purse, she seemed gradually more annoyed and distracted. Was it because I declined to compete for the county title? I don't know. Probably it started then and went on from there.

My wardrobe changed. My hair. My attitude. I refused to sleep in rollers. I had Flower Child hair; but not for politics, for fashion. Between me and my mother it was a problem of styles, at first, anyway. I wore pants to school, bell-bottoms with peasant blouses, and left my sweater sets at home. She got furious over this. I talked back. I argued. By fifteen and sixteen it got worse. I had questions about God. How could He really care whether I wore a halter top or not? How would the length of my skirts matter on the Last Day? The questions were what made my father furious. He sent me for a talk with Pastor Hanneman. I got caught calling him Hiney-man behind his back. Soon I was sent to him weekly.

"A true Christian wears fashions that please the Lord," the pastor said. "If you do not allow Him to guide you, we must ask: Are you, in fact, a true Christian?"

I wanted to be a true Christian, but I didn't see how I could and still be Charlotte—wearing what I wore and feeling what I felt. It was a test I was failing daily. In our house, all through high school, it was tense and getting tenser. "Turn that off," my mother said, about my radio. "Shh," my dad said, when I spoke. "Have respect! Sit up straight! Comb your hair! Right now! Clean up this mess! Charlotte! Charlotte! Charlotte!" I had to get out and I did. I got to college.

"Hey, Charlotte." "Hi, Charlotte." " 'Lo, how you doin'?" This was the routine of my fellow Cabot students passing me on the way to breakfast. "Hi!" I said. "Hi, Hi, Hi." I prepared for the approach of each one I passed, looking down at my feet, then boom, right up into their eyes, smile like a dare: Do you like me? It was a sorry kind of game, hoping the sun behind me made my hair a halo. I watched how they looked at me, the handsome boys with Greek statuary faces glancing away as I came toward them, the snow squeaking under their thick boots, and then just before it was too late, there would be a hard little narrowing of their eyes, into a frank smile of...what? Something like lust, or appreciation, that made me grateful each time, but also gave me a scared feeling, like trumping some-body. Like they didn't know what they were seeing. Who they were smil-ing at. Sometimes girls talked in pairs about me behind their cupped hands. Still, I saw their lips curl.

My mother's lessons played like tapes in my head. *They're just burn-ing up with envy of you,* she'd say. *If you have a problem, you can be sure it's jealousy, because they're looking at you, your blue eyes and golden waterfall hair, Charlotte sweetie. You have what everybody wants, women to be you, men to have you. All your life, wherever you go, every-one will love you.*

But I did not expect anyone to love me, to be quite honest with you.

That morning as I walked to breakfast I saw somebody across the big field coming toward me carrying skis. As he came closer I saw that it was a black man. *Strange, to see a black man carrying skis,* I thought. And then I was immediately arguing with myself: *Well, why is it strange? Because when have you ever seen a black man ski? They don't ski. Never seen a black person on skis. But why wouldn't they ski? Everybody skis here, this is a college known for skiing. What do you mean, "they," anyway?*

These thoughts were unsettling, so that my face was not properly arranged as he approached. I was staring outright at him, a tall, square-shouldered student with dark brown skin. His eyes were—green. I had never seen that, realized it was possible. *Green eyes, my God,* I thought, and couldn't help my mind's big leap backward two hundred years, willy-nilly, thinking of Thomas Jefferson and Sally something, his slave's name was; picturing the smiling woman in the red head wrap on the Aunt Jemima pancake-mix box coupled with the pigtailed president on the nickel head, making a brown-skinned child with green eyes. And in that instant, when the guy with his skis passed me, I was squinting as if blinded by snow glare. I stepped off the path to let him go by. In the space of that brief second, there appeared to be a smirk on his face, or an exhale of disgust.

Maybe he thinks I thought he was going to rape me, or take my money. But of course I wasn't thinking that! Just because he's a black man? Why would he assume that? That's not the way I think. But perhaps he assumed nothing. Maybe he was passing me on the path and I was getting out of the way of his skis. I was letting him pass as I would anyone carrying skis. Anyone.

Now something about my morning was spoiled. I was rattled. He had smirked at me. As if I had done just what he thought I'd do. *Isn't that just like a white girl,* he was thinking now. In my white town there was not much in the way of black people. We didn't have any black kids in our school. Not even one. Some lived in the town of Napa, down 37 from us. But we only saw them in the street, in shops or a restaurant, once in a while. On TV there was Redd Foxx in a cap, and Flip Wilson in a waitress uniform. There was Martin Luther King, Jr., and pictures of German shepherds leaping at the throats of black girls in pastel dresses and white gloves. At home there was five-year-old me singing *Catch a nigger by the toe,* and Mom, furious, saying "Don't you ever use that word! We are all God's children. We are not racists!" There was my grandfather watching the news when Dr. King was killed, saying *I don't see what all the fuss is about. He was a troublemaker.* In school we had standard assignments about being created equal, about George Washington Carver and the peanut.

But when did you ever see a black man ski?

Thinking about it made my head feel boiled. I went to the dining hall and drank saccharine coffee and studied the Bible. This was not for any reasons of faith, or an attempt to find meaning to what had just transpired on the pathways of my college or my life so far. It was for my Religion class. I was reading the Old Testament for credit, for my mom Barbara and my dad Arthur, to convince them I would not continue my spectacular fall from grace, and that here in the pure, sparkling whiteness of Vermont I was living a righteous life with God, still renouncing Satan with all my might.

Of course, I had failed to do the assignment. I was frantically reading Deuteronomy at breakfast, guilt and hangover and caffeine perking in my veins in equal measure. *Take heed lest you forget the LORD your God....*

To me, God was real. Not real the way He was when I was little. Then He was my friend. In Sunday school we sang *Jesus loves me, this I know*. In church, Diana and I would be sobbing, sometimes, just sobbing. Because it felt like He loved us so much. *He holds you in the palm of His hand*, the congregation sang, and the pastor asked all the little ones to come up and receive His blessing. We closed our eyes and raised our arms and the pastor put his hands on us. The music was loud and emotional. *He will raise you up on eagle's wings, bear you on the breath of dawn*...I sobbed and Diana sobbed, up there by the pulpit in our smocked dresses and our hair ribbons. We were overcome. I loved it. I invited Jesus into my heart. The grown-ups looked at us with damp eyes and their hands raised, witnessing, little knowing that Charlotte Halsey was thinking of God as a kind of amusement park, hoping to get a ride, an eagle ride; imagining myself in His hand, as if He could scoop me up like Gulliver holding a Lilliputian. It sounded so cool. I loved God then. My friend, God.

Now He was real in a different way. For example, He knew I had a hangover. I pictured Him watching me in the cafeteria, watching every moment, Him and Father Time and Santa Claus—basically the same guy: same basic beard. With one yank you could get it off, that beard, leaving a gray gum stain behind on the chin. I was always having these blasphemous thoughts about serious things—God, black men with skis—but I was good at tamping them down, finding the proper line to toe.

Toe the line. That was my father's expression. God was definitely real to my father. You could be talking about anything: school, what's for dinner, a football game, and there was God being an expert on the subject.

Me: Who's winning?

Dad: Not the 49ers. He just must be saving them for next season, I don't know. Or He may wait for the fourth quarter. They must not have prayed hard enough about winning, Sunshine.

Sunshine. Honey, Angel. He had sweet little names for me then, but later not so sweet: *Heretic, damned, lost.*

My dad was gorgeous as a young man. Like James Dean, I'm not kidding. Not with the lip-hung cigarette, of course, but in certain pictures he has bedroom eyes, a sidelong glance, with his hair sculpted and also his cheekbones. He was called Art then, not Arthur. Art Halsey. I can see exactly what my mother saw in him. He was kind and gentle, my dad. He said I was God's gift. He said we all were. Peter, Charlotte, Diana, Sean.

The four of us. We were precious. He was affectionate. Big bear hugs and *Hello, precious, how's my Sunshine this morning?* But there were problems. His temper. *Don't you dare!* A confusing person. So friendly, *Hey, how ya doin'?* slap you on the back, kiss on the cheek, *Don't you look beautiful?* one minute, the next, thundering and rampaging around like bad weather. Or withdrawn in the backyard hammock. Eyes closed but not asleep. Rubbing his temples. What did he think about? God, I guessed. But I didn't know half the story then, what kid ever does?

Are you okay, Daddy? When I was small—five or six—I used to go out there and climb into the hammock with him. He smelled of aftershave and the stomach acid tablets he chewed all the time. *You okay?*

Sure. Just tired, just tired.

But really he was melancholy. I wanted to cheer him up, make him happy.

Which was what I was still trying to do, long-distance, reading Deuteronomy in the dining hall. It was boring, with all its silly food rules, what to eat, what not; and scary, with its warnings close to the bone for me, *if you forget the LORD your God and go after other gods, you shall surely perish....* I was trying hard not to think about the Last Day, or have the irreligious thought about God's beard, or that Deuteronomy sounded like a medical procedure to remove something *(have you heard? he's just undergone a deuteronomy ... or is that deuterectomy?)* when I saw Jack Sutherland, with his tray full of breakfast, emerging from the cafeteria line and searching for somewhere to sit.

You could see a shift of attention in the room. You could see girls sliding their eyes toward him, boys watching them notice him. Somebody said, "Oh, God. It's him," as if she meant Him, as if Jack were sent to Earth for a Holy purpose. Their attention influenced me. Everybody seemed to want him, so I would want him, too. I wanted him to sit with me. Then, I wanted him to be my boyfriend. I waited till he got about a table away from me, till he was within eyeshot, and then, just at the right moment, raised my gaze to his face, just hoping he would feel it.

3.

Jack was tall and fine as what you read about in fairy stories when you are young. You could use words like *dashing* about him. You could talk about him as if he were riding around on a steed, or a unicorn. He was a Californian, like me. He had the same devil-may-care personality of the dangerous boys I went to high school with. In the way he carried himself, the set of his eyes, narrowed down a little with his mouth torqued up on one side, you could see he had some private, possibly cruel amusement going on in his mind. He wore baseball caps backward on his head, and there was a fountain spout of yellow hair sticking up from under the plastic fastening in front. Veins like vine tendrils climbed up his lean muscly arms. I admired that. Also he was a champion ski racer, one of the best on the college circuit, which meant he was a kind of celebrity at Cabot.

I think now that I had what Claire called the Magpie Syndrome, after the magpie, a bird that likes flash, goes after anything shiny. In a magpie's nest you are likely to find lost earrings, scraps of foil, a car key, somebody's glass eye, filaments of tinsel. None of which are all that comfortable to have in a nest, but they are the heart's desire of the magpie, for whom glamour is all seven of the virtues.

In the cafeteria, I looked up from my Bible at Jack as he walked with his tray and smiled just enough. He stopped at my table and swung his long denim leg up over the back of a chair to sit. "Hey," he said.

"Hey, Jack."

"Git your nose out of that book, kid," he said. He put some twang in his voice that made him sound vaguely Texan. "You look all serious."

"Ja-ack. It's the Bible."

"*Sumimasen*," said Jack. "*Charlotte-san sumimasen yo.*" Jack was a Japanese studies major. He told me once he picked Japanese because he knew he could make a lot of money in Japan. Yen were apparently all over the place, ready to be changed into dollars. People said Jack's Japanese was nearly flawless, not that I would know, but it made me laugh, to hear this squeaky-mouse language coming out of his cowboy personality. It reminded me of a song my uncle Paul used to play on the piano that went: "*Chinky chinky Chinaman, washed his face in a frying pan, combed his hair with a garden rake, saw his sweetheart in the lake....*" He used to sing it every Thanksgiving, clowning around with his upper teeth bucked out over his bottom lip, eyes squinting.

"*Ohayoo gozaimasu, Charlotte-san. Genki desu-ka?*" Jack was asking me a question.

"Speak English," I said. He grinned at me. "How's your team doing?" I said. "You guys winning?"

"Fierce! Fierce, fierce, fierce. You been on the hill yet this week?"

"Excellent," I told him.

"Supreme bumps, huh?" Jack said.

"Yeah," I said. "But not like home."

In the California Sierras the snow was soft and feathery. The mountains had endless, wide trails. I learned to ski by going on church trips and getting invited on weekends with the families of my school friends. My style was not fancy. I could perform what was called *wedeln*. I managed to be graceful. But here in Vermont there were nasty little dark rocks coming up to eat the bottoms of your skis, yellow slicks of ice stuttering your edges. Sometimes I had to sideslip the whole way down. "There's just no comparison," I said.

"Naw, you're right, never good as home," said Jack. "You goin' back, Christmas?"

"Yeah," I said. Mom and Diana would get the Christmas tree out of its plastic bag in the attic and put it in the living room, dolled up with tiny white lights and white ribbons. On the lawn, Dad would put out the manger with the plaster Baby Jesus in it—*the Baby Cheese*, I used to think he was called, talking about the Son of God as if he were cheddar or Muenster.

"Home," I said to Jack. "Sure am. Are you?"

"Nope," Jack said. "The whole ski team's staying here for training up at Stowe. Got a race Christmas Day. Hardcore, right?" He wiped his mouth with the back of his hand and drained a glass of juice and grinned at me. He was giving me looks, winks and smiles.

"So how's the team doing so far?" I asked. *Always ask the man questions, Charlotte. Be a good listener.* My mother's voice again.

"Best in the West, Beast of the East," said Jack. "As usual. Division One champs again, for sure."

"Downhill? Or slalom?" *Be knowledgeable about the things that interest men, sweetheart.*

"Who, me? I'm a slalom man," he said. "I like to ski gates. Gates! It's technique, not just balls, you know?" He was tapping his temples. "I gotta have my thinking cap on at all times! Downhill is pure balls. But slalom gates—that's a brain trip."

"Are you the best?" I asked him, tilting my face up at him. "I bet you're the best."

"Could be." He winked.

"So who's your competition? Don't tell me you have competition!"

"Smilo," he said.

"Smilo?"

"Smilin' Milo Robicheaux," said Jack. "New guy. Freshman. Like you."

"Milo Robicheaux?" I said, surprised. "I think I met him, last night." *Call me Mortified.* I thought of the midnight pounding on the door, the voice coming through the crack, the eloquent apology. "He didn't sound like a ski-team star," I said. "He sounded like...a butler. Well, first he sounded like a gangster, and then he sounded like a butler."

"Charlotte!" Jack said.

"What?"

"I can't believe you said that."

"What?"

"A butler? A gangster?" Jack was shaking his head.

"Why?"

"Well, he could get offended, you know?"

"I don't even know him. He speaks very properly, is all."

Jack snorted. "You're too much, Charlotte-girl." He leaned in and smiled, tousled my hair the way you do a child's. He stood up and stretched so the tails of his shirt came untucked, and I could see a dark cyclone of hair around his navel.

"Yup, Smilo is Top Dog," said Jack. "Top Doggie, presidential material, Rhodes Scholaresque, all-round genius, athlete, mother-pleaser kind of man." There was a jokey edge to the way Jack said that, "A real mother-pleaser kind of man."

I remembered this later. *Not my mother*, I thought then.

That night there was another party. Jack told me he was going and maybe he'd see me there. Parties were happening all the time at the college: little ones in rooms in the dorms, big ones in the fraternity houses and in the basement of the student union and in the dining halls. I liked all of them, especially the big loud crowded ones that were light on conversation and heavy on dancing. I liked to feint my way through the ogling press of people to get to the beer keg or the punch bowl. I liked the drinking games and especially the language that went with them: juicehounds chugging and funneling, doing shots, getting hammered, shitfaced, wasted, toasted, barfing and booting. All of it seemed wicked, beyond adult rules, beyond the worst fears of my mother and father, and also somehow hilarious and ridiculous. The air of those parties was always moist with longing and possibility. The boys' arms would come snaking around my shoulders. They'd get my neck in the crooks of their elbows and say "Ooooooh, Charlotte, gimme a kiss." And often I would, if I felt like it, or if I was drunk enough.

This particular party I went to with Claire. She was a waify girl from New York City: pale and skinny, with a dark chic cap of hair. She had big long-lash eyes that got bigger when she was drinking. And she usually was, starting at about four o'clock in the afternoon, with a beer from the window ledge, where she kept it cooling. Lately it froze, and sometimes fell in six-packs down three stories into a leafless clump of lilac bushes. Claire would have to go dig for it then, fishing it out of the snow and holding it aloft so her friends in the room above—me included—could cheer. We liked beer, too, but we nursed ours.

Claire had to drink. She told me why one evening the first week of school, tossing it out as the answer to some normal question as if she were throwing a grenade. "My mother is dead," she said, "I found her. I was twelve. She hung herself in the barn at our summerhouse." And then the subject was closed. "Don't go talking about it." Right after she told me, she put a record on, with the volume knob turned all the way to the right. Dancing around our room with a rum and Coke. *The lunatic is on the grass.*"

Claire tried everything to pretend it didn't matter, to remember it wasn't her fault. So, besides the substances she abused, she used mean jokes and curses, followed by hugs or the touch of her hand, as protection. When she found out I was her roommate she said, "Shit, I had to get a fucking California fucking beauty queen." And then she gave me the finger. "Just kidding," she said, and hugged me. She hugged everyone all the time. She tried whenever possible not to sleep by herself, because nightmares followed her like ducklings. Sometimes when she wasn't sleeping elsewhere, I woke up in the dark and saw her sitting up in bed, the red ash point on her cigarette flaring. "Hey, stupid," I always said to her. "Go to sleep. I'm right here." She told me this helped her. She told me she didn't know what she would do without me. I loved Claire.

Around nine o'clock that night, she came over to my desk, sucking the top of a brown glass bottle, and said, "Are you coming with me tonight, or not?" I was. I always did.

We glossed our lips and pulled on big Frye boots the color of golden retrievers. We wrapped ourselves in puffy down parkas. We left behind all the serious students, sitting at desks in their little quiet pools of light, studying. We went rowdily out into the dark campus, along the road to the Delta Upsilon house.

"Will Scott be there?" Scott was also on the ski team, a guy with thick, bowl-cut hair. He played his guitar in coffeehouses. His body was thin and wiry from skiing around slalom gates but his hands on the guitar strings were red and meaty. He sang huskily and slept with girls who came up and murmured compliments. Including Claire, last weekend.

"Ummm," said Claire. "Don't care."

"You said you thought you probably might like him."

"Fuck him."

"Oh," I said. "Okay."

"You better not." Claire curled her lip at me.

"I never would, Claire, you know that," I said.

"Ahhhh, yes, but everyone wants Charlotte," Claire said, meanly. "Scott included. Including Scott, et cetera, et cetera."

I punched her shoulder. Claire got this way with me when she was nervous. "Besides," I said, "you know what I want."

She started to sing *Jumpin' Jack Flash is a gas, gas, gas*. Of course I had told her about Jack, about the way he touched my head, winked at me.

"You'll get him, too," she said. "If anyone could, you could."

We got near the frat house with its gingerbread-trimmed porch and could feel the shake of the party even as we walked up the sloping path, over the muddy snowpack. Every time the door opened, a phrase of music escaped toward us. We could feel our hearts' staccato and the color rising in our cheeks as we bounced up the steps where a big-shouldered guy greeted us by saying "Laaaaay-deeeez! Yes!" and stamped our hands with ink in the shape of a naked woman.

"Aw," said Claire, disgusted.

"Grow up," I said.

We threw our coats on a pile upstairs and went right down to the beer. Claire filled her cup and started talking to a guy in a hat with flaps that hung down like dog's ears. They disappeared to the bathroom and did God knows how much stuff up their noses. I waited, sipping beer and looking around at the jammed pack of people, swigging at their cups. The girls in sweaters and jeans raked at their shiny hair with their fingers. The boys squared their bodies in flannel woodcutter shirts, darting their eyes around the room like snakes' tongues. I could feel a sifting of men coming toward me, Dan Hirsch, Ted somebody. I didn't want to talk to them, backed my way away from them, looked around without appearing to look at all. Jack said he would show up. I was only interested in Jack.

Just then somebody came up behind me and roped me in by the neck, pulling me to his itchy sweater so my cheek was stashed up somewhere next to his armpit. Jack. It was him. "Whooooooo!" he whooped and laughed and beamed his blue headlight eyes down at me. He smelled like smoke and scotch. "Charlotte!" he said. "Dance with me."

We started dancing right there in the front vestibule, fast and happy; three, four songs in a row, so that other people started dancing, too, and a space cleared around us. Somebody turned the hall light out. The music slowed down. It was dark but you could still see. Jack was smiling out of one side of his mouth. His eyes were half closed. Earth, Wind and Fire started up, singing "Heart's Afire," rhymes with desire. Jack loomed in all of a sudden, with his hands on my shoulder blades and his face right there in front of mine. He planted his lips on my lips and left them lingering.

I had meant for it to happen. But not like that. Everybody was watching. Even I was watching, kissing him and imagining what we looked like, wondering what did he want, really? Jack's lips were dry and friendly, tasted of whiskey. Soon he had me packaged in his woolly arms there in the Delta Upsilon entryway, our mouths turning against each other like doorknobs. When I pushed away for air and opened my eyes I saw everyone trying not to notice us, and I had the brief thought that the others were all standing around holding little urine specimens in their clear plastic cups, and not beer.

"Jackie," I said, and fell against him laughing. He turned me around, dancing with my back to his chest, walking me through the crowd that way, to the beer keg. Broken shards of plastic cups crunched underfoot in a gray sherbet of old snow and cigarette ash and spilled beer.

He had one arm around the front of me, the friendly announcement grip: my girl, see? Or maybe not. Maybe he was just trying not to fall. "Whoa, Charlotte!" he said, laughing and laughing. His nose was against my ear. His breath there felt nice. It made the hairs stand up on my forearms, on the back of my neck.

"Dance with me again," I said. "C'mon, Jack."

I pulled him along after me, to the room where the music was. Somebody had rigged up a dark light with an orange paper shade that made us look like people in photograph negatives, big white eyes and ashy skin. The Talking Heads were singing "Psycho Killer," and as we danced we shouted the words, smiling as if we were all in on a private joke, punching our fists in the air. *"Better run run run run away...."* Then the music heated up and I started to move around all over the place. I liked dancing. Loved dancing. I was having a good time. When they watched me the women on the sides of the dance floor leaned together to speak behind their hands. Somebody said, "Look at her." The men looked over their beer cups at each other, eyebrows up quick, then down. Jack noticed this, he liked it, I could see.

Back in the alcohol room, a black guy wearing a cap grabbed Jack's arm. "Sutherland!" the guy said.

Jack stopped and hugged him and clapped him on the back and said, "Smilo!"

That's the same guy with the skis from this morning, I thought, but when I looked again he had his back to us, moving away. The same guy. He had glanced my way, had seen my double take. "Who was that?" I asked Jack.

"Smilin' Milo Robicheaux," he said, and he started talking in this *Gone With the Wind* Butterfly McQueen voice: "Dass Mi-lo dat I's mention to you dis mo-nin'," he said. "Dassa ace collegiate downhill champeen of de en-tiyuh U-nited States." He leaned in toward me and whispered: "He's, uh, *black*." He raised his eyebrows, as if repeating a piece of sexual gossip. Winked.

"No kidding," I said.

"Well, you're the one who said he sounded like a butler," Jack said. "Right?"

The night before. That had been Milo speaking through my door. I hadn't seen him. It was the British flavor in his voice that made me choose the word *butler,* nothing else. "He didn't sound black," I said. "I mean, you know what I mean."

"Yo, whas' happenin' sistah? Damn you dance bad, girl," Jack said. He was shucking and jiving and holding his hands with the wrists bent downward, one of them resting by his crotch. "Wish I had me a watermelon."

"Jack, *stop*." But he was funny. He was a riot, popping his blue eyes and rolling his walk and sticking his lips out. I was giggling. I couldn't help it, snickering and looking around to see if anybody was watching. "Ja-ack." I laughed. I knew that he wasn't supposed to be funny but he was. So I kept giggling at him, saying, "Stop! Ja-ack, you're terrible."

"What I don't get," he said, "is how come when, like, one of them gets up and imitates a white guy on TV or something, everybody thinks that's great, that's hilarious. And the white guy they imitate is always some prig faggot kind of a guy with no personality or anything, like if you're white you're, like, dead, and we have to sit there and take it, laugh, ha-ha. But if we do it, right? if we imitate one of them? it's racist. Am I right?"

"You're being racist right now!" I said.

"Das right, sistuh Charlotte," said Jack.

I giggled again. I was uneasy. "Shhhhh!" I held one hand over his mouth and covered the other one over my own mouth. I couldn't help laughing. He popped his eyes. He licked my hand. He grabbed it where I held it by his lips and he licked it.

"Oh, spare me," he said. "Spare me, spare me, spare me." He got down on his knees and put his face against my waist. "Spare me a dance, Miz Charlotte, you know I's in love with you. And I have been ever since the day I saw you."

"Stop, Jack," I said, but I was flattered. I pulled him up and jitterbugged him around. He got twisted up and missed the connections to my hands.

"You're leading," he said.

He got me from the back on the next pass, wrapped his arms around me, moved them up to my face with his hands over my eyes in a blindfold. "Don't lead," he said, and kept my eyes covered. Leaks of reddish light came through the spaces between the weaving of his fingers. I felt the callus on his palms and the hard metal of a thick ring he wore. My head was pulled backwards awkwardly on his shoulder. It made me panicky. I pawed at his arms, trying to pull away. He was laughing. "She was trying to lead me," he said to someone I didn't see. "She has to learn not to lead."

"The blond leading the blond," the person said.

Jack took his hands away. "Peekaboo!" he said.

I blinked back into focus, rubbed the back of my neck. A guy was standing there: green eyes, brown skin. "Or is it the bland leading the bland?" he was saying pleasantly. His shirt was white, tucked into his khakis, which were tucked into the leather tops of the duck-hunting boots that all the students wore, as if Cabot were some swamp.

"This is Milo Robicheaux," Jack said. "The skiing phenomenon? Milo, this is Charlotte Halsey."

We nodded at each other.

"Hey, Smilo?" Jack said, unwinding me from his arm. "Talk to Charlotte a sec, willya? 'Cause I gotta go take a leak." He kissed me on the cheek with a cartoon pucker of the lips and winked at Milo. Then Jack went off outside to the cold bushes behind the fraternity, where guys pissed in the clean snow in fancy patterns or wrote the initials of their girlfriends in yellow letters.

"Milo Robicheaux," said Milo. "Nice to meet you."

"Again, you mean," I said. We had to lean in near each other to hear. I shook his hand, which was delicate and dry, with long fingers, the hand of a pianist. "Don't you mean it's nice to meet me again?"

He made his eyebrows go up in a question mark, and I said, "You introduced yourself once already, through the door."

"Oh," he grinned at me. "That must've been my evil twin."

"You have an evil twin?" I said. "Is he a champion skier, too?"

"Now what makes you think I would have a twin who's a champion skier?" he asked back.

"Aren't you?" I said. "Aren't you some kind of ace downhill racer?"

"Me and Robert Redford," said Milo.

"That wasn't really Redford skiing in that movie," I told him. "That was a stuntman."

"Are you suggesting it's not really me on the downhill course?" he said. "Are you suggesting I'm an imposter?"

"No, I am not." He was getting me flustered, he was smiling in ways that seemed to carry other meanings, private jokes and references. Perhaps he remembered that morning on the path, somehow knew what I'd been thinking. *Black man with skis.* But what was wrong with thinking that? Surely nothing. I didn't know anybody black. My head hurt. There was Milo Robicheaux smiling at me pleasantly. He was attractive. Was he teasing me? He fingered his lips, just absently. He was very handsome. The party was swirling around us in the dark beery room. The music ratcheted up, faster and louder.

"Aren't you going to ask me to dance?" I said. I am not good at banter. He was wrong about me. I was not what he thought, whatever that was. I would show him by dancing with him in front of everybody. "C'mon," I said.

"What makes you think I can dance?" he said, and another stutter of time passed while I considered whether he was mocking me or he thought I was mocking him, or whether I was. Was I?

He pulled me out into the dancing. The DJ spun a new record, and the Average White Band funked a thick bass line through speakers the size of steamer trunks. Milo could dance. (*Of course he can dance, they're good dancers* was the thought that just popped into my head, but I ignored it, tamped it down.) His moves were spare, he was fluid, the way athletes are.

I suddenly felt that my arms were flailing too wildly, that I was leaping and hopping like a jackrabbit.

I copied him. He was smiling at me. The music slowed down. The orange light was warm and dim. We drifted toward each other and his arms came up to circle my hips. I'm not sure whose idea it was, to keep dancing through the slow song, but there I was, with my head on Milo's shoulder and my pale arms around his neck. His dark brown neck.

I have never touched a black person before, I thought. *Not even to shake hands.* There was the safe rub of his white cotton T-shirt under my cheek, the laundry smell of it mixed with sweat and smoky air; there was the warm weight of his jawbone resting on the crest of my sideturned head. *I have never.* Holding my breath. Down along the length of my jeans were his tan trousers, the buckle of his belt above mine. I felt his arms solid around me, the skin of his fingers damp and light on my back. We danced in an ambling circle, like tired people resting. His knees touched my knees. My arms were around him. He was just enough taller than me. It was nice. There was none of that cheap pressing-together of the hips or any wandering of the hands up and down the spine. There was just me, without meaning to, lifting my head and pulling back to look at him, and smiling right at him. And him smiling back, down at me. We stayed like that, dancing and smiling, our faces close but apart. And then, as if we had determined something, I dropped my head to his shoulder again, with my face now toward his neck, so I could feel the temperature of his skin on my cheek, my ear pressed close to his collarbone. I could see the dark dots of his sparse beard whiskers shaved down close to his jaw.

I had thought to ask him, chattering Who is Angela? Why were you looking for her that night? Why were you kicking the doors? But I didn't. I didn't say anything.

After a minute, the music got fast again, and Milo lingered his arms around me till the beat was nearly too fast for touch. Just then Jack came back from taking his leak.

"I can't leave you alone with a woman for five seconds, Smilo," Jack said, and pulled me.

"Hey," I said, pulling back.

"Waahht?" Slack-jawed Jack.

"I was dancing with him."

"Oh. *Well.* Excuse me." Jack stepped back elaborately.

Milo raised his two hands, flat of the palm down for peace. "Nice to meet you, Charlotte," he said. "Later, Jack." He winked at us and moved off into the crowd of people.

We left the party, Jack maneuvering me through the crowd. On the way out the door I saw Claire, back against a corner. The guy in the flap-hat was still talking to her. He had his hands on the wall above her shoulders so she was in a kind of arm-trap. She was trying to open her eyes. She kept pushing the guy away, but then he would have to catch her because she was falling. "Claire!" I said.

She focused briefly, saw me and rolled her eyes. "Oh God," she said, and I started over to her, but Jack pulled me outside and down the steps.

"What a slamhound," he said.

"Who?"

"That Claire. She'd do a tree."

"She's my friend."

"Oh. Sorry," he said. "She did Scott, you know?" Jack took my hand and reeled me out away from him. He watched me as we walked, our breath cold puffs. "You're so fucking lovely, Charlotte," he said to me. "God."

4.

He did not take his jeans off or his boots or his shirt. He lay me flat on the bed. He pushed me down on the mattress, kissing. I had my eyes open, waiting for him to say my name or touch my cheek. He didn't; didn't see I was watching him. Shadows fell on his face in stark stripes when he moved into the light. He kissed away, with his lips turning opposite to mine, left, right, left again. His hands spelunked around my body. I waited, hoping to feel love, hoping Jack would open his eyes and see I was there. He just screwed on ahead, unbuttoning buttons so his shirt fell open, pulling mine off me, greedily unzipping me and then himself and that was that. As it was happening, when he called my name as I lay there, eyes open, I was thinking: *Yes. He's calling out for me.* I felt I had won some prize. I was safe. He was calling my name, he needed me. But I was surprised by how, immediately after, when he was quiet, my throat clotted up with sadness.

I felt him by my shoulder, breathing through his nose, could feel the fast pump of his heart through the rib cage, my own heart knocking against his, and was sad. He had called out, "Charlotte!" which made me think he was vulnerable to some truth about me, that he knew me somehow. I moved aside to look up at him, still waiting, thinking *Now he will say something. Now I will know if this is it.* But instead I looked away when he rolled and pushed up on his elbows to see me.

"God, Charlotte," he said. "It's disgusting how beautiful you are, everyone says so." As if he hated me. He fell back and fell asleep.

His hair was long around his face, soft. Mixed in with my hair on the pillow it was hard to tell whose was whose. The lids over his eyes had a sheen of sweat, the bones of his face lay under the skin in clean lines, a blue worm of vein at the temple. Jack was beautiful himself, as a postcard. His long elegant body stretched the length of the bed, muscles under the flesh like ridges of sand shaped by waves.

You lie there next to somebody like that, you think maybe you'll find out some private truth, examining him up close without his knowledge. You research the face for information: Who is this, lying there? What has just happened? What does he think of me? I was eighteen years old and I was wistful for love. Just what that meant, I was not sure. *All you need is love. God is Love. Hunk a hunk a burnin' love,* John Lennon and the Gospel of John mixed up with Elvis. Love was due to arrive soon, I hoped, perhaps announcing itself in full bloom, in the shape of someone I kissed, some look flowering in the cold Vermont night.

Watching Jack, I checked to see if it was going to be him, wished. But I couldn't tell, even now, our skins touching.

His bed had a smell of wool and gym clothes. I sat up and pulled my T-shirt down, got my jeans back on. Jack rolled up on his side, didn't wake when I stood up.

Big posters of ski racers papered the walls of his room: Billy Kidd with his scrags of hair jutting out under his hat, Jean-Claude Killy blurred in midair. Golden ski trophies were lined up on a shelf next to a collection of beer glasses, steins, and pilsner flutes and mugs: Mad River House, Oktoberfest, Squaw Valley.

A picture was taped up over the desk. It was a Japanese erotic print, of a man and a woman, their long black hair pulled back and held up with chopsticks. They were lying on pillows in painted kimonos, little white socks on their feet with a space sewn for the big toe. The man had his leg up and the woman held her skirts high, showing exaggerated genitals yearning toward each other, like pets on leashes. But their faces were formal, revealing no sign of bliss.

Jack woke then and saw me looking. "Hey," he said. "Yeah. Japs doing it."

"Tch. Jack."

"Come here."

I went and sat on the edge of the mattress. Jack's shirt was pushed up to his ribs and his jeans bunched down, hanging off one foot. He didn't reach to pull them up. He was smiling at me, naked and frank.

"I should go now."

He propped himself up on his elbows and tried to sit. "Whoa," he said, "I'm still partially wasted." He rolled his eyes and swung his feet over the edge, holding his head. "Okay, so, I'm experiencing technical difficulties," he said. "Give me a kiss before you go, huh?"

I kissed him, lips to his cheek.

He held up his hands in the shape of a camera. "Click," he said, winking, pressing his finger down as if releasing a shutter. "Click, click."

"What are you doing?"

"Snapping your picture." He was grinning, charming.

"Why?"

"Proof," he said. "Evidence. I mean, I wish I could, you know? Snap, snap. Photo evidence. Else no one would believe it: I got Halsey. In my bed. Shit."

Jack stood up. He pulled his jeans back on, buckled the belt, and wrapped his arms around me. "Charlotte Halsey," he said.

When he said my name, hope flared up and burned me again. *Now he will really look at me, he'll see.* Because if Jack really looked he would see my nervous stomach, my troubled sleep. He would see Charlotte who was not certain about much except that Christ was not her Personal Savior. Who was? I wondered. Jack?

"Charlotte," he said again, but his eyes missed somehow, they closed before they got to mine.

"Yeah," I said. "That's me."

"You're my Charlotte."

"We'll see about that," I said, for safety. I smiled and winked, since winking seemed to have important meanings for him. "See ya, Jack," I said, and let myself out.

Walking back to my room, with the bleak sun just leaking over the tops of the mountains, I pulled my arms up inside my parka and wrapped them around my shoulders. My legs were spongy and my lips hurt from kissing. He said *You're my Charlotte*, yet I did not feel possessed, or swept away, not smitten or lovesick, more like: flawed. Perhaps I was incapable of tidal-wave emotions or was just mistaken about what love would be like. Everybody wanted to win Jack Sutherland, so what was wrong with me?

Back in my room, I fell onto the bed.

Claire stirred and rolled over. "Where you been?" she asked.

"Jack Sutherland."

"Oh God, he's a god," said Claire thickly. "My God."

We got whispers after that, all around Cabot: *Look who's with who. Catch that. Check out Mr. Ski Team*, I heard them say. *She's taken. Yeah, and look who's got her. What, are you surprised?*

Jack sat with me now, at breakfast and dinner, stood with his arms around my waist while we waited in the cafeteria line, walked to classes holding my hand. It wasn't my idea anymore. But I didn't stop it. *Of course she'd be with him*, somebody said, overheard by Claire in the girls' room. The envy surrounding us—because that's what I believed it was—played on me so that I began to like it. *They're just jealous of you, Charlotte, sweetie. You have what everyone wants.*

"Shit, Charlotte, you got him, you got him," Claire said. After a week or so of this, I guessed I had got him, and came around to the belief that being with Jack was fate happening, love falling. "You're so fucking lucky," said Claire.

"He's really fabulous," I told her. I was on the bandwagon then. We became an item. Jack and Charlotte. It seemed we moved in our own pool of light, matched as siblings: hair, height, eyes, the West Coast in our voices. We kissed at parties, danced till late, fell drunk into bed, grappled at clothing. This was our great love: not much talking, not much that happened in daylight, just the receipt of gossip and glances, just drinking, loud laughing, bed: a carousel of parties.

Jack only ever told me the bare bones about his life: He was a Squaw Valley kid, a mountain rat, he called himself, raised by his mom the ski instructor. "We had, like, skis on our feet when we came out of her," he said. "Me and my brother Karl have been skiing since Day One," he said. "Karl is into freestyle," which is how he explained that his brother lived in a van, traveling wherever the snow took him, working just enough to pay for lift tickets and beer. "My mom is into freestyle, too," he said, explaining: "Not ski-wise, but you know, kind of free. Follows the snow." The only way Jack could talk about anything was in terms of how it related to skiing. He once mentioned how his dad left, for example: "One day he just goes and moves out and leaves, because he was more into *Alpine* skiing, and he thought it would be better if he just went back to Switzerland, because that was where Alpine was happening." As if skiing was the reason. The dad was a wealthy Swiss guy and now he owned some chemical company there. *Big Swiss Cheese* was how I thought of him. "I call him whenever I win," Jack said. "He doesn't like to hear from me if I lose. Used to pound the crap outta me if I didn't place." He said the last part under his breath and didn't elaborate. It was the one time I heard any sadness, under the bravado in his voice. But Jack hardly ever lost. That year, his junior year, he was winning all the slalom races on the college circuit. He was competing in the national races, too, on the weekends, whenever he could. "I knew I'd get you," he said to me once. "I'm used to winning."

About a month after I started up with Jack we went to a bar in town called the Red Hat. It was one of those places like a packed cave. All the tables and chairs there were rutted with the carved initials of Cabot College students going back to the 1940s. The floorboards were damp from a marinade of spilled beer. The walls were covered with framed pictures of skiers who had won fame for the school, big white Cs on their navy-blue sweaters.

Jack pulled me past the bar into the back, where lamps hung down over pool and foosball tables, making cones of smoky light above each one. A group of ski racers was sitting in the corner, and when they saw Jack, they started snorting like warthogs: "Owgh, owgh, owgh."

Cabot skiers were known as party animals, a term that made me think of pets wearing conical hats with elastic bands under their furry muzzles. "We're party *beasts*," Jack liked to say. "Not animals. Beasts."

"Owgh, owgh, owgh," the guys at the table snorted. "Jack-ee, heeeeyyyy, Jack. Hee-eeeyy, Charlo." Jack sat down, pulled me onto his lap. Parker, a ski jumper with a hairless babyface and legs like telephone poles, handed us mugs, foam up to the rim.

Jack raised his glass and shouted: "Beasts on the hill, beasts off!" and we all had to smash our glasses together and snort like warthogs some more.

I enjoyed this, I loved it. All those evenings made me feel like part of something, a happy warm litter of skiers with our private jokes and snorting toasts. None of this behavior would have been allowed in our house, where first of all, there was no drinking. Alcohol touched no Halsey lips. Until mine, that is, starting in about the ninth grade, behind the rows of bleachers and in the backseats of cars, in the basement dens and woodsy tree forts of my friends. We did not get drunk, not really, but we drank. A beer lasted all night between us. It was thrilling and wicked if unoriginal. My parents would have worn out the knees of their pants in prayer, or the seat of my pants in punishment, had they known. Which they did not, not until the Dave incident. "Charlotte?" my daddy would have said. "She's a pink lemonade kinda girl."

Most of the ski team saved the bestial sort of partying for Saturday nights like this one, except for Jack. He was known for winning no matter how much he drank the night before. He could hold it, they said. It had no effect on him. The only other racer who came close to Jack's caliber of party beast was Milo Robicheaux.

Milo had the reputation of being a straight-arrow wildman. Meaning he never lost control, no matter what extreme thing he was doing: dancing on the roof; skiing behind a car at 45 miles an hour; walking a second-story window ledge from dorm room to dorm room. Everybody liked Milo. "Heeyyyy, man, how are ya?" Milo called everybody "man," even me. "Hey, man, Charlotte, see ya later." But all the guys on the team talked that way. Everything they did, Milo did, too, just with more fuel. He skied tucked into a shape like an egg, at speeds that would crack and break him if he fell. Milo was a downhiller, which meant he had to fly without wings, sixty miles an hour. To miss a turn meant a date with rocks, with trees, with massive internal injuries or paralysis or coma.

He had fallen that day at practice. A bad one. Everybody had seen it. The whole team. And now they were ranking him about it. He had slid down the whole mountain, got up and skied away.

"You took a digger, man." This was Scott.

"A grave digger," said Andy.

"It wasn't any digger," Milo said scornfully. "I was upright. I was up-right at the end. Admit it."

"You were upright," said Scott.

"A digger is when you don't get up, okay?" Milo said. "It's when you leave a dent in the hill. Technically, that is the definition of *digger*. Am I right?"

"But you were *tumbling*," said Jack. "You were wiped out."

"You were the Agony of Defeat," said Andy. "You did the course face-down."

"I got my weight back too far," said Milo, "coming over that bump. I got my wings flapping? Whoaaaa, baby! I nearly pulled it out. But, fuck. No recovery."

"I was watching you, man," said Jack. "You were a tumbling dice." Milo laughed. He was liking the stories about himself. He was backflapping with his arms like wings, showing how he had tried to recover.

"Yeah," said Jack. "When you slid the slide, on your belly? I was sure your whole face'd rub off, and there'd be, like, a black trail streaked behind you in the snow, you know?"

Everybody laughed. Rub off black in the snow, they said, that's funny.

I looked at Milo to see if he thought this was funny.

Yes, he was laughing. It was okay. You could see his teeth. He whacked Jack on the back, ha ha ha. "Yeah," he said, winking. "Well, don't you know, the day *you* fall like that, my pal, Jackie boy, it'll be a *red* trail streaking out down behind you. It'll be *blood*." He smiled, just charming, and everybody laughed. He had Jack in a neck-collar hug. He was giving him a scrub on the head with his knuckles.

"High five, bro," said Jack. And Milo high-fived him. He was such a good guy. He was everybody's favorite on the team, like a mascot. "You are one bad-ass dog, Milo, dude," said Jack.

"Ruff-ruff," said Milo, and growled with his lip curled.

I laughed when he did it. Just quietly. Milo saw that I laughed. The way he noticed made me turn my eyes away. It was a look that said *You know he's an asshole, don't you?* I sipped my beer and nuzzled around in Jack's neck, played my finger around the collar of his shirt. Milo got up and left after a while and Jack told more stories. I think now that whenever Milo was around I stuck closer to Jack, touched him more, smiled at him, like I had something to show, or hide, or prove.

What Milo remembered about those times is that I was cold. "Frosty queen," he called me to himself.

We had conversations about it like this:

"I was not cold. I had a boyfriend."

"You did not give me the time."

"You never asked the time."

"Had you ever melted the freezer burn off that pretty little shoulder I would have asked the time, the date, the place, and so on. You were cold."

"You were skiing. That's all you did. You skied, and then you left. You skied and went away to be famous."

"If I was famous then you bet you'd have jumped my bones."

"Don't go down that road."

He claims he does not remember dancing with me. He does not remember anything about the Red Hat except drinking there. He remembers hating Jack. He remembers looking for Angela.

Angela was a black woman, a student at Cabot. When Milo told me about her we were lying in the dark. My head was on his shoulder and I said, "Do you remember the night you practically broke down my door? Before we met?"

"Yes, I do," he said.

"You were looking for Angela."

"I was looking."

"Who was Angela?"

"She was sharp." There was a long minute while Milo let all the air out of his lungs. I jump-started him in the ribs with my elbow.

"Angela was like a knife in your heart to look at her," Milo said, and I didn't mind then, that he was talking about some other woman, because this was a conversation we had when we were first together. It wasn't complicated yet. "She was beautiful," he said, and I didn't dare speak, because as he told me, something else was happening. The air in the room became delicate as porcelain, that might break with the wrong words. I knew, by the way his voice was tight in his lungs, that he was telling something he had never told.

"You have to understand you don't see women like that where I grew up in New Hampshire. Not in the White Mountains, that's for sure. Aptly named. Except for my sister. Angela looked like Bobbie—small and lean with big muscles in her legs. She was a runner. She was from Chicago. She had wide eyes like a deer's eyes, you know? Big. Scared, you think, when you see her sitting alone? In the library? But no, turns out not scared, *mad*. Pissed. A mouth from Chicago that was nothing but lip. I was running after her that night."

"Why?" I said.

"She wouldn't go out with me. Told me I was nothing but a white boy."

"Why would she say that?" I said, and picked up his hand in the dark.

"Because I am a white boy, Charlotte, don't you know that?"

When he said it I could feel him smile in the dark. Next to my scalp where his jawbone rested, the flesh of his cheeks went back up toward his ears.

"Really?" I said, and wondered, why would he say a thing like that? I asked him, but he never explained, not in so many words.

The glass in my hand was getting warm and the beer in it was flat. "I'm going to the girls' room," I whispered in Jack's ear, but he pulled my head onto his lap. He didn't like it when I left. He liked me there, where he could have his hand under the back of my sweater, or holding the back of my neck, like a glass. Down on his lap where he'd pulled me I could see the pills of cotton on the red plaid of his shirt.

When I sat up a little, there was Milo across the room talking to freckly Katrina. She laughed at whatever he was saying to her, with her lips pulled back off her teeth like a horse's.

"Bathroom," I said again to Jack, and got up, sidestepped my way out from behind the table and leaned over a little bit so the opening of my shirt lined up in front of Jack's face, just for him to see. He reached in the open neck and grabbed me on the breast.

"Jack!" There was a split minute there where I nearly sobbed. I had bent over him on purpose, privately, because I was interested in being wild, or seeming wild, and what he did made me feel caught, cheap. Not wild at all.

"Be right back," I said, trying not to mind. I even winked at him. I saw

Andy leering after me, digging an elbow in Jack's ribs. Jack grabbed him by the hair. "Don't scam my girlfriend, asshole," he said. I turned and walked across the room with a backside sway for their benefit. *'Cause it's all right now, in fact it's a gas;* they watched me, head-bopping to the Stones on the jukebox. If I wished for some other kind of admiration, I didn't know what it was, and it's true I liked them looking at me. If they didn't look at me I'd have felt like a loser. A dog. A hogan. That's what they called ugly girls. *She's a real hogan.* Who knows where they got the word.

The bathroom at the Red Hat was down a narrow, dim staircase. The stalls were gross with soggy paper and cigarette butts and grim sex graffiti on the walls, about skiers and their poles, and there by the door handle was some small writing on the pale pink paint that I read because how can you not read something? and it said: *big black dick.* Jesus. It made me wince. I left without even washing my hands.

Coming up the stairs the jukebox was stopped and I heard voices. A guy was saying "Why not?"

A girl said: "Oh . . . it's *no offense*, you know . . ."

When I got to the top of the stairs, I saw a couple talking in a dark alcove near the fire exit. The guy had his back to me but I could tell it was Milo. The girl was Katrina. "Uh-huh," said Milo. "I get it." He turned away from Katrina and I saw he had seen me, he had the look of somebody caught. I went to the bar to get another pitcher of beer.

Is Katrina Milo's girlfriend? I wondered. *Big black*— Once you read something like that you cannot unread it, you can't keep your brain from coming up with these things, little loose wires. I didn't want to think it, but there it was. I tamped it down, banished it. Katrina and Milo. I couldn't imagine it. Katrina with her freckles, kissing Milo with her perky lips. Milo seemed too, I don't know, intense for Katrina, who liked to write her name with a little smiley face dotting the *i*.

It's not like I paid a great deal of attention to Milo then. Just idly sometimes. I tried to imagine Milo with the various women who hung around the skiers, and I couldn't. Some of them were incredible ski racers themselves, and some didn't ski at all. There were the beautiful ones, with the blush of apples in their snowy cheeks. Their hair was long, restrained by plain velvet bands, and was often some shade of blond. They wore no makeup, or makeup that looked like none. Their earrings were tiny and gold. The ones who were not beautiful made up for it in spunk and adorableness. They were muscular, with button noses, and treated the men, even their boyfriends, like brothers, punching and backslapping and tussling. Probably they would have said I was different. I felt different. I had clothing that showed my skin, earrings that hung down, heels that were probably too high for snow. I was from California, is how they would have explained it. They were from New England, most of them. Milo, too, from New Hampshire.

"Who's Milo with?" I asked Jack once.

"Oh, he's active," said Jack. "Don't worry about Smilo. He's getting it all the time."

"Ja-ack," I said, "don't be crude."

"Why fo' you wanna know?" he said. "Milo gets hisself plenty a trim."

That whole time in college, I never saw Milo Robicheaux really with a woman, although he was always flirting, always had a girl to dance with, somebody different hanging on his arm, always somebody white.

I brought the beer to the table. Katrina was back sitting there and Milo now, too. But not next to each other. Maybe all his girlfriends were black, I thought. Perhaps he had a whole other, private black life that I knew nothing about and couldn't possibly imagine, one that was beyond the limits of a white person to fathom. But I never saw him with the other black students on campus, who mostly sat apart, mostly didn't mingle with the whites much, and apparently not with Milo, either. This was not something I thought about, as in: why, or if anyone cared. It was the way things were. So maybe, probably, Milo did go out with white girls. *And why not?* Who would have a problem with that? The fact he was with us, made us all feel . . . what? Noble. We were hip or full of brotherly love and we didn't have a problem because Milo was with us. He was our friend.

"That Milo guy seems white," Claire said once. "It's like he's a white guy. I never even notice that he's black."

Right, he was just Milo, one of the guys on the team. How could Claire not notice? Was I the only one who noticed? Was that *wrong*?

"Snacks!" Milo said cheerfully, when he saw the beer I brought. "Heeeyyy, Charlotte, man! Be so kind as to give us some of that refreshment."

I put the pitcher down and Milo reached across for it, pouring beer for me and around the table. "Beasts!" he shouted, that winning smile on his face. "Beasts on the hill and beasts off!"

Jack started to force-feed me sips of beer. "I don't want any more," I said, and pushed the glass away. "I'm tired." He kissed me but there was beer in his mouth, which he let go and made me swallow.

"Mouth-to-mouth resuscitation," he said.

Milo and one of the other guys got up to dance, pulling women off bar stools. I pulled Jack. "Dance," I said.

"Fuck dancing," he said, kissing me and pushing me back against the red vinyl of the banquette where we sat, so the table moved backwards as his hips came up and he tipped me sideways. We were capsized down now, lying on the bench. I was giggling. I was going "Jack! Jack!" and laughing, and I was kissing him back. It was normal then, at that hour, at our age, in places like that, for people to be making out. Claire was, with Scott. They were over at a different table, had been for an hour, and you could see his hand under her sweater. Nobody really looked but everybody knew. And Jack's was under mine, but not the back now, the front. So, since I was pretty drunk, and the room was rocking pleasantly, as if buoyed up by water, I had this distant feeling of watching from afar, watching myself lying down there on the bar's back bench, eyes shut and Jack's hair hanging into my face. Kissing.

But then I heard somebody rummaging under the table by my head, crawling around on the floor near where Jack had me pinned on the bench. Somebody said, "Goddammit." I started to push Jack off, but he pressed me back down and put his hands up by my eyes so I wouldn't stray away from him. And then he heard, too. Some guy was under the table searching for something. We both opened our eyes, me and Jack, and saw that it was Milo.

"What the fuck you lookin' at?" said Jack, and he got up so fast I was suddenly cold. "What're you lookin' at, asshole?"

"Lost my wallet," said Milo, standing up. "Can't find my goddamn wallet."

"Keep your eyeballs in your head, pal? Okay? Is that clear?" Jack said. He had his finger pointed up near Milo's chin. He was taller than Milo, stringier. They were staring at each other so you could just about see fur raised up on the backs of their necks.

"Calm down," said Milo.

"Keep your eyeballs in your head, okay?" Jack glanced over at me where I was sitting up, dazed and blinking. I was straightening out my sweater when I realized it was open from Jack's adventures with the buttons and that my breast—one pale one—hung out like a bare bulb in the dark bar. "Button up, Charlotte," Jack said. "Milo's never seen it."

Now. Now it'll happen.

Milo just moved his nostrils. He tensed toward Jack but pulled back in time and stayed still, staring Jack down, and I could see he hated Jack so much. Hated him. Narrow eyes, tight lips whitening. He turned, practically military, on his heel, and slammed his hand against the wall, hard.

"You're an asshole, Sutherland," he said. "Ya prick."

Big white prick.

"Milo," I said, "I'm sorry—"

"Shut up, Charlotte," said Jack.

And I did. I shut up.

5.

Everything went back to status quo status after that. They were very *har-har-har*, pat your back, *hey man how' ya doin'* kind of guys together. Jack, Milo, the other racers, all got along fine. Skiing was not a group-effort sport so it was easy for them to have team spirit, even though what really mattered was: Every man for himself.

And for Jack it was him for himself and me for himself. Every crumb and scrap of me for him, no leftovers. After a month or two, I was beginning to feel this. He wanted me to live in his dorm room, put my clothes in his closet, my books on his shelves, myself in his bed. He liked to wrestle me. He liked to get me pinned with my arms twisted behind. He could do pretzels with his legs. Mostly this was horsing around. But then when I said *Mercy*, sometimes he kept on, sitting so my lungs were half crushed, rib bones nearly touching front to back. "Jack! Jack! Stop it!" struggling words out. He'd maneuver around, holding me down, looking straight at me, with this flirting smile. "Make me," he'd say. "Say you'll do whatever I want." He enjoyed this. "Say it."

"I'll do whatever you want," I said, gasping.

"Say you're mine."

"You're mine," I said, and smiled at him. I said it because it still seemed like a wish that could come true. And his beauty was like a spell. It mattered. I won't say it didn't. I fell for his face every time. Girls looked at me, asked, Oh my God, what was it like to be so lucky as to have Jack

Sutherland to sleep with, gorgeous all night and in the morning? "I'll do whatever you want."

"That's a good girl. There's my Kitten."

Kitten was this name he gave me in the Burlington Airport before I flew home for Christmas. We had been together since early November. We were sitting on the floor of the airline terminal because the hard metal arms of the chairs dug into our ribs when we held on to each other.

"Three weeks apart," he said. Jack was staying in Vermont, training at Stowe, and then going to Canada for a Nor-Am race. It was a big deal for him.

"There's always the phone," I said.

"I'll forget what you look like."

"I look like this," I told him, and made a gargoyle face.

"That's funny," said Jack. "Like, weird funny, not funny ha ha ha."

He said, "Here's your assignment: You have to think about me every day, all day." He demonstrated. "Like: breathe in, *Jack*, breathe out, *Jack*, breathe in, *Jack*, breathe out, *Jack*, et cetera. Okay?"

"I do that anyway," I said, fibbing.

"Do it more, then, when we're apart." He got a package out of his backpack. "I want you to sleep with this," he said. The package was wrapped in pink paper with a white ribbon. "This reminded me of you."

Inside the package was a stuffed kitten. White fluffy fur. Pink bow, a bell around the neck. Blue glass eyes. I hated it. I couldn't think why, I just hated it. But Jack, he got tears in his eyes, watching me open it.

"So cuu-ute," I said, rubbed its stuffed animal fur on my cheek.

"Merry Christmas." He thought I loved it. He tried to say something, got choked up, tried again. "I'm not a sentimental guy, Charlotte," he said. "But when I think of you, in my mind? I call you Kitten. You're my kitten," he said. "I'll miss you."

"Me, too." I wanted to miss him. Hoped. *Kittens are born with their eyes closed. People drown them, tie cans to their tails*, I thought, and wanted to tell him to see if he would laugh, but it wasn't the sort of thing he would laugh at.

"Secretly I was expecting you'd give me a little something," he said, moping. "A memento."

"I was going to get you something from home," I told him, but he looked disappointed. "Wait. Here." I reached up to the crown of my head, where the longest hairs grew, and gave a sharp tug so several came out in my fingers, long cellophane threads. "Keep these," I said, as if it were something dramatically meaningful you would do if you really loved someone.

"Your hair." He stretched the strands taut. "Charlotte's Web," he said. "Some gift."

"I don't have anything else handy right now."

"I'll lose these."

"You could eat one." As a joke.

"Charlotte." Jack looked at me.

"No, I mean it." Suddenly I did mean it, and waited to see what he would do, as if I were conducting some perverse sort of test. "You have to eat one."

"No way," he said.

"Yes way."

"You're crazy," he said.

"Crazy about you," I said. The words went with the movie in my head, with the scene about the parting of lovers.

"Really, you have to," I said. "Eat." And he did. I must say I was surprised. I gave him sips of soda to wash it down.

"Good," I said, laughing. Which was cruel of me but I didn't care. He was crowding me. He was going too fast.

"What was that for?"

"It was romantic."

"Oh." He thought about it. "You mean, so now I'll have a little bit of you with me always." His face was troubled. "Forever, right?"

"Right." I felt guilty then so I said it. "Aww, Jack. You know I love you." That was the first time. He was so happy he kissed me all the way to the gate. *I love you, too, Charlotte*, till all the passengers were loaded onto the plane. I pulled away then, backing down the loading tube. Jack stayed behind with his hands jammed down into his pockets, velvet ropes keeping him back.

Home in California, my sister Diana demanded a picture of Jack. "Ow," she said, looking at one of him on the mountain, his eyes little chips of the blue sky behind him. "Mr. Right."

I shrugged.

"How can you *not* be in love? Jesus, Charlotte!"

"I am, I guess."

"You guess?" Diana shouted. We were in our bedroom, lying around.

"Don't shout, Di," I said. "Mom."

"Mom would love this."

"Probably."

Diana was sixteen. She had kept on with the pageants till last year but quit because she had not done well. She was very tall, nearly six feet, and pretty, I always thought, more than me, because of her lips, which were full and what they call bee-stung. Plus there was something vulnerable in her face, despite the fact she was constantly smiling. But it would take awhile for her to handle all that height. She was clumsy, tripping on her own feet. Still, Mom was loyal to her, drove her around to dance lessons, took her to the preliminaries for Miss Napa County. Diana didn't get past County. She had kept up with Kids for Christ but she didn't care about it. "Bunch of dips," she said. "They're not normal kids. They're brainwashed." She went because of our parents, because Mom and Dad had been so disappointed in me. She didn't want to be another Charlotte in their eyes. She had one more year left in high school. She wanted a boyfriend but she didn't have one, although she did have a prom dress already, my dear little sister.

"How can you *guess* you are in love?" Diana whispered. "Don't you *know*?"

"Everyone says we're perfect for each other?" I said.

Christmas dinner. The whole family. Charlotte and Peter home. The enormous roast beef festooned with parsley, dark and bleeding onto the platter. The polished silver, the crystal water goblets. The crèche on the sideboard with the pies. All of us were dressed up and famished after church. Peter got us all holding hands for the blessing. It was quiet. The smell of the roast was torturing everyone. Especially Sean, who was nearly fainting, yawning to cover the sound of his stomach growling, and trying hard to sit up straight. His wrists hung out of his handed-down sport coat. He was constantly eating, constantly hungry, wilting now like a plant. He was my favorite, Sean. He had a new shaving shadow on his fourteen-year-old jaw. Christmas Eve he stayed up with me and Diana and listened to music, Lou Reed and the Velvet Underground. "Shh, Sean, Mom will hear," Diana kept saying. "Shhh."

"Relax, willya, Diana?" Sean said. He was taking after me. He had already gotten in trouble for driving a friend's car without a license, Diana told me.

Peter said: "Hear us, Lord O God, that You may make us thankful and worthy of Your love on this day Christ our Savior was born." He went on about how we were not worthy, we were low and had to do better to get up there to the level of Jesus. I peeked at him while everybody else sat with their eyes squeezed shut. Seeing Peter pray like that, I remembered how I used to go in his room and watch him sleep, his metal race cars balled up in his hands. Two years older, he was like a supernatural being to me, a really handsome boy. But since he'd started at Bible College in Virginia his hair looked too combed, parted 60 percent on one side, 40 on the other. And buzzed short. Normal guys his age had hair down the back, at least hitting the collar. He looked preoccupied all the time and talked a lot about his Personal Savior, which to me now sounded like something you might find under the seat of an airplane. I supposed he was always heading for the ministry, even when he was little. Once, when he was eight years old, we took his turtles out of the turtle aquarium and let them go free in the backyard. One got lost and Dad ran over it with the lawn mower. We had a funeral. Peter did all the readings. And he really cried. He said, *All life is precious.* I remember I hugged him and said, "Don't worry, Pete, you still have me." I love him, of course, but he is not the same brother. Religion used to be normal with him. Now it's extreme. *All life is precious.* He said that to me, too, when I got In Trouble. He was furious. More even than Mom and Dad. "God forgives you," he told me. "I pray to be strong enough to forgive you, also."

"You are the Light and the Way, O Lord. Amen."

Sean attacked his plate. Mom played with the glass beads on her neck and said, "Tell us about all your beaux, Charlotte honey, the boys you've met at school." She always called them *beaux*, as if she was Scarlett O'Hara.

"There's just Jack," I said.

"He's going to ski in the Olympics," Diana said.

"Maybe," I said.

"He's incredibly handsome," Diana said. "Charlotte has a picture." They made me drag it out and show it around the dinner table.

"Nice-looking fella," said my dad, who was still so nice-looking himself, hair graying with what is called "distinction" for a man, and his eyes pale as a husky dog's. He looked at Jack's picture, and I wondered if he thought of himself at our age, how he looked, what he felt then. "Nice-looking."

Sean made kissing noises.

"Is he a Christian?" This was all Peter wanted to know lately.

"He's an Episcopal," I said. "He's also from California."

"Episcopalian," Peter corrected me. "Like Catholic, only not strayed as far from the Lord, I think. Don't you? Dad? Am I right?"

Here we go now. God, scrod, Lord, bored. I was thinking of how I could mention Deuteronomy and get points for studying religion when Diana decided to rescue the conversation.

"You should see what Jack gave Charlotte," said Diana. "Mom, you'll love it. You should see."

"Di-*an*-a," I said.

"What, sweetheart?" said Mom. Diana went and got the fluffy stuffed kitten. She brought it out holding it like it was alive, stroking its neck.

"Tch. Ohhhhhh. Look." Mom's face softened up and she made the sounds many women make at babies or lambs or Easter chicks. "Ohhh, that's so precious. He really gave you that?" She was so pretty, my mom, with her jonquil-colored hair in parentheses around her delicate face. Her eyes were the same arresting blue as the fluffy kitten's and when she took it from Diana, its fur matched the angora of her new white Christmas sweater. She looked at me and put her hand over my hand on the tablecloth. "Charlotte, I'm so happy. So proud of you." She looked at Jack's picture just shaking her head back and forth.

"I'm glad you're happy, Mom," I said, and patted her, too. And to my surprise, she held my hand, clenched on to it, her thumb rubbing back and forth like a windshield wiper, warm and soft.

"I'm proud, sweetie."

"Thanks."

She was proud. She did her best to love me, her idea of me, which was all she could do, and I loved her, too, the way she held my hand for dear life, squeezing it. For one minute I felt there was a door I could have gone through, to find her in the room on the other side, where we would be dressed in identical mother-daughter dresses, sharing recipes for gelatin-mold salads, or needlepointing, our heads bent close to our work. My mother loved me. She saw Jack in the picture and he looked just like she wanted him to look: handsome, strong, important. Safe. She was proud I could get a man like that. Then she snapped out of it and said: "Don't do anything to ruin it, now." She looked right at me with her eyes hard, like: *You know what I'm talking about, my girl.*

I did, too. I knew perfectly well: *Dave Mueller.*

On the face of it, Dave was a lot like Jack. I picked both of them out for identical reasons. Dave was the choice guy in our school. Captain of this and that. Good-looking and a little dangerous because of it. He could break your heart. He was eighteen and I was sixteen, senior and junior. My official eligibility for dating had just been granted that year by Barbara and Arthur. I was allowed out till ten. Before then I had been out, of course. But they thought I was with Kids for Christ, strumming guitar and singing "Kumbayah." But no, mostly I wasn't. And even so, some of the Kids had my same interests. Skipping out of meeting. Heading for the woods. Christ spent some time in the wilderness, I often said, and we must emulate him in all things.

Let's go, Dave. I have to go home now.

He wanted to find his watch. It was a spring evening. It was our three-month anniversary. We were supposed to be at the movies but we were lying in the DeNunzios' apricot orchard in the tall wild mustard. It was cold. *Crazy about you,* Dave said. The air made gooseflesh on our bare skin, even under his big jacket crusted with letters and insignia.

I swear he lost his watch on purpose. There was no need to take it off. He had taken it off along with my bell-bottoms, my sweater, his black jeans. He wanted to keep going. He wanted whatever he could have. Whatever I would let. I had never let anyone. There had been plenty of chances and I had let a lot, but not that. I was afraid. Lately in school I heard people saying things. Frigid slut. Tease. *Christian virgin saint whore.* They wrote things on my locker.

That night was a night full of complicated problems for me. It was getting tiring, all this holding out. I liked the feelings. Loved them. I liked the weight of Dave lying on me. Tongues and murmurs. But I was scared. Pebbles or apricot pits were digging into my back. What about sin? What about babies? God, not yet, not that. What about marital love, pure and sanctified? To save yourself for your husband to have and to hold. The gift of yourself. I didn't believe I was a gift exactly, but what if it was true? What other way it could be was not clear, nobody talked about it, except as if it was some kind of hunt. *Did you nail her? Did you lose it? Did he pork her? Did you get him? Did she do him? Did he pole her?* In sex ed they said *intercourse*, and we just howled. Intercourse! The word was hysterical. I knew all the facts. The birds, the bees. The four bases. But I had no clue about anything. What I wanted versus what I was supposed to want, allowed to want. How to say yes. Or no. How to be safe. It was terrifying, wonderful, great. How the sucking swampy quicksand of sin and wrong choices lurked ready to drag you down, and how the risk was so intoxicating. Yes, no, yes, no, yes. This but Not That. Here but Not There. Oh my God. I loved how it felt to not know whether it would happen that night or not yet. All the while my parents waited up, reading quietly in their hospital-cornered bed, trusting me, that I would be home with my nice young man. Ready to spring like big cats, claws ready, if I was not. But I was always right on time. Always brushed and combed and composed.

I said I had to go. I said Hurry, hurry. He said *please*. He said—no, gasped—*Charlotte, I'm desperate for you*. What happened was this time we stayed, we lingered, and one thing led to another thing and then another thing and then to the thing. I still have trouble talking about it plainly. Then there were no words. There were the school nurse words and the girls' room graffiti. You didn't say *make love*. That's not what was happening, anyway. Nothing was being made, at least not that I knew of then. It was desperate. Nothing you could help or stop. Why would you? Why would you want to?

I was not ashamed. Not even sorry. I was glad. I didn't care what they thought. I believed they had no idea what they were talking about. The stuff about wrack and ruin. Cheapening what is sacred. It was fine, I thought. Over with. Dave was nice with me. He worried he hurt me. He didn't hurt me. Not that time. That time he was nice.

I got pregnant. Despite the odds against it. But of course. I was the one in a zillion chance. Somebody always is, and it was me. Bingo.

No way could we have it, keep it. We couldn't even *say* baby, either of us. Dave drove me to Sacramento for the procedure. It would have been fine except my mother found out. She saw I was queasy. I was late. The clues added up. The pads did not disappear from the box on schedule. She kept track, estimated on a monthly basis. How many for her, for me, for Diana. I was green at breakfast and at lunch. Sleepy. One Saturday I said I was going off to a neighbor's house. Dave's father mentioned we'd borrowed the car all day. I came home gray and weepy, bleeding. She figured it out, told my father.

It took a whole year of lies to get them to send me to college. It was all I wanted. None of the women in my family had been. It's not that I was a student, really. I had good grades. You got them by showing up, by filling in the answers, by spelling well. I wanted to go to college. To say I had. To get away and figure things out on my own. Just to get away.

"I'm sorry for what I did," I said. I blamed it on Dave. I said he forced me. This was not true. I knew how to hang my head down at just the right angle and tell them, "I know I strayed but I've realized the errors of my ways and I am back with you in faith." It was easy. I just repeated what the pastor said in the service on Sunday, all my life since we started going there. It wouldn't work to argue with them, claim they'd been wrong. Their answer then would be to make me stick around Conestoga. I could go to Pacific Union College right nearby. Stay home and be safe with them. Get a job where Dad worked at the pharmaceutical company, filing or something.

When Jack called from Vermont my mom was thrilled. Her cheeks flushed. "It's for you, Charlotte honey," she sang out. "Woo-hooo," and then hissed: "Long distance," widening her eyes. "He sounded so nice," she said later. "Big deep voice."

His voice did not sound particularly deep to me. "Hey, Charlotte," he said, "I'm clocking great times." He was burning up the training camp, he told me. Coach had been talking to Team USA about him. They would be scouting him at Lake Placid. "The U.S. team," he said. "Think about it." His voice sounded staticky. It was hard to picture him. There were patches of silence in our conversation. "Charlotte? Are you there?" I was there, but I didn't really have anything to say.

. . .

When school started up again in January, Jack came back from training camp and started in on a new campaign. "When are you gonna get your little coed luggage set and fill it up with your jeans and your new diaphragm and your toothbrush and unpack it all over here to live with me?"

One night we were in his room, supposedly studying after dinner, and he wouldn't drop the subject. "Spacious room," he said. "Fireplace. Large closet. Warm bed. Me. Come on, Charlotte."

"I can't," I said.

"*Na-ze ikenai?*" he said in his harsh samurai voice. "*Onna, naze ni?*"

"What?"

"I said: Why not, woman?"

"Because my mother would find out. I'd have to leave."

"Why?"

"Never mind. I'd have to leave school if I did that."

"Did you know that in Japan the wives live in the houses of their mothers-in-law and have to do whatever the mother-in-law says, and also walk two paces behind the men, and also they cover their teeth when they smile?"

"What do they cover them with?" I said.

"Their hands," Jack said. "Like this." He put the flat of his hand sideways across his face and bucked his teeth out over his bottom lip and said, "*Ahhhh sooo. Ahhh sooooo desu.* If I make the U.S. team I'll get to ski in Sapporo."

"They ski in Japan?" I didn't know.

"Yeah. They go *banzaiiiiiiii.*"

He leaped at me, onto the bed where I was sitting, and started wrestling with me, till he hammerlocked me down and said: "Charlotte, go get your stuff. It's moving day."

"Maybe," I said. "I have to go to my room anyway, because I have an art history test tomorrow and I need the book."

"Let's go to the Red Hat."

"Jack."

Jack wouldn't let me up until I said, "I will be back in just one hour." He made me say it over and over so that when finally I got out of the hammerlock there was no blood left in my arms.

. . .

"Where the hell have you been?" Claire looked up from her book and her beer. She was bitter. It had been a week since I'd slept in our dorm room.

"Jack," I said.

"What, there was a wedding?"

"No."

Claire looked at me and held her beer out. "You need this," she said. I took it and drank some but it was warm. *Tastes like dog saliva*, I thought to say, and then did say it, so Claire laughed. I missed her.

"Your mom called," she said. "She's been calling, actually, a lot." Then she imitated Barbara, with her voice high and full of exclamation points and extra syllables: "Hi-iii there! Is this Claire? Oh! Hi! Charlotte's told me all about you! From the big city! New York! My, my! I don't know how you could grow up in a place like that! Remarkable!"

"So. Any message?" I said.

"She asked me not to tell you she was asking this," said Claire, then took a deep breath, "but she wanted to know did you entertain men in your room?"

"Holy Lamb of God," I said. Barbara was checking on me. *Avon calling.*

"That's not all," said Claire. "She said she'd be grateful for any information I had about that sort of thing."

"She wants you to rat me out?"

"Yeah. She asked were you still drinking and I said, 'Oh, no, Mrs. Halsey, she's too busy studying.'"

"Jesus," I said. "She should've been in the FBI or a narc or something."

"Aw, she wasn't so bad, Charlotte," said Claire. "She sounds nice. She's around, anyway." And she was suddenly so glum and blue. I wanted badly to snap her out of it.

"Believe me," I said, "your setup with your mom has its perks."

Claire looked away into the dim yellow desk light of the room. "No, Charlotte," she said, "it does not." She started to cry then. "It has no perks."

Geez, I'm an idiot, blurting without thinking. I had wanted to cheer her up and now she was sobbing. "I'm sorry, Claire, oh God, I'm sorry," I said, and hugged her.

"I just miss you, Charlotte," she said, shrugging me off. "You're always with him."

"Where have you been?" Jack wanted to know as soon as I got back.

"Just in my room," I said. "Just talking to Claire."

"What took you so long? Why didn't you come back? You said one hour. You said an hour."

"So I was gone two."

"Have you been drinking?"

"Just a beer with Claire. Just one beer. She's my friend."

"She's a slut."

"Shut up."

"What did you say? What? Did you say to shut up?"

"Yes."

He came over and held my jaw. "Don't say shut up to me," he said. "Sweetheart. Don't."

I moved his hand down from my chin. He smiled at me. "Now unpack your little things," he said. "See? I made a space for you." He stood behind me while I put my clothes in his dresser. He rubbed the cords of my neck, kissed me behind the ear. "I love you, Charlotte," he said.

I folded my underwear. Hung my jacket in the closet, my vest, my long skirts. What in the world was I doing? He loved me, he said. He wanted me. My mother would call, she would find out.

Well, maybe I wanted her to.

Jack was happy. I was his roommate. Whenever I needed to spend a night in the library studying, which, believe me, was not often, he got worried. Whenever I went without him anywhere, to meet Claire for a drink, he wanted to know: "Why? Where are you going? Who will be there? What will you be doing, huh?" He always said this with his fingertip lifting my chin, as if he thought that to want me all the time, every second, was love.

Finally, it was bound to happen, that I would try to get out of it.

It was a race day in late January, snowing and windy. Jack had not had a good race. He lost time on the third gate where there was rock under slick ice. He edged badly and caught the basket of his pole on the bamboo gate. He came in second and his time was off from the practice run. "They changed the course on me," he kept saying. "Goddamn, Charlotte, they changed the course."

A guy named Franz had taken first in the slalom, some German ringer from the University of Vermont. Milo Robicheaux was first by entire minutes in giant slalom and downhill. Jack was second in all three. A U.S. Ski Team coach was on the hill. He was scouting. Jack was desperate to impress him, but everybody said: "Good run, Jack, too bad about that gate!"

I hadn't seen it. I was waiting at the bottom, the girlfriend at the finish line. This was my talent. Loyalty and ornament. Eyes watching Jack like Patricia Nixon's watching Dick. My mother admired her so, the way she stood by him. *Pat's the real hero*, she liked to say.

All afternoon Jack would review the mistake for me on the way up the chairlift, clacking his skis. Then we were off the chair and down the slope again, freestyle runs. Jack's furious schussing and aerial tricks off the bumps got hoots of envy from the regular-joe skiers on the way down. When he stopped short to wait for me, the power of his legs pushing snow sent up big sprays like peacock tails at the end of his fancy tracks.

"Charlotte!" he said, when I caught up to him. "Get your nerve. Get your nerve. You're chickening on those moguls, you're not bossing them, you're not."

"No," I said, "I just want to ski."

"You just want me," he said, kissing me. "Say it. Say it, you just want me."

"I just want you, Jack," I said peevishly. "Only you. But I'm cold." I pouted and smiled and kissed him. "It's no fun, Jack," I said. "I'm tired. I don't want to ski down again. I'll break something."

Another guy from the team passed by then. Andy. "Hey, Jack, hey, Charlo," he said.

"Hey," I said, and started to follow him in.

Jack looked at me, snow melting onto his eyelashes. "Charlotte," he said, half desperate, "it's over for me—the Olympic thing, I think it is."

"You'll win the next one," I said, and put my mouth up. He kissed me and nipped the chapped-lip skin so a dry flake pulled off bloody in the cold.

"Ow," I said.

"Aw, Kitten, sorry," said Jack. "Stay and ski with me. I need you."

"I'm freezing *and* bleeding," I said. "Hey, Andy," I yelled after this other guy. "Andy, wait, I'm going in, too."

"What do you mean, I'll win the next one?" Jack said loudly. "What would you know about it?" Andy left and Jack started stabbing the hard-pack with his ski-pole tip. "You're going inside to look for somebody. Some guy to whore around with." This was the way he'd gotten lately. Worse even. The word *whore* was new.

"You like to go where you know they'll all look at you, right, Charlotte? Because nobody can see you with that woolly hat on, right? And that scarf up around your face, and that big jacket? With all this snow coming down? No one can see you. You're just going in there to get some looks, eh?"

"No," I kept saying. "No. Stop it. No."

I was getting my skis off, bending low over the bindings. He was stabbing the snow right by my head.

"Go sit by the fire, little ski bunny," he said, singsong. "Sit by the fire in your big fur boots till somebody comes along. Hop along now, Charlotte."

"Just stop it, Jack," I said, and stood with my skis. "I'm just going to get warm." I turned and started to walk away from him.

"Charlotte."

"I don't want to ski with you anymore," I said. It could have sounded like I said *be* with you anymore. That's what he thought I said. And I might as well have. He knew. He was right. I *was* leaving him.

But I don't think he meant to hurt me. He said he didn't. I was about ten feet away when he took his ski pole and threw it at me, chucked it like a spear. It hit me in the shoulder. I shrieked and started running.

He skated after me on his skis. He nearly caught me. He shouted and grabbed for my scarf so I thought I might die of choking but I just unwound it from my neck and left him holding it. People stared at us, then looked away to be polite.

"Stupid girl!" He was getting his skis off as fast as he could but I was gone by then, into the base lodge, running through a seething warm stew of families and wet wool. My shoulder was going throb, throb, throb, though I didn't think it was bleeding. I wasn't in pain so much as shock. *He threw his ski pole at me*. He had never done that before. Never hit me or hurt me. In the bathroom I sat in a stall gulping, out of breath. I peeled off my big jacket and waited to think what to do. I didn't want to go back with him to the campus, didn't want to go back with him, period. I calmed down enough to be angry. I struggled my turtleneck up and twisted my head back and down to look at my injury. It *was* bleeding, the skin broken in a small red stab, not too deep. I just began to cry then.

Jack. You know, it seemed he should be such a flawless boyfriend, with his tously gold hair, his friendly demeanor, his fighting spirit on skis. He was a brilliant athlete. He could speak two languages. He had talents and abilities. I didn't know what I had.

I thought about this, running in the parking lot through the snow, away from the base lodge, crying. What was I good at? Running. Looking for Claire's car, trying to find it in the darkening parking lot, huge ski boots lumphing, leaving tracks. Jack would be coming after me. What I wanted was just to hide in Claire's car, drive it away. I ran with the high boots punishing my calf muscles, searching for a white car in a parking lot of white cars, all of them covered in snow.

I didn't want to explain to Jack. I didn't want to talk to him or have to comfort him, try to make splitting up seem like a good idea for him, too. When I broke it off with Dave Mueller I could see little adjustments going on in his eyes as I yapped on, preaching about being too young to be serious, despite *what happened*. All those bubble-wrapped advice-column words about loving him but not being In Love. *I think we should see other people.* When I said that Dave's eyes got wide and bright as Bambi's, just before his mother gets killed by hunters.

Better, I thought, not to have to see Jack like that. Maybe I could transfer, go to another school, take a leave, leave altogether.

I found Claire's car and tried the handle. It wasn't locked, just cold; the thumb-catch was frozen so I had to thaw it out with my breath. I climbed in and sat sweating and panting behind the wheel, feeling under the mud mats for the key. But the key wasn't in its usual place. I checked behind the visor, checked the glove compartment, where I found a can of frozen soda and a bag of chips. No key. My breath fogged up the cold windshield of the car, making frost flowers on the inside of the glass. When I stopped sobbing it was quiet, getting dark. The car was covered with snow that looked black from inside, or yellow sometimes, as the headlights of other cars passed. It was so still. The crackling of a potato chip, when I ate one, was loud as a brick through a picture window. I listened for footsteps and thought about what to say to Jack.

In the study lounge of my dormitory there was a poster tacked on the wall. It had a picture of two butterflies flying in separate directions. *If you love something set it free*, the poster read. *If it comes back it's yours, if it doesn't, it never was.* These words might work on Jack. He could set me free. It was funny: me and Jack as butterflies.

Now somebody was coming. Snow squeak and boot-buckle rattle and ski clack. No voices. I cracked my window down to see who it was and saw Milo Robicheaux passing with his heavy equipment, trudging to the team van parked not far away. He was by himself and whistling a little tune in the snow and the dusk.

"Hey, Milo," I called out softly.

He stopped and looked around, couldn't see where I was.

"Hey." I cracked the door open so he saw me in the light.

"Charlotte!" he said, smiling. "Hey, man. Now what finds you here in the middle of such a vast parking wasteland?"

"Waiting for a ride," I said. "From Claire."

"Why don't you come back with the team? Van's parked over there."

I just shook my head.

"We're celebrating," he said. "Though you must of course already know."

"What?"

"Me and your man," he said. "We're anointed. We're summoned for trials. Olympic trials. Both of us." He was beaming. He was so happy.

"Congratulations!" I said. "That's great!" I got out of the car and we stood there, snowflakes landing on his face like stars. "That's wonderful." His arms were full of skis and boots and poles, balanced on his shoulder.

"Thanks," he said, shifting the skis down now, resting their heels on the ground. He couldn't stop smiling. He was bursting with his news, about to tell it, but then he looked hard at me, his face serious all of a sudden. "You okay?" he said. "Charlotte?"

"Yeah," I said. "I'm fine." My hand went up to my shoulder, rubbed it. "So," I said. "That's great! You did it."

"Sure you're okay?"

Tell him what happened. What Jack said. The ski pole flying through the air. "I— See, Jack, we were—" My voice caught on the words. I was about to tell him, but I stopped and my eyes watered. Milo's hand came up to touch my shoulder and I winced. The fabric of my jacket rustled where his glove brushed it. I saw worry in his eyes, like the glimpse of a bird in thick woods.

"What's wrong?" he asked.

But we heard a commotion heading toward us. It was the guys on the team. "Hey! Smilo!" Milo turned around so his back was toward me. He said, "Heeyyyy!" They started lobbing snowballs at him. Claire was with them. And Jack.

"Hey, Milo! Way to go, man! We were looking for you!"

Jack hung behind. I saw he had my skis with him. The others swarmed around pounding Milo on the back. Andy picked him up like he was carrying a baby in his arms and Scott was pegging him with snowballs. Claire gave him a big kiss. "Milo, you fast machine, you!" she said. "Olympic tryouts!"

Jack watched me. He stood back. Then he came and put his arm around my shoulder. "You heard about it?" he said.

"Yes," I told him. "It's so wonderful, Jack. Congratulations."

He pulled my ear to his mouth. "I'm sorry, Kitten," he whispered. "I never meant to hurt you. I was kidding. You know that, right? I just care so much, you know?" He was grinning at the guys when he whispered these things, so they would think he was saying something hot and private to me.

The thing to do, at a time like that, is to kiss the victorious boyfriend, as everybody there would expect. It was not the time to talk about freeing the butterflies or the ski pole flying through the air. When I kissed Jack all the men whooped. "Ow! ow! ow!" they snorted.

Then Jack went over to Milo and said, "Yo, bro, slap me down some skin," and he held out his hand. Maybe I was wrong, but Milo had that smirk around the mouth, just for a second, till he slapped Jack on the back and whooped it up and said: "Lake Placid, watch out!" Everybody laughed. He was a nice guy, and they all liked him a lot.

"What were you talking to Milo about?" Jack wanted to know later. We were in his room. I was thinking about telling him. Breaking Up. About packing. Where to begin. He had just shown me the letter from the U.S.

team. It was a form letter. "Dear _____," it said, with Jack's name ballpointed in. "You are invited to tryouts for the U.S. Ski Team, in Lake Placid, New York, on February 20, 1974." He kissed the letter. He took my hand and pulled me down on the bed, where he kissed me and then put his hands up around my neck. "Pretty," he said, "Charlotte, my kitten."

"Jack?" I said, pulling his hands away. I was just going to start my farewell speech.

"What were you talking to Robicheaux about?"

"Nothing."

"That was not nothing, Charlotte. I *saw*."

"I just said congratulations to him. Same as you."

"*Not* the same as me. And don't forget it," said Jack. "One. Of. Us. Is. Your. Boy. Friend. Right? And: It's. The White One." He had my wrists gently pinned on the mattress. "So, if you ever go near his black ass, Charlotte?" he said. He smiled with just one side of his face.

I waited for the punch line but he just winked at me. "Right," I said carefully. Hair was standing on my arms. "I'm not interested in him," I said. "Only you." I decided to be safe. It was not the time.

Breaking up is fraught with peril. With Dave it was. I made my speech about being too young. I was kind and I held him and felt it was all so tragic and awful. "I'll miss you, Dave. I'll think of you all my life," I said.

He got very sad and then he got angry. He said why had I been leading him on all this time? He put his arms around me, saying *Let me hold you one last time*. But then he wanted more than holding. *You don't mean it*, he said. *You're mine*. I pushed him away gently. I didn't want to kiss him, I wanted it to be over. He wouldn't quit taking off my sweater, pulling at my pants. *No, I really don't want to keep going*.

But he was angry and wanted his money's worth, or whatever. *You think you can just dump me?* He pulled and yanked, popped buttons. Mud got on my sweater. I was pushing him off while trying to be nice. *You know I care about you, Dave. You'll find another girlfriend. I'm not right for you.*

He got rough. He was going to go through with it.

I just lay there saying *Please*.

He said *You should say thank you*.

That time he did hurt me. I was sore, crying. He wouldn't drive me home.

So I knew it was not the right time for talking to Jack. It wasn't safe. We never talked. Not about the ski pole he threw at me. Not about why I wanted to leave: how it felt like he was lying when he said he loved me. When he held my face in his hands, it felt to me as if he was holding *his* face. *You're my Charlotte*, he said. *This is my face, my hair, my girlfriend, my Charlotte.*

He meant it to be sweet but it didn't feel sweet.

I just waited for an opportunity, biding my time. Jack was heading for tryouts at Lake Placid. The school was letting him take a leave for as long as he stayed in contention. I would write him a note, I decided, use the butterfly line, leave school when he was gone. We talked about how hard it would be for me to be apart from him. I knew what he wanted me to say so I said it. I told him I was so happy for him. He was going to win. He was going to be really fantastic. The night he left we celebrated by getting drunk on champagne, popping corks whizzing around his room. It was funny. Also fun. I knew it was the last time. He drank champagne out of my belly button while the room whirled around my head. It was wild. I was one wild girl.

After he was gone, I wrote the note and left it on his bed. I didn't even pack all my things. I left the heavier sweaters behind and some books. I went back to my room, and in the study lounge of my dorm, I saw that the poster of the butterflies had been altered. Somebody had blacked out the last phrase and changed the words so it made me laugh. It said: *If you love something set it free. If it comes back it's yours. If it doesn't*, hunt it down and kill it.

6.

Fifteen years later Jack still looks the same. He's frozen in time. I didn't see him again until recently. Just before it happened. The assault.

We went out for dinner, me and Jack. Was it the day before? I don't remember precisely. I know the timing matters; I'm trying to decide what exactly to tell the police. Or if I should.

Jack called and said he had just moved back to the West Coast after years of being away. Milo was furious. *Good*, I thought. *Fine, be furious. Be enraged.* I rubbed it in. I made it worse. I let Milo think whatever he was thinking about Jack and me. Insinuating things. I never loved Jack at all but let on I always had, always would. Why? Because I'd had some news about Milo. Because Milo deserved it. He deserved jealousy and suspicion and hurt. Also, a broken heart, cuts and scars, shattered nerves. I always did want equality in all things for me and for Milo. We were *created equal*. So it was only fair that he have what I had: regret, guilt, sorrow, penance. *Equal justice.*

But more than anything I wanted Milo back. In my arms, in our family. Wanted reconciliation, wanted to be reborn in the cleansing spirit of his love. Milo's. Ours.

This was, of course, before the, whatever, *incident*, before I almost died. Before I woke up in the bed in L.A. County Hospital all intubated and sedated and wrapped like a mummy, throat and hands cut up with chips of bottle glass still in the skin, Mommy and Daddy there by my side,

Mommy saying *I knew it, I knew it would come to this. Dear God, my child.*

The night Jack called, Hallie was some kind of miniature banshee, pitching tantrums and wolfing food. Ketchup stained my shirt and rice grains were sticking to my little pencil-leg black jeans like maggots. The phone rang through the bedlam and I picked up and said, "Hello," sullen and heartbroken because of my husband and what he had told me.

A voice, a man, said: "Charlotte?"

"Hello?"

"Charlotte-san, *o genki desu-ka?*"

"Jack?" I was flustered. "Is this Jack Sutherland?"

Just then Milo came downstairs into the kitchen.

"Jack!" I said, for Milo's benefit. "Oh, my God, it's you! Oh, *Ja-ack*. I always knew this day would come."

I could see Milo's eyes slitting down and his nostrils winging out in anger and disgust.

"Hey, Kitten," Jack said brightly.

Oh, boy. That voice. It brought Jack right back before my eyes, the way he smiled sideways, his bold gaze. My God, the sound of his words got to me so my legs were weak in the kitchen. Even the name didn't bother me: *Kitten.* It was an endearment, and it seemed a long time since I'd heard an endearment.

We agreed to meet. I theatrically carried the phone to the armchair in the corner, away from Hallie and Milo, and curled up, with my legs twined around each other. I played with my hair while I talked, not looking at Milo but sure he could see me, turning my cheek to the receiver and whispering, just loudly enough for him to eavesdrop. I saw Milo was listening, pretending to spoon peas into Hallie, pretending to listen to her story about the snake.

I put on a big show. Audience of Milo.

Me: Spago, sure, yes, the restaurant. I know it, of course. Drinks are fine. Okay, *and* dinner, why not? (scandalized) *Jack!* I don't know about *after* that. We'll see, we'll see about after, won't we? (thinking) *Because I am a married woman, don't you know? Still, maybe I just would, for old times' sake. For spite. For pain management, as they say during these painful days. Manage your pain.*

. . .

When I was in the hospital, recovering, they gave me my own personal morphine dose control pack. I could crank it up or not, however much or little I wanted. This was pain management for beginners, and I became good at it during my three weeks in the hospital. I had a burning in my throat, pain in the wounds on my neck and my arms. I couldn't speak at all, did not breathe through normal channels. My tube itched and festered in its little iodine-painted spot in my trachea. Sister Morphine, as the Stones sang it back in college, back in the Red Hat, that Sister Morphine was like a serene nun of reassurance and calm. I needed her cool hand, to distract me from the fact that somebody—my husband!?—had tried to kill me.

But of course there is no handy home morphine dose control pack, not for emotional pain, anyway, and so, back then—before the assault—Jack and other bottled anesthesia would have to do.

I hung up the phone and saw that Milo was furious.

"I know you always hated Jack Sutherland," I said, "but really, you're turning white with anger, Milo." This was the kind of joke I would never have made during most of our marriage. Because I knew it was what hurt him the most, this accusation of whiteness. But now I used it. I got him with it, and you know there *was* in fact a white line between his lips, he was pressing them together so hard.

"Fuck you."

"Daddy!" said Hallie. "Bad word."

Milo grabbed his blue sport coat off the back of the chair and left the kitchen, left the house.

Good, I thought. *Good*.

The rest of the evening, with Milo gone, I was gentle and quiet with Hallie. I read her stories and sang her old Bob Dylan songs for lullabies. *Shut the lights, shut the shade, you don't have to be afraid, 'cause I'll be your baby tonight.*

When I saw Jack, the next night, I was relaxed and cheerful, and if I do say so, looking nothing like the dishwater mother of a small child or the pale white jilted wife of Milo Robicheaux. I was quite beautiful, on purpose, hair streaming down my back, still gold as Rapunzel's, even at thirty-four, and I wasn't self-conscious of it. Didn't put it up, didn't tie it back. I did not worry that anyone would look at me for any reason but that I was pleasing to the eye. Did not worry anyone would say *There goes that white wife of his.* I was not white that night, I was just me, Charlotte, out with my former boyfriend.

And as I said, it was amazing how Jack had not changed. He was still wearing jeans. He still had that square chin and his sculpted cheekbones, still muscular, his hair blond as mine and long, past his earlobes. People were sure we were sister and brother. The waitress asked. We talked and laughed and drank champagne, just as we had that last night fifteen years before.

He said he could see I had had some lonely days. *You've had some hard times*, he said. My eyes filled with tears, because he was right, and he picked up my hand and laced his fingers with mine.

But I would not have dinner or go off with him. He wanted me to but I wouldn't. *Charlotte, stay*, he said. *You're beautiful as ever.*

I'm telling you I wanted to. Just to have somebody hold on to me, to praise me and say everything would be all right. But I couldn't. No. I was married to Milo and it wouldn't be right. Why? Just because Milo did that sort of thing? No. I wasn't like that. I wouldn't stoop to his level.

Except that is not the whole truth. What I just said about not stooping to his level. It is not "nothing but the truth so help me God." But it is the *essence* of the truth. The missing parts of the truth about that night with Jack could be seen as offering Milo a motive for the crime of attempted murder. The other details could be seen as giving sense to a senseless act, and I will not dignify it with that. Cutting me was senseless. Who has it served, to have me cut here in ribbons? Our family a shambles.

Perhaps somebody will say I asked for it. Perhaps I did, in a way. Somebody has in fact already more than suggested: I deserved it. I had it coming. Darryl Haynes is who. Milo's erstwhile agent. His "friend." *You play, you pay*, Darryl said. One of his little maxims. *The snake will have whatever is in the belly of the frog.*

But I prefer my mother's maxims: *Sometimes, Charlotte honey, a woman has to tell a little fib. A little white lie never hurt anybody, right?* It's interesting to me, how lies she thinks are "good" she calls *white.*

unwittingly played in these events. There are no words to ade-
quately express my regret, nor a good enough way I can convey my
deep wishes for this tragic matter to be resolved happily. May God
be with you.

> *Sincerely,*
> *Geneva Johnson.*

Geneva Johnson must have been well brought up, I must say, to have so graciously apologized for sleeping with someone else's husband. *Unwittingly.* This is the word I question.

And it would have to have been *his* fault. Milo would have said things so that she would think it was okay for him to be with her and not with me, his wife. He was good at lying. Must have been, since I didn't know anything about *her*, she was a secret for years. It was *years* he was seeing her, the papers say. The papers seem to know more than I do. They have it all figured out. He tried to get rid of me so he could be with her, is one theory.

But he *was already* with her, wasn't he? He had been with her. It's just that I found out, and became—I became . . . what is the word?

I don't know a word. My love went out of me.

When is Snowflake gonna get sooty? Darryl asked. *When's he gonna get himself a taste of that brown sugar?*

A part of me doesn't even hate Milo. A small part, about the size and the sad color of a blueberry, doesn't hate him. *He will have his medicine,* Darryl said, and he was right. Geneva Johnson answered a question I couldn't answer, fixed something in Milo I couldn't fix.

Because I am a white girl.

You hate your black self, Darryl told him. *You cannot be a real black man with that white wife of yours. Your fine black mother is black! Your black sister is a queen! And look at you, chasing that vanilla frosting. Snowflake, man, get yourself a real woman.*

Milo used to shrug him off. At first he did. "Charlotte is my wife," he told Darryl. "She is going to be the mother of my children."

"Her daddy would put a necklace round your neck and string you up," Darryl said. "In a second he would." Darryl always went on like this. He'd kiss his lips at me and say, "It's nothing personal, Pink, you know that, right, Charlotte?"

He called Milo "Snowflake."

I wish Milo had never, never, never met Darryl. If wishes were horses I would have won the Triple Crown by now.

Get him some of that Brown Sugar.

Brown Sugar. I look at Geneva Johnson's picture and I think she is beautiful. Next to her I am Styrofoam floating. I am Wonder Bread.

"That's my daddy!" said Hallie, pointing.

I can't explain to Hallie. She can't read yet, and how I talk now is mostly by writing notes on pocket-size pads of white paper. She asks me questions and I can't answer them in a way she'd understand. If there is such a way. The child psychologist suggested we write her a story for her grammy to read aloud, so she'd know. The "Where Is My Daddy?" story. The "Why Mommy Can't Talk Now" story. Well, I said, in my note, how would we write that? What would we say?

It's twisted and sick, the story. It would be Dick and Jane, warped. *Daddy had to go away for a while. He's in jail. The police say he tried to kill Mommy with broken glass, so that is why Mommy went to the hospital. That is why she can't talk. If it's true, he won't be coming back soon. Even if it's not true, we're still all doomed. And maybe we were always doomed, which is what our parents said we would be. They had plenty of company. Everybody thought we were headed for nothing but hell and damnation. Looks like they were right. The end.*

7.

I left school. Just dropped out. Left Jack when he was away at tryouts. It was late February 1975. First I went to New York with Claire. There was no plan, exactly, but soon it became clear we were not going back. Claire had had it with Vermont. She thought she would go to NYU or City College. Not me. I was through with it. Six months of higher education was enough, since all I ever really wanted was to leave home. We started out staying at Claire's father's apartment on Fifth Avenue. It had dark velvet curtains and thick carpets and was supposed to be temporary for us, just a week, but it was going on months now.

I needed a lot of things: a place to live. Money. Another bottle of aspirin. Maybe a haircut. I needed some arms around me. A job. I was still only eighteen years old, guilty and nervous but having a good time anyway. I owed people cash. Also apologies. Jack. My parents. They didn't know where I was. They hadn't heard from me. Not since Vermont. Not since a girl answering the hall phone said, "Try Jack Sutherland's room, she's mostly living there." This did not please them, to put it mildly.

They had gotten hold of me the night I was packing up my stuff in Jack's dorm. My father asked was I living there? No, I said, which was about to be true. He said he knew I was lying. He said: *You are no longer in His light and His love. You are lost in the shadows.* He wanted me home right away. He would stop all payments for school.

So, go ahead, I told him, and slammed down the phone.

Years later, my sister told me that phone call had just about killed our father. He started drinking again briefly. Drinking *again?* He drank *before?* Yes! She had found out. The Story of Dad. How long ago, whiskey was the warm river that carried him into the arms of God. It was the story of a party and a bad accident. How one night my dad drove his car smack into somebody else, a young woman. She was seriously damaged, clinging to life. But Dad had only bruises, and a hangover. He lost his license for two years, paid the fines and the hospital bills of the young woman, who would never really walk well again and whose disfigured face would never be rectified by plastic surgery. He was fine, except for his guilt and torment, and my mother saying *You will never touch a drink again. Never.* Oh, it explained a lot, that story. The brooding silences and the temper. All the praying. After the accident, Barbara had to drive chastened Arthur everywhere, until he got his license back. One of the places she drove him was church. The Assembly of God. They went one Sunday with toddler Peter and newborn me. Pastor Hanneman put his hands on our heads and took away our baby sins and all my partyboy father's, too. Pastor said Jesus would take the sins, had died for them. My father fell hard for the pastor's hushed voice, the words *Come, the Lord says, and rest in Me. Won't you rest? I will hold you in the palm of My hand.*

Daddy needed a rest, for sure, and he climbed into the Lord's hand that day in 1956. My mother told the story to Diana in the maelstrom of worry about my disappearance from college. They were all furious and frantic. Sick with fear. Crazy worrying that because I drank and sometimes got drunk I had inherited the alcohol talent from my father, along with his height and his cheekbones. When I finally heard the story, years later—I was just about married when I heard it—I thought: She's right that Dad and I are the same. We like drink and are not quite drunks until something goes wrong. Then we take long numb baths in alcohol and self-pity.

So go ahead, I said to him. *Cut me off.*

It just killed him. I had to say it, though.

You are no longer in His Light or His Love, he said to me. He meant God's light and love, but he might as well have been talking about his own.

During those first months in the city I thought I might never talk to my family again, since all the news I had for them was about waitressing jobs, bars and parties, a fast life in a fast city. I didn't call. At the time I blamed my father for cutting me off, but *I* cut *him*. I cut everyone but Claire.

I especially cut Jack, who was now a junior member of the U.S. Ski Team, trying for the '76 Olympics. Him and Milo. I'd heard about it from Claire, who'd gone back to Cabot to pack up all our things and bring them to New York. "Just tell Jack I'm traveling," I said. "Say you're storing my stuff for me." I certainly didn't want to go with her, to have to explain why I was leaving. I hadn't said boo to Jack or congratulations. Nothing. I dropped out of his sight. Just bolted. It was not a moral thing to do, or even polite, but it was easier for me to just go, to give myself as many breaks as possible.

Claire did not see Jack when she went back to Cabot, but she did hear things. "He told everyone you're coming back to school, Charlotte," she said. "He told everyone you left because you were upset he wouldn't be there. He told Geoff he would see you this summer in California."

"Oh, boy," I said.

"Apparently Jack told people he got some letter from you saying you'd be back."

"Not exactly," I said.

"You'd better write him again, Charlotte," Claire said. "You can't string people along like that."

"I'm not stringing him," I said.

But was I? My mother told me years later that Jack had called them in Conestoga off and on, looking for me. They didn't know where I was, they said, they wished they did. He called Claire's once, too, and she said—because I asked her to—that she hadn't seen me for months. She thought I was in Paris, or maybe Rome. I was glad I hadn't been the one to answer the phone, glad Claire lied to him that way; it seemed easier.

At the time I didn't consider that Jack would really feel anything about me leaving. I had no idea he still carried a torch for me, which was my mother's theory, years later. He was just trying to save face, I thought, telling people that I would be back. Maybe he *believed* he loved me but he would see immediately that he didn't, not really. He would soon have someone else, like snapping his fingers.

"You should at least call him," Claire said. "Poor guy."

"He'll live," I said. "Trust me."

I didn't think about Jack again. He was in the past. That's what I thought, anyway. It was time to think about Charlotte. What I needed. Sleep, a job. Definitely a haircut. My hair was all the way down my back, childish and dull, it now seemed to me. New York women had coiffures, and style. I leafed through magazines and shopped for a new way to look. I concentrated on getting a haircut as if it would change my life.

And it did change my life, my haircut.

Claire said you could get one for free at Vidal Sassoon Salon. They wouldn't charge you to cut it, but you had to let them do whatever. You would be a test model for the haircutting students at the Sassoon School, like a lab monkey. They would snip away, with their novice scissors, practicing on your head. Vidal himself supposedly would do the critique.

I didn't care what they did to me. They could shave me. They could lawn mower my hair. I was heading for something. Not Vermont. Not California. My vague direction seemed to be toward trouble. Toward something not very well thought out, surely ending up in the sucking ooze-pond of sin and regret that my parents warned me about. I didn't care, as long as it was new and different.

Late one afternoon I headed toward the Sassoon Salon. *Sassoon Saloon festoon a baboon.* Walking toward Madison Avenue from the subway I made up rhymes to ward off panic. *Croon a soft tune at Sassoon's Saloon.* I worried that I would be grotesquely out of place, a laughingstock of the Sassoonerites, in just my pea coat and jeans and my too-small muscle shirt featuring silk-screened Vermont dairy cows. And this cornfield of hair down my back. Perhaps I was just some kind of hogan, as Jack would say. Thinking about him and his expressions, I was glad to be far away, in the thrilling city. That afternoon the late sun hit the buildings and the April wind whirled the garbage around, newspapers and plastic bags sailing giddily up. Every other woman on the jam-packed sidewalks of midtown had on skirts and hosiery. Their hair was right. They had suits and dark lipstick. Handbags. They did not look like hogans or escaped children running from their parents or their boyfriends. They did not have on cow T-shirts.

At least the ones I looked at did not. I was not really noticing the old ones, or the Chinese ones, the fat ones or black ones or Mexican ones. The women I was checking out were white, around twenty, like me. They were thin. Looking at them was like research for me. I was deciding how to fit in, what kind of shoes, what kind of hair, who looked good.

I noticed and was wary of all kinds of men. They said things to me in the street. New York men were always muttering. They were not like the men in the Sierras of California or the Green Mountains of Vermont. They scared me. The Spanish ones made hissy noises or kissed their lips. *Hey, mami,* they said, *Ssssssss.* Passing a scaffolding of white construction workers I could hear clapping and hooting, whistles of wolves. Guys in fancy suits, most of them, whatever their ilk, didn't say anything; still, I saw their eyes sliding sideways at me. Black men were the ones who talked at me most often, who stopped before I passed them, arrested mid-step, standing there staring me down. *Take it to the limit, blondie, lookin' fine. I would like to get to know you, oh, I'd like to make your acquaintance.* Sometimes the things they said were funny: *Your baby gonna need a daddy, why not me?* Sometimes they just said *Unh. Unh, unh, unh,* as if they had just tasted something delicious.

This was not my imagination. It didn't happen that much to Claire, who was beautiful. Her dark hair was long now, cascading down her back. If we walked together she was amazed at how often I got hassled. I didn't know why it was so, whether it had to do with me: What I wore? Or whether it had to do with them—because they hated white people? because I was extra white? I knew this was not the kind of thing to talk about, even to Claire, or remark about. There was a newspaper column I read when I first got to New York, in the *Times,* by a black man who got sick of white women grabbing their purses when he passed, as if they thought all black men were muggers. I felt mad for him. I tried not to even touch my purse when I passed a black man in case he would think I was grabbing it in fear. I tried to look straight ahead, maybe smile pleasantly to signal I was friendly and not a racist. But I couldn't help flinching from strangers, taxi drivers who said *You're very beautiful,* looking at me in the rearview mirror, guys in bars asking the time, asking for a light.

And I couldn't help, I confess, liking that they looked at me. I was terrible and vain. Preening inwardly. *You know you look good,* one guy said to me. *You love it.* I did. I was noticed. I needed that. It was all I had, I thought. At least they noticed me.

When I got to the salon, about fifteen women were waiting to be chosen. There was a big piled-up red hairdo next to a straight blue-black sheet of Chinese hair. There was a starched white head, a curly brown pelt, and a girl with dozens of tiny pale braids close to her scalp like a black child but she was a grown white woman. This was a fashion at that time but to me it didn't look right. You could see the exposed scalp, the color of newborn mice, and all the veins. She stared at me. "You'll get picked," she said, and I admit I thought she was right. I would get picked. It's not like something I controlled, so why not? I'd get a free haircut.

All the women waited politely on chairs with purses on their laps. They read the magazines. But I sat on the floor in a corner away from them and wrote a letter in my head. *Dear Mother and Father, You would hate it here. It's loud and the air is one big bus fume. There is no sign of God that you would recognize. Surely it would be some comfort to you to know I feel Him watching me just constantly as usual without giving me any breaks. God is telling me right now that certainly I should not let this man coming toward me with his comb and clippers cut my hair all off. I don't mind homosexuals. I know you do. This guy with the scissors, he's friendly. He's joking with all the women waiting to get haircuts. He's looking every one of us right in the eye and smiling in a friendly way. What is evil?*

I was just daydreaming this, wondering if I'd ever get the guts to send a letter at all, even a postcard to say: "Don't worry, I'm fine."

The man with the comb was getting closer to me. I could see him glancing over, while he was talking to the others. Eventually he crouched down in front of me, sitting back with his heels flat. He had black hair, chin length, that he tucked behind his ears every few seconds with a C-shaped motion of his fingers.

"Hi," he said, "I'm Kevin." His smile was lovely. Safe and quiet. His manner was like that of an animal trainer, serene, reassuring. I said hello. He squinted at me and lifted my chin with two fingers, so I felt the end of a fingernail in the soft underskin of my jaw. He tipped my head left and right. I was tempted to open my mouth, show him my fillings. *What if I whinnied like a horse?* I thought, and imagined what he'd do then. For some reason I thought he'd laugh.

"You are very beautiful," Kevin said. He felt my hair, slipping it back and forth in his fingers like testing a fabric. "Your hair is amazing. The color."

"Thank you."

"What style are you looking for?" he asked.

"Just do whatever," I said, shrugging. "Isn't that the rule? We let you just, cut?"

"Come with me," he said, pulling me to my feet.

The other women in their chairs watched. They wished they were going with Kevin. We went in the back of the salon. The student hairstylists were waiting there, wearing green smocks like hospital scrubs.

"This is—" Kevin said, and looked at me.

"Charlotte."

"Charlotte. She'll be our model tonight. I'll cut her, and then the other volunteers will come in for you to work on yourselves. I'll do the critique, and I'm looking to grade you on choice of style, how the style you choose goes with the customer's face and overall type. And of course, execution."

He was going to cut me. He had said *execution*. It sounded grim, but I had a fatalistic urge about this haircut. They could do whatever they wanted to me.

Kevin sat me down and put a cape around my neck. He brushed my hair and I closed my eyes. It was very soothing, to be brushed. I know why animals like it. My mother used to hold me on her lap and brush my hair, talking. *Your lovely hair, my Charlotte.* She'd sing quietly. "Swing low, sweet chariot," or "Michael, row the boat ashore." They were just soft songs, me in my mother's lap. Nothing more, though, no idea of what the songs were really about, or where they came from. *Comin' for to carry me home.*

It's only now that I think this way.

I was in a kind of trance, despite the bright light and mirrors, the students in a half circle behind me. I listened for the sound of the scissors.

He cut off nine inches. It fell in dead furry hanks onto the floor. He talked to the beauty students while he was cutting, about the shape of my face, the way my hair grew. I didn't listen to him. My hair was gone. Somebody was sweeping it into a mangy yellow pile. What was left hit the top of my ears. I couldn't say anything. *I look like a palm tree. Or a boy.*

Kevin spiked my head up with clear gel. My neck, when he took off the cape, was long as the neck of a goose. "Well?" he said.

"Well." My lip trembled, as if I'd been punished.

"You look amazing," he said, in his kind animal-trainer voice. "Come and talk to me after class. I'll just be twenty minutes."

I went back into a mirrored office to wait with tears in my eyes. It was just hair, I told myself. I guess I had liked it, pridefully, more than I had admitted. I believed what they said about it, *Like spun gold*, in the fairy stories and the magazines. *A woman's hair is her crowning glory*, my mother said. It was seemingly my only glory, if it was, actually, a glory. I didn't have another, as far as I could tell.

"Don't cry," Kevin said, when he finally came in. "Your hair is even more beautiful now because it surrounds this face, which is extraordinary. Trust me." He asked me some questions. He was interested in my experience as a child in the California beauty pageants. He wanted to know had I ever done any modeling.

Yes, I told him. At home I did the garden club fashion shows with my mom and the church ones. Once I was in a catalog. *It made me throw up.* I didn't say that, but I remembered it, the photographer rolling his eyes while I leaned over and vomited, and my mother whispering at me to *just cooperate!*

"Did you enjoy it?" he asked me.

"It was okay," I said. "Yeah."

"I'd like to have this cut photographed. It's extraordinary," Kevin said. "If you photograph well you could have a career. You have a Look. I'm serious, let me know if you're interested." And right then he offered me a job in Vidal's salon, which I took. I was a kind of hostess, answering the phone, making appointments, greeting clients. In my short hairdo, I helped women in and out of their haircutting capes. I made coffee and served chocolate lace cookies on doilies. I shopped for clothes with my pay. I bought three different colors of Charles Jourdain pumps with heels that caused me to be six feet tall. I bought black things, jackets and sweaters, jeans, skirts, eyeliner. I saved just enough for rent money. Claire and I got an apartment in the far East Eighties, a neighborhood of singles' bars and Laundromats and Germans.

Claire was doing better. She stopped sleeping around and started going to school at New York University, waitressing on weekends at the Whiskey Dog Saloon on Second Avenue. This was a good job for her because there was something about carrying trays of drinks, with the smell of spilled alcohol on her skin like perfume, that kept her from drinking so much herself. She was getting better about that. She had a new boyfriend named Carl. He was from North Carolina and worked for an investment firm in Midtown with around four names that I could never remember. Claire and I called it Pork Belly and Sow. Carl was bland, yet nice. Just what Claire needed. He laughed at her jokes. He called her "sugarlips," and held doors open and always insisted on walking on the street side of a woman so that should a bus or a taxi splash through a puddle or jump the curb, it would be he, Carl, that was soaked or flattened grimly and killed gallantly and the woman would be saved. Claire appreciated gentility. She was studying history and was never going back to Cabot College. Claire thought maybe she could be a lawyer like her father. "Only without the little bow tie," she said.

As for me, it seemed I would be a beautician. Kevin started training me that spring. He took me along on various photo shoots where he did hair and makeup. This seemed like the right profession for the daughter of an Avon lady. I knew my way around the brushes and combs and pins and gels by instinct. I was nineteen years old, without much of a plan other than to see what happened, but everyone kept telling me: Charlotte, you should model yourself. *On whom should I model myself?* I would say back to them. The idea of modeling was terrifying to me. All I could think of was my pageant smile, how long it lasted, hours and hours of rictus of the cheek, my teeth flashing. Being a model was the same as being a pageant contestant as far as I could see. I would throw up behind the runway.

Kevin talked me into it. "In modeling you don't have to be cheerful," he said. "Not constantly or even often." He talked about beauty and fashion as if it was some kind of art. *Fashion is the way we show our souls,* he said. *Our moods and feelings. A great model is a model who communicates a vision of the soul, a vision of who we are, how we live, what we value, what we hold as beautiful.* I never heard anyone talk the way he talked. He was a kind man, and smart.

"Charlotte, girl, you need to use your gifts," Kevin said to me one night after the salon closed. I was sweeping up hair, watching all the colors of curls and snips mixing in my dustpile. I was growing mine again.

"I don't think so," I told him.

"My dear, do you want to be sweeping *hair* all your life? Or do you want to take the world by storm?"

"Sweep hair," I said.

"Bullshit," he said. Then he talked to me soothingly, cajoling. It was sweet talk but of course with him, vis-à-vis me, there was no bedroom agenda. He was safe. So when he kept telling me I was a natural, I was lovely, I was born for the camera, I liked it, the way animals like being brushed. He was feeding me treats, compliments like biscuits.

"I don't like to be stared at."

"Then get yourself some Coke-bottle glasses, wear a sackdress and jackboots. You'll be hiding till you're old. They're staring at you *now*, my dear. You turn heads. It's a law of nature."

Kevin finally got me to go down to Chelsea with him to have some pictures made. A photographer stood me up against a white drape and asked me to tilt my head, look backward over my shoulder, look up, look down. He snapped pictures without conversation. It was quiet except for the strange bird sound of the camera shutter advancing the film.

It was amazing to me how I loved it. Right away I did, even just shooting portfolio shots, the first time. I liked the way the light felt around me, warm on my skin and face, with everything black around the edges, the camera clicking in the dark. The glare made it hard to see the rest of the room, the photographer snapped in shadow, so I couldn't see his face. I felt free, as if I were alone. I combed my hair with my fingers and closed my eyes.

"Let your face tell a story," said the photographer. He put music on so I would move around.

I let my face tell the story of singing in church with my sister when we were small, how we were carried away by the words and the feelings. *What wondrous love is this, O my soul.* All I had to do was imagine that certain song and it appeared on my face. In the photographs from that first shoot I am smiling. I am relaxed with my eyes closed, or flirting right at the camera. My head is back laughing. My hair is short. I look to be about fifteen years old. Pictures of a happy girl.

Later, when my career really was rocketing along, it got harder. My face told the same stories over and over and got tired, wooden. Photographers said: more mystery, more sultry, more wholesome. But those were just words, without stories. I didn't do that as well and it showed. Still, that first time, there was something there. Even I could see it.

I was pretty in those photographs. Young. I knew nothing.

Kevin took the prints without my knowledge to the Wilhelmina Agency. He was a friend of Wilhelmina's. I got a contract right away and quit working for Vidal. I did runway work and magazine shoots and for a year the Estée Lauder people signed me up to be "the face" of their makeup. Later I was the Charlie Girl, for the perfume. I went to parties with movie stars and politicians. I went on a date with the son of the Aga Khan and another one with an English rock star and one with Warren Beatty. Actually a few with him. I met Milo again, at a party in a nightclub. All because of a haircut.

8.

The next time I heard of Milo Robicheaux was on television. It was after I had been in New York a year, some Saturday in January. Having stayed out until four or five in the morning, I woke up at noon. My head was crawling like some kind of ant farm of pain, with all the intricate passageways of blood vessels and chambers throbbing. I resolved again not to drink anymore. I was hungry but I had resolved again not to eat anything. I turned the TV on and got back in bed, watching with the sound off and my head crawling with hangover. I eventually noticed footage of a mountain, white trails snaking down its slopes. This was Innsbruck, Austria, and the TV showed big banners over the finish line. Olympic skiing, 1976.

And there he was: Milo Robicheaux, breathing hard and smiling, talking soundlessly to a sports reporter with that big ice-cream-cone microphone under his face.

I jumped up and turned the sound back on. But the picture cut away from Milo. There was a guy in a booth talking now.

"Just an amazing run by twenty-year-old Milo Robicheaux, the American," he said. "A stunning upset of the Austrian Franz Klammer, making this, I believe it would be, if the time stands, the first gold ever by an American in the downhill and the first gold for a *black* American in the Winter Games. This could be history in the making, folks."

"Hey, Claire," I called. "Come in here."

She came in from her studying with her glasses down on her nose and we watched, sitting on the bed.

They showed Milo again. He was looking at the time clock. His name was up on the board. Robicheaux, Klammer, Heine.

"Holy shit," Claire said.

"He looks good," I said to Claire.

"He looks the same," she said.

But on TV Milo seemed huge to me now, suddenly, even though his image on the set was small enough to fit in my hand. He was smiling in the crowd, looking up at the race times with his eyes excited and nervous, joking to his teammates.

"He always was such a handsome guy," I said.

"Oh," Claire said, pouncing, "*now* you think he looks good."

"What's that supposed to mean?"

"Now he's famous you think he's cute, eh?"

"Claire," I said. "Fuck off, Claire."

"Sorry," she said. "I love you. I take it back." She leaned over and kissed me on the cheek. "Sorry."

Milo had his skis off now. He was holding them and talking to somebody, another racer with a stubby blond ponytail and freckly skin. Milo put his arm around this guy. We watched them confer and nod while the announcers went on about him.

"Hey, Carl," Claire called. "Come here and see this."

Now Carl was in my room, too, his neat corduroy pants crinkling at the knees where he perched on the windowsill, safely away from the bed. He didn't approve of me, I knew. "Claire gets so silly with you," he said. Which usually just made us worse, putting napkins on our heads in restaurants. It made him uncomfortable. "Calm down, girls," he was always saying. "Down, girls, down!" He made me want to bark loudly or slobber on his coat, just to bother him.

"What's this?" he said now.

"Someone we knew from Vermont," Claire told him. I liked how she called us "we." "Look at him, Charlotte!" she said. "Milo Robicheaux! I mean, we used to *party* with this man. Just a year ago we were at the Red Hat with that guy! We were throwing snowballs at him in the parking lot!"

We watched while they replayed the footage from Milo's run. There he was, crouched in the starting gate, his legs coiled to spring. The picture was black and white, the camera tight on his face. I couldn't recognize him as Milo, not with the helmet and the goggles.

He dug and skated hard out of the start.

"There he goes," said the announcer. "Milo Robicheaux. Nobody thought he had a shot at a medal here today."

Milo was tucked right away. He stayed shaped like a bullet, bent low, with his ski poles snapped under his arms and his head down.

"Here he comes up to the *Mausefalle*," the announcer said, explaining that *Mausefalle* was German for Mousetrap. "This is where three others lost control today, one badly injured." The announcer explained that no other downhill course had a jump with a pitch that steep. He named some very damaged racer who was being choppered right that moment to the hospital with a broken neck.

"Oh, God," said Claire.

Milo hit the edge of the Mousetrap and hung in the air, still tucked but sailing, a stick-man on my cheap television. *He's traveling at about sixty miles an hour*, they said, *forty feet off the ground. Look at him, he's in control.*

He was a dark speck surrounded by white sky. They slowed it down so he hovered, took forever to land. It was not exactly beautiful, given the long spiky skis on his feet, the speary poles behind him; he looked spidery, but for some reason it seemed poignant. *Look at him*, I thought. *He can fly.*

His knees soaked up shock as he landed, and he hurtled on, careening around curves like a car on two wheels. Then he was streaking through the finish and piling into the big foam pads at the end of the course and falling. They showed him being helped up by the crowds, dusted off by his teammates. His chest was heaving. He was gasping for breath, leaning over with his hands on his knees. Finally he stood up, pulling off his helmet and goggles.

"Oh, my God, are you telling me that was a black man?" Carl said.

We looked at him.

"It is!" he said. "Holy shit!"

"That's who everybody was talking about," Claire said. "What did you think?"

"I thought it was the other guy. I thought it was the blond ponytail guy you were talking about. I thought this one was, like, the caddy, or something."

We glanced his way silently so he got nervous. "Well, he was holding the skis!" Carl said, palms up and shrugging. "And, I mean, list me the Negroes you have met while skiing."

"Shh," Claire said. "Quiet, Carl. Listen." She loved Carl but he was embarrassing her.

Milo's time stood. He won.

"Whoooeeee!" said Carl. "I never would have believed it. Just amazing. They're getting into everything, you notice that? What with whatshisname, Ashe? in the tennis? and now this with skiing? It's really..."

"Really what?" Claire said. "Really...?"

"You know," said Carl, "unbelievable. I mean, it's great. And you gals know this guy?"

"Yeah," said Claire. "We do. We used to hang out with him."

On TV Milo's teammates picked him up and put him on their shoulders. He was grinning. Beaming. It was wonderful to watch. Wherever he was, said Claire, Jack would be green. She was right, but who cared? Milo deserved it. He was amazing. It was a Historic Moment. We were all quiet. Milo was radiant. There was sweat on his face in shiny beads which I remember surprised me; you don't think, somehow, of snow and sweat mixing. Or perhaps it was something else, how the picture was both familiar and stunning, too. In the close-up, white specks of snow showed in the black field of Milo's hair. He was looking at the time clock with his chest still heaving, shaking his head in disbelief.

"Not many blacks *in* the sport of skiing, Billy, am I right?"

"You're right, Jim. In fact, there are *no* other black racers on any of the teams that ski the World Cup. It's been a bastion of white athletes much like golf." It was Billy Kidd, the former champion, talking.

"This is really a breakthrough for young Robicheaux."

"I believe this makes him the first black man to win a Winter Olympic medal," Billy Kidd said. "Am I right?"

Claire was nodding just slightly as she watched. It was apparently okay with her for the sports guys to say it but not for Carl.

They cut to a news conference.

"How did a young man like you learn to ski?" somebody asked Milo.

"From my mom and dad," said Milo, "Milton and Hattie Robicheaux of Rugged Mountain, New Hampshire." He gave the thumbs-up sign, right at the camera, probably right at his watching parents. He was winking.

"How are you feeling about the fact you're the first black man to win Winter Olympic Gold?"

"It feels good to win," Milo said, not exactly answering the question. He looked happy.

"What do you think this means for black people in the United States today?"

"One would hope it means barriers are falling." Milo was pleasant and smiling. "One would hope it means progress. It's great to bring home a Gold."

"He even talks like a white guy," Carl said, watching him. "He seems white."

"Oh, yeah, definitely," Claire said, "I mean, even I am blacker than Milo Robicheaux."

"What's that supposed to mean?" Carl said.

"I remember he didn't even know—I had to tell him," she said, "who Malcolm X was."

I didn't know who that was, either.

"I always thought that, actually," Claire said. "That he seemed white, Charlotte, right?"

"You did say that," I said. "Yeah."

"He doesn't even look black," Carl said, squinting at Milo in his USA team sweater with the blue field of white stars and the red stripes on the sleeves.

"Are you blind or something?" I said to him. "Maybe I just have a hangover, but you are not making sense."

"What I mean," said Carl, "is look how he sits."

Milo was just sitting there, relaxed and confident, answering questions. Was there a white way of sitting and a black one?

"Down South, you know what they call a guy like him, don't you?" Carl said. "We call a guy like that an Oreo."

Claire said, "Ca-arl."

"It's not a pejorative, Claire, it's an adjective."

"That would be a noun," she said. "A pejorative noun."

"You both," I said, "quit fighting."

"I don't see race," Claire said. "I just see the person." Carl did see it, she explained, because he was from the South, where, according to Claire, they're not color-blind like in New York.

She seemed so sure it was wrong to notice. I wondered: Could you become color-blind once you were fully grown-up? Or, if you had been raised to see differences, could you unsee them?

Oh, a kid'll eat the middle of an Oreo cookie and save the chocolate crunchy outside for last...

Carl whistled the tune of that song—the commercial jingle for Oreos—as he hung around the apartment that day. I didn't even know I knew the words, but when I heard Carl whistling, I couldn't shake them. The tune stuck in my head, so that later, when I would read something about Milo, or see him on TV, the Oreo cookies' song popped into my mind. Thanks to Carl. In the supermarket, even now, when Hallie wants to buy them, I won't. I just hate the word, *Oreo*, the idea of somebody's dry chocolate body, like cardboard; their creamy white insides, sticky white heart.

After that, I followed Milo in the news. Not like some kind of groupie, or a dumb fan. It's not like I didn't have all kinds of things happening to *me* in those years, preoccupations and boyfriends and big nerve-wracking shoots and trunk shows and traveling all over Europe. This is the time— I was twenty, twenty-one—during which I began to use sedatives. Just Valium, once in a while, for sleep or nervousness in flight. I didn't have any habits or addictions, just a cheerful readiness to partake of whatever pharmacopoeia was available and whatever party was happening. This is the time when my weight was managed down to about 109.5 pounds, which at five foot eleven made me thinner than I had been since the tenth grade.

But what I am trying to explain is how Milo dawned on me, how it happened with us. I read about him. I became a *Wide World of Sports* viewer. From that time, from 1976, Milo won four Olympic Gold Medals. He cleaned up in '76 and in '80, both. Between Olympics he won three World Cup ski championships. No one could beat Milo Robicheaux. He was a phenomenon. It wasn't skiing. Who cared about skiing? It was a back-page, footnote sport. Milo, though, was front page. He was racking up endorsements and press and money. You could see him in ads for cars and sportswear and shaving cream. In the shaving cream one, you saw what you thought was a snow-covered mountain with a graceful skier tracking down the slope. But it turned out to be Milo's face, covered with foam, a razor making fresh tracks in his beard.

People all over the world knew him. He was on the level of fame between household word and insider information.

The first time I ever claimed to know him was late in '76. I was getting made up for an Estée ad, and the girl next to me, under a beehive dryer, was reading *Esquire* and there was Milo, on the cover. "He's gorgeous," she said. It was Milo without his shirt on, sitting on the seat of a chairlift with his medals around his neck. This photograph later became part of an Olympics calendar and a best-selling poster.

"Oh, I know him," I told her.

"What's he like?"

"He's nice." I always said that. "A nice guy." I'd see somebody reading about Milo, or hear somebody mention him, and I'd say, "Oh, I know him, he's nice."

I knew things now about Milo that everyone knew, the way everyone knows how many husbands Elizabeth Taylor has had, about her little hair-ribboned lapdogs and her jewels. I knew, for example, about his cars, more than ten, all of them red; how many car accidents he'd had (seven) speeding in the Rockies or the Alps, wrecking the cars but somehow never getting hurt. I knew what Milo looked like when he was a little boy, with a rascal grin on his face, missing teeth, bow-tied and blue-blazered in the yearbook, center front in the ski team picture. They never needed to describe where he was in the team pictures, or put one of those little circles around his head. He was always a lone brown face surrounded by white ones.

One magazine had a picture of him on his first pair of skis. He was four years old and standing indoors by a Christmas tree, with his stripy pajama legs spindling up out of new ski boots, beaming and hamming it up for the camera, already in a downhill position, knees bent, chest resting on thighs, ski poles up under his arms.

We have that picture on our refrigerator now.

From interviews and profiles and gossip columns, I knew the Milo Robicheaux story. It was about a young black child growing up in a small

New England town, Rugged Mountain, New Hampshire, where his parents had settled after coming north from Louisiana with young Milo and his sister. About how from an early age the boy showed great athletic promise, and when he was given his first pair of skis, there was nothing, nothing! that could keep him from the slopes. His mother, shaking her head, fondly recalls the time her darling devilment of an angel son strapped on his skis and went straight down a hill in back of their house through the woods! and how he came to a perilous deathly rocky overhang! and jumped it! and just missed a giant balsam fir with a massive trunk! only to fall and crack his head open and require fifteen stitches on the crown of his cute seven-year-old head. How in school, despite his being the only black child among whites, Milo was popular and well loved, an industrious kid with a paper route and a lemonade stand and a house-painting business; everybody's pal and a good student who won spelling bees and accolades as well as national ranking as a junior skier, and finally a full scholarship to the prestigious Vermont Ski Academy, proving ground of racers. This is where his mentor, the German, Hans Licht—who died in a tragic auto accident when Milo the young champion was just seventeen—groomed him to become a world-class skier. And of course a paragraph or two about Milo's remarkable parents, Milton and Hattie Robicheaux, who insisted on their son trying Cabot College for at least one year and were concerned when he dropped out for an Olympic career because they had worked so hard on his behalf. The story told of his dad working as an industrial engineer and his mom driving Milo to ski races and practices in her wood-paneled station wagon, how she preferred to wait outside, reading in the car with the heater running in the cold parking lots of ski resorts, because she was tired of being mistaken for a lost person or for kitchen help when she went indoors to the lodge.

The story was about cold days on mountains, hours of practice, up and down slopes, training to ski straight down, without pausing, a downhill racer.

The story was about Milo, how fiercely, fiercely determined he was. Everybody said it. The magazine writers and sports producers got neighbors and kindergarten teachers to say it: *Noticed it right away, even as a little boy, how much, how badly Milo Robicheaux wanted to win, to be the best, how hard he worked, how he did not rest, how he trained and worked at it till he got it right.*

Many versions had the tale of how little Milton Robicheaux Jr. had woken from a sound sleep one night at the age of five and gone to his parents' room to tell them he no longer wished to be called Milton. Thinking to indulge her son in what she thought was a passing whim, his mother had looked in a name book the next morning and said: How about Milo for a nickname? The book said that Milo was the name of an ancient Greek wrestler, a six-time Olympian. From that morning on, Milton Jr. determined to be Milo, and got it into his head to become an Olympian.

Every Milo story also included anecdotes of his escapades with his ski team guys. *Milo could get laid in any town anywhere in Europe,* said his teammate Rick VonDrehle. *Milo would just be driving along and women would lift up their sweaters and show him their naked breasts.* He was linked to a French actress named Clivia. I saw their picture in *Paris Match.* She had pouty French lips and dark brown hair that fell over one of her eyes and Milo's arm around her shoulders. Underneath it said *Clivia Nobili arrive au Maxim's avec son fiancé champion du ski Milo Robicheaux.* You didn't need to speak French to understand that they were engaged. But then it turned out they weren't. She wasn't mentioned again. He was linked to this one and that one. It was all very vague, not many details, no interviews with former girlfriends, just that *Robicheaux does not deny he is popular with the ladies.*

Oh, there are lots of stories. The one about the U.S. assistant coach who had to resign because he joked that Milo ran on *watermelon fuel and fried chicken grease.* The one about the Austrian skier who painted the word *niger* on Milo's race bib and got suspended from the circuit. And how the French named a race course after him—*le cours Robicheaux.* They loved his name, *Robicheaux,* and liked to pretend he was really French.

But here in the U.S. he was the biggest. He was an American success. He met the president, Ronald Reagan, and was held up as an example to youth and everybody else, that everything was okay here in America because a black man could be on the U.S. Ski Team and be a world champion and be invited to the White House and could shake the hand of the most important White Man in the world.

The 1981 White House picture was taken just before Reagan was shot and just after Milo's knee was injured at Sarajevo, and just before we met up again in New York. I saw it on the front page of the *New York Times*. "President Greets America's Athletes." Milo appeared to be the same guy I remembered: smiling, upbeat. In other pictures, in his various ads, he always seemed to be giving some kind of okay sign, thumb and forefinger circled, or a V for victory. He telegraphed winning and happy messages, so that even with the sound off you could see that life was grand for Milo Robicheaux.

And it seemed life was grand for me, too. Perhaps we two were, at the time we met up again, the most well-known faces ever to have passed through Cabot College, not that that was any big deal. I'm not trying to brag. I'm talking about being well known, known *well*, how it is that you *know* somebody.

I knew everything about him. What he or anybody else knew about me, I couldn't say, but by 1977, when I was twenty-one, my face was on the fronts of magazines, on the sides of buses and buildings, in the windows of stores. Not that anybody knew my name. Strangers looked hard at me in the street, stopped me and said, "Do I know you?" they said. "I thought I knew you."

"I don't think so," I said, and smiled at them politely.

But it was a good question. "Do I know you?" Sometimes I wondered if there was anybody to whom I could say *Sure you do, you know me well, I'm Charlotte, your Charlotte.*

Even my parents. God knows I did not contact them for two years after I moved to New York, but I don't think that's the reason they didn't recognize my voice when I did call.

"Hello, it's me."

A long silence.

"I'm in New York, and I'm fine."

"May I help you?"

"It's me. It's Charlotte."

"Arthur," I heard my mom whisper. "It's her."

She cried a long time (twenty-two minutes and forty-five seconds, I found out later from my phone bill). I said how sorry I was to have made her worry.

"Did you get the pictures? Did you get the magazine?"

"Yes." She was sobbing. "Yes we did."

I had sent her the first *Vogue* cover. This was late 1976, after two years of fending for myself in the wild. I had sent the magazine to show I had survived, that I had harvested nuts and berries and licked leaves for rainwater, that I had come through the wilderness just like Jesus, so maybe I could now get back in their good graces.

"We're very proud of you, darling."

My father got on the phone, briefly. "We've prayed for you, honey" was all he could manage to say.

"Thanks."

"Let us pray now."

My mother cleared her throat. They began praying across the phone lines: *Dear Lord, Our Father, help Your little lamb Charlotte who has strayed so far from Your flock to return to the embrace of Jesus Christ...* I had a picture in my head of them as they whispered: the squint-wrinkles at the points of my father's eyes, my mother's hardcap of blond hair, her perfect mouth tight with worry, surrounded by pucker lines, like the mark of a bullet through glass. I knew them, what they wanted and how they loved me. I did not know how I could be their child, though, how I had turned into me, coming from them.

Hanging up, I was sad, despite the fact of being reunited, sort of, with my parents. They were proud of me. I was a fashion model. My face was on the cover of magazines. I was using God's gift, which is what I thought they wanted me to do, to earn money, raking it in, actually. So, while I dutifully visited, and took my mother to Paris each spring for the collections, and called them faithfully in the years after that, it was out of guilt. As I dialed their number there was always a hope that somebody else would answer, my real parents, or my same parents' newly revealed true selves, the ones who had made me.

I still prayed, but in my own way. I had a practical attitude.

Dear God, please let me get a taxi, please don't make me throw up at the shoot, please don't let me eat anything before I go, please let the clothes fit me, let these circles under my eyes be concealed under this concealer. And also if it's not too much trouble for you, could I just fall in love? to see what it's like? just to feel it? sanctified or pure or not, I don't really care about that part.

The pastor used to tell us at our teen meetings to always go on dates with Jesus Christ. "No other man satisfies like Jesus. You will behave yourself to save yourself for Him. Think of Jesus as your date!"

I was having a lot of dates all those years in New York, but not with Christ, who would surely have been mortified by many aspects of my life then, but especially the dates. For example, when I was twenty-one, twenty-two, for roughly two years I went out with one of the more famous photographers. This is the boyfriend who would later sell to tabloid newspapers the intimate nude pictures of me that he took. The ones whose negatives he said he destroyed, and all the prints.

After the photographer, with a few brief mistakes in between, I gratefully moved on to this much older guy who had made a fortune in the record business. He was more than forty and boyish with a long gray ponytail. His name was Simon. He was English and said "bathing costume," not bathing suit. He called rich people "toffee noses." I went out with him for a year just to listen to the way he spoke, the way he called me *sweet* with the *t* hard at the end. "Oh, Charlotte," he said, with his eyes closed, "do that again," like *Eau, Shaaaa-lot, dyew that a-gaine*. It was gorgeous, that accent, so that even ordinary words were gilded with it. Simon was getting fat at the tops of his hips. He liked cocaine very much. He was constantly speedy, like an ant picked off its trail and put down somewhere else, going! off! frantically! but with purpose! He was an important man and had a lot of money that he made by his wits. He knew many people I needed to know: the French designer, the Italian photographer, and especially the American Couture King. Simon knew countless things I didn't know, had read thousands of books, many of which he gave me: novels, Hemingway and Steinbeck, *The Executioner's Song. The Bluest Eye*, a biography of Bob Marley, one of Elvis Presley, a lot of music ones, about Duke Ellington, Miles Davis, and Mick Jagger, whom I met because he was a friend of Simon's. Other books he recommended were beyond me: Tolstoy, Pope and Milton and Byron and poets in general. *You and your blond education*, he said. *Don't they teach you anything in American schools?* He played me jazz and took me to museums. *How's my sweet nothing today?* he said sometimes. *My dizzy blond.* He made me feel stupid as a baby, but also that it didn't matter, he would take care of me.

"This is Charlotte," Simon liked to say. "She's a model. She's very hot right now. She's a rising star. She's done *Vogue*. She's had the cover. Surely you know Charlotte?"

People always looked at me very carefully when he said this, searching my face for hints like doctors search for signs of jaundice or melanoma. None of them knew me but they said they did. "I thought you looked familiar!" they said, and grasped my hands warmly or kissed me on both cheeks. "Charlotte, of course! I thought I recognized you."

Don't I know you? Milo said that.

This was in the spring of '81. I was twenty-five and so was Milo. There was a party for somebody's new restaurant. It was a grand affair. Simon knew the owner, who wanted a lot of models there for the press to write about. The girls had to sit around like exotic plants. I told the agency and they sent the ones who were just starting out, the beautiful new ones who thought parties like this one were exciting. I was bored, though, and trying out the table closest to the kitchen, closest to the back by the rest rooms, not our usual table in places like this.

"Don't I know you?"

I was looking down, playing with the ash at the end of my cigarette, rolling it in the ashtray. It was dark at this party and I hadn't seen him in the room, wasn't looking.

He touched my arm. "I know you."

Funny how I felt that he did know me. Right then. Or I wished he did. I remember that wish, how he said the word *know*.

"Milo Robicheaux," I said. "My God."

Oh, he was so startling. He knelt so he was below the level of my eyes. I smiled down at him and blew the smoke in my mouth up to the side. I just looked at him. His green eyes, smiling face. I felt odd, light in the head and sort of sick, as if the nicotine was making me high, but I was used to smoke so it wasn't that. I stubbed the cigarette out.

"I thought you looked familiar," he said. "It's you."

I was smiling without any kind of guard up. We stood and I reached across the little cocktail table and hugged him, awkwardly, so my chin hit the lapel of his jacket and the ashtray fell on the floor.

Sorry, sorry, oh Jesus. I was apologizing already.

I was saying compulsory things. *Well, well, well. I've been hearing about you. Long time no see. Looking good. So, you're a famous face now. Yes, but not as famous as you. What's next for you? Are you living here in New York?*

He didn't say much, nodding at me, looking happy. *Yeah, guess so, yeah, we'll see.* But our conversation, the party around us and the introduction to these two white guys in suits he was apparently with were not what was really going on. What was really going on was a simmer of memory, of five years ago and Jack and the Red Hat and how we'd been acquainted, how once we had danced at a different party and what had happened to us since then. You feel all that past lurking as you nod and say pleasantries. I felt it while I was looking at Milo, at his eyes, watching his lips move while he talked. The past. I could see how he was the same but not the same. He was twenty-five. Not a boy. His face had more flesh on it. His hair was shorter. He seemed like a man. A sharp dresser. Punky black jeans and a narrow tie. Pointy shoes. He was smooth. He was startling. Handsome.

"Jed Moscowitz, Mark Raleigh: Charlotte Halsey," Milo said. He remembered my name.

The men were agents. They were from ICM. *Are you secret agents?* I asked, smiling at them. Charm floated off me. *I don't know how you stand working with this guy,* I said to them, wink, wink, tilt of the head at Milo. *Robicheaux's been a wildman since he was a kid. Oh, yeah, sure. We go way back. A wildman. Smilin' Milo they used to call you, right?* I was right back to being one of the girls, Lynnie or Katrina, little sisters, ski team babes.

"I'll catch up with you," he said to Mark and Jed, practically like: *Dismissed!* They went, and Milo said, "Let's go out for a drink or something."

"Okay, sure," I said. "Maybe sometime next week?"

"I'm talking about this minute," he said. He whispered in my ear. "Right now."

I smiled at him. I asked what about Jed and Mark.

"Fuck Jed and Mark," he said. "I am in charge of Jed and Mark." He took my elbow. "Come on."

I loved it when he did that. I loved the feeling of being steered by him, with his hand on the skin of my elbow. I could feel the warmth of it, there in the cold air-conditioned party. He led me through the crowd, handsome and important.

"Are you here with anybody?" he said.

I was. Simon.

"No," I said. I was giggling. I didn't care. People I knew looked up from their dancing, from their drinks and saw me go. I turned my head toward Milo and looked at him like he was the only person in the room. Who knows where Simon was at that moment? Having a spot of tea. Putting powders up his toffee nose, I didn't care. Even people I didn't know were looking as we left. They pretended they weren't watching but I read the lips of somebody who said: Milo Robicheaux, the skier.

"Where are you taking me?"

"Eighth Avenue," said Milo, as if the street were a destination in itself.

We went outside and walked down Eighth. We saw beer neons in the window of a bar and went in. He steered me to a table, pulled a chair out for me, and sat himself across.

"My God," he said. "Look at you."

"Look at you," I said back.

We just stayed for a while without saying anything else, looking and grinning. I felt stopped from thinking. The waitress came and Milo asked for beer so I did, too.

When she brought the mugs, there was a moment where both of us were deciding whether we were going to smash them together, the way it was done back at the Red Hat. All this past was pushing at us, weighted like water, so that by some simultaneous unspoken agreement, we smashed the mugs together and said, "Owgh, owgh owgh," but sort of sarcastically, without the pig-snorting noise. It was as if we were quoting those others, the Cabot ski gang, not really doing it ourselves, which made us both laugh, and beer foam went up my nose so I started coughing and he had to come around the other side of the table to thump me on the back. Or maybe he didn't have to but he did.

"You're out of practice," Milo said.

"I haven't been oinking much lately, no," I said.

"And so do you miss it?"

I laughed at him. We both just cracked up and snorted the way they did back at the Red Hat. Neither of us could believe we'd been there, doing that.

"I've heard all about you," I said, like a confession.

"What have you heard?"

"You know. You're a champion, you've won all these golden trophies, medals, you walk on water, blah blah."

"So, what happened to Jack?" he said.

"You tell me," I said, "I don't know."

"He fell and got a head injury. He didn't make it to Innsbruck."

"He had a head injury before, if you ask me," I said.

Milo laughed but there was something in his face I couldn't read, some flicker. "He said he was heading for New York," Milo said. "He said he would be coming to stay with you."

"Well, he didn't," I said blithely. "He didn't come so he couldn't stay." I poured more beer. I didn't want to talk about Jack. "How's your knee?" I said.

"You know that, too?" He said it with his eyebrows raised. His eyelashes were long, almost feminine. "I'm on my second surgery," he said.

Milo had wrecked his knee a few months after he won in '80, his fourth Gold. The sports shows replayed him falling over and over, tumbling down a twisted course in the mountains of Yugoslavia during some post-season race that didn't count for anything. They stopped the tape to show him with a Gumby knee bending unnaturally back and up. They had a close-up of his face all twisted up in pain. He'd have to retire from the circuit. He was moving to New York to be a sportscaster. It was in the papers.

"So you're moving to New York?" I said. "You already live here?"

"How do you know?"

"Everybody knows."

"What other salient facts do you have on me?"

"Your whole life story!" I said. "I know everything! All about you!"

"You think so?" He was smiling but only out of one side of his face. "You think so."

It was if he was saying: You couldn't possibly know. What could you even begin to know?

It frightened me a little bit and jerked me suddenly into feeling like a White Person sitting across the table from a Black Person, instead of just me, Charlotte, sitting across from Milo, an acquaintance from college. So I drank quickly and a lot, and was afraid that whatever I said would be the wrong thing, that I would just reveal the bottomless pit of what I didn't know. My blond education.

He asked me about myself. He said he'd seen me in some ads. He said he was never sure if it was me, that I could look so different. "Sometimes you look like you, and sometimes you look...I don't know," he said, "like someone else."

I put my teeth over my bottom lip like a beaver's teeth and crossed my eyes. "What do I look like when I look like me?"

He laughed at that. "You're funny," he said. "I always harbored suspicions that you might be funny."

"I'm not," I said. "I'm a very serious and boring uptight priggish kind of person." I brought my elbows to the tabletop and rested my chin on my laced fingers like I was the queen.

"I heard you had made it big in New York," he said. "La de da. *La haute couture.*"

"Not like you, though," I said. "Everybody all over the world knows you."

We talked a long time, it seemed to me, although it was probably not more than an hour. We talked about safe subjects, about Milo's new job at Network Sports. About modeling and New York and apartments and restaurants we liked. We talked about traveling in Europe, where he'd been and where I had. During which time I wondered what it would be like to kiss him. To be kissed by him. I sometimes did this while talking to someone handsome, just idly. I looked at Milo's lips while he was talking and thought about my lips touching them but suspended the thought because it seemed...suddenly not so idle, somehow. His lips were ample and fleshy and it struck me how it would be to kiss them.

And I thought, *Don't think they're ample, you can't think they're ample or large because you're not supposed to and his nostrils are elegant wide brown nostrils but no, you don't notice that. Why not? Because it's a racial characteristic, because it means you see the race of the person when we are all color-blind and if you are not color-blind you are a racist and evil. His teeth are white when he smiles. His smile is nice, like ripples on sunny water. Don't think about the lips. Why? Why not?*

I drank more and more. I wondered what it would be like.

After a while he looked at his watch and said, "Better get going, I'm afraid. It's late." He pushed his chair back.

"Yes," I said, standing up, but I fell, spilling beer. "Whoa!" I said. "I'm completely useless."

"No," he said, catching me so that I was against him, lingering for a second. "No, I don't think completely."

And I wondered what did he mean by that. *Not completely useless.* Did he mean I was good for a screw? Did he mean it like Simon meant it? *You're good, you know, love, what? This is Charlotte, she's a terrorist in the bag,* wink, wink, wink; or like all the other ones at so many of the parties, who said, *Let's go home. Come home with me?*

I stood myself up, blinked and straightened. He saw that he'd said something that bothered me somehow.

"Listen, how about if I call you and we go hear some music or maybe go for dinner?" he asked. "Next week?"

"I don't know," I said, to erase the chance he thought I was cheap.

"Hey, I don't know anybody else in this town."

"Okay," I said. We walked outside.

"Hullo! Well, there she bloody is! We've been hunting all over the bloody place for you!" It was Simon, with some friend of his. "Where've you been?" he said, coming toward me and taking my arm and glancing at Milo. The friend hung back and Milo did, too.

"It's bloody late," said Simon. "Let's get going."

"This is Milo Robicheaux," I said.

"Oh, right, skiing chap, right?" Simon said. "We've heard of you. You're an Olympian. A medalist—" He was going on and on.

"Si-mon," I said.

Milo smiled. "I'll see you, Charlotte," he said, and waved at us, striding ahead down Eighth Avenue, sticking his hand out to get a taxi. A taxi passed him. And then another one. I didn't see him after that; he was swallowed up in traffic, and Simon was revved up, talking and talking, rubbing his hands together as if he were cleaning them.

"I'm going home," I said. "Good night, Simon." I stuck my hand up for a cab and one pulled over. I got in without Simon and went home and went to bed, lying in the dark with my head hurting and thinking about all kinds of things I wasn't supposed to be thinking about. Lips. Eyes with girlish lashes.

9.

Three days later, a Friday, he called me up. "Charlotte Halsey? Milo Robicheaux here." He asked would I kindly please excuse him for calling at the last minute? He inquired was I free that very evening? He wondered might he pick me up in front of my building? At 11 P.M.?

When I hung up I was happy. Which made me nervous.

So there he was in the lobby, sharp in a dark blazer over a white shirt, loafers with no socks, silver buckle on his belt. There was me in my silvery silk Von Furstenburg jumpsuit cut low to the navel revealing a white bandeau underneath, getting off the elevator with blotches of shyness blossoming on my chest and neck. I was expecting him to say something—*You look lovely*—along the lines of what was usually said.

But Milo said just, "Hey, Charlotte." His face split into a smile I remembered. As if he thought everybody was downright delightful or privately amusing.

"Your doorman here has been most hospitable," Milo said on the way out, but his voice now had a little tang in it, so I wondered what hospitality Paulie had offered, exactly.

"That doorman?" I told him, "Paulie. Well, he's kind of a real skankball."

Milo laughed at me. "Skankball," he said with his eyebrows up. "That's a nice one." He opened the door of a waiting car and climbed in after me. "By the way, this party? I don't really know anyone there." He'd been invited by the hotshot winner of last year's U.S. Open Tennis Championship. "We don't have to stay long," he said. The party was in a new club housed in a former church, with the original sacred detail still intact, down to the stained-glass windows showing the Baby Cheese grown up into Christ, people and sheep gathered at his knees. It was the closest I had come to any kind of church in a long time, and as we pulled up, Milo cryptically said, "Be prepared." I was half expecting some kind of a biblical moment.

A searchlight beamed at the car as we stepped out and a popcorn of flashbulbs went off all around. The bouncer beckoned us and the people parted as if Moses were going dancing. As we passed, one or two called, "Heeyyyyyy, Mi-lo!" and put up their hands to high-five him. Holding my hand on his left, he slapped their outstretched palms on the right. He had a smile for everybody.

"Way to go," they said. "All right, Milo."

I pushed up on my toes to whisper by his ear, keeping my face turned by habit out to the cameras: "I had no idea!"

And I didn't. That he was known, yeah, but not how it felt, angling through a crowd like that, stares of hunger, people wanting something. *Who's she?* I heard someone say, his celebrity splashing onto me. *Ooooooh, look at the girlfriend. Is she somebody?*

I was not his girlfriend. But I liked their thinking it, liked the giddy feeling of the crowd pressing around us, the lights glaring. It was thrilling, and reminded me of that first time Kevin took me to be photographed, how that made me bold, freed me up from being ordinary. They thought Milo was so important; they seemed to love him.

Way to go. All right, Milo.

The bouncer led us up some stairs and then behind some velvet ropes where the private part of the party was happening. The Tennis Hotshot was there, in fact, with a model I recognized from the catwalk at the spring Saint Laurent show. She had her seventeen-year-old hand on his red-haired arm. In a corner I recognized the *Post* columnist, who was a friend of Simon's, wearing a cowboy hat. I blew her a kiss to see if she remembered me and she waved. People were checking out Milo through the murk of smoke and low light. We got drinks. He shook a couple of hands, introduced me by shouting. He and the Tennis Hotshot gave each other an elaborate high-five.

The Saint Laurent model said, "Hey, Charlotte—"

"You girls know each other?" the tennis player asked.

"Charlotte and I worked together?" said the girl. Her name was Vanessa.

Tennis Hotshot looked at Milo with an eyebrow lift, followed by an eyeball roll. Translated into English, it meant: *these model babes.*

"So New York's treating you well, Milo?" the Hotshot said. "You meet Charlotte here?"

"No, actually," Milo said. "Charlotte and I have known each other for a while. Since college, in fact."

Hear that, Vanessa? I am not some runway rodent, as we say in the trade, not like you, darlin'. I am Milo's old friend from college. It felt good to be the old friend from college, instead of having Vanessa's part, a *little something just picked off the rack,* which was my usual assignment.

Milo got more drinks and led me to a table by the entrance. Everybody who came in stopped to say hello, and he introduced me by saying *This is Charlotte Halsey, the face of the eighties.* He smiled when he said this, as if he was kidding me. For a while, it was like the Milo Robicheaux Booth at the county fair. There wasn't room for anyone to sit with us. People squatted down on their haunches or leaned over the table. Sometimes, in between getting slapped on the back and smooched by all the arriving guests, Milo looked at me with smiles complicated by appraisal. Sometimes he put his hand on my arm. His touch was dry like a doctor's, fingers long with knotted knuckles. His knee was crowded warmly against my leg under the small round tabletop. The tequila was making me dangerously cheerful. My smiles were starting to go all over my face.

But out of the blue Milo got up. "Excuse me for a moment," he said, and left. He crossed the room and disappeared into the party.

I waited. I smoked.

Men came over to me, kept appearing like ants on a cake crumb, saying *May I join you?* so that I was forced to repeat pathetically that my date would be right back.

Maybe he's not coming back.

The party, except for me, was milling and mingling around, laughing and dancing. After twenty minutes I got up and walked out, past the velvet ropes, into the public part of the club, wallflowering myself along the outskirts of the crowd. Maybe I was not fascinating enough for Milo. Maybe I was merely shiny in my silver jumpsuit, like tinsel. I saw him by the dance floor, talking to a woman I recognized as some new actress. She had an exotic name like Cassandra or Mignonne. She had almond-shaped eyes and Slavic cheekbones, and also her hand on Milo's waist. She was laughing and pulling him to dance with her. She was go-going all over the place, and he was Mr. Suave, Mr. Small Steps with the Music, slowing her down with his arms around her and looking at her through desire-lidded eyes. Or was he looking at me? I saw him see me.

It got me. It made me want him, to get him. I bit through the skin of my lip so blood salted into my mouth. *You chump, Charlotte, liking the pressure of his knee.* I was hurt, plus furious, ingredients that with me are a recipe for recklessness and bad judgment.

As Milo was dancing, Tennis Champ passed me. I smiled at him. He wheeled around and circled my waist with his arms. He shouted something about *beautiful* in my ear, over the music: "...Always, always thought that, since I saw you tonight." I leaned on him on purpose. "Worship you," he mumbled. I closed my eyes as if I were falling asleep, and he pulled my head down, dancing with me, way too slow for the music. He kept sniffing, the sharp sniffs of a coke-nose.

God, he said. *What's your name again?*

He smelled of new tennis balls and aftershave. His ears were freckled as birds' eggs and his arms were feathered with reddish hairs. While he was shuffling around he managed to offer me what was in his breast pocket, flashed a foil packet like a fish lure and danced me in the direction of the bathrooms. I smiled at Tennis Champ and told him, *Not right now.* But I kept dancing with him and let him kiss me a little bit, when he tried it, kissing back mechanically. It was for spite, getting back at Milo. *As if you are so famous you can dump me before you even have me. You don't have me.* I got away as soon as I was sure Milo had seen me with my lips on the other guy.

Maybe an animal behaviorist could tell me the scientific reason I do these things, committing follies of jealousy like throwing down gauntlets. All I knew was, Milo started it.

Also, maybe it worked.

That time, anyway. I tried it again, years later, which may have something to do with where I am now, here at my downfall.

I went to stand off by myself, looking down from the choir loft of the disco church into the mess of dancers below. *Forget this place*, I thought.

Go home and find Claire. Then I felt breath on the back of my bare neck, warm and scary so the baby hair stood up all along my arms.

"Let's get out of here," Milo whispered. His hands cupped my ear and his words condensed in steam on the skin of my temple. "We're leaving."

"Okay."

Outside, Milo hardly said anything, just shot me a tight smile as we strolled through a neighborhood of shuttered warehouses and loading docks. I didn't know where we were. The streets had foreign names: Gansevoort and Lispenard.

"Look," said Milo, "I have no idea where we are. I'm just walking, okay?"

"Yeah," I said. "Kind of like, just dancing?"

"*Exactly* like just dancing, right?" he said. "Or maybe, like just kissing Tennis Boy back there, or last week just dumping your English 'bloke' at that restaurant."

"Or your date? *Moi.* Tonight? At a nightclub?"

We were sort of kidding and sort of not.

"So?" I said, sliding my jawbone in a boxer's grin.

"So," he said, "come with me." He pointed to a bar across the street and hustled me against the light and in the door. The bar seemed to be for truck drivers and loading-dock workers and was nearly empty that late at night. We sat in a dusty booth and ordered beer.

"You were supposed to dance with me," I said.

"Sorry," he said. "People come up to you. They want—who knows what they want? Once in a while I can't deal with them."

"Actually I did dance with you once," I said after a minute.

"Did I ask you or did you ask me?"

"I think it just...we both, I don't remember. I think I asked you."

"Well well well," he said.

"What's that supposed to mean?"

"I hadn't remembered you as that sort of person."

"What sort?"

"Who would ask," he said. "You were—how shall we say?—taken."

"No, I wasn't," I said. *Taken.* It had a hard sound to it, like describing a seat or a parking space. "I wasn't. Not when I danced with you. Not—"

"It was a long time ago," he said, smiling. "It's hard for me to remember details, after all that time on the road."

"Seven years?"

He nodded.

"Do you miss it?"

"Nah," he said.

"Why not?"

"The road is the road." He shrugged. "Basically it's a skanky VW bus full of eight guys. Tons of equipment, waxing and sharpening every night, team meetings, dirty laundry, beers and bars and broken bones. See this?" he said, and leaned in across the table as if he was going to show me something secret.

I sat forward.

"Look, there," he said, and gave me his hand. A dark scar creased the side of his right pinky finger and ran down the edge of his palm. I traced it with my nail, but as a nurse would. I felt his hand thawing where I held it. He shifted in his seat and pointed to a dark metallic dot by the tip of the finger. "That's a piece of wire," he said. "Holding together the bones. Feel it."

I did, wincing. The wire was hard under the skin.

He withdrew his hand and told me the story of how he caught a glove on a gate in '79, shattering the finger and nearly ripping it right off, and how he kept skiing anyway, finishing with just the one pole. He kept talking, loosening up, telling about his racing life. Mountain towns. Groupies. Ski bums. All those Euros with their unfiltered cigarettes and that great beer. "Really great beer," he said. "Plus the unbelievable cult of the sport, like baseball is here. I loved that," Milo said, softly now. "How people had skiing in their bones."

"You *do* miss it," I said. "Why wouldn't you live there?"

"It's not part of the plan," he shrugged. "If you're not moving forward, as my father would say, you're standing still. You don't think about what's behind you. Just like you don't think about crashing."

"How can you not think about crashing?"

"If you think about crashing," he said, "you'll crash."

"What do you think about, then?"

"Aggression," he said, grinning. "Aggression. Control. Attack."

Milo was waiting to see what I would say now, watching me so I was nervous and wished for props, matches and smoke. I began stacking up packets of sugar in towers, arranging them in rows like cards.

"So what do you miss?" he asked.

"Me?" I said. "Nothing."

"Nothing?"

"Nah."

"No one?"

"No one." I wondered if he was fishing somehow about Jack, checking me about the old days.

"Not even your family?"

"If you're not moving forward," I said, "you're standing still. Right?"

"Forward toward what?" he asked. "What's your plan?"

"I don't know," I shrugged. "Whatever happens, happens."

It sounded weak and careless. Milo seemed to think I should have a plan. He clearly had one, with his eyes glittering, hooded by smiles, some expression I couldn't for the life of me understand, whether it was playful or mocking. A twist of his mouth.

"Surely Charlotte Halsey has a *plan*," he said.

"Look—I'm still working on the not-thinking-about-what's-behind-me part. The not crashing. I'm trying—it's not like I have any—"

"What's behind you that you're not thinking about?" he asked.

"Nothing," I said, flustered. "Nothing interesting, anyway."

"I doubt that," he said.

"Whatever happens, happens!" I said gaily. "That's my plan and it's fine with me as long as it's not—"

"Not what?"

"Not where I come from. Not—" His questions filled me with panic, as if I had only a few seconds to hide all the evidence, dress in something presentable. "I don't really want to go into it," I said, and saw with dismay that I had shredded one of the sugar packets so it was spilled all over the table.

Milo smiled at the mess. "Well, when you're ready," he said kindly, "then you'll tell me."

Kindness was not something I expected. It made me want to tell him, the whole story, about the family fire and brimstone, all of us Holy Halseys terrified of damnation, eyes closed, hands raised. Milo was watching me with his lips on the rim of his glass. *Don't think about lips*, I thought. I played with my hair and tried to think of something to say that would save me from all my unreliable ideas about kindness and lips, the question of what would happen next. I was suddenly tired and I shivered from nerves, wondering about him.

"Here," Milo said, and sat forward to take off his jacket, starting up to put it around my shoulders.

"I'm not cold," I said.

"No?" he said slowly, and sat back. "Sorry, I thought you were."

"I'm sorry if you thought I was," I said.

"No," he said, "that's not what I meant. I—"

I swallowed and without warning my eyes glazed briefly with tears so I looked away.

"What?" he said, concerned. That kindness in his face. "What?"

"Nothing."

I could see Milo was surprised by me. His eyes were bright as the Emerald City of Oz. I don't know what he had thought I was like, but it was something different from what he found out about me now. We were quiet. I ran my tongue across my mouth, nervous and fast. Milo looked away.

"It's late," he said. "Let's go."

We left without speaking. At the light out front, a Checker cab was loitering, and Milo flagged it. I waited to see where we were going. Milo said, "First stop," and gave his address to the driver. Then he looked to me to give mine, so I did. *Okay then, I'll go home.* The quiet was thick and strange. Milo's face was worked up with something he was thinking, or deciding. He turned and looked at me just as we got to his block and spoke, but his words got lost in the siren of an ambulance passing.

You're too scary, I thought he said.

"What?"

He smiled. The taxi stopped on the corner of Fifth Avenue just above Washington Square. Milo opened the door and got out, leaned in again, gave me fare money, put his hand on my arm.

"Good night, Charlotte."

"Oh." I swallowed. "Good night then."

He reached up, toward my hair, with his thumb and forefinger, and pinched at something small there, as if he were removing an insect or a speck of dirt. He opened his hand flat to show me: a crystal of sugar on his fingertip. He smiled and put it to his mouth. "Sweet," he said then. "Come in with me."

I got out of the cab and Milo paid the guy. We didn't speak. He put his hand on my back and steered me toward an old ornate building. Brass awning posts, flower urns brimming with petunias, doorman dozing on a bench, mirrored elevator. We had to watch each other's reflections trying not to watch, pretending not to look.

"I've only lived here a month," he said, closing his apartment door behind us but not turning on the light. "Have a seat."

I sat on a couch, which was all the furniture he had, he said. The room was echoing and dim. Silver street light filtered in the windows. Milo was in the kitchen, humming something. He came in after a moment and handed me a glass of water, then opened a window so a breeze blew in. I watched him as he looked through some records stacked against the wall and had a feeling like vertigo, as if I knew everything that would happen and didn't know at all. Milo put some music on, a man singing blues, but in another language. He stood up and crossed the room and sat down, not exactly next to me. He leaned back and closed his eyes.

"Do you want anything?" he asked mildly.

"No, thanks," I said. "I'm okay."

Long rectangles of light moved across the ceiling as the traffic passed on the street below. Milo hummed a little, barely, with just his breath. We didn't talk. We stayed quietly, our heads back, watching the light wheel above us. It was peaceful, and tense as the skin of a balloon filling with water. "Here," he said softly, and reached across so his hand was open beside me. I put my hand out, and he pulled me toward him, moved his arm around my shoulders. We sat there in his dim living room like that, my ear against his rib cage, right over his heartbeat. We could hear our own breathing. I closed my eyes. Milo was stroking my head now, just absently. "Charlotte," he said quietly, as if he were trying my name out, practicing it.

He sat forward to see me then and looked in my eyes, not blinking. He leaned in and I lifted up my mouth and he kissed me.

"A long time waiting to kiss you," he said.

"Really?"

"Since I saw you."

"Three days?"

"Since Vermont."

"No. I don't believe you," I said.

"Because you didn't notice me then," he said.

"I did. I did."

"No you didn't," he said. "You notice me now, though," with another kiss.

"I do, yes, I notice you definitely, Milo."

"Along with everybody else and their grandmothers."

"Grandmothers don't notice you like I do," I said.

And we teased back and forth like this, kissing with something hidden underneath, like a fish just below the surface of the water, circling, so that I was unsure and scared of what was happening, and wanting it to happen anyway.

"Years," he said.

"You could try to make up for lost time," I said.

He picked me up and carried me then, just lifted me.

Save me! I whispered.

I'll save you, he said.

He put me down on the bed and held me. He was not in a hurry. I was not. He looked in my eyes while he undid the buttons and unhooked the hooks and his face was full of something I don't know what to call, and my throat was so swollen with this same feeling I could barely swallow.

"Are you all right?" he said.

"Yes. Are you?"

"Yes."

Everything happened wildly and desperately then. *Charlotte*, he said. *God*. There's no way to remember what I said, whether they were actual words or just sounds. I could feel the bones in his cheeks and the bones in his jaw against the bones of my face. He pushed my hair back off my forehead and held it, gripped me there with his fingers laced hard through the strands to the roots. I had my hand up to cradle his cheek. He looked in my eyes, and I looked back, both of us fierce, as if the first one to turn away would lose.

Thinking of it even now fills me up with longing. Oh my God, Milo and Charlotte, we had a good time, we had a beautiful time, I must say, so that tears were in our eyes, looking at each other, who knows why? Maybe it was relief, or awe, at how raw we were, our feelings, crying and saying things. Jesus. We were exposed as mussels dropped on the rocks by gulls.

We lay there later, stretched out alongside each other, breathing hard. Light came in from the street and I could see that he was smiling, forks of wrinkles at the corners of his eyes.

"Milo," I said.

"Hey," he said.

We fell asleep on our backs with our faces turned up, fingers woven in the dark gray dark. I loved him right away, so much, and he loved me, so help me God.

10.

In the morning, the sun poured in the window over us and we looked at each other, lying there like stripes. We did not talk. We didn't dare. The air was fat with questions and the fact that we were mostly strangers. Around noontime, Milo said, "If we don't get up, we'll starve." So we stood. My legs felt so wobbly I had to lie down again. Milo put a robe on, went in the shower. I looked around. There on the floor was my silver jumpsuit crumpled, my pointy silver heels. They looked wrong in the daylight. Like witch clothing.

I rummaged around his dresser. Right away I saw it. Stuck in the mirror was a snapshot of a light brown-skinned woman with her hair in soft waves around her face. She was pretty. She was outside somewhere, with leaves in the background. Her brown eyes looked sunnily at the camera, looking out with love, I thought. She was his girlfriend, surely. Beautiful. Sitting on a lawn chair, wearing a yellow summer dress with thin straps, dangling brass earrings shaped like suns.

I had to draw a deep breath. I had to blink. I had to lecture myself and jump back from conclusions. *I wouldn't be here if she was everything to him.* I decided not to ask. I didn't want to know yet. The picture watched me. I imagined him kissing her and then argued with myself. *She's some old flame. She dumped him. She's his sister. She lives in France. She's dead.* Whoever she was made me cautious, suspicious. But I wouldn't ask. I would find out but not by asking.

I opened the drawers of his dresser. His socks were balled up and in rows, the shirts folded in a way that spoke of housekeepers. I saw knee braces and Ace bandages, a jockstrap, a black bow tie, a condom in foil! an old passport, a stopwatch, airline tickets. I don't know what I was expecting but there was nothing I hadn't seen in the drawers of other men. I put on a T-shirt of his and some of his boxer shorts, plaid ones. The shirt said *Lake Placid, New York. XXXII Olympiad*, with those Olympic rings interlocking.

I went out into the empty living room. The moldings and mantelpiece were carved and intricate. One whole wall was windows, and the sun came through the arched glass in shafts, lighting up a soft glitter in the air, spangled motes hanging there in the Saturday morning. Unpacked brown cardboard boxes were neatly lined up around the room.

He had tried to decorate a little, pathetically. It was touching. There was a poster tacked up, of the Montreal Jazz Festival, 1976, and another, framed, of Milo racing, his body shaped like an S of yellow spandex. Not much else. I looked for clues but he hadn't unpacked them. I couldn't very well start going through the boxes, although I thought of it. When he came out of the shower I was reading *Ski* magazine on the bed.

"I am going to make you breakfast," he said.

"I thought I already was your breakfast," I said, coy as all get-out. "And your lunch."

"You think I'm some kind of cannibal?" he said.

This made me lurch around and look at him. "I didn't say that," I said.

"Just checking," he said, grinning. Like: *Gotcha.*

The whole time I was in the shower I was washing myself with the word *cannibal*. I worried that I had said something wrong. Oh boy, there seemed to be a miniature cannibal with a bone through his nose standing on the soap dish in a grass skirt and watching me through beads of water. I scrubbed my face too hard, till my skin was pink as bubble gum, and shiny.

In the kitchen, Milo handed me coffee, and I nursed it gratefully. He watched me cradling the mug and said, "I remember you always had a hangover at breakfast."

"I did not!" I said.

"That's what I remember," he said, pouring cereal.

"Oh, and you didn't?" I said.

"You never saw me with a hangover," Milo said. "But I used to see you. Hiding in the corner with three big coffee mugs and circles under your eyes."

"I like caffeine," I said. "It's a staple food." I was trying to be funny but Milo was looking at me again as if he was trying to figure something out, which made me wary. "What else do you remember?"

"Not much." Then, as if it had been on his mind, he said, "Your friend Jack is in Japan. Did you know that?"

"Well, he's not my *friend*, you know?" I said. "We lost touch."

"So to speak," Milo said.

"So to speak," I said. "Ha ha."

"He's in Japan. That's where he ended up."

"But, I don't really care about Jack."

"He was hurt," Milo said. "You know that story, right?"

"No, I don't," I said. "I don't particularly like Jack stories."

"Oh, well." Milo smiled, backing off. "In that case I will not encumber you with this one."

"But you have so perked up my curiousness," I said, "I mean, that I really would like to be enlightened—you know, find out."

"You mean I have inflamed your curiosity," Milo said.

"Right," I said. "You have inflamed everything." I was red, under his gaze.

Milo took a breath and told how Jack hurt his head. The story was not about a ski injury. Not about Jack wiping out and slamming into a rock-pile or catapulting off an overhang. It was about a basketball game. A pickup basketball game in a gym at Lake Placid, winter, 1975, which was the year after we all left Cabot.

There wasn't a flake of natural snow. The skiers were hanging around waiting for machine-made snow so they could race. Meanwhile, in order not to become slothful and fat, they lifted weights and ran stairs and played basketball.

"So there we are, stir-crazy out of our minds," Milo said, "and you have to remember that every one of us is an asshole, every man jack of us. We're all big motherfucking egomaniacs. We can't play basketball to save our own asses because we're *skiers*. But we don't let that stop us. No. We decide we're going to play hoops."

The teams were divided up: technical racers against the downhillers. Slalom racers versus schussbombers. I didn't need Milo to remind me that made him and Jack on opposite teams.

"And each guy is highly accustomed to winning," Milo said. "*Highly accustomed*, okay? or he wouldn't even be at Lake Placid. Each guy wants to be in *el big time*. Also: We hate each other's guts. Now, no two guys hate each other more than me and Jack Sutherland."

"I used to notice that."

"Not from me you didn't," Milo said. "I was sweet as pie to that guy. From day one. We were buddy-buddy. Teammates on and off the field, as they liked to put it in the magazines. By the way, I am sweet as pie to everybody, in case you hadn't noticed, which is a practice that was drilled into me by my parents." Milo made his voice low and slow and very dignified, which is what he did when he quoted his father, and he said: "Son, never give anybody any *extra* reason to give you trouble."

So Milo liked everybody no matter how he really felt about it, and everybody liked Milo. But his neck got wiry with anger, and his voice flattened out as he told about how, in this pickup basketball game between the maniac mad-dog downhillers and the fancy-dance slalomites, Jack Sutherland called Milo Robicheaux a name.

"He called me a gorilla, which is something he'd been circling around for a while, if you didn't know," Milo said. "He said, 'Step aside, ya big gorilla.' "

"Jack said that?"

"He did," Milo said. "And I looked right at him, right in his face, and I went like this." Milo made a kiss with his lips and silently mouthed the words *I love you.*

Sometime in the next part of the game, Jack was going up for a rebound and Milo was guarding him, and as Jack went up to park the ball in the hoop, Milo leaped and tipped it away, and there was some kind of collision between them, so that Jack went flying and cracked his head smack against the big metal pole supporting the backboard and landed on the sandbags, bleeding.

"We rushed him to the hospital," Milo said. Jack had a fractured skull. Double vision. Extreme headaches. Dizziness. "He never got better enough to race again," Milo said. "Not that year, not on the team."

"I never knew that. I just thought he got cut, didn't make the team."

"He left the country. He teaches skiing in Japan."

"But he always wanted to do that," I said. "He speaks the language."

"Nobody heard from him."

"I heard from him. I mean, he called my family in California. He's—"

"You said you lost touch." He interrupted me.

"This was years ago," I said. "But—"

"I thought you lost touch," Milo said. His voice was brittle and quiet. "Anyway, there's more."

"More what?"

"He said I pushed him. He blamed it on me."

"Did you push him?" I asked.

"No," he said tightly. "And you know damn well I didn't push him."

Milo stood up and put his coffee mug in the sink. He closed all the cereal boxes and put them away. I tried to help, tried rinsing the dishes, but the water running was too loud. We were suddenly awkward and stiff with each other. "I'll get you a cab," Milo said.

It was hot out, already afternoon, more like August than May. People wearing shorts and sandals were passing me in my shiny jumpsuit, sweat on my legs underneath, my feet pushed up in strappy heels. We walked past the doormen with their rubbernecking eyes, out to Fifth, up to Fourteenth Street. Milo walked alongside in his tasseled loafers with no socks. His steps were too long for me in my shoes. For every stride of his I took three shiny silver baby ones, mincing along. He was in a hurry, hustling toward the cab. His sunglasses were on but you could feel him staring straight ahead; you could feel a zone of tension around him. The faster we walked the more I wondered what I had said, what was the matter. Was it the people checking us out or the word *cannibal*? Was it being seen with me, my showoff silver clothing, or my question *Did you push him?* What? I didn't know.

He held the door of the cab. "I'll see you," he said.

"Call me up," I said.

It's like being swept under a rug before the police come.

"Milo," I said. "Hey."

He bent his head in the open door of the taxi, with his face arranged in a polite question, like *May I help you?*

"Milo." I just said his name, quietly, like calling him back from wherever he had been, to see what he would do. Reading his face I thought I saw a brief, soft feeling there, like the one I'd seen in the night.

"See ya," I said, and grinned at him.

He laughed. "See ya."

So when the cab sped off across Fourteenth Street, I still had my face curled up in relief, in a smile. When it faded, I closed my eyes against the rush of wind coming in the window, leaned back against the hot blue vinyl seats and felt a cramp take hold in my abdomen. I crossed my arms over my chest and felt dizzy. Sick.

At home Claire did not have to ask. She knew. She looked at me when I came in the door, Saturday afternoon, a grin ready on her lips. I looked right back at her and made my eyes bug out to show her she was not wrong in her conclusions.

"Whoa," she said.

"Yeah."

I lay down on the couch, and Claire sat in the armchair.

"Oh, boy," she said.

"Yeah."

"So, you like him."

"He's nice."

"Well"—she sighed—"as you know, Carl and I took a while to figure out that we really had enough in common to get married." Claire had had the ring for a year, planning the wedding forever, ad nauseam, though it wasn't supposed to happen for another year still, when she finished law school.

"What the fuck are you talking about, *marriage*?" I said. It was all I could do to keep my eyeballs from rolling back in my head. She was obsessed with weddings. To me the simple tragedy of Carl was that he had made Claire boring. She wouldn't go out. Hardly ever and just with him. She wore sweater sets and flat shoes with her jeans. I gave her tube tops and stacked-heel shoes and vinyl hotpants—she was tiny, she could wear anything, but she wouldn't. "It's not me," she'd say. Or, the truth: "Carl wouldn't go for it." For gifts, he gave her brooches. Brooches! Gold ones in circle patterns, with maybe a pearl. As if she was some dowager with a hump who ate tiny mayonnaise sandwiches without crusts. I would never say just what I thought of Carl. Or admit that part of me was jealous of Claire, the reports of her increasingly calm state. I was not calm. Just a few weeks before this I had lurched in from Rio de Janeiro at one o'clock in the morning with Simon and half the girls from a shoot and our whole entourage. We stayed up listening to music, smoking and eating all Claire's food, messing up our whole gorgeous apartment that she mostly was responsible for, since I was hardly there. We were carrying on till dawn, and Claire just glared sarcastically at me in the morning and said, *You're a fucking lunatic, Charlotte, you strumpet.* She gave me the finger as usual. There were never any hard feelings. But it was difficult for me to see how the new calm Claire or the old wild Claire would be much help to me in sorting out Milo.

"Anyway," she said, smiling, "is it true?"

"What?"

"You know." Her eyebrows went up and down. "What they say."

"Fuck you."

"Fuck you back. Don't be coy with me."

"Well, it's not about that."

"Oh, *right,*" she said. "Where did you go?"

"A party. A bar. His house."

"What did you talk about?"

"I don't know. Beer. Skiing."

"Oh," she said. "You kids have so much in common!"

"We do," I said, defensively. The way she sat, draped now on the chair, her mouth screwed skeptically over to one side, made me doubt myself. *She won't believe me, no matter what I say.* The doubts and the questions started right there, the first morning.

Then I told Claire about how Jack hurt his head, about the basketball game and the injury and what Milo said: *You know damn well I didn't push him.*

Claire listened and she was shocked. "I knew Jack was hurt," she said. "But I didn't know Milo had anything to do with it."

"He didn't."

"You don't know that," she said. "Just because he says he didn't." She shook her head. "The two of them. They always had some kind of tribal thing going. Some rivalry."

"Claire," I said, "*tribal?*"

"All I'm saying," she said, "is it's not about that right now, at this point in your, shall we say, *reacquaintance* with Monsieur Robicheaux. But it will be. Mark my words."

"Mark your own words, Claire," I said, cranky at her.

"I'm not saying *I* see it," she said. "Other people do."

"I don't care about other people," I said. "It doesn't have to be about that."

It. Thing. That. We knew what we meant. We couldn't say any of it.

"Look. We had a good time," I told Claire. "We had fun. I like him. Milo is ... He is—"

"Handsome. Also famous."

"Tch."

"What?"

"I like him."

"Fine," she said. "Good. I like him, too. I always thought highly of him. But." She gave me her psychiatric nurse smile, full of reassurance and *don't say I didn't warn you*. It was a smile of *Yes dear*. "I think you should just adopt a wait-and-see attitude."

But it was all waiting and no seeing. Milo didn't call me. Not the next day or the next. A week passed. More. He didn't call. I thought I would dry up and die if he didn't. My hands were cold, yet sweating, I couldn't eat; everything tasted dry as pet kibble. I was obsessed with him, with that night. What we said, the sugar on his fingertip, how he put it to his mouth, a crystal on his finger. It killed me. I nearly passed out thinking of it. I wanted to call him but I couldn't. It was medieval, truly, it was pathetic. But I was afraid he scorned me now. He was not calling, so neither was I. Equal and mutual not calling.

A woman never throws herself at a man.

I thought of it, hurling myself at Milo. Or hadn't I done that already? Wasn't that the problem?

"He's probably out of town," Claire said, to be nice. Her other hypotheses were: "You're too gorgeous." "He's ill." "You probably scare him," or "He's dead."

I looked for him on the news, where he was not ill or dead at all, but bantering away with Tracy Austin and all the young players on the U.S. Women's Tennis Team. Tracy's ponytail wagged when she talked. He looked right out of the screen, handling the microphone, already a pro after two months.

He wasn't calling because he was busy. He was afraid of me. *You in-timidate men, sweetie, the way you look*, my mother had said to me often. I had all kinds of theories. The theory of the photograph on the dresser. The theory of *You know. That.*

Just because he didn't call me back? That meant it was about skin? It was about skin. Of course it was, some of it, in the beginning. I can't say it wasn't. Claire's question, *What they say, is it true?* the rumors and the history books and the second-guessing, all that was there, like the graffiti on the bathroom wall. It was there when Milo and I were maneuvering around the party, there when I wrapped my arms around his back and felt the valley along his spine, made by the hard muscles on either side of it. I felt those muscles, like warm stone, how they fit in the bowls of my hands, how they ran down to meet the high curve of his backside, and I thought, *This has nothing to do with skin.*

He didn't call me.

Nothing to do with skin. Ha! I was already angry over it. Petulant. I hated that I had to think about it. Interrogating myself. Claire wagging her eyebrows, saying *So? What's it like?* made me furious. But. Okay. I will admit. Between me and Milo that night, was me, thinking: *A black man.* I thought this even before his name. *A black man.* I confess it. I've never admitted it. Your race is there in the bed with you, and his, too. The first time, it would have to be; the minuscule differences, especially, or, what I mean is: the *idea* of the differences, what we think they mean; the different hair, his for me, springy under my fingers. (Mine for him? No, for him it wasn't new.) Smells. Like ripe fruit in the sun, like pine. Like Milo. Then, I wondered, was it him? Or was it *them*? Did smells have race? Did sounds? I outgrew these questions, but back then I didn't know anything. I was not White then, when I met Milo. I was green. Green and dumb as a grassy lawn.

11.

At work I was a wreck and couldn't concentrate.

"Charlotte."

"Charlotte."

"Hey!"

"Put your heart in it, sweetheart."

After two weeks of waiting I was booked for a big show during New York Style Week. The Couture King wanted me on the catwalk, to be one of his new faces and then later to do a big campaign, including TV spots. My booker wrecked her vocal cords, screaming, to tell me. Kevin called to say how proud he was, how happy. It was a great moment for me, he said.

"I guess so," I said.

"What's wrong?" he asked. "Baby?"

"Men," I said.

"Tell me about it," he said, wearily.

For one whole day we had to shoot promo stills, for previews, for press releases. By the time we finished work, around eleven, I was wrung out and cranky. My scalp hurt from hot combs, and my arches were collapsing in the shoes. They had given me the clothes I had on at the end of the shoot, a short leather jacket, leather pants, but I was too much of a hellhole to say thank you. No, I wouldn't wait for Anthony, didn't want to go to the Mudd Club with Gillian. I was going home. I didn't even change out of the leather stuff. Makeup was still on my face and my hair was teased in a wild way. I was marginally sane.

On Eighteenth Street I looked for a cab but there wasn't one. *So just walk.* I didn't want to go home, anyway, where the phone was blatantly not ringing, where the answering machine was blinking regularly as a heartbeat, but without that particular recorded voice, *Hey, Charlotte.* I didn't want to go anywhere near home. Claire and Carl were there, with their closed door, their linen napkins folded, their wineglasses washed by the sink, everything poignantly paired. No, not home. Shaughnessy's. There it was, like an omen, a bar I had never noticed. A fairy godmother must have put it there in my path. I went in and sat on a stool. I normally didn't ever do this, didn't go out alone, didn't drink alone. I never was alone.

I sat four stools down from Plaid Shirt and Gas Station Shirt, both of them with mustaches and wolfy eyes, staring as if the most succulent of the three pigs had just walked in and laid down on their plates. I would not look at them. I swiveled my stool away, toward the corner. So what if I had on leather pants? They could just go wank in the bathroom for all I cared. *Wank is a Simon word. Fuck Simon. Don't want bloody Simon.* I had two dark rum and tonics with lime. I lit a cigarette and dragged the smoke into my lungs. *Milo isn't going to call me up or come and see me or otherwise hold me in his arms again,* I thought. He wasn't. It had been two weeks. Longer. He had shown up and settled some score with me and then gone on ahead. He wasn't my savior. Not my redeemer. Apparently any saving or redeeming would have to be done by me. It was a frightening thing to realize. I had never gone after anybody. People had always gone after me. I had never tried for anyone. Never had to. *Never wanted to.*

I paid for my drinks and left the bar and walked downtown to his building. It was right there. Just six blocks away. Petunias in the urns. Same doorman.

"Excuse me, would you just ring Mr. Robicheaux's apartment."

You would not be able to tell the degree to which I was fortified by rum. Not by looking at me. What the rum made me was charming when I wanted to be charming. I wanted to be. I had decided.

"Okay," he said, obviously impressed by my leather ensemble. "May I tell him whom is calling on him?"

"An old friend from college," I said.

Yeah, sure, said his expression. "Your name?"

"Charlotte Halsey," I said, as the doorman dialed Milo's apartment.

"He says come up," said the doorman, eyebrows waggling like woolly bear caterpillars.

Milo answered the door barefoot but still in his suit, the tie half off and the collar unbuttoned. His throat was beautiful. Dear Lord. I couldn't help thinking it. And his feet. Long long toes.

"Hello," he said, rearing back at the sight of me.

"Hello," I said. "You're home."

"Just got home," he said. "I was—"

"Let's go out," I said. "Want to?"

"Out?" he said, but he was smiling.

"I finished a shoot," I told him. "I just got done. Just a few blocks from here. I've been working all day. See this?" I said, and twirled for him, showing him my leather stuff. "I got this for free."

"Least you didn't pay money for it." He looked at my shoes with concern.

"Free shoes, too," I said. "Let's go somewhere. Let's go out."

"I just got in," Milo said. "I was— Why don't you come in? Come on in for a minute."

"Oh, no," I said, pretending to be scandalized. "Never. Not me. Put on your shoes and come on, Robicheaux."

He took a breath and blinked and looked at his watch. "Okay," he said, "I'll be right there."

We went down the street to a joint where students went to be serious and smoke and as we walked Milo asked me pop-fly questions: "What's new? How are you?" Fine, just fine, I said. I told him I had something to celebrate but I didn't say what. I didn't ask him anything. Didn't say: *Where have you been? What is going on?* My strategy was to blunder ahead blithely, to make jokes, to acknowledge nothing of What Had Passed Between Us.

"I've been out of town," he said.

"Me, too," I lied. I said I'd been in Paris.

He said he'd been all over: L.A., Denver, Boston. "My sister lives in Boston."

I didn't say, *Did you think of me?* I said, "You have a sister?"

"She's two years older," he said.

I made Milo tell me about her while we drank our drinks.

"My sister Bobbie," he said, "is so smart she could talk a dog off a meat wagon." Which was an expression of his mother's. His proverbial sainted mother, Hattie. She and his wise father, Milton, along with the brilliant Ph.D. sister, Bobbie, were the rest of the Robicheaux family. He quoted them. As he talked he got a nice look in his eyes. He used the words "we," "us." *We always chopped our own tree at Christmas. We had a big garden, every year, each of us had our own specialty.* Milo grew corn because he liked to eat it. Bobbie grew rutabaga. Rhubarb. Sassafras. *Not because she would eat these things but because she liked the words. She just wanted to say "I'm growing my own rutabaga."* He was proud of them and missed them, I could see. It made me jealous, hearing about his happy family in New Hampshire, running around in the wholesome air. And his stories lowered my guard. *I was not wrong,* I thought, watching the way he leaned toward me, the animated movements of his hands, his unsettled and unsettling gaze. He was interested in me.

When you're ready, you'll tell me.

"My own personal parents are aliens from another planet," I said.

This troubled him immediately. He furrowed his face and asked quietly, "What do you mean by that?" I remembered he didn't like to say anything bad about anyone.

"We were all raised to be saved," I said, "and there was no saving me. I was hopeless, you know?"

"Saved from what?"

"Sin. Damnation. Et cetera," I said. "Mostly et cetera. You had to really watch out for that."

He wasn't quite sure if I was kidding.

I didn't know how to explain except to quote the Book of Matthew. I took a deep breath, made my voice whispery and urgent like a preacher's. *"You will see the Son of man coming on the clouds of heaven with power and great glory. And He will send out His angels with a loud trumpet call..."*

The words made me remember a picture in my old room, of an angel in white robes helping some children across a stormy sea. I told Milo about that, too, the picture, and how I used to tell Diana, *That's you and that's me,* picking out two little girls holding the angel's hands. *He's taking us to the shore.*

"Whoa," Milo said, fascinated. "Are you some kind of a Bible-thumper? Are you a Jesus freak?"

"Don't call me that," I said. Snapped. "Just don't."

"Sorry," he said, and backed off right away. "It was a joke."

And right there we had this moment of checking, back and forth for safety, like looking both ways in a crosswalk. We looked away fast. But I saw it: that other night. It was there between us, hanging in the air with the murk of bar smoke. We didn't mention it. The moment passed like a big truck on the road, leaving a wake of wind.

"I wasn't raised in any church," he said. "We only went to church summers, back in New Orleans. My parents didn't like the ones near us in New Hampshire," he said. "So I'm something of a pagan."

"I'm not even a pagan," I said. "I'm a failed pagan." I told him how even though I didn't believe any gospel, I still looked for signs, prayed, tried to identify some angels, but never did see one, not even once. I told him about my mother the Avon lady and my sister Diana the Sunday school teacher. About my father's temper and my brother Peter, the pastor. I didn't say much about Sean, who was a taxidermist in Oregon—he still is, really, a taxidermist. I mentioned Kids for Christ.

"What did you do for fun?" he asked me.

"Needlepoint," I said. "Prayed. Polished our nails."

"Not really." Milo looked as if he couldn't believe any of this about me.

"Yeah, really," I told him. "At least, until I had a religious conversion."

"What kind?"

"I'm not sure what you'd call it," I said. "If it's called 'born again' when you find religion, what would it be called when you realized it was all a lot of crap?"

"Born again," he said, and smiled.

I liked that he said that.

We stayed out till three in the morning, until Milo looked at his watch. "Holy smokes," he said, like a Boy Scout.

"I have to go." I spoke before he could. "I have to get some sleep."

On the sidewalk outside, we were quiet for an uncomfortable moment.

"Thanks for dragging me out," he said.

"Anytime."

He noticed my outfit again, the leather. "You don't look like a failed pagan at all, not in that." He poked the jacket. "You look like you just need a helmet and the Harley and they'd sign you right up."

"Ha ha."

"I have an old chair that needs upholstering," he said, poking again.

"It's fashion!" I said primly. "It's designed by the Couture King of the USA." Then without really thinking about it, I invited him to come to my show, the King's new fall line, featuring Charlotte Halsey. "It's next week."

"Next week."

"You're invited. So come."

"Okay. I'd love to."

We did not kiss. He said good night.

"Good night," I said.

"Sleep well," he said. But I saw he knew I wouldn't, and maybe he wouldn't, either. He hailed a cab for me and I headed uptown toward home, happier for the moment. He was coming to my show, anyway. *Love to*, he said.

To get on a runway for the Couture King, you have to be no bigger than size 6, you have to be five ten or taller. You have to be exotic, which is the word they used at the time. I was not *exotic*, just muscular, with biceps and quadriceps and lats, as well as a big long crop of whitecorn-colored hair. In those days, in the ravaged aftermath of Twiggy, I was extreme.

The shows are always bedlam. You walk out onto the runway with straight pins sticking into your flesh. You have Band-Aids taped across your nipples. Or nothing. You are blinded by lights; music pumps you up and propels you out from the pit of backstage. Backstage is frantic. People are pulling clothes off you, pinning you, stapling you with staples, into the next thing. You're naked half the time. Dressers think nothing of taking off your bra while you're taking off your shoes.

"Thirty seconds."

"Watch my hair."

"Left earring."

"Touch up the chinline."

"Suck in, babe."

"You suck in."

"You're getting fat."

"Not as fat as you, precious."

Everyone in the seething place is pretentious and frivolous and calling each other darling constantly. Absolutely everyone is sweetie or babe or hun. Everyone obsesses; everyone's skin is thin as onion peel, everyone has to have their waters bottled and iced just so, with mint, with lemon, with the blood of their rivals. The girls are cold-shouldering each other and hugging everyone in sight. We're sliding our eyes at each other to see who's wearing what, if hers is better. Dressers are dabbing you and wiping your armpits dry and blowing your hair. Compliments are flying around like common colds. *Fabulous, marvelous, stunning, gorgeous.* They mean nothing. You can't go on without them. *You own it you own it.*

You do. You have to. You take those words and you flaunt that piece of fabric around as if it's yours, right out of your closet. You wear it like it's ordinary but you're not. As if by wearing it, Mrs. Horseface Old Money and Mrs. Helmet Hair Captain of Industry and Mrs. Facelift Society Page will have everyone look at *her*, the way everyone on either side of the apron is looking, clapping, murmuring about *you*. I liked that feeling. I craved it. I was so pumped and excited to do this show. There would be a lot of press. *Women's Wear Daily*. The Dragon Lady of *Vogue*. Jackie Onassis and Princess Grace. Milo. I made sure he was in the front row.

The Couture King gave us a pep talk before the show. He is a pompous blowhard phony with sideburns and big black-framed glasses. *Elvis is alive*, I used to say behind his back. *Look, girls, it's Elvis.* He thought we couldn't get enough of him. He was on his third wife, each one younger than the last by a factor of three. He kissed us and held us, each individually. "Charlotte," he said to me, "you're the embodiment of my work, with that American face, all those biceps in your arms. Those long legs."

Pretentious pug, I thought. *You say that to everyone.*

"It's you," I said. "You make anyone look good."

The first piece of mine was a long metallic taffeta dress, purple with a ruffled train, slit up to Kingdom Come, with a tight strapless bodice. It had a small bolero jacket cut high. My legs led and my face was impassive. Bored. I walked. Milo was washed out by the lights. I knew just where he was, though, felt his eyes at the height of my ankle. He was there. I slipped the jacket off to show the back detail, to show my shoulders. He would remember them.

I walked out nine times. Sportswear, more evening wear. Last was a short slip with a lace-bra top. It was made of shimmering green gauze the color of caterpillars, worn with enormous bright red beads, red sneakers. I flexed my biceps gracefully at the end of the catwalk, one at a time, half fighter, half dancer. People clapped. The press said later I was an embodiment of the new confident woman of the '80s. The New Athleticism. Feminism Comes to Fashion, they said. Ha. Right.

I don't remember where we went afterwards. I do remember Milo was bowled over, he said he'd never seen anything like it, me on the runway.

"I never knew you did that, that you could do that."

"Do what?" I said. "It's just walking a line."

"Some lines are harder to walk than others," he said.

"Yes. True." *And some lines mean more than what they seem to mean, and some are just lines.*

"I mean it, Charlotte. You're gifted. You looked different every time you came through the gates."

"The gates?"

"Well, that's just how I think of them," he said. "Starting gates. Anyway, you cranked out there."

They weren't lines. He had respect in his voice.

We went home separately. It was old-fashioned and unspoken, as if we had agreed about it.

"So good night again," he said, something mischievous going on with his smile.

"Yes," I said. "Good night again."

We had several weeks of this hellish pretend Victorian courtship. It took forever, as long as the gestation period of an elephant or a whale. We talked on the phone sometimes. We met once for lunch. For dinner, a couple of times. We didn't go out after, we didn't go dancing. Once we tentatively kissed in a taxi. We were riding uptown and when we got to his corner, Milo gave me fare money and opened the door. One of his legs was on the sidewalk already when he leaned back toward me. He meant to kiss my cheek, but our lips touched. I remembered his from before, dry and muscular. I nearly fainted. He stopped and pulled away for a reason I didn't know, didn't ask. Whatever it was made him look ill.

"See ya," he said. He looked just terrible.

. . .

"He's using you," said Claire. "You'll never learn."

She saw Milo a couple of times, when he came to pick me up. He was charming to her, and she was shy in front of him, in her old sweater and glasses. "Claire!" he said, and hugged her. "You look great, you look just the same!" He was always in a hurry. He kept looking at his watch. "Let's go, let's go." He held my jacket for me. He looked in the mirror in the entryway and yanked at his tie knot. "See you, Claire," he said.

"He's definitely using you," Claire said when she saw me home early, in the door by eleven.

"For what?"

"He needs someone flashy, picked you."

"Why wouldn't I be using him?"

"Maybe you are," she said.

There was no talking to Claire for some reason. She seemed to think Milo was just another folly of mine. "You'll need a broom to sweep up what's left of your heart if you hang it out there for that guy," she said. To tell you the truth, I wondered if she was jealous, or threatened. She talked about the handwriting on the wall, and how I should wake up and smell the coffee. Later she had this comfort to offer: "There must be someone else."

"I thought that, maybe."

"Why?"

"Picture, on his dresser."

"Of whom?"

"Girl."

"Do you ask?"

"Sort of. I go, so, Milo, who's the babe in the picture? And he says, you're the babe in the picture."

"He says that?"

"Said. Once."

"Slick," she said.

He didn't seem slick. Not to me. He was dazzling. Everywhere we went, people asked him to sign things, shake hands, smile for the camera. He was a new New York Darling, polite and dashing. He had millions and millions of dollars and all the accoutrements: apartment in New York, house on the beach, Park City condo. The talk shows booked him in their guest spots, newspapers and magazines wrote about him: his recovery from his injuries, his appearance at this or that city sports clinic, his probable role in an upcoming film, his new career in broadcasting. They all loved him. He had chemical qualities that made you want to watch him. The way he carried himself was graceful, contained. He did not look left or right, he looked straight ahead. He was aloof until he wasn't. When he looked at you, you almost had to turn away, because the touch of his gaze was so steady. It was like being recognized.

"That's what I thought about you," he said, when I told him this later. "Every time I turned around you were watching me."

"I was," I said. "I couldn't help it."

"It got to me," he said. "It got me."

But it took so long, to get to him.

In June we went to Sweetwater's. It was maybe five weeks into our renewed acquaintance. Sweetwater's was a jazz club near Milo's office, and this was our second time there. It had good music and sloe gin fizzes. Milo and I watched the sax player that night and started talking about how you get good at something. Music. Skiing. Being a stupid fashion model.

"It's not stupid," Milo said.

"You have no idea how stupid," I told him.

"So quit."

"It's all I can do," I said. "When I got here, everyone said my face was the only thing I had that could save me."

He looked frustrated with me. "That's not all you had," he said.

"What else?"

He reached around me and ran his fingers down either side of my spine. "Spine," he said, and ran his fingers up again so they bumped on the knobs of bone.

"Spine?"

"Yeah."

"Not me."

"What kind of attitude is that?" Milo said. "That's no way to talk."

I shrugged.

"You know what you need?" he said. "You need to see the story."

"What story?"

"The story, the *story*. What's your story?"

I didn't follow him.

"Okay. Listen," Milo said, and he started telling me about his network job. "Somebody's always saying to me 'What's the story, Robicheaux? You gotta find the story.' See, the way I always thought about the story was: Who's winning? Who's ahead? Who's got the technique? Who's got the speed? But now, as a reporter, they're always saying to me: 'Yeah, I know she's *fast*, I know they *won*, I know he *leads the league*, but what's the *story*?'"

Milo looked at me as if I was supposed to get it, but I still didn't, so he kept explaining. "I mean," he said, "is the athlete winning after overcoming a childhood handicap? Is she skating to honor the memory of her father, the former Lithuanian skating champ? That kind of thing."

"Oh," I said, "now I get it."

"So, what's your story?" he said. "The story of Charlotte."

"Born in California?" I said. "Came East to make my fortune? And someone gave me a job? And here I am? Is that a story?"

"No!" he said. "Not if you tell it like that. The story is: You got out of there, didn't you? Smalltown, California. Charlotte Halsey got out. Wherever you came from. You had your *religious conversion*, I believe you called it."

"I guess," I said.

"Not: You guess. You *know*."

"But everybody leaves home."

"Not like that, they don't. Right? Takes guts. Can't have been easy."

Nobody ever praised me that way. Milo was the first person I knew besides Claire who never went on and on about my looks. He didn't flatter. *Guts and spine.* I liked that, since mostly I'd thought of myself as invertebrate, holding my shape with an exoskeleton of hair spray.

"Thank you," I said. "I never heard that story before."

"You tell that story, now," Milo commanded. "Whenever anyone asks."

"I'll try."

"No," he said, "not try. Say: I will."

I tried but no words came out.

"Say it, Charlotte, say: I will."

"I will."

My eyes filled up with tears.

"What's the matter?" Milo asked, with alarm in his voice and that tenderness I'd heard before. Which made it worse.

"Nothing."

"What did I say?"

"It was nice, what you said."

"It wasn't nice," he said, watching me. "It was true."

"What about you?" I said after a while. "Your story. Didn't you ever want to give up?"

"I have a motto," he told me finally. "Keeps my nose to the grindstone."

"Motto?" I said. "Like: Semper Fi?"

"Yeah. Like that."

"What is it?"

"You don't *need* it, you just *want* it." He whispered it but like a military order. Then he laughed.

You Don't Need It, You Just Want It. That was his motto.

"Did you make that up?" I asked him.

"Yeah," he said, "I did."

It was a way to deny himself things, he told me, certain kinds of pleasure or comfort. When he was a little boy, he'd get cold, skiing, wish to go inside for warmth; he'd wish for a new bike but would save his money for skis; he'd want to blow off the last practice run and go get hot chocolate with whipped cream, but he'd tell himself: *You don't need that, you just want it.*

"It's what I say," he said, "to stay out of trouble."

"Oh," I said. "And am I trouble?"

"I don't know," he said.

"I don't want to be trouble," I said simply. "I don't."

We left. Silver sprays of rain glittered out of the darkness, the streetlights like shower nozzles. Milo put up his umbrella, held it over our heads, hailed a taxi. "Good night," he said. "Charlotte." And then without warning, he pulled me back from the open door of the cab and kissed me. The umbrella made a tent around our heads, rain battering it. People were coming and going, stepping around us. We were kissing like mad, stealing each other's breath. The taxi honked and then pulled away. The umbrella tipped in the wind and turned inside out. Milo dropped it. A man passing us pivoted around and stared, our umbrella flying at him as he walked backward, looking at us still kissing in the downpour. We ignored him, the pop-eyed fool. We knew where we were going, that night, anyway. When we got there, we didn't get up for a while.

12.

After that, we went out all over town. We were seen together. They wrote about us: boldface Milo Robicheaux seen squiring boldface model Charlotte Halsey. It was a gas, all that boldface squiring around with Milo. We were wild now, laughing, flirting, staying up all night dancing, getting out of limos, drinking sparkling alcohols out of flutes. I was reckless, wherever we went. My arms were always around Milo's neck, like ropes of pearls. For weeks I did my best not to think about anything serious, jettisoning questions and worries the way balloonists throw out sandbags, to stay aloft. But it scared me, how much time I was biding, waiting for the end of the party, wishing for later, the dark of his room.

"I like this room," I said, lying there one night.

"I like you in this room," he said.

"Why did you wait, then?"

"When?"

"After the first time."

"What."

"To get me back in here."

He shrugged.

"You weren't going to call me."

"Maybe not, no."

"I was starting to think you hated me."

"I did hate you, actually," he said lightly. "For making me interested."

"So why did you wait, if you were interested?"

"You Don't Need It, You Just Want It," he said.

I whacked him across the bare chest with a backward shot of my forearm.

"Ow," he said, annoyed. "All I meant was, I just was not in the market for any more of these cross-cultural encounters of the so-called ebony and ivory kind. I've had quite enough international experience, if you know what I mean?"

"Me American," I said. "You American."

He lifted his eyebrows at that. "You think so?" he said. "Because I had been thinking that in New York, I'd finally be somewhere I could find what you could call . . . a soul mate."

I sat up and pulled the sheet around me, listening.

"At first," Milo said, "I thought that you would be . . . how shall I say this delicately? An easy target, or maybe, like a little short-term therapy. To settle an old score."

"What score?"

"Just to see if you'd notice me now."

I was noticing everything about him now. The moons on his fingernails. The hair on his arm.

"But then, Charlotte, you turned out to be a little complicated. A little scary."

So he had said it. *Scary.*

"I didn't know what I'd be getting myself into," he said. "So to speak."

I hit him another time, socked his shoulder.

"Cut it out," he said. "Listen. What I'm saying is: I dislike confusion."

"Are you confused?"

"No," he said, "I'm not." And he pulled me down and kissed me so I had to stop talking. Which was why he kissed me, I knew, to keep me from asking things, to be heedless of anything but the turmoil of limbs and sheets and sweat drying pleasantly on the skin.

He was not confused, he said.

But I was. *He* was the scary one, with all his evasions. Why was he with me? What was so scary? *Because I'm a white girl?* I couldn't ask. The question would give the idea respect it didn't deserve, would insult him, would make it, color—I still had trouble naming it—a problem when it wasn't, not for me. Or I wanted it not to be a problem. I actually believed it was a choice I had.

The girls were all curious about Milo. "How's Mr. Olympics?" "Hey, Charlotte, how's Anchorman?" We were shooting the Couture King's new spring sportswear line, standing on the steps of the library between the big lions. It was August, early morning, and they had the newspaper open to the picture of Milo and me on Page Six. A girl named Jenny was reading, *The lovebirds were seen kissing on the dance floor of the Peppermint Lounge.* Everybody was hooting and teasing me. "Whoa, Char, hot date!" "Kissing on the dance floor!"

But then there was Glenda. She was one of the few black models they used a lot in the '80s, so beautiful she made you want to put a bag on your head. She was tall and ethereal with ginger-brown skin and brown eyes with yellow in them. She came from the islands—from Trinidad? I wasn't sure. It was as if the sun had lightened her eyes. These days she'd be one of the top faces, I'm sure, but even in 1981 they'd only put one black girl on the cover of a major fashion magazine. Ever. Black covers wouldn't sell, they said, and tongue-clucked about what a shame it was, that readers weren't interested. They blamed the readers. Glenda had worked on a couple of jobs with me and we were friendly.

"So," she said, "what's going on with you and Milo the Skiing Brother?"

"Oh, just—I don't know."

"Well, what do you want?"

"I like him," I said, looking down at my feet. "That's all."

"Well, just be careful," she said.

"Why?"

She wouldn't say at first but I kept after her. She explained to me kindly, as you would explain something difficult, like death, to a child: "It's this thing with them."

"Who?"

"Black men."

"Come on," I said.

"Listen: They have this thing about a blond model-type woman, okay?

Or any kind of white, you know? It's some sick status thing." She seemed weary when she said this.

"We knew each other in college," I said. "I've known Milo for years." Glenda was making me uncomfortable. I was picking at invisible pills in the weave of my sample coat. "He *already* has status, all by himself. He has two *gold medals*."

"Right, but he doesn't—" Glenda made a bitter mouth, lips tight. She was shaking her head as if there was no way I could understand. "The other part of it is, it's kind of like a self-hating thing, or sometimes a re- venge thing, against white guys, like, *Nyah, nyah, nyah, I got your woman* type of thing."

I said nothing.

"The point is, Charlotte, is he really interested in *you*?"

To me it seemed he was. Also I didn't care. *I am interested in him*, I thought. "I don't know," I said. "I just like him. I don't even notice the black-white part. I don't want to think about it."

"But," she said, "you're going to have to think about it, if you keep it up."

The nerve of her. *It's not her business*, I thought. But Glenda was right; she saw it was on my mind: why Milo liked me, why I felt so disorganized by him. I saw the looks people shot at us when we were out around town. Every color looked. Or was it that I was looking now myself?

The truth is: I liked what people saw, me with a black man, a famous man. I saw him with my old magpie eyes. Milo was a prize. I stood out next to him, a pearl on velvet. Not that I'm proud of it now, but I thought that way then. I thought, no, *knew*, that for me to be smitten by a black man was automatically illicit, a bad-girl thing to do. Nobody ever told me this, but I knew. My parents—they would not take well to Milo, despite their teaching that we are all God's children.

"He's that black one," my mother said, when I mentioned who I was dating. No questions, nothing to say after that. Well, fine. It's true I was glad to shock them.

But it's also true that my heart leapt up. Every time. I was glad to see Milo, his smiling face finding me across a room, sliding his eyes across the table, beaming from the window of the waiting car. I liked his company, his jokes. *I have a chair that needs upholstering*. He made me laugh. Still, every day was a mined meadow of motives and feelings, wondering how to sort out the rights and wrongs of my interest in a man.

It was wrong to see color. But I saw it anyway. On my way to go out with Milo that summer I saw people sleeping in doorways and checked for some of their skin showing from under a blanket. More often than white, the skin would be brown skin. I saw harrowing sights that were apparently quite ordinary. Children begging! Ulcerated sores on legs! Occasional pools of blood! Women holding out cups, or their brown hands, shaped like cups. What did any of that have to do with skin? With me or Milo Robicheaux? And what did *he* think, as he walked along? I didn't ask. I went through the doors of some swank-filled restaurant or some nightclub or into the vaulted rooms of Lincoln Center, and the air changed. It was conditioned, cool, scented with perfume or the aroma of fine cuisine. It was still and calm or full of music. And Milo right beside me was *proof*, wasn't he? that I was not responsible for what I saw outside, in the sweltering or freezing streets. That I was, in fact, better than those white others, doing my part.

I never said any of this. Not to anybody.

Also it's not like I was the only one. Invitations arrived in the mail at Milo's Fifth Avenue address, from white people inviting him to sit on the dais, to present the award, to sponsor the cause. Hostesses of dinner parties wanted to sit next to him, introduce him to the assembled guests. His friends were all white, though you wouldn't call them close, just colleagues from work, other athletes, people he interviewed, his agents, Jed and Mark. Wherever we went, he was nearly always the only black person. He didn't seem to care, so why would I?

Still, all that summer I was wary and nervous about Milo. What did I mean to him? What, as my father would say, were his intentions?

One Sunday morning in August these questions woke me up full of panic. It was worse than an alarm going off. I sat straight up. There was Milo sleeping. His muscles made hard hourglass shapes against the sheets: shoulder, biceps, forearm; thigh, knee, calf. He was just a man. Only Milo.

I gazed at him, thinking that, *just some man*, but twisted with this frightened feeling. I tickled his ribs with my fingernail, nudged him. He opened his eyes and smiled, seeing me there.

"How do you feel about me?" I said. My lips were right by the whorl of his ear.

"I feel about you," he said, groggy, running his hand down my flank. "I'm feeling about you."

"Milo, but—"

"Don't say butt," he said. "Say buttocks."

"Milo." He was impossible.

"Say *fesses*."

"What?"

"That's French for these parts."

"How do you know?"

"I know." He wowed his eyebrows, half asleep. "Now shh," he said. "Close your eyes." He dozed again with his face in the crook of my neck.

"Have you ever been in love?" I asked.

"No," he said. He was nearly snoring.

"Tell," I said. "What about that French one? The actress."

"She was French," he said, annoyed. "She lives in France."

He kept trying to shut me up in the usual way but I wouldn't let him. "What about the one in the picture?"

"What picture?"

"The one that used to be on your mirror, in the yellow dress."

"Oh," Milo said, "that's my sister. That's Bobbie."

Not the girlfriend, I thought. *The sister.*

He opened his eyes. "Were you worried?"

"She's pretty," I said, a little smile on my lips.

"Ha," he said, seeing it. "You were worried."

"It was right on your dresser."

"You were snooping around!" he said. "What else did you snoop?"

"Nothing," I said. "There's nothing *to* snoop. Your stuff is still in boxes. You're a big question mark. You leave no evidence!"

"Good," he said.

"You don't even have fingerprints."

"Oh yes I do," he said. "And I will leave them all over you."

"But answer," I said, holding his wrist. "How do you feel?"

"Do you see anyone else here in this bed?" he said, annoyed. "You're the one who's in it." He kissed me so that I was silenced by hints of his teeth and his tongue and the weight of his legs saddling me, so I didn't care if it had meaning as long as he kept on. I realized then I could not judge him by his words, his cryptic answers, or his evasions but only by how he acted, what he did. And that morning he grabbed me by the hips and pulled me under him. He centered me. In the morning light I watched his face the whole time and he never opened his eyes so I saw. That he was helpless, that I had him right then in those moments. Seeing the curl of his lip and the turn of his head to the side—the way a musician does when he is listening to the feel of each note—seeing that took me right along with him. So when he did open his eyes, and saw me, saw how gone I was, watching, some flicker of panic or terror crossed his face as he was carried away by the *oh God*, the drowning, narcotic feeling, and me saying *Milo, Milo*.

Later, he turned to face me, considering something. "You *watch* me," he said after a while. "You're always watching."

He was right. I was. I thought that if I could only watch him, asleep or awake, that would be enough; I would know him. I would be happy, saved from longing. But it had been weeks now, months, and I was not saved. What did it mean, that I was with him, and every moment felt a sense of danger? I knew he could hurt me, break my heart. And what's more, I liked that feeling. It was thrilling. Was that love? We never said the word at all.

One Friday night, in late September of that year, VD showed up. VD had skied with Milo from way back, from '76. He was an Olympian but not a medalist, a wild downhiller from Wyoming. His name was Rick but his last name was VonDrehle, so of course, everybody called him Venereal or Disease or plain VD.

"He's my best friend," Milo said.

I first saw Rick at the Odeon, a place whose name never failed to make me think of *odious* and *deodorant*. VD at the Odeon. The two names went together in my head now like a title. Milo and I were at the bar, me leaning my head on him, dripping my hair on purpose down the front of his dark linen jacket and him looking over his shoulder for Rick, who was late.

"Hey, hey, hey," Milo said, smiling. "Look at him." He was pointing with his head toward the door. "Shit. You could spot that guy a mile off. He does not have a clue what to do in here."

Rick was rangy with no fat on him. He was such a mountain man he had on some ancient red flannel shirt worn as a jacket, a bandanna on his neck, jeans drooping off his backside. His dark red hair was mostly held back in a shocking pink ponytail holder, except for the parts that ringleted around his freckled face. He had a big nose, with a bump on the bridge of it. He kept looking down.

"Hah! He hates the city!" Milo said. "Hates it. He is lost in here." Rick was looking at his shoes or the floor, not looking for us. Then we saw he had a dog with him.

"Shit!" Milo said. "He's got Cheyenne."

"What?"

"His dog.

"Hey, VD!" Milo shouted over the bar noise.

Rick saw us and came over with a yellow Labrador and a crooked smile. "Smilin' Milo! Heeeeeeyyyy. Wassup?" Rick said, in black English, which, as far as I'd noticed, only white people talked with Milo. You never heard Milo talk that way. Milo said *shur*. He said *rully*, as in *he's a rully fine athlete*. He said *ex-cel-lent* in three syllables, about whatever pleased him.

"Rick, man," Milo said. They hugged each other a long time. Cheyenne wagged her tail and tunneled under a bar stool.

"This is Charlotte Halsey," Milo said.

"Hi," I said, and shook Rick's hand.

"And that's Rick's woman, there." Milo pointed at the floor. "Careful, she might start sniffing you."

"Fuck you, ya whoremonger, Robicheaux," Rick said, taking Milo affectionately by the neck. "You never could tell dogs and women apart." He looked over at me and said, "With the very dramatic exception here of Miss Halsey."

"Dog or woman?" I asked.

VD blushed. "Not dog," he said. "Definitely."

Milo laughed and we went and sat in a booth by the back, where the smoke wasn't so thick. Rick was coughing.

"So will ya look at you, Ice," he said to Milo, reaching across and feeling his jacket. "Look at these threads. You're a fashion dude now, eh?"

"She's the fashion dude," Milo said, and pointed at me.

"He said you were some kind of model," said Rick. "Do you, like, know any other models?"

"What he means is that he would be willing to stay in New York if only you would introduce him to your coworkers," Milo said.

"No, I can't stand the place, man," Rick said, "not even for women." He explained he was in town on the way to Italy. He looked sheepish, as if he were admitting something.

"Italy!" Milo shouted in his announcer voice. "Italy. Italy. Italy." This had some coded meaning for them, apparently.

"*Italia*," said Rick. "One sixty-nine!"

"One sixty-nine," Milo intoned. "Number One Hundred and Sixty-nine! Sixty-nine!"

This made them both howl. Milo had tears in his eyes. "Sixty-nine! Italy!"

They went on like this till Milo could hardly speak, he was laughing so hard.

"What," I said finally, "is the meaning of one sixty-nine?"

They explained it was once Rick's number, a really bad seed number, a back-of-the-pack, rutty, icy race number that had something to do with a young lady named Lucia. The 169 girl. Apparently Lucia had had a *nocturnal opportunity* to wear Rick's racing bib, which Rick had not been able to forget. Now he was going back to Bormio to find her.

"The problem is," he said sadly, "I don't know her last name."

"Well, what this calls for," said Milo, "is a road trip."

"Road trip," VD said, happily now.

We ended up in Milo's car, barreling at midnight toward Lake Placid, where former assistant U.S. Ski Team coach Bill Winks had a ski school. They weren't even sure Winksie was home. But the idea was: We were going to go see him, ask if he remembered the 169 girl's name. It was a seven-hour drive.

VD was folded up in the miniature backseat of the Jaguar. He had Cheyenne and the beer. Milo wasn't drinking anything; he was driving with the radio cranked, weaving in and out of traffic in time to the music, slowing down fast to fit between hurtling cars in other lanes. I kept gasping, saying *Oh, dear God* under my breath, holding the dashboard and covering my eyes.

"What is this? A slalom?"

"Yeah! See that?" he said, grinning. When we got to the clear stretch of thruway Milo said: "Now comes the *schussbomb*, which is for serious people." He stepped on the gas.

"Yow!" said Rick.

"Milo!" I said.

The needle hit 100 miles an hour. It was dark with hardly any traffic. Milo was quiet. Rick sang softly to Cheyenne in the back. Slowly I let go of the dashboard. Milo took one hand off the wheel and put it on my neck. "Road trip," he said happily.

"Drive," I said, and returned his hand to the wheel. The pavement rose up hypnotically in front of the headlights, the heater wafted cooked air up around me. I fell in and out of sleep, breathing up the smell of beer, hearing the low music, the hiss of a can opening, Cheyenne whimpering, Milo and VD laughing, their words a warm soft buzz. *Kitzbühel, Bormio, Rossignol. Piece of ass. Blow job. Snow job. White girls. Fuck you. You never did. Fuck you. Why? None of your fucking business why.*

I don't know when I realized they were actually fighting.

"It's true, though, right?" said Rick. "You never did."

"Shut the fuck up!" Milo hissed.

"She's asleep," Rick said. "Sorry. I'm wasted."

They were quiet a long time. Milo was driving faster, angrily. I could hear the engine pulling, tires bobbling on the rough patches, a deep breath.

"I grew up where I grew up," Milo said. He sounded sick and tired. "I'm with who I'm with. Who I meet. I'm not apologizing for that."

"I was the one apologizing to you, Ice," Rick said, remorseful. He kept saying he was sorry. I heard him whispering to the dog. *Cheyenne girl, I'm a jerk, you know that? Big-time human dog, that's me.* He cracked another beer and fell asleep, snoring. The car was quiet. I sneaked a look at Milo and saw his hands on the wheel were clamped hard, his long fingers pianoing and agitated.

Well, the coach was not home. His big house, when we finally found it, was empty and dark, so we made our way back to the Olympic Motel in town, where we stayed for the rest of that night. We woke up late, and on our third round of drinks the next afternoon in the Saranac Bar, Milo started in on VD again about Italy, the 169 girl.

"Hey," I said. "What about Milo? Did he have, say, a 122 girl?"

"Code of silence," said Milo. "*Omerta*. Say nothing."

"It is well known how *well known* our friend Milo was all over the goddamned globe," said Rick. "But I must say that you, Charlotte, are the first actual girlfriend Milo's ever had."

"Right," I said. "Like anyone would believe that."

But Milo wasn't laughing now. "Drop it." Anger snapped in his eyes so I couldn't tell whether it was because he just didn't want to talk about girlfriends or that he didn't think of me that way.

Rick flushed and backed off the subject. "Milo is just a ski machine," he said. "That's all he's ever really had time for." We drank considerably more wine and went to bed, drove seven hours home the next day.

"So Rick said I'm the first girlfriend you ever had."

Milo looked up from his steak. We were out to dinner the next night, in a restaurant with paper sheets for tablecloths, sets of crayons in shotglasses.

"VD doesn't know jackdog about anything," Milo said.

"Am I?"

"*Are* you?"

"Am I what?"

"Are you my girlfriend?"

"As opposed to what?" I said.

"As opposed to, say, my sack rabbit?"

"Your *sack rabbit?*"

"My squeezebox?"

"Your what?"

He was smiling.

"Milo," I said, "I just asked if it was true. Am I?"

"Well, am *I?*" he said back at me.

"What?"

"Maybe I'm *your ethnic phase?*" He said this with his most alarming sweet charm, calm and quiet.

"Let's go." I threw my napkin down, stood up, pushed the chair back-ward, got my wrap from the coat check, headed home. We were near enough to walk there. He ran after me but I wouldn't speak.

"Is he bothering you?" somebody said, as I walked fast away from Milo.

"Shut up," I said to the stranger.

"I was just trying to look out for your safety, honey. Ya bitch."

Milo took me by the elbow and we went up to my apartment. Claire was gone for the weekend, so I wouldn't have to pretend nothing was going on when something clearly was. *Here it comes*, I thought. *Now I'll find out.*

"You are not my *ethnic* phase," I said, sitting on my bed. "How dare you? How can you think that? It's so tiring, and sick, having to think about it."

He nodded patiently. "Yes it is, isn't it?"

"Yes," I said, exhausted.

I pressed my thumbs into my eyelids, colors swimming in front of me like gasoline on puddles. I stood up and walked to the window. Down below was the city, sparkling like fairyland, with the dark rectangle of the park a blank in the middle of it.

Milo came over behind me and rested just his forehead against me. The hard bone of my skull pushed back against the plate of his brow. The in-hale and exhale of his breathing filtered through my hair.

"So what did Rick mean?" I asked again. "That I'm your first girl-friend. Am I?"

"That depends on you," he said.

I turned him around toward me. "Is this what you want to know?" Kissed him. "Can you understand what I'm saying?"

"What are you saying?"

"I'll be what you want. Whatever that is."

"Yourself," he said. "Yourself."

"Whoever that is," said invertebrate Charlotte. "You tell me."

"Tell what?"

"Who I am," I said, fishing. "What you want. What Rick meant. He said I'm your first . . . first?"

"Fuck first!" Milo said, his voice low, the words like sparks. "You're not *my* first goddamn anything," he said. "I'm the one who's always the fucking first. First this. First that. I'm everybody's goddamn first."

He got up and left.

Out in the living room I could hear him. A smash. Cursing. The sound of keys. He was pacing. Another crash. The telephone picked up and hurled. This was the first time I saw his red temper. It was familiar, like home, this sudden anger. *One fell swoop.* I couldn't tell what it was, exactly, that had set him off. The word *first.*

Five minutes went by. Fifteen. The refrigerator door opened. I heard ice cubes. Milo came back to my room and sat on the bed with his back to me. He did not say he was sorry. He had a glass in his hand, and smelled of scotch.

"I wasn't asleep in the car when you were talking to Rick," I said.

"So, now you know," Milo said quietly.

"Not really," I said. "I want to know. You know all about *me*, my checkered past."

"My past is not checkered," he said. "It's snowy. Basically, really snowy."

"Does that make you sad?"

"Fuck, I don't know," he said. "It makes me nothing. It is what it is and I don't think about it unless people try to think about it for me."

I put my hand lightly on his shoulder but he flung it away and moved off, the way people do when they are afraid that sympathy will make them weak. He sat on the windowsill and looked out. When he started talking again it was to tell me the story about Pearl, about the summer he turned fourteen.

Pearl was a little girl he knew as a child in New Orleans where he was born. She was some kid he played with in the summer, when he went South visiting relatives. Milo loved Pearl at first sight, although at the time they were four years old. He never *said* he loved her. But he even remembered how she had her hair the first time he laid eyes on her: in soft twists, held at the ends with big white beads on rubber bands. He said, *I thought you could eat the beads; I thought they were gumballs.* When he heard her name was Pearl, he thought those were the pearls in her hair.

The story he told me was about how Pearl wanted to see real snow and how he tried to get her some.

In the middle of the winter, when he was nine years old, Milo took a plastic Tupperware container from his mother's kitchen. He zipped it inside his parka and rode a chairlift to the top of Loon Mountain and filled it with snow. The way he told me I could see him doing it, see him putting the container back in his parka, bombing all the way down the expert black diamond trail, a little boy whooping and jumping spread eagles. He got home and stored the snow in the freezer and kept it there all winter, till school got out, despite his mother yelling "Get this thing out of my Frigidaire!" And he took it to Pearl all the way down in New Orleans, packed in a cooler.

When Milo was telling me this he was smiling at himself. In his face you could see the excitement he felt at showing Pearl the snow. You could see the crestfall of his old disappointment when he opened the lid of the container and saw a small lump of gray ice, lingering dully in a puddle.

"Pearl was laughing," Milo said. "But I couldn't stand it, I was so mad. I tried to tell her, with snow, you had to feel it, see it coming down on you, see the way the flakes are different, you know." He wanted Pearl to know how it felt, speeding down a cold slope so the wind makes tears come out of your eyes. "But it was not something I could get her to understand," he said. "Snow, New Hampshire, what it was like in the White Mountains. She just didn't understand what it was like."

"What was it like?" I said.

He lifted his eyebrows up and lowered them down as if the effort to explain was sheerly too much for him to bear. As if he had given up explaining. "All I did was ski, anyway." He shrugged. "That was it for me, since I was five, six."

Where was Pearl now? I asked him. He shook his head and said he hadn't seen Pearl since he was fourteen years old, the last summer he spent at home. New Orleans. He called it home.

"You loved her," I said.

"I was a kid." But he smiled. "Yeah, I had plans for her that year. I had bought her a little ring, a little silver ring with four bands in a puzzle."

"I remember those," I told him. "I had one."

"I thought about her all winter long," Milo said. "How pretty she was, buying the ring, keeping it secret in my desk, taking it apart, putting it together, taking it apart. Supposed to be doing my homework."

"So what happened," I asked, "when summer came?"

"Twenty-six hours of driving. Straight on after Louisville, Kentucky, where we always stopped the night. We never stopped after that because in those days you couldn't stop in the South. Take your own gas can, food. Piss in the woods. Finally got there. Rushed right over to Pearl's house, the minute we drove in, and she had some fellow on the porch with her, some big older dude. And he sits just staring at me, saying nothing, till I turn right around back to my grandmother's.

"Later Pearl comes over and she politely explains this guy told her not to go speaking to me. 'Sorry, Milo,' she says, 'but I can't come out with you this summer like we did before.' And that was it."

He sat on the deep sill of the window looking out. I thought of walking over and pulling his head to my shoulder, to soothe him down. But there was no getting near him. He was stiff and charged with telling me, making me understand. What the snow was like.

"I don't care about the past, anyway," I said, after enough time. "Just the present."

"The moment, you mean," he said.

"Yes, the moment," I said. "This moment. The one after that."

"And then?"

"Quite a few more moments following those."

"Which adds up to what? Tomorrow morning? Next week?"

He was looking hard away from me now, playing with his watchband, jabbing the metal fastener into the different notches on the strap.

I went over and leaned on him, ran my hand along his backbone, under his shirt. In the dark I could feel sweat on his body, feel his heart pounding with old anger. He stood up and I rested my head on his chest, listening to the banging in there, stroked the length of his arm till he calmed down. "Shh," I said. I seduced him. Took off his clothes. Handled him and whispered things. I was wanton, just abandoned any concern over what might come out of my mouth. *You know I never cared about anybody like this, just you, love you.* I said that without thinking of whether it was true. Milo did not say it back. I saw his eyes close and he winced as if the words were hitting him somehow, maybe ecstatically, I couldn't tell. He wrapped his arms around me so that the breath halted in my lungs.

God, he said, but not that he loved me.

I would make him. *I love you*, I said. I was relentless and savage. Debauched and reckless. I could make it all right for him, make it up to him, all that time in the White Mountains. He needed me. Me. I could save him. I warmed him up, nursed him, salved his wounds. *Milo, don't ever leave me*. Got him worked up so much, that then—that was the night he said it. *I love you, Charlotte. Do you hear me? Jesus!* He said it in the dark like it made him so angry, to feel that way about me.

13.

Milo's parents didn't like me.

We went to see them in October. It was Milo's idea.

"We'll go for just a weekend," he said.

"And sleep there?" I asked.

"Why not?"

"I'll be nervous," I said. "I'll be a wreck."

"Don't be."

"They'll hate me."

"If you think they'll hate you, they'll *really* hate you," he said. And that was the end of the conversation until the Friday we left. I was packing at home and he called.

"Just pack some hiking boots or something like that."

"That's all?"

"Sweaters."

"Okay."

"And nothing—" He stopped. "You won't need anything frilly."

"See?" I said. "You're worried they won't like me."

"Charlotte," he said. "Don't be nervous."

Well, he was the nervous one. Not that he would admit it. Driving up he was quiet, singing, sometimes, with the radio. After about an hour, he looked over at me and said, "So, you're the first girl my parents ever met. That I've brought home."

So Rick was right! I thought to say, but didn't.

"No way," I said. "How is that possible? You're twenty-five years old."

"I've lived on my own since I was sixteen," he said. "My parents never really met any of my dates."

"Well, are they ever in for a treat!" I said.

"Like I say," he said, "be yourself. Here, put your hair back up."

Be yourself. Put your hair back up. As if he had no confidence I could pass the test, sleep on a hundred mattresses and still feel the tiny hard pea under the feathers, prove I am worthy. His parents were the king and queen. They loved Milo and his sister, Bobbie, fiercely. They were like a sci-fi force field around their children, making them strong and protecting them. When Milo and Bobbie were little the parents did not hit them, ever, and later, never cut them off, no matter what they did. Not when Milo brought me home. Not later when Bobbie had a child and never married its father. But that didn't mean they would like me, or what I was: *a college dropout mannequin with a blond education. Just what a mother wants for her son,* I thought. Not to mention the wrong race. It worried me, staring out the window at the landscape.

"It's pretty," I said, after a long quiet.

"Looks fake, right?" he said.

He was right. Rugged Mountain was a town with quotation marks setting it off, down in a valley with the White Mountains looming all around, blazing with fire-colored leaves. The buildings were old and darling with gingerbread woodwork. Hand-painted signs hung over stores that were all charmingly named: A Bear's Place, Drop O'Joe, The Ragged Sleeve, Pock Hollow Hardware. There were three churches on the main street. Grinning jack-o'-lantern leaf bags sat out by the driveways of white houses with wooden shutters, pumpkins and hay bales piled on every porch.

"Pease Engineering," Milo said as we passed a gleaming corporate campus on a hill. "Where my dad works." I watched Milo's face as he drove, washed with the feel of his town, narrating: *That's where we used to ride our bikes for sandwiches. That's where we used to go for sodas after baseball practice. See that building? I painted that building, the whole thing one summer.* We saw a sign saying Rugged Mountain Ski Area 3 miles. *We'll go up there maybe later,* Milo said. *I'll show you around.* We passed a coffee shop called Clark's Route 4. *That coffee shop? I worked there*

one summer. They put my picture in the window when I won. They have
good pie.

When I got out of the car Hattie came toward me smiling, her eyes full of kindness. She put out her hand and said, "Charlotte, how lovely to meet you. Do come in." Formal and charming like her son. She was beautiful. Her dark hair was pulled up elegantly and had a dramatic white streak in it from the forehead back along the right side. She wore dangling brass earrings twisted with silver, a long skirt. Her eyes were wide and hazel in her pale brown face, like her son's eyes, but hers with circles purpled under them. She stood very straight and she looked right at me when I talked, so sometimes I felt I had to look away. As if she could see things I didn't want her to see.

Mr. Robicheaux—even years later I could never call him Milton easily, it was not formal enough—was intimidating, tall and trim and dark as Milo with a straight back and salty trim beard. He peered down at me over his half-glasses when he shook my hand. "Miss Halsey. How was your journey?"

"Just fine, Father," Milo answered, like Beaver Cleaver.

Then Mr. Robicheaux looked at my bag and looked at his son. "Milo?" he said, his eyes drilling holes at the luggage. Milo jumped, picked it up, and carried it in. He went right upstairs and left me alone with his mother.

Hattie tried but she did not like me. I bustled around in the kitchen while she worked on dinner and attempted to help out. "Sit, sit, sit now," she kept saying, as if I were an annoying young beagle. I didn't want to sit. In my house everybody helped out in the kitchen, except the boys. I didn't like what I thought she might be thinking, with me sitting. *I'm not waiting on her. Just what does she think I am anyway? Next she'll be wanting me to starch and iron her petticoats, make sausage curls in her hair.*

All that self-conscious second-guessing that I had stopped lately with Milo was happening again here in his old home, with his parents. I was not exactly anyone you would want in the kitchen fooling with the sauce, but I was raised to help out. To me it showed respect. I set the table but Hattie rearranged it. She thought I didn't see her but I did. There were carrots to be peeled and I offered to peel them but she wouldn't show me where to find the peeler. *Sit, sit, I'll do it.*

Milo was outside with his dad. I saw them through the window heading for a barn. I was all set to go join them till Hattie came to stand next to me, fondly watching them. "They pretend it's work," she said, "but in fact they love to cut wood, the two of them. Milton enjoys it." Which I took to mean I ought not disturb their sacred manly chopping by the woodpile.

She was always polite and warm to me. She embraced me when I arrived, when I left. But there was something deliberate about her manner, willed. I could see her lips press together whenever Milo would touch me. He did it more than usual, on purpose, I think, picked up my hand and held it there, on top of the family dinner table, smack in the middle of polite conversation about how he and I met a long time ago at Cabot College and ran into each other again in the city. I saw her skimming glances toward us and our hands, even as she smiled and asked politely, "And what did you take your degree in, at Cabot?"

"I'm embarrassed to say I didn't finish," I told her. "I started working instead."

"Well," said Hattie. "Milton and I both worked all through college." She didn't intend to sound critical, I know, but that's how it came out.

"Charlotte's a fashion model," Milo said.

"How nice," his mother said, as if it wasn't.

Milo rescued the conversation so we all talked gratefully about baseball and had a lovely dinner by candlelight with classical music playing. Guitar music. Segovia, Mr. Robicheaux said, when I asked him. I looked around their house and realized that it surprised me, black people listening to classical music. Black people with silver candlesticks, oil paintings on the walls, old leathery books on their shelves, sport vehicles in their long wooded driveway, a grand old staircase with carved banisters. The house was a hundred years old and had once been part of an inn. I had been to Milo's apartment in the city and to his enormous place at the beach, but that was different. He had these trappings because he was Milo Robicheaux, the skier, the famous man on TV. Although he had told me about his family, I'd had only a vague idea of what to expect. You have to remember this time was way before you ever saw any ads or shows about black families where the parents were doctors and their children went to the country club. So for some reason I had imagined Milo's parents having a small plain house with a picture of Jesus on the wall, or one of Dr. King.

There were no pictures of either of them, but many old ones of dark-skinned people in starched collars and bustled skirts, the fashions and the sienna tinting making them look the same, to me, as the few pictures of my own family from that time. And then there was the pageboy hair of Milo's young sweater-girl mother, flipped over her Peter Pan sorority collar, and the side-parted hair of his young bow-tied dad, from the fifties. They had met at college in New Orleans, the first in their families to go, and Hattie had worked as a postal clerk to put Milton through graduate school for his engineering degree. Then, when Bobbie was seven (ribbons and white gloves) and Milo just five (mini Boston Red Sox uniform), the Robicheaux family moved to New Hampshire. The walls and mantelpiece held many snapshots of all the darling ages of Milo and his sister. After dinner I lingered over one of them, a black-and-white theatrical portrait of teenage Bobbie wearing what looked like a toga, a crown of leaves on her head. She had her mother's pale complexion, and her hair was unleashed around her head in the picture, lit from footlights. She was beautiful in the way goddesses are supposed to be, strong and serious.

"That's Bobbie when she played Antigone," Hattie told me. "At Boston University. She directed and acted in an ensemble that performed the plays of Sophocles, the *Oedipus* trilogy, *Electra*, and those." She pronounced it Eed-a-pus, and I had no doubt that was the proper way to say it, whoever Oedipus was. She took the picture from my hands and gazed at it. "Mercy me," she said. "I'm no actress, but I still remember one line she taught me: 'There is no happiness where there is no wisdom; Proud men in old age learn to be wise.'" She turned to me and smiled. "I've learned a great deal from my children."

"She's very beautiful," I said, not knowing what else to say, distracted by wondering if what she quoted was some coded message to me. "She's stunning," I added, for good measure.

"She's a brilliant girl," Hattie said, as if correcting me. She had corrected me for real, earlier, when in conversation I said "Milo and me." "Milo and *I*," she said, her hand on my wrist. It took me a second to realize she was talking about my grammar.

Milo came over to us then, to rescue me again. "Yeah, Bobbie's the brains in the family," Milo said. "I'm just the brawn."

"Oh you, stop," his mother said affectionately. "You can do whatever you put your excellent mind to and you know that."

"Ha!" Milo said. "I got your goat."

"Now quit, Milo," said Hattie, girlishly swatting him. "I just try to encourage you children."

"You're going hunting with us tomorrow, right Mom?" he said, goading. "We're going out for whitetail."

"Have you lost your mind?" Hattie said.

"C'mon, Mom!" Milo said, and poked her in the ribs. "It's buck season."

"The day I go hunting," Hattie said, "is the day pigs fly." She went into the kitchen with a pretend scowl, trying to disguise the look of smitten indulgence on her face.

They made me jealous, the way they all liked each other, joking around. My brothers—none of us—would dare tease our mother that way.

"We're going hunting?" I asked.

"You bet," Milo said. "A-hunting we will go. Dad's coming."

"I wasn't aware," said Mr. Robicheaux, from his chair, "of such a plan."

"That's because I just made the plan," Milo said. "You need to get out and bag a whitetail!"

"All right," he said. "I'd enjoy that." Clearly both Milo's parents were among the many victims of his charm.

"Are you a hunter, Miss Halsey?" he asked me.

"Not me," I said. "I'm a gatherer."

He smiled at that, and it was his son's smile now, so maybe, I thought, the father might soften toward me someday.

"I've never been hunting," I said.

"Tomorrow's your chance then," he said.

"Oh, Charlotte will never come," Milo said. "She likes to sleep late."

"No, I'd like to try," I said.

"You won't like it. It'll be cold."

"So what?" I said.

"Four A.M., Charlotte," he said. "Heavy gear. Guns. Ugly boots."

"She doesn't have to carry gear," Mr. Robicheaux said.

"I can carry whatever I'm supposed to carry," I said. "I don't mind."

The more Milo tried to talk me out of it, the more determined I became. To be honest, I didn't *want* to go hunting, I was revolted just to think of it. But it bugged me, Milo saying I would never go. And I certainly couldn't stay at home not helping Hattie all day. *Sit sit.*

"I'm going," I said.

"Atta girl," Milo said. He found and cleaned and polished his gun, excited and humming. "You can use Dad's old rifle," he said. "Right, Dad? Charlotte can use the Remington?"

"Sure, son."

"I don't think I'll be needing a *gun*," I said. "I'm just hunting. Not actually shooting."

"The only kind of shooting Charlotte knows about," Milo said, "is: click, click." He winked his eye like a camera shutter. "Charlotte's a big-time fashion model."

"So you said." Mr. Robicheaux got up and put his pipe away. "See you first thing." He went to the kitchen with his wife so neither of them, I thought, would have to watch the two of us, climbing the curving staircase hand in hand, up to the second floor.

Milo's room was a boy's room. Ships and snails, rocks, posters, trophies, a closet full of mitts and bats. What you'd expect, except for the little sayings. In between some snapshots, about a dozen slips of paper were stuck up on the bulletin board, each one typed up like something out of a fortune cookie.

Man is the origin of his action.
   —Aristotle

Trifles make perfection and perfection is no trifle.
   —Michelangelo

There is no such force as the force of a man determined to rise.
   —W. E. B. Du Bois

Not only do I knock 'em out, I pick the round.
   —Muhammad Ali

"Where'd these come from?"

"Various places. My father mostly. My sister sent me some of them. The Ali one I cut from the newspaper."

"You were sweet," I said.

"Not goddamn sweet."

"You had a part in your hair!" I said, looking at his yearbook picture. "You had a little necktie!" He growled at me but he was smiling, pushing the twin beds together into one big bed, the wooden wheels scraping and shuddering on the floorboards so I kept saying *Shhhh!!* and he kept saying *Why don't you relax, why don't you?*

Not long after we turned out the light, I realized that something I needed was in my purse, and that my purse was downstairs in the kitchen, and there was nothing to be done but to go down and get it. I put jeans on under my nightgown, which, to put it mildly, was unsuitable for going down to the kitchen. But once I got out on the back stairs landing, I heard them talking, whispering, really.

Drink this, you'll feel better.

Both tablets?

Yes.

Don't know what's wrong. Indigestion probably.

Not surprised.

Don't know what he could be thinking.

Not thinking.

Thinking with his you know what is what.

A woman like that.

Well, now, Hattie, let's aim for fairness.

All right, you're right. Let's aim.

Here there was a silence, till Milo's father finally spoke.

She's going out with us tomorrow. Said she's game.

Fair enough, his mother said. *Maybe she has some kind of gumption.*

Maybe.

He'd like that, she said. Then: *You have to drink it all, Milton, you can't get away with just half.*

All right, all right.

It will be all right.

You think?

I do.

He's a good boy, Hattie.

Then the sound of the TV. I was shocked, standing there on the stairs for the longest time. I liked *them*. I was doing my best! What else could I do? I tried to calm down. Tried to remind myself I was the first girl Milo ever brought home. I tried to aim for fairness.

"Milo." I shook him awake.

"Hmm. What's the matter?"

"Nothing," I said, but he knew, he said later, that I was bothered. "You have to go downstairs for me." I made him go get my purse. I heard him downstairs, mumbling something, laughing, kissing his parents.

"Night, Mom, night, Dad."

"Night."

"Night, my Milie."

Milie. Whatever she thought of me, I liked that she called him that, *My Milie.*

"Hey, Milie," I said under the covers. "Hey, you little Milie."

He growled at me. "Don't call me that." But I could see he liked it.

"You don't have to go hunting," he said.

"I'm going," I said.

Milo's father was waiting for us in the car at five in the morning, the engine running, a cloud of exhaust escaping into the dark. I got in the back and watched them load gear in the headlights, their breath steaming above the beams. It was an old routine with them. Clearly I was making a huge mistake, would get in the way, bring bad luck the way a woman on a ship made it sink. But to change your mind was womanly. It lacked gumption. Moreover, it was too late to turn back. Mr. Robicheaux got behind the wheel, Milo up front next to him. We drove for a while and parked off a dirt road. The weak daylight revealed brown woods full of scrub and occasional stands of pine, in hilly country. We climbed out and began unloading gear.

"Okay, Charlotte," Milo said, "put this on." He handed me an orange vest like the ones he and his father were wearing.

"Oh!" I said. "Fashion!"

"That, young lady, is so you won't be mistaken for game and shot by our fellow sportsmen," his father said curtly.

"Right," I said, and put it on.

"Won't the deer spot us from miles away?" I asked. "Don't we want some camouflage-type jacket?"

"No," Milo's father said. "Deer are color-blind."

"At least someone is around here," Milo said, straight-faced.

Milo's father paused and allowed half a smile to play around his mouth before he laughed. Which made all of us loosen up. After a while his dad started whistling. Milo pinched me on the backside when he wasn't looking.

"Okay, let's get on with it, Charlotte," Milo said. "No talking and follow what we do. Stay behind us."

"Yessir," I said, saluting him.

"Dad, you go first," Milo commanded as we set out.

I saluted him again and kowtowed so that Milo's dad was laughing.

"Charlotte's worse than Bobbie," Milo told him. "She's a wise guy. We never should've brought her."

"Well, if she loses us a trophy," his dad said, "we'll just have to leave her to find her own way home, the way we did with all those others."

Their jokes at my expense made me happy for some reason.

We set out, looking for *rubs,* which meant antler marks on trees, looking for *spoor,* which meant droppings. I kept getting the giggles. "Is this spoor?" I whispered. "How about this? This looks like spoor!" But the men were apparently not amused anymore so I stopped. Milo was completely absorbed, walking silently, his gun tucked under his arm, his eyes flicking left and right. He paused often and stooped down or just listened. His father, too. They communicated by nods of the head, juts of the chin, pointing. At first it was fascinating to watch them, but mostly the hunt was boring, like golf, only without the occasional suspense of little white balls lofting up and possibly going down holes. We concentrated on holding still. *Lying down would be pleasant,* I thought, even in the backseat of the car, with the oily blanket and the duffel bag for a pillow. "I think I'll just—"

"Shh!" Milo exhaled softly. He and his father were frozen still and I saw why: In the clearing was a girl-eyed buck with his head up, checking the wind. Mr. Robicheaux's gun was up just like that and he shot him, crack, crack. Pop-gun noises.

He just fell.

My breath was stopped. "Oh dear God," I said. The deer lay there, heaved once and shuddered so you could see its ribs rise and shake clear across the clearing.

"Got him," his father said.

"Oh geez, Dad, that's sweet!" Milo cried in the same breath.

"I thought he'd spook," his father said. "Thought she'd spooked him."

Both of them looked at me, turned away with my hand across my mouth.

"What did she think we were out here doing?" his father said. "Antiquing?" It seemed he was annoyed but it was hard to be sure. The huge buck was whiffling a little, dying in the leaves not fifty feet away from us.

"It's okay, Charlotte," Milo said reassuringly. "The deer's just sleeping." And he walked over quickly to the big animal and slit its throat. "That's it then," he said, beaming, and wiped his hunting knife on some leaves, put it back in its sheath, hanging from his belt.

"Yessir," his dad said, walking over now, too. "A broadside shot."

"He's a good big one," Milo said. They were both over there suddenly talking like John Wayne. "Ya hit him a good shot square on, Dad. Eight points."

"Yep," his father said, "an eight-point buck."

"Look at the rack on him!" Milo said. "Nice rack!"

"We're at least a mile from the road."

"Yeah," Milo said. "Dress him here." He came back over to me and asked was I all right.

"You just...killed it?" I asked.

"Dad pretty much killed it. I euthanized it."

"Miss Halsey, would you prefer to go back to the car?" Mr. Robicheaux called to us from where he stood over the deer.

"Maybe you should, Charlotte," Milo said.

"No, I said I'd come. So."

"Okay," Milo said.

"You'll have to show me, you know, what to do, skin it or whatever."

"Atta girl," Milo said, beaming.

"I think maybe we should walk her back," his dad said.

"No!" Milo said. "She said she'd stay. She said she'll help."

"Well," I said, "I'll try it."

His father didn't say anything. They began to dress the deer. With my teeth grit, I got through it, basically by pretending to be a pioneer woman traveling in a covered Conestoga wagon like the one my ancestors rode in my imagination to California, enduring unbearable hardship without showers, getting malaria and dysentery, losing the trail, and of course, having to hunt. I had no problem, like some professional colleagues I could mention, with wearing fur or eating meat. These all seemed the natural order of things to me, and I didn't see why I should pretend otherwise simply because my food came from restaurants. Somewhere somebody had to kill it.

What bothered me was the warmth of the deer. How, even with the heavy gloves they gave me to wear, I could feel the live, ebbing temperature of the animal. It made me nauseous. But I helped them. I asked them to show me what to do. Milo was impressed. "Bobbie would never do this. Wouldn't even try," he said. *Who could blame her?* I thought. It was a messy business. The men knew what they were doing, how to gut, how to skin, how to section the haunches. Milo's knife worked easily under the hide, between the bones and through sinews. He knew his way around with a knife.

Milo's mother came out to the car as we drove in. "You got your buck, then," she said, eyeing the deer strapped to the roof. "How was it?"

Meaning, I thought, *how did the fashion model deal with all the blood?*

"Charlotte did fine," Milo told her. "She was great." He and his dad went to wash up for breakfast.

"How was it, really?" Hattie asked.

"To be quite honest," I said, "I didn't care for it."

"No," she said, "it's nothing I'd enjoy, either. Come on, have some breakfast."

"I don't think I'm really hungry," I said. "Not right now."

"Are you all right?" she asked, a crease of worry on her face.

"Yes," I said. But I pictured again the way the deer went down, the look on its face, and my eyes teared up.

"Oh, my," she said, "I worried about this." She put her arm around me and held it there awkwardly for a second.

"I'm fine," I said.

"You did your best," she said. "And that's all you can do, right?"

"I hope so."

"That's what I always told my kids: Do your best." Then she smiled brightly. "And after that: just don't think about it! Because, you know, the venison is quite delicious in a stew, so I simply don't think about the rest."

"Okay," I said. "I won't, either."

She told me later that her heart softened to me a little that morning, seeing me try, but hating the whole thing, same as she did. Maybe she saw something about me she hadn't seen at first, hadn't expected. I hoped so anyway, even as I saw something about her, about Milo and his family, that reminded me in a strange way of my own: how you just don't think about whatever it is that's bothering you. You put it out of your mind. I wonder now if that was a lesson we all learned much too well, me especially.

14.

We left New Hampshire early on Sunday afternoon. Milo was driving like he was at the helm of the Batmobile, tapes cranked so loud the car was throbbing. "So my parents liked you," he said.

"Not entirely," I said, but smiled. "They think I'm a floozy."

"You were great," he said. "You were fine."

"But I heard them talking about me," I said.

"They worry," he said, and told me his father had said something the first afternoon, out by the woodpile. *Son, you're not thinking, son. You are asking for trouble, you know that.* This is what Mr. Robicheaux told Milo, out of my hearing. *We taught you to be proud of yourself, who you are. Your mother is a beautiful woman, Milo. Your sister is.*

"So, what you're saying," I said, "is they actually hate me."

"They'll get over it," he said.

I checked to see if he meant that, but he was fooling with the controls, the window washer and the airflow, and didn't look at me.

"You have to understand, Charlotte. My parents are proud of me, but I'm not completely what they had in mind."

"No, that's *my* parents," I said. "You're confused."

"Mine, too."

"How can you not be everything they had in mind?"

"For one: They were furious with me when I left school for a *sport*. A sport!? they said. You think you can make your way in this life off a game? Out of playing?" He was imitating his mother now, I could tell. "No son of mine will be a college dropout."

"We had big fights. They were livid," he said. "Since I was supposed to be summa cum laude, Phi Beta Kappa, Ph.D. like my sister. A doctor or a lawyer or president or king. My mother had apoplexy. My father said, *You make your bed, son, you lie in it.*"

"Poor Milo."

"Poor Milo my ass," he said. "I never minded lying in any of the beds I made for myself."

"Funny," I said. "Don't change the subject."

"Well, they came around," he said. "They always do."

I thought about that, hoping not to be some kind of exception to the rule.

We hit a traffic snarl outside Bridgeport. I-95 was a red glitter of taillights stretching ahead in the skeleton dusk of October. A jackknifed tractor trailer, the radio explained. The cars were inching. Milo was restless and irked. He had a big story to do the next day, about advances in arthroscopic knee surgery, a subject he knew well. He would be interviewing Joe Namath and his own personal doctors. He drummed his fingers on the wheel, opened his door, got out, stood on the pavement and craned his neck to see where the trouble was. I said, "There's nothing we can do about it." But he was anxious to get home. Five in the afternoon already. He gassed the engine in neutral for thirty minutes and idled along. Finally he pulled onto the shoulder, passing everyone on the right and careening down an exit ramp for a shortcut he was sure he'd find.

The road off the exit ran along parallel to the highway, past weedy lots and ramshackle buildings, no traffic lights. Milo grinned at me when he saw it was empty of cars. "Ahh, sweet," he said, and floored it. "We'll be home in time for supper." The way he said it was cute, like Dorothy Gale, from Kansas.

Then we heard the siren.

"Shit," said Milo. The speedometer was sinking down from 70. A cop car was screaming after us and flashing lights.

"Listen, Charlotte," he said. "Stay very very cool and calm." He pulled over, found his wallet. The cop spoke at us through a speaker on top of his cruiser. Milo arranged his hands piously on top of the dashboard. A big torch of light ricocheted off the rearview mirror into our eyes. A policeman stood now behind the driver's window, shining the beam on Milo. His partner was there, too, on my side, shining one on me.

"Well, well, well, what do we have here in the Jaguar?" the officer said in a jovial voice.

"We got wabbits," his partner said, as if we were in a cartoon.

"I realize I was speeding, Officers," Milo said. "I regret it."

"You *regret* it," said Cop One. We couldn't see his face, only his taut midriff, his porkchop-colored hands.

"Yes sir, I do sir."

"And do you *regret* the crime of fraternizing with a prostitute?" he asked. He was clearly the Senior Cop. His partner seemed younger and newer, laughing too much.

"Maybe he just regrets how obvious it is he's a pimp," said the young one.

"Oh that's nice," I said sarcastically. "Charming."

"Shh!" Milo said softly.

"Sit tight, campers," said the senior one. "We be right back." He took Milo's wallet with him.

"My work ID is home on the table," Milo said quietly.

I could see it, the laminated photograph with the raised Network logo on a beaded chain, lying on the hall table with piles of mail, a tin of mints that Milo liked, the picture of the U.S. Ski Team in a frame. But why did it matter? "They're just jerks," I said.

"Don't talk," he said tightly.

I was scared because he was. It surprised me. Suddenly a sheen of sweat was on him, the smell of it. This was only a ticket. I've been stopped for speeding myself but I'd never been scared before. Annoyed but not scared. The car was still. We could hear the creaks of the engine cooling under the hood, behind us the metal groan of the police car trunk opening, shoes crunching on gravel, keys clinking.

Milo looked a warning at me. "Don't take the bait," he said. "Don't take the bait, that's how the fish ends up on the plate." There was something like a plea in his eyes. "It's a little saying in our family, you know?" and

I remembered the other one, his father saying *Son, don't ever give anybody any extra reason to give you trouble.*

Okay, I nodded at him.

"Get out of the car, please, muthafucka," said Cop One, when he came back. "Excuse me, I mean, *Mr.* Muthafucka, get out of the car."

Milo did. They told him the things they tell criminals. Hands on top of the car. Feet back. Apart. He complied while I sat in the car with my tongue dry, mouth open, some new truth coming in the shocked O of it, like flies.

Milo was not shocked. He was scared but not shocked.

"My name is Milo Robicheaux," he started quietly.

"Don't get smart," the first cop said.

"No chance a that," said the young one.

He was feeling Milo all over, putting his hands on his legs, sliding up the inseam and down the flank, up to the waistband, brushing the chest. He emptied the pockets. Keys, roll of mints, a dry-cleaning stub.

"It's only a speeding ticket," I said.

"Shut up, please, miss," said the first one.

Now I had to get out, too, put my hands on the roof. "Excuse me, what are you doing?" I said, when he came over and started searching me. "You can't do this to me!" Warm meat hands on my hips, down, then up the rib cage, feeling, feeling, and I thought, of course, that's why there is the phrase *copping a feel.* "Hey!" I said, just indignant. "I can't believe this. You don't have the right to do this! It's only a speeding ticket." I started to cry. "I know my rights! I know my rights! You can't do this!"

"I think we will be the judge of what we can and cannot do," said the older one.

Maybe I thought I knew all about it; had heard how things like this still happened, even in 1981, but only south of the Mason-Dixon Line, the cops with their blunt snouts and small pink eyes, picking on regular innocent people. At that time, you never heard stories like what happened to us. If you heard them you would say *Half that stuff is made up and the other half, well, it's justified based on who does the crime, statistically;* or you would rationalize on behalf of the cops: *But their jobs are so dangerous, they risk their lives every day;* or, maybe if you really thought about it, you would cluck your tongue and say, *Isn't it outrageous?*

Well, it is. Outrageous cop hands under my shirt, his calluses on the skin of my ribs, cupping, weighing me like a handful of coins. *You can't do this to me.* And it was in there somewhere that I realized with horror that the other half of that idea was: *You can do it to them.* And then they did.

One cop told Milo to *lie his ass down* on the ground, on his stomach. Milo lay down. He wilted to his knees, then elbows, then belly. They put handcuffs on him. Over the roof of the car I could see him lying facedown in the gravel, trussed like a rodeo calf. "Stop it!" I shouted at them, so one of them came back to me and said: "Maybe your little party should realize that you are under suspicion of being in a pantload of trouble so you had better do as the officer says, which is: Do not speak unless you are spoken to."

The first cop stood over Milo and put his foot on the small of his back. *I love your small,* I said to Milo once, running my hand down his spine, and now the policeman's foot was on it, in the hollow there. He started sneering questions at Milo while dangling his nightstick by his head. *Where you going? New York? Where you been? To see your "parents"? Your quote unquote "parents"? I don't think so. You meant connection, right? See your connection. Mr. New York Big. Who's your connection? You got a Bridgeport link?* Milo answered, "No sir," docile and almost pleasant, as if he were halfwitted and perfectly accustomed to lying in his suede jacket with his hands behind him so he had to arch his head up to keep his face off the pavement. They were putting a Breathalyzer in his mouth, a yellow plastic job with tubes and numbers. "Exhale!" said the young one. He read the results.

"Clean," he said. "Lucky surprise!" But then he put it back between Milo's lips, pushed it back toward the throat and left it there.

"Listen," I tried to say, "that's Milo Robicheaux, he's an Olympic gold medalist. He's a famous skier."

"Oh really now." They laughed at me.

"Go Speed Racer!" the younger one sang.

"He's a network sportscaster," I said.

"Oh, now he be a sports-castuh!"

They said for me to shut up. Milo was craning his neck up, looking at me to do what they said, the plastic contraption still in his mouth. The senior officer went and tapped Milo on the head with his nightstick so it made a little woodpecker sound. "Nuh uh uh," he said. "Head down."

Milo gagged on the Breathalyzer and worked it out of his mouth. "Officer?" said Milo. "Sir?" but the word was sucked in by a sound of a bat on bone. I saw Milo's head sink, heard a moan soft as the lap of waves. He lay there, breathing hard.

"Milo!" I could see he was curled up with his knees to his chest. "What did you do to him!" I was making it worse. Livid and panicked. *They can't do this. They can't be real cops, maybe they're thugs disguised as cops. Maybe they're going to steal our car, they can't be real cops.* I tried to get calm. I tried smiling, looked at them like *Just between you and me, you and me, we understand each other*. They were leering. The senior cop called over to his partner and said, "Ask her, what's the matter with white guys?"

"What's the matter with you?" I shouted.

"Charlotte." Milo was on the ground warning me through his teeth.

"You want to lie down next to him?" the young one asked me.

"Yes!" I said, "Yes I do!"

"Fine," he said. "Now I know you're a pro." He looked at me as if he had bought tickets for a show, waiting. We were about the same age. He slightly resembled my brother Sean, with elfin eyebrows that arched up, laugh creases at the corners of his eyes, daring me.

I took my hands off the car roof and walked slowly around the front of the car, toward Milo. "C'mon," the policeman said. "C'mon, c'mon." They were both laughing. "That be far enough," said his partner. "Two more baby steps and that be fi-ine right there."

I lay down on the ground. Knees, all fours, flat down. I was near Milo. Not next to him. I couldn't see his face, could only hear his breathing, stuttered over clenched muscles. The shoulder of road under me was graveled and smelled of oil.

We had to lie there while the cops worked, searching the car. They kept saying *You all got some 'splainin' to do*, in accents like Ricky Ricardo. They were whistling that Stevie Wonder song, "Ebony and Ivory," laughing and enjoying themselves. The senior cop opened the trunk and rooted around our bags. He piled my underwear on the hood of the car; he and his partner were opening my lipsticks and pulling up the tongues of my running sneakers, shaking Milo's shaving cream, unballing his socks. The only other things in the car were a pair of ski poles, bent for racing, and an old press release about the Seattle Mariners, addressed to Milo Robicheaux at the Network Sports Desk.

"Hey," said the officer who found it. "Look."

Their tune changed. Right away. They helped Milo up, got me to my feet. They let us go. No harm done, they said. They explained they worked nights, see, so they weren't too familiar with the weeknight sportscasters. Honest mistake not to recognize him. They didn't give Milo a ticket. They were practically sweet about it, giving him a good ol' pat on the shoulder, hey man, brother, no hard feelings. *I remember when you won*, the younger one said, as if he was about to ask for an autograph. *This is a known drug area*, said the senior cop, as if that were a perfectly logical explanation for why you would hogtie people, crack them on the head for speeding, cop a few feels while singing little jingles not so far under your breath.

Milo was stony and quiet. He took his wallet and his keys. He walked stiffly. I was crying. We got in the car and he sat behind the wheel for the longest time, pressing his eyes, breathing in. He reached up to the crown of his head, felt it, brought his hand around to the light to check for blood. A swelling the size of a plum was there under his hair.

"Oh," I said. I touched him but took my hand back fast. He wanted nothing to do with nursing. He turned the key and put the car in gear, got on the highway, without looking back. The traffic was gone now, the road clear. He was silent. Red and white shadows of headlights and brake lights were moving on his face, and I saw his cheek was dented by gravel. At the first exit we pulled over and got a drink in an empty truckers' bar. Milo put his head back and swallowed, plain scotch.

He would not look at me. He looked up at the ceiling, closed his eyes, exhaled, shook his head. His breathing was too fast. Too loud. He touched his head again, where he'd been hit, looked at his hand and got up and went off toward the vending machines.

I put my head down on my arms. Below my feet I could see a straw wrapper on the dirty linoleum, a dropped crust. I was head down like that, when he came back twenty minutes later. I could feel him standing next to the table.

"C'mon," he said. He didn't touch me.

"Are we going to do something about it?" I said, miles down the road.

"For instance?"

"Report them?"

"To whom?"

"To the police."

"They are the police."

"Not all police."

He looked at me. "Let's just say I do report them and the alleged other police, the nice, good-boy police, are shocked and outraged. Then what?"

"They should be disciplined," I said passionately. "Fired. Arrested. Anyway, the Network would do a story. You could talk to somebody there. This can't— You don't— It was—"

Milo shook his head, small hopeless shakes, as if trying to explain to me was like trying to explain to someone with a head full of feathers. He took several starting breaths before he said, "It was a common little offense. It happens all the time."

"What?"

"D.W.B.," he said, three letters hanging out there.

I asked, what did that mean? Was I supposed to know?

"Driving. While. Black," he said.

Anger and damage were filling up the car now like ashes, gray flakes landing on me from the direction of the driver's seat. Milo held the wheel as if letting go meant losing control of more than the car. He wouldn't look at me. He blamed me somehow, I thought. He pressed his lips together to keep words in, breathed through his nose.

After a while, in the tight quiet of the front seat, Milo began telling me a list of stories.

Once in a grocery store in Saratoga where I went to buy some sodas and some chips I was told Sorry, they weren't hiring.

Once in another grocery store in Burlington where I went to get eggs, I was told that the applications for the stock boy job were in the manager's office.

Once in Dexter, Colorado, walking to a restaurant, I was stopped and asked if I was lost. When I got to the restaurant, the hostess asked: May I help you? as if she was not in the habit of having people come in expecting to eat.

Once on Madison Avenue I was locked out of a store and no matter how many times I rang the bell or flashed my money the salesgirl would not let me in.

Once at Logan Airport a woman asked me to carry her luggage, pressed a ten in my hand.

Once at the door of my own house at the beach I was asked if the man of the house was at home.

Once in front of my building I was mistaken for the security guard, once for the super, once for the trash collector.

Once the police stopped me walking on Library Walk at Cabot College and asked me for my ID. When I didn't have it, they took me back to my room to get it.

The only difference in the stop this time, in Bridgeport, Milo said, was the press release in the trunk and the fact that he was, in fact, caught actually speeding.

He stopped his list without ever saying the word *white* or the word *black*. As we drove over the Triboro Bridge into Manhattan, he glanced at me sideways. I was resting my head on the window, looking at the blur of road, the red glitter of taillights lined up for the tolls, and I was struggling. I was having real trouble with what to say.

"I'm sorry," I said, which sounded weak.

He bounced his head angrily, still not looking at me.

"It wasn't *my* fault," I said.

Which made it worse. I thought he might eject from his seat, rocket straight up in fury. He smacked the wheel.

Finally he said: "Why did you do that?"

"Do what?"

"Lie down. Why?"

Well, because, you were lying down, I thought.

"You provoked them," he said.

"I didn't. I just—"

"Never—in that situation you just don't— Insane thing to do! Why did you do that?"

"I—"

"Why?" Milo asked. "Why?"

"It seemed like the right thing to do," I said. "It *was* the right thing."

Milo watched me in the stopped traffic, checking my face and checking the road, gazing off and coming back to check me again. I kept my face open and plain, so he could see whatever it was he needed to see, that I was telling the truth, that I had not been mocking him or provoking the cops. Somewhere in that currency of looks passing between us, in that awkward space between the car's bucket seats, some trust rose up. We didn't say anything more for the moment, but it felt as if we had. So much of what we came to believe we had spoken aloud happened like that, promises and meaning taken from the degrees of smile or squint, the slack or trim of the muscles in the face, the uncoiling of silence. We came to believe we knew feelings the way one can know facts, as inalienable truth, trusty and loyal as dogs.

"I wanted to be next to you," I said, "so I lay down."

Milo opened a window and the car grew cold with night air. He reached a hand across and tucked it under my leg. I was crying but not making any noise.

"It just makes me— I can't. I'm so angry," I said. "It makes me so furious and enraged." Which sounded like nothing. Like insect wings against glass.

He asked me then, a little bit cruelly: Did I know, by the way, that in 1960-something, a fourteen-year-old boy visiting Mississippi from Chicago, just a child really, had had his terrified face beaten in and his genitalia *cut off* and his eyes *gouged out*, and then, had a cotton gin tied to his neck, and had gotten his body jettisoned into the Tallahatchie River, just because someone said he whistled once, at a white woman? His father had told Milo that story again, that very weekend in New Hampshire, as if Milo didn't already know it, hadn't heard it told at his father's knee many times before, back in the days when the ponytailed girls from Rugged Mountain High School used to call Milo up. "The phone would ring, and it would be Wendy Morrison or Karen Cook on the phone for me," Milo said. "And right when she hung up, that boy Emmett would be at the table with us Robicheauxs, eating dinner."

We Halseys never had a guest like that at our table. What would he have to do with us? We had heard the story, probably, somewhere. Emmett Till, his name was. It was terrible, unspeakable, but what happened to him had nothing to do with us. Now, though, winging along toward home, I had the feeling Emmett was there in the car while Milo told me about him, and come to think of it, he had been that whole weekend, and would be often after that, tagging along wherever we went, terrified for eternity, still just a boy really, a terrified boy ghost.

15.

I don't know if I can stay with you," I said to Milo, a couple of weeks later.

I said this on top of a mountain where we had gone for the weekend, to a small resort up in the Berkshires. It was Milo's idea to go there. He was edgy and needed air, he said. "Let's go be alone."

So we went. But it was strained. It had been strained. Or strange, or something. Something was off.

Milo had been flying around the country, working. He had gotten up the morning after our Cop Stop and kissed me good-bye for four days.

"Don't go," I said. I was crying. He wasn't safe. Nothing was.

"Charlotte," he said, "I have to."

"No, stay."

"Get over it," he said, the tough coach. "Put it behind you."

He finished the knee surgery story with Joe Namath, the two of them rolling up their pants legs for the cameras, comparing scars, comparing surgeries, then started his next assignment, profiles of Heisman trophy candidates for the '81 college season. In between he was working out at the gym, lifting weights, running along the Hudson. What he had not been doing was talking about it, about what happened. He hadn't told anyone, he said, when I asked.

"What would I say?" he said. "Who would I tell?"

"Your parents? Your mother?"

"Now why would I want to do that?"

"She's your mother?"

Milo nodded. "Precisely," he said. "Don't dwell on it. Move on."

He was the expert. But, I thought, he'd never had a choice but to move on, whereas, I was used to choice.

I couldn't put it behind me. I was too angry. The fucking cops. How could they! How dare they! Even a week later, when I saw a cop I stared as if I'd never seen one before, swallowed, felt betrayed. And even that bothered me. What was I expecting them to be *loyal* to? Me? Had they betrayed me? No thought was comforting. I told everyone. Claire of course, and Kevin, all the girls. Claire cried. She worried about me. About Milo. *It's not safe to be him,* she said. I told my sister, who said, *It must be an aberration.* My voice cracked, telling her. I couldn't get over it.

Milo was over it, it seemed. Sick of me going on about it. There was something hard in his eyes I couldn't read, something like victory or possibly accomplishment. *So now you know.*

Up in the Berkshires he ran miles in the afternoon and again in the morning. He came back to our room where I was still sleeping and sat on the edge of our bed. I woke up to see him gazing down, fondly and seriously, as if he was trying to figure something out.

"What?" I was groggy and worried my eyes were puffy.

"Shh," he said. "Don't wake." With his fingertips he pushed the hair off my forehead. "Shh, now." He looked away and went back to unlacing his running shoes, peeling off his sweaty knee brace, a so-called flesh-colored one that looked dirty on his shining leg. I put my hand lightly on his wet back. "Don't touch me," he said, "I'm sweaty."

"I don't care," I said. Since the day the police stopped us, Milo and I had spent a lot of time staring at each other glassily. He was gentle with me. If I was teary in front of him, or pensive, he stroked my head. He said he loved me, and I believed him. The way he said it now was different, or maybe the way he looked at me, with something in his gaze small and helpless as a baby rabbit. *I love you,* he said. I said it back. We had gotten used to the words now. But they still worried me. What was that going to mean, *love?* Was it even true what I said? What he said? I was brooding a lot about what it really was, love, and kept thinking of the naked white baby Cupids with wings shooting darts at people, and checking to see if I felt pierced. Love was an arrow. It had to point somewhere, to something.

Claire said, "You'll either get married or you won't."

"Stop with the marriage stuff. I'm not you, Claire."

"But it's true, either you will or you won't." She was hoping it was *will*, I could see. She liked Milo. She no longer thought he was using me. When he came over she hugged him and offered him things to eat.

"What if it's won't?"

"Then you'll have to split up, right?" Claire saw things so clearly sometimes it gave me headaches.

In terms of weddings I had never gotten past the fashions, the plain white sheath or the antique veil, the big spread I did once in *Brides*, wearing a lace train longer than Amtrak's Northeast Corridor line, with seed pearls clinging to my bodice like larvae. I had never considered the scary aftermath of a wedding, what the real purpose of it was: having a life with somebody. Children. I never thought about them except to think I would most likely have them someday, or a pet. Now, thanks to the Connecticut State Police and Milo's parents and my friend Claire, the questions for me boiled down to: stay or go? And what would happen if the answer was, stay?

"You know," Claire said, when I was telling her about the police, "if you stay with him you just have to accept that's part of your life."

There was that *that* again. But I saw clearly now, she was right. It was there. You couldn't accept it. You could send it away but it would always come back, like the cat that knew how to find its way home from hundreds of miles away.

Let's go somewhere and be alone.

We couldn't be alone except in private. It was annoying. In the Berkshires I got tired of the small-town looks of the desk clerk, and the dining room families, and the dough-faced maid who jumped back when Milo answered the door wearing spandex bike shorts on his way to go running, and you could see the word *trash* practically tattooed on her face as she sniffed and tidied around our things. The maid was followed a half hour later by the morning desk clerk on the phone who said, "I have a Mr. Robicheaux to see you?"

"What?"

"Mr. Robicheaux says you're expecting him?"

"That's my boyfriend!" I shouted at him. "He forgot his key!"

"Excuse me, ma'am," said the clerk, "*is* this Room 302?"

"Right."

"Well..." He was stumped. He said: "It's just a precaution but could you describe him for me?"

"No," I said. "You describe him for me."

"He's a black gentleman," the clerk said.

"Really?" I said. "I guess I need glasses."

It was fun, in a sick way, chumping the desk clerk, leaving behind the empty tube of spermicide for the benefit of Doughface. It made me feel righteous. But it was not fun, for example, having to dine in the Lodge Room, where pastel families were having their surf and turf and looking over their elbow patches at me and Milo in the corner. Maybe there was a time when I would have said, *It's just innocent curiosity. Of course they look and why not? Maybe they'll learn something, think of the educational value.* But it was exhausting, being a human public service announcement.

"Are you okay?"

"Sure!" I said. "Just tired." *Move on, don't dwell on it.*

"Wake up," he said. "We're going hiking."

We climbed and climbed and ate a picnic at the top of the biggest hill. It was the last warm day of the year, crisp and blue. The foliage was raging. Milo and I stood looking out over the valley and he put his arms around me.

"You do seem tired," he said wickedly.

"Maybe I do."

"What you need is to lie down," he said, as if it were a medicine he was recommending. He sank me to my knees, spread his sweatshirt out for me in the grass by a big tree and pulled me over him, kissing. His long eyelashes curled in a fringe. Shadows from the leaves overhead dappled his skin. His fingers tapered up to the tips near my eyes and when he felt they were open, he smiled and brushed my lids down, shut them as I imagine the coroner does on a body. And it was like that a little, in the sense that I forgot about my earthly worries. Milo unbuckled his belt and unzipped my jeans and flipped me under him so I felt cold grass on my bare back. I gave in, like going under the influence of a drug, without saying what was on my mind, just liking so much how we couldn't help ourselves.

We rested. We lay and looked up through the branches and felt the cool air drying our skin. Milo was looking at me, but now I wouldn't turn my face to his, serious and weighed down again. Because I couldn't trust anything, especially not myself. How could I be lying there next to him with these snakes of doubt worming around in my heart? It was not honest.

"Milo." I hid my face in his shirt so my voice was sad and muffled.

"What?"

"I don't know."

"What don't you know?"

"If I can stay with you."

"What does that mean?" He got very focused and sharp right away, like a doctor in an emergency.

"I am confused," I said.

"Fine," he said. "Let's go home." He got up and buckled his belt. He looked at me where I was lying, cold and exposed. "Come on." He picked up his backpack and went back down the path without looking back.

"Milo!"

But he was gone. I could see him running ahead of me, dodging low branches along the path. He was a blur in the tree trunks, then he was the far-off crack of a stick underfoot. He had packed up the room and was paying our bill when I caught up to him. "We don't have to *leave*," I said, out of breath. We were supposed to stay another night. It was only Saturday.

"We do. You do. You have to leave."

"I just said—"

"Why would you want to stay?" he said. "For what?"

"Milo, I just said—"

"Either you know you can stay with me, Charlotte, or you leave."

We got in the car. He backed up quickly and pulled out.

"Milo?"

"Say what's on your mind, Charlotte. I'm listening."

But I could see he was closed up. He hit the gas and held the wheel and his tongue curled up over his lip as he steered the narrow road, faster and faster.

"Milo, it has nothing to do with what you think."

"Oh, yeah, I know," he said. "I know."

"What?! What do you know?" I said. "You don't know. You won't talk about it. You won't discuss it. It just happened and it's like it never happened."

"I don't need to talk about it," he said. "I know what it is and what its name is and how long it's lived here and you know, too, I think you do."

"I'm confused," I said with a trembling lip. "I don't know where we're going."

"We are going home," he said. "Jiggety jog."

"You know what I mean."

"Where do you want us to go?"

"Where do you?"

"That," he said, "depends on you."

"Why?" I shouted at him. "Why does it depend on me? Why not on you, too?"

"I told you my feelings," he said.

I was quiet all the way home. It got dark while we drove, and started raining. I rested my head on the window glass and stared into the lights of all the cars coming toward us. I let them blind me.

First of all, I don't owe you anything, don't owe you just because you're famous, or black, or an acquaintance of my stupid school days, or because I've been sleeping with you, or because I said "love." I don't have to love you for those reasons. And what's more, everything doesn't have to be about color, you know, buddy. It's not like I haven't had confusion about white boyfriends, or haven't dumped white guys or said I loved white guys and then taken it back, so why are you accusing me? Of what? I'm just trying to be honest and never hurt you or especially myself again because God knows I'm lonely, too, in the world. Yes! even fashion models can be lonely! It's funny, right? You laugh. You have no idea. No idea how exhausting and hurtful it is always having to think of color color color.

Right. He had no idea.

"We didn't have to leave," I said.

"Oh really," he said.

"I'm sorry—" I reached my hand over toward his leg.

"No," he said, and stopped me with a look.

I'll tell you one thing: Men detest pity. They hate it more than bleeding. Most men prefer you to throw the china at them in a jagged-edge rage rather than feel the cool compress of your being sorry for them, whether it's because of something big or something small: their sore throat or their crummy childhood. Perhaps Milo thought I pitied him and so was forced by masculine dread to push me away. But in fact it was only self-pity, just me, thinking of how tragically misunderstood Charlotte was and trying to figure out what Charlotte wanted to happen. It was too late for Charlotte to decide that now, however. Milo had already done the deciding.

He said one thing, finally, when we were almost home: "Look, Charlotte, the way I approach life is as what we used to call a lights-out race. It's all or nothing. All out every second till your legs are on fire and tears come out your eyes and never losing that tuck for one unnecessary goddamn second, and never catching an edge or otherwise fucking up, because if you lose your tuck in the wrong place you will lose your race, and if you catch an edge you will either get badly whacked or permanently. *Wham!* into the rock! *Wham!* off the cliff! You don't get to make mistakes. You don't get second chances. You mess up, you lose. Confused? you lose. That is my philosophy and my style, too, and I have got no room for *I don't know.*"

"Fine," I said, thinking *That's fine for you. For you it's yes or no. It's stay or go, it's black or it's white. But not for me. I spend most of my time in the gray area. Maybe this maybe that. I can't make up my mind, probably haven't got enough of a mind to make up, dumb blond vapid bimbo airhead.*

Milo drove straight to my building. Pulled up in front. He grabbed my bag from the backseat, got out, and held my door open. "Charlotte," he said, clipped and polite, "thanks for the weekend."

He handed me my bag.

"Milo, don't," I said.

"Don't what?" he asked me.

"I just—"

"Figure it out, Charlotte. Work on it."

Milo drove off. He never looked back.

I stood in the dirty rain with my bag, leaves and sticks still in my hair from where we had lain down in the woods, and watched the taillights of his car cutting in and out of the traffic. I started getting the chills, stunned at the feeling I was going to be sick, holding it off, swallowing in the elevator up.

Crashing into the apartment, I found Carl and Claire having dinner. They had candles and wine. "What are you doing here? What's the matter?" Claire asked me. I ran past them, ran to my room.

I sat perfectly still, except for trembling, on my bed. *Just sitting here in this black depression of dark gloom and panic. Only you can't say gloom is dark or sorrow is black because why shouldn't these be white?* I was not blinking. The newly terrifying idea of Milo driving off and leaving froze me there, with this Ping-Pong of black thoughts and white thoughts relentlessly cropping up now, whatever I did. Would they always crop up, from now on? Could I ever get away from them?

Claire came in after a few minutes and sat on the bed edge, put her hand on my knee. "Charlotte? What happened?"

I told her.

She predicted he would be back. She predicted the phone would ring in an hour or in the morning or in just a few days when Milo got home from L.A.

"You're wrong," I said. "This is a lights-out race. It's all or nothing. You keep your eye on the finish line. There's no room for mistakes. You fuck up you wipe out. You hit the wall. It's all about knowing what you want and going out and getting it."

"Wow," said Claire, "he said that?"

"Something like that."

I got on a plane the next morning after no sleep. I already looked bad and soon would look worse. First class was full of us models, heading for six days in Palm Beach. Half of the others were about twelve years old. I knew they had packed their stuffed animals in among their blow-dryers and their sable powder brushes. They were excited, chewing gum and reading *Women's Wear Daily*, *Vogue*. "Isn't this a gas?" said Andie, my seatmate.

I smiled at her and said, "It'll be fun." But it wasn't.

I missed Milo. I lost my appetite, which was the only dividend. I slept badly and had problems on the shoot, trouble moving, finding the right feelings for the pictures they needed. I kept bumping into things and tripping. For the first time in years I got a Bible out. There was one there in my room at the Palm Beach Hotel and I have to say, it comforted me that week, thinking *Hello, Mr. Bible, what have you got to say for yourself?* I used it like a fortune cookie, opening it at random with my eyes closed, pointing down to see if it would tell me what I wanted to hear: Turn the other cheek, don't look back. I was doing this the night before coming back to New York, sitting on the terrace of my hotel room drinking dark rum, looking out at the dark sea, at the far dots of light from tanker ships working their way up the coastline. What was Milo doing? Who was he with? I couldn't picture him except with me, holding me, dancing.

You have to leave, he had said, handing me my bag, driving away.

I held the Bible, turned the pages, thumbing blindly, landing on a passage. The Book of Ruth.

Entreat me not to leave thee or return from following after thee: for whither thou goest I will go, whither thou lodgest I will lodge. Thy people shall be my people, and thy God my God. Where you die I will die, and there will I be buried. May the Lord do so to me and more also, if even death parts me from you.

While I was reading this, an image of Milo strayed into my system with the rum and biblical language, Milo fast asleep with one arm flung up over his head and his face turned in profile on the pillow. He slept sometimes like this, with his mouth open, so the rhythms of his breathing were deep and peaceful and dear to me.

Entreat me not to leave thee. It didn't matter to me that Ruth in the Bible was talking to a woman, her mother-in-law, or that the passage was about the Moabites and the Ephrathites. It was the words "entreat me not to leave thee." Men did not tell me to leave them, as Milo had. They entreated me to stay. Dave had. Jack. Simon. All of them. Milo was the only one. *Go*, he said.

I still believed in the Lord's Will, even though now I called it Fate. At the time I pretended that finding the passage from Ruth was a big stick of Fate, pushing me to be with Milo: *Thy people shall be my people.* But I know now it was my own will, choosing him happily, and I thought he was happy to be my fate and have me be his.

I chose Milo. He was a good man. He was raised right. He loved his family. He was strong and he worked hard and played by the rules. He used his gifts and never gave up. He was brave. I could see that. He knew his own heart, an all-or-nothing kind of man. He had no room for *I don't know*.

Charlotte, she was headlong. I was. Heedless. He liked that about me. I unhinged him, he said I did. I couldn't say no, never knew my head from my heart. I wished and thought wishes were truth. I was raised wrong, raised on appearances, the virtue of beauty. I loved my family but wistfully, in spite of them. I worked hard but only to escape. He said I had backbone. He said I was confusing. He said I was funny. He had said it was up to me. I remembered that, in the mildewed Palm Beach hotel room.

But he drove off and had not looked back.

It was that: the idea of never seeing him again. It was unbearable.

When I got home I went straight to his place from the airport and waited outside his building, waited there for two hours, till he came back from work. He saw me standing there leaning against the brass post of the awning, leaning and waiting, and he knew. Where it was going, where the little arrow pointed. And so did I. We thought we knew.

16.

"What are you doing here?" was what he said when he saw me. I smiled, but barely.

"Charlotte, what are you doing here?"

"I'm here," I said. "I'm here is the answer."

"To which question?" he asked, his eyes wary.

"You said you had no room for *I don't know*."

"So," he said, "do you know?"

"Yes."

"Well," he said.

I saw he had a Band-Aid on his thumb and doubt on his face. I walked close to him and put my forehead against the top of his arm, his damp raincoat. He didn't move. It was like leaning against a tree. I couldn't see his expression now so I can't say whether he was dismayed or glad, or if there was anything grudging about the decision he made.

"Well, come up then," he said finally. "If that's what you've decided."

"It is," I said, and when I pulled back to look at him, he was smiling and kind of shaking his head as if he couldn't get over me, like I had convinced him of something in spite of himself and his best intentions.

So I went. He looked happy about that. We didn't talk any more about what happened on top of the mountain, him leaving, sending me away, not one pearly word. Not about the whole thing with the cops, either. We just let it lie the way we left the remains of the deer behind in the woods, and moved on, into his building and upstairs, where Milo came up behind me and crossed his arms around in front of me. "So you're back," he said into the collar of my sweater.

"I missed you too much," I said.

"Did you?" he asked, warm breath on my neck. "Good."

I had mostly been living in his apartment ever since, almost two weeks. It was December, hurtling toward Christmas. I had been home, but not to sleep, just for clothes, or mail, to see Claire. One cold day I fetched a winter coat. Wearing it back downtown, hood up, I could not get warm. I had chills in the taxi. My teeth rattled and the muscles of my arms were clenching and unclenching, and now I was a miserable pile of chills in Milo's bed. He came in from work to find me there with my knees pulled up under my wings, up to my chin, under the covers with my coat still on.

"What's the matter with you?" he said. We were supposed to be going out. He felt my head awkwardly. It was obviously something he wasn't used to. He pushed the hair off my face, stroking my forehead with the pads of his long fingers as if he could cool me that way, brush the fever off.

"You're boiling," he said.

"I'm freezing."

He didn't know what to do. He wasn't a nursemaid kind of man, he said. I thought he was going to coach me from my chilly nest, bark at me: Up and at 'em, Snap out of it, Hup two three four. But he sounded worried. He lay down next to me, under the blankets, in all his clothes. Heat came off his chest and legs and thawed out the parts of me they touched, but most of me was shaking.

"I'm cold," I said. My teeth rattled and my head was pounding as if something was being installed in there with heavy equipment.

"It's okay," he kept saying. "Hang on." He was sort of panicky and tender. He got up and covered me with a comforter, a heavy one, of gold velvet, with tassels. It was new. The pillows were new and the sheets, too. Milo had been buying things. Whatever he wanted, whatever I did. His house was filling up with a wacky mix of furniture and stuff that we bought on weekends and found in window displays walking around town after work.

Whatever you want, Charlotte.

If I said I liked something he just bought it, which was brave of him, since his own taste, if you could call it that, tended more toward the hunting lodge, with his downhill skis crossed over the mantel, a trophy deer head on the wall. I tried to mock him away from his natural snowshoe inclinations. "Milo, you may not have plaid," I said. "Plaid is banned."

Whatever you want, my darling, he said.

In this way, in the space of a few weeks, his apartment no longer echoed. It was beautiful. The bedroom! *It's a goddamn boo-dwah,* I said to him, and he had to correct me, pronounce it properly, *Boudoir, pour toi, chéri,* in his perfect French. We ordered the bed right out of a magazine, dripping with tassels, laden down with dark persimmon-colored shams and silk pillows in flaming shades of orange and red.

"Milo," I whispered hoarsely, from under the covers. "Milo." But he didn't hear me. He was leaving the apartment, or maybe not; he was gone forever or maybe he never left. I couldn't tell. I was hallucinating and freezing and sweating simultaneously.

He came back with aspirin and a thermometer, which he put in my mouth. "Under the tongue," he said, as if he weren't quite sure, or it scared him. He read it after a while. "A hundred four," he said. He wanted to call a doctor but the only one he knew was Danny Morehead, the U.S. Ski Team orthopedic surgeon.

"Hey, Danny-boy," he said, into the phone. "It's me. Yeah. (Pause) Knee is fine. (Pause) My girlfriend is sick. (Pause) No! She has a *fever.* A hundred four. Chills, all that. Lying here shaking. (Pause) No, she is not knocked up. No! Never mind, Morehead, she's *sick.* Ill."

He listened for a while, talked some more, but I just lay there thinking how he called me his girlfriend. How he called me that now. How I was practically living in his apartment. How he called the doctor about me, as if I was someone in his family.

I fell asleep, woke up, fell asleep again. The night passed in sweat and shivering, running for the sink, vomiting, lying on the bathroom floor, burning so that the cool tiles felt like medicine on my skin. Milo was right there the whole time. I was sure the whole thing was repulsive to him.

"Go away," I said, humiliated.

"No, now," he said. "That's okay."

He fed me sips of water and put toothpaste on a brush for me and had a washcloth for my head. "Thank you, Florence," I kept saying, and he made me laugh by folding a little white nurse cap out of a paper pharmacy bag and wearing it around on his head.

In the morning when I woke up he was still there. "It's noon," he said. He sat on the edge of the bed and felt my clammy head. My fever was gone by then but I was exhausted and limp.

"You're not pregnant," he said, out of the blue, "are you, Charlotte?"

Well, that startled me. "Not as far as I know," I said. "Why?"

"Just—you were sick. Morehead was ragging me. I don't know..." He shrugged.

"So what would you do?" I asked. "If."

"If what?"

"I were."

"What would *you* do?"

"I asked you first," I said. "Do you even like children?"

"Of course," he said, as if children were so obvious a thing to like that if I didn't know that fact about him, then I didn't know anything. We never talked about children. I couldn't name a child I knew, except some faraway nephews, Peter's children.

"You'd run, I bet," I said to Milo. "You'd head for the hills."

"Well, I like hills," he said coyly.

I like hills. Maybe it was only a joke. I didn't press him; any small hint of his leaving sent me into a frenzy of doubt, having watched him drive away once already. *You're not pregnant, are you?* His question startled me and started me thinking *What if I was?* I put my hands to my stomach, felt how my hipbones made a bowl under the skin, a cradle. *What if I was?*

Maybe it was the power of suggestion, but a few weeks after that, I was late, and I recognized the symptoms from before: the breathlessness, tenderness of the breasts, a hint of blood, and then nothing. Not for a week. Longer. It made me quiet and still. *What if I am?*

"What's the matter?" Milo asked me, home from a party one night, late. We were sitting on the edge of the bed, me sliding stockings off.

"I don't know," I said. "I think maybe I might be, actually."

"What?"

I just moved my eyebrows, but he knew.

"God," he said. He put his hand out and rested it on my leg, watching me. Looking at his worried face I knew right then what I wanted. A baby. Ours. Wanting it felt like a sudden hot blast from the oven. A baby. I let myself picture it. A light brown child with dark eager eyes; a girl, with downy hair and fat rolls and shining pink gums without teeth, just a flash of this baby smiling and squalling before I banished it. Tamped it down. No. He wouldn't want it. He would run. It was impossible. Was it?

I was religiously careful but not every time. Milo hated all of that stuff, the chemicals and the apparatuses and the timing and thinking about it. The terminology alone! *Barriers* and *methods* and *interruptus.* Just the word *spermicide* is heinous to a man, I think. He pretended he didn't hate the subject but he did. I was always very good after what happened in high school. Still, there are always equipment failures, human failures. When I was drunk.

We sat on the bed. My sloughed-off stockings were a dark limp pile in my lap. You could smell stale party smoke off Milo's jacket, off my hair.

"Why—what, why, do you think you—" He couldn't bring himself to ask the whole question.

"I'm late," I said.

His eyes dropped down to my waist like sinkers on a fishing line. "Oh, boy," he said.

A boy would be nice, I thought, *but I imagined a girl.*

"Don't think about it right now," I said. "Let's not." But I did think about it. I had been through this once before, don't forget; not that he needed to know.

He asked in the morning and I said: *Still late.* He said, *Can't you do a test?* I snapped at him, *I'll do the test when I damn well want to do the test.* I couldn't help snapping. I was nervous and sure by now of what the test would show: a twister forming, funnel clouds in a dervish heading toward us. The stick would turn pink, meaning yes, I was. If I said I wanted it he'd clear out. *I like hills.* He hadn't said otherwise. If I *took care of it*—which I would if I had to—he would leave anyway, because I would be depressing, not fun anymore, full of sorrow and anger and resentment over wanting it, not a terrorist in the bag or any kind of party animal. He would tire of me. I didn't entertain other possibilities—such as him sticking right by me with his little paperbag Florence Nightingale hat on. If I imagined that, or the idea of a real living baby with us both as its parents, I made myself stop because that little family would be impossible, I thought.

After three more days I finally did the test. Alone. I didn't want him there. I took the vials and the droppers and set them up on the bathroom sink, watching the hands of my watch tick around.

The stick was pink. Of course it was.

I was shaky but I didn't cry. I put the test stick in my pocket and went across the park to get Milo at work. They knew me there at the Network, let me in and up the elevator without a pass. I went through the newsroom to his office and closed the door. Some production assistant went to fetch him out of an editing room. His big carpeted office was full of pictures: Milo with Carl Yastrzemski. *To Big M from the Yaz*, it said. There was Milo and Reagan; Milo and that football player, the Refrigerator, along with Lawrence Taylor and some other very big, padded men. There was Milo's typewriter, coffee cup, phone, roll of mints, leftover sandwich. His little compact of pancake makeup.

He knew right away. He closed his door and put his hand on my cheek, scanned my face. We left and went to the park across the street and sat in the miserable cold. December 10, I think it was. Pigeons were the only ones out, strutting around us hopefully. Milo's face was furrowed with worry. I took the pink test stick out of my pocket and gave it to him. "Aw, Charlotte," he said, so it made me cry.

"Don't worry," I said. "I'm not dragging you into anything."

"I didn't say—" he said. "Come on." He took my hand and went to a pay phone where he called in sick. Then he hailed a cab and we went home to Milo's apartment. I opened his wine closet and got out a bottle of red wine, poured it, took a big swig, and then another.

"So I'll just go and take care of it," I said.

"Is that what you want?"

"It doesn't matter." *Look, I've done it before.*

"It does matter," he said.

"To you?"

"Yes. It's not some small thing."

"It's small right now," I said. "But not for long."

"Charlotte."

"I'll just go and have it done." I said this again so he would talk me out of it, or into it. I said it before I had to listen to him say it. I assumed that was what he'd want. "I'll just do it."

"Well, maybe," he said.

I checked his face and saw the relief and the decision there. So, it seemed we had agreed, to go and have it done. As if this were hair or nails we were speaking of. He didn't want a baby, not with me, not at that time. He swallowed and looked away. I tried to take a breath but I was crying.

"No, no, no, oh no, now," he said, gathering me up.

"I just wish—" I tried to speak but my throat was swollen so the words would barely fit through. I had to say them with my eyes closed.

"I just wish I didn't have to," I told him. "I don't want to."

"Aw, honey," he said.

"I wanted it," I said, hiding my face. "You know?"

"No," he said, "I don't know." And I could see he had no idea what I wanted. I hadn't told him. He let me cry in his lap.

"What do you want?" I asked him.

"Jesus," he said, blowing out so his cheeks filled. He picked up my glass and drank.

"Hasn't this ever happened to you before?" I asked from down in his lap where I couldn't see him.

"No," he said. "Not that I know of."

"I would think it would have."

"No. Has it to you?"

I waited and didn't answer.

"Has it to you?" he asked again.

"Yes," I said, after a long while.

"When?" he asked.

"When I was sixteen," I said. Telling him made me see myself back then, how young sixteen is, my dolls still in their doll beds in my room, how far gone I was, buttons popping, before I could admit to myself what was happening. The bleeding for days after. I told Milo what my parents said about me, how I was Damned, how furious they were. "They never really got over it, what I did," I told Milo. "It was like I betrayed them and became a stranger."

"Are you sorry?" he asked me.

"No," I said quietly. "I'm not sorry."

"And is that the reason why you think you want it this time?" he asked uncomfortably. "It's not some—because of your religious belief?"

"Of course not." I was angry he would think it. "I'll do it again if I have to."

The pink home laboratory test stick rested on the coffee table next to the wine bottle. Milo picked it up and fingered it. "If we had a baby most likely it would not...look like you," he said carefully. "You've thought about that?"

"Well," I said, "why would it look like you, either?"

"Perhaps it wouldn't," he said.

"It would be beautiful."

He smiled.

"Half you, half me," I said.

"But who would know by looking?" he asked.

"Who cares?"

"Plenty of people," he said.

"You? Do you care?"

He shrugged.

"I don't," I said. "I don't care about anybody else."

"What do you care about, then?" he asked.

"You," I said.

He pulled me up on his lap, swung my legs over his knees so my feet dangled. He put his head against me with his ear near my heart and tightened his arms so my ribs shifted. We stayed like that a long while, breathing.

"Let's get married," he said straight into the fabric of my shirt.

"Okay," I said.

"Okay," he said.

"You don't mean it," I said.

"I never say anything I don't mean," he said.

We woke up in the morning and there was a new membrane of shyness between us. *Were you serious?* I whispered uneasily. Milo nodded and smiled but didn't take up the conversation. He went to work as he always did. *See ya, babe.* He came home late that night from covering a basketball game and before we fell asleep, he squeezed my hand under the blankets. Will you see a doctor? he asked me. Yes, I said, on Monday.

He's having second thoughts, I was sure. I worried until a couple of days later, when something happened. I will spare you the details except to say it woke me up. Cramps and pain, some sort of early miscarriage. I was disappointed but also relieved. A little teary and blue. I was not pregnant but still altered somehow.

I went out to the kitchen and made coffee and looked out the window, watching pigeons wheel and strut along the window ledge across the way, watching the drab light fill the city. I was feeling thick and achy. I wanted to go back to sleep, but I had an early call that day and so did Milo. He was headed to the airport, flying down to Miami for preproduction on all the holiday football games. I would have to tell him. He would think I made up the whole thing. Invented pregnancy. He'd think I was a lunatic. I went and lay down next to him and watched him for a while, then whispered what I had to say, shy and uncomfortable.

He stirred and blinked and looked at the ceiling. "Hmm?" he said, fighting out of sleep. "What?"

I told him again.

He blinked and I could see what I had said sinking in, dawning on him just as the morning was coming around the edges of the window blinds. "Oh," he said, raising himself up on his elbow. His eyes were baffled and then shining a little bit. Filling in. He put his head down again on his arm. I couldn't see more than that, just that welling up of something. Disappointment, was it? Or relief.

"Aw," he whispered, "Charlotte."

"Mm," I said.

"We'll get married anyway though," he said. His voice was soft and groggy, as if he was dreaming. It was barely light in the room.

"Okay," I said.

"Good," he said.

Talking in his sleep, I thought. I still didn't expect he meant it.

Later, when I went to a doctor and described to her what had happened, she told me it was nothing to worry about, that I had had what was called a *chemical pregnancy.* Pregnant just long enough for hormones to show up in the system, to change my chemistry, turn the stick pink. I asked her about the blood, the first early spot of it. Oh, she said, that was probably what we call *implantation bleeding*, where a pregnancy attaches to the wall of the womb. In your case, she said, it was not sustained.

But it seemed to me something *was* sustained, that some chemistry *was* altered. Ours. Something did attach, plant itself in my head and Milo's, an idea or a feeling.

"I saw how you wanted that baby," Milo said later. "I never believed you would. Not *you*. Forget it." But it changed him and decided something, when he saw how much I wanted it. I wonder sometimes if we would ever have gone ahead and married, if it hadn't been for that phantom baby, showing us something about ourselves. We'd have broken up. We'd have gone on as children ourselves.

Who knows.

Another thing I wonder now: Is that near baby another ghost that haunts us? Does Milo believe with regret and hindsight that I tricked him? Made up the part about the test, the evidence? Does he sit there in jail now and trace his troubles to that first small stain of blood, one that was only a rumor to him? Does he think the whole thing—vials and droppers, crying in his arms—was merely the first time he was wrongfully accused? I don't know, maybe he does.

17.

The ring Milo gave me, at Christmas, was beautiful. It had powers, I swear. When I had it on I felt I was not *just some girl* but somebody's true love. Milo's. *My ring.* It had a diamond in a teardrop shape, offset with small chips. I am looking at it now, sparkling on my hand. I have always loved it, since he put it on my finger, and I have never taken it off, nor the wedding band, either, not even now.

Milo told me, It won't be easy.

So? I said. It would be the same as any marriage and as different as any marriage.

Oh really, he said, with sarcastic eyebrows.

"Don't think about crashing," I said, quoting his own words. "Or you'll crash." I did a lot of the cavalier talking about this subject, which worries me. "It will be okay," I said. "You'll see. We'll be happy. We're happy now, aren't we?"

He smiled and said, "Yes. Yes we are."

He wanted to believe me. I wanted to believe myself. We got seduced by the idea of ourselves. We got filled up with We Shall Overcomeism. We thought we were our own personal melting pot, deserving congratulations and gratitude, if not the Nobel Peace Prize: two public figures united in a living, breathing example of how Love was The Answer. If anybody had a problem with us, well, it was their problem, right? Not ours. We were our own little world, unto ourselves, hands cupped around each other's faces to block out everything but our wide bright eyes.

I love you, Milo.

I love you, Charlotte.

We were really darling. You have no idea.

Also, we were terrified. What the hell were we doing, marrying each other? We were out of our minds. Oh God, the thought of our families.

I called my sister Diana first, for practice.

"Heaven help you," she said, when I told her the news.

"Don't you ever swear?" I asked her, annoyed.

"You are just going to kill Dad. Just kill him."

"Dad will be fine."

"You don't know that. You have no idea."

"Aren't you going to say congratulations, or anything?" I said.

"Oh honey, I'm sorry, oh Charlotte, yes," Diana said. "That's nice you're getting married, that's great."

She went on for a while about what kind of dress, and sure, she'd love to be the bridesmaid, but soon she was right back to how I was going to kill our parents. Especially Dad. This is the phone conversation when she told me the Family Secret. The story of Dad and the Bottle, the story of The Accident. She made it clear that my phone calls had the power to throw Dad right off the wagon into Johnnie Walker's arms.

All of this was nothing more than a covert argument as to why I shouldn't marry Milo. Good practice, I told myself, for calling Barbara and Arthur.

"Are you sitting down?" I said into the phone. It was just after Christmas.

Mom knew right away what I was going to say.

"You're engaged!" she said.

"Yes! How did you know?" Already relief was escaping into my voice: She sounded excited. I could hear her planning the wedding just in those words, *You're engaged*. She loved a wedding.

"And who is your intended?" she asked.

"Milo Robicheaux," I said quietly. Of course they knew of him. I hadn't mentioned anyone else for six months. "Milo."

"Well," said my dad, after a long time.

"Oh, Charlotte," my mother said, tears starting, "I think you're making a mistake. A terrible mistake."

My mouth tasted like metal. If you have ever accidentally chewed a piece of foil, that is the feeling I had, listening to my parents. I wanted them to say Oh, how wonderful, darling. Congratulations, you have our blessings. My little girl.

We are not prejudiced, my father said.

We believe all men are created equal, my mother said.

But society, my father said.

God loves all His children, my mother said.

What about the children?

You cannot do that to a child.

"Do what?" I asked finally.

"We admire your idealism."

"It's just you have no idea what you are doing," my father said.

"Your career will suffer," said my mother.

"I'm getting married," I said, through the metal taste.

I hung up the phone, sitting on the side of my bed for the longest time. I hated them. Diana said it would kill them, and I half hoped it would. They could stew in their own juice. I would disinvite them. It was touch and go, with Mom especially. Even six weeks after I told her, she was grasping at straws. She called up and said, "What about that nice young man?"

"Who?" I said.

"The skier, the other skier, the good-looking one. From college."

"Jack Sutherland?" I said.

"Yes, him," she said. "He's called here, you know, looking for you."

"Pardon?"

"Yes, he did, he's called you," she said. "But at first we didn't know where you were, either, back then when you were . . . lost to us."

Oh, she means way back then, after college.

"And then he, this time I just thought— Well, he—"

You just thought maybe I said I was getting married but it doesn't matter to whom, so you can go dragging out fossils of old boyfriends from six thousand years ago.

"Listen, Charlotte, he—"

"Mom, I don't want to hear anything about Jack Sutherland," I interrupted her. "Ever again. That was a long time ago."

"But he called you. He was in town, in San Francisco, last week, he said, and he thought he'd come up to Conestoga for a visit."

"And what did you tell him?"

"I had to. Tell him."

"Thank you."

"I felt so badly for him. He sounded very disappointed when I told him. I must say I think he still carries a torch for you."

"Well, he can just light himself on fire with it, for all I care," I said.

"Charlotte Halsey," she said, "I am ashamed of you."

She quoted me Isaiah: *And if thou comfort the afflicted soul, then shall thy light rise in obscurity.* I could picture her, eyes closed, preaching into the phone. "Jack's mother recently died," she said, "and he is quite alone in the world. He was genuinely concerned about you."

Jack's mother was dead, so I should marry him?

"I don't ever want to hear or think about that guy again."

I stopped her. I got off the phone. All I really heard was her saying *Don't marry that black one, marry the white one, any old white one.* I didn't listen to what she was saying, about Jack calling—more than once, was it?—and coming for a visit, carrying a torch. But lately I've wondered: If I had let her keep talking, maybe only my feelings would be hurt now, and not my throat, my voice, my family.

All my mother accomplished was to make me not care what anyone thought. I just wanted Milo more. Only Milo. His was the one opinion I cared about now. Oh, and his parents. I cared deeply what they thought.

Milo drove up to see Milton and Hattie without me. "If you're with me they will just be polite and not honest," he said. So he went for a weekend and they were just—*dumbfounded* is the word he used. "Your liaison" is what they called our engagement, as in "your liaison with this woman." A liaison was one thing, according to them, which they could abide, but marriage was another. Here's how the conversation went, according to Milo, who played all the parts and did all the voices of his mother and father talking to their son around the family table:

"My mom says, 'Oh, Milo honey, you don't have to *marry* her.' And my dad says, 'You don't know that, Hattie, maybe he's got the young lady in some trouble.' 'Milton!' my mom says. So he asks me, 'Have you gotten her in trouble?' and I say 'No sir, not so far as I know, sir,' and they can't really think of another reason why to get married, so I ask them why did *they* get married, and they say: love. And I say: '*Right.*' Just like that, waiting so they see what I mean."

Then Milo's father said, "There are practical considerations. Would she be a good mother?" And his mom said: "Yes, what about the children?" and she explained how it was very very difficult for children of *mixed parentage* to feel that they belong to one community or another.

"What did you say then?" I asked him.

"I said"—and Milo seemed especially proud of this part—"I said, 'And what do you think it's been like *community*-wise here in the woods of New Hampshire?'"

I smiled at him. "Poor Milo," I said. "No community."

"Don't start that," he said. "We won't be teaching them any of your poor-me shit."

Them. He meant our kids. It thrilled me, to hear him say that. Little Boy and Little Girl. *Tiny sneakers with Velcro,* I thought. I had seen a pair on a child, now that I was looking at things like that.

Milo thought his parents would come around. And they did. It didn't even take them a day to recover. The phone rang the evening after Milo got back and Milo answered. "Charlotte, it's for you," he said. The look on his face was half a smile with a twist of lemon around the mouth, as if he weren't sure what was going on.

"Hello?" I said into the phone.

"Charlotte?" said Hattie, on the other end. "Congratulations to you and Milo. We just couldn't wait to say how happy we are for you."

"We're sure you're going to be very happy together," Milo's father said formally. They kept saying "happy" like a wish that could come true. "We're very happy for you both." Even though of course they weren't, exactly. It was so moving to me, how their faith in Milo was the strongest I had ever seen, despite all the time I'd spent among the faithful. It made me jealous. Thou shalt not covet, but I did. I wanted that sort of faith for myself, *the substance of things hoped for,* the Bible says somewhere. *Evidence of things not seen.*

It was Bobbie who worried me most. The sister. She appeared in my dreams before I ever met her, wearing that toga and crown of leaves from the picture in her parents' living room, her muscles rippling, beams of X-ray vision coming from her eyes. Milo talked about Bobbie as if she had wings.

"Of course, well, you know, Bobbie is a teacher. Bobbie has advanced degrees in child psychology. Bobbie runs a youth program. Bobbie counsels pregnant teenagers. Bobbie was on the front lines during the Boston Busing Crisis of 1976," about which I was too ashamed to admit I had no idea. Brilliant Bobbie lived in Roxbury, Mass., with Marcus, her boyfriend, a counselor in the Boston prison system. Beautiful Bobbie read everything, in three languages, standing on her head. She did not suffer fools.

Surely she would hate me.

Milo had told me how New Hampshire had been a rocky state for his sister. How she sat alone at lunchtime many days of her school life, was hardly invited home with any of the little girls, oh, it made him so mad, how she was never asked on a date, his gorgeous sister, only asked, maybe once in a while, to baby-sit the neighbor's child. Three years older than Milo, quieter, she could not be rescued by a pair of skis. She hated skiing, hated the people who skied. She left home at sixteen, moved to Boston to board with family friends, attended school there, and Boston College. Bobbie used to want Milo to come live with her. She said, *Oh Milo, you're just missing so much by staying in that white state.* But when he asked her if he should give up a shot at the Olympic Team, at the World Cup, she always said, *You're right, Milo. You'll be okay.* "Bobbie has faith in me," Milo said. "Except she thinks I live too much in the fast lane."

Bobbie was going to be traveling with us in that fast lane for the weekend. She was coming to New York. We were going to take her out, show her the town.

I became preoccupied with all the bad things I had: the blueness of my eyes, for example, and the disaster of my hair, which would never be forgiven by her. I knew it. She would be thinking of plasticky Barbie dolls, and Miss Flyaway Clairol, Dum-dum Doris Day, and especially Rapunzel whose suitor is blinded. Plus my skin-deep profession would not impress Her Loftiness. She would be aghast at all the makeup and hair products she would find in her brother's guest bathroom, which I had appropriated prenuptially along with the closet, now full of my shoes, stilettoed and stacked and strapped. She would open the louvered doors to hang up her simple yet classic clothing and she would gag at the sheer amount of my frivolous stuff.

I told all this to Claire.

"Charlotte," Claire said, "you haven't even met her. You are not giving her the benefit of any doubt. You are projecting, plus condescending."

"Condescending how?" I demanded.

"You assume that Bobbie Robicheaux is programmed by her appearance to judge you on your appearance. You assume that what *you* look like and what *you* do is the preoccupation of every woman. When: it's not."

"Right! Everything I do is condescending!" I said. "I'm a big snob, right? Looking down on everything, including you! That's what you think."

Claire delicately scratched her nose with her middle finger and then left that finger up in the air pointed in my direction. "Why don't you go play on the thruway with the other trucks?" she said sweetly.

"I hate you," I told her.

"I've heard that a little too often lately," she said, and suddenly her face was stretched out, the jaw pulling down and widening her eyes, lashes batting against tears.

"Oh, Claire," I said, "I don't hate you. I love you."

Claire had broken up with Carl. She has a terrible, fatal knack for timing and finding things she isn't looking for and doesn't want to find. She had come home unexpectedly from a canceled class and discovered Carl fooling around with some Amanda. She told him to get out and never call her again. This had happened just after Christmas.

Now, six weeks later, Claire was jumpy and blue but brave and taking antidepressants. She had been getting better but I had just now made her worse. I was always worried that the sadness that ran through Claire's system would suck her down so far she would think she had no other choice but her mother's.

"Don't you think," I asked, "that it's actually lucky you found out about Carl now instead of—"

"Really lucky," she said. "I'm a lucky duck!"

"Quack," I said.

"Quack yourself," she said. "It's like saying to somebody 'Oh, aren't you lucky you were stabbed in the back and not in the vital organs.' You are not lucky! You're *stabbed*."

"I'm sorry, Claire," I said.

"Yeah, Charlotte, you're always sorry," she said, sadly. "Thanks, though." She hugged me. It was a bad time between us, since her wedding plans were a shredded confetti in the wastebasket and mine were piling up in brochures on my bedside table, notes by the phone, samples on the kitchen counter.

Bobbie was arriving. I was nervous, waiting for Milo to bring her home from the airport. When I heard the elevator coming up, my hands got cold. "Bobbie!?" I said, opening the door with a big hostess smile. She was slim and small, standing in the doorway next to her brother. She looked like their mother, with the same white stripe of hair running from the left side of her brow to the crown of her head, which was braided in serious rows close to the scalp, with more plaits hanging down her back. She had style. A gold cut-velvet scarf around her neck, dark bangles up her arms, dangling pendants made of cowrie shells on her ears. She had a strong handshake, spoke slowly and calmly, exactly as she did in my dreams. She did not smile unless she felt like it, I could see. "Charlotte," she said, "it's nice to meet you." So far she had not felt like it.

I shrank down into my bones to become shorter, quieter. "Thank you for coming all this way," I said.

"I had to," she said. "Baby brother's getting married." And now she broke into a smile just like Milo's. "This is a golden opportunity."

"Bob-bie," Milo said, like warning a toddler.

"I'm going to tell Charlotte the truth about you," she said, "*Milton*."

"Oh, God," said Milo.

I liked her already. She put me at ease, on purpose. It was possibly a ruse, so my guard would be down. She was in control, no question. What she actually thought about me I couldn't tell, but she was giving me a chance. I could imagine what Hattie had told her about me. *A woman like that.* She sat down in the kitchen. Milo poured wine. Bobbie said: "So, you probably want to know all about Milton, here."

"Quit it now," Milo said.

Bobbie stuck her tongue out at Milo. He was helpless.

"If you let her tell me," I said, and reached across the table to him, "I promise never to call you, uhh, *Milton*." I patted his arm. The big diamond on my finger seemed garish, a traffic light flashing against Milo's arm. I saw Bobbie looking at it and pulled my hand into my lap, like hiding a sore.

"I'll just tell Charlotte about Lydia," Bobbie said.

"Go ahead!" Milo said. "Tell her everything!" He got up from the table and rummaged in the cupboard for some chips. He found some, ripped the bag open so it spilled on the floor. "Goddammit!" The chips crunched and stuck to his shoes.

"Who is Lydia?" I asked, imagining some kind of ex-wife.

"Should we help?" Bobbie asked.

"No!" Milo snapped. "Leave me! Begone the both of you harpies."

"Lydia," Bobbie said, "is the name we gave to Milo when I used to dress him up in one of my nightgowns and pretend he was my baby sister."

"I'll kill you, Bobbie," Milo said. "Slowly and painfully." But he was laughing.

"He was only about five," she said. "With hair bows."

"Lydia," I said, wishing I had a picture of him as her. "Aw."

"Lydia would like a stiff drink," Milo said, and poured again.

Bobbie and I had a frivolous conversation about the dress, Bobbie's bridesmaid fitting, the flowers, the menu, the kind of champagne. I was sure the whole topic only confirmed what Bobbie already thought: *See the silly bimbo my brother is marrying, Miss Diamond Teardrop Solitaire with her baby's breath and her bubbly Dom Perignon and her train of lace.*

"So," I said, "who are you counseling these days?"

"Oh, God," Bobbie said, "Tanisha. Accchh. Too depressing." She waved her hand as if directing traffic away from this Tanisha. "Tell me again?" she asked. "You think pale green dresses?"

It was obvious she couldn't stand me. Wouldn't tell me anything about herself, or counseling Tanisha, didn't trust me not to dress her in something sallow.

"So," Bobbie said to Milo, "are you two gonna jump the broom?"

"Jump what?" Milo asked.

"Lord," Bobbie said in dismay. "You don't know?"

You could see how it was with them: big sister, little brother. Milo was prickly around her. She was bossy.

"Even if I did know," he said, "I'm sure you'd be telling me over again, anyway, Schoolmarm."

"It's an old African wedding custom," she said.

"Oh, here we go now," Milo said, exasperated.

Jumping the broom, she explained anyway, meant: Sweep out the old and sweep in the new. You got a broom, swept around yourself in a circle, then jumped over it, a symbol of starting a new life.

"Then what?" said Milo. "We all start cleaning up? Couldn't we do it with vacuum cleaners, just to be modern?"

"Milo," said Bobbie, "you're still a flaming asshole."

"You two quit," I said. "I'll tell your mom."

They smiled at me.

"No brooms," Milo said to me. "My sister's always got some radical preposterous ridiculous idea."

"All the girls are doing it now," Bobbie said. "It's popular."

"Don't notice you doing it," said Milo.

"Marcus and I are not the marrying kind."

Milo raised his eyebrows at that. "You mean *Marcus* isn't the marrying kind."

"Maybe I'm the one who's not," Bobbie said.

"Really?" Milo asked her, surprised. "Why not?"

"Questions," she said.

"About?"

"*Patriarchy*," she said ominously.

"Whoa, whoa, never mind, never mind," Milo said quickly. "Don't talk about that stuff. Jesus."

"Relax, Milie," Bobbie said. "All I said was I had questions."

She was scaring me. She clearly had all kinds of ideas like broom jumping and words like *patriarchy* up her sleeve, ready to pull out whenever she needed them. No wonder Milo was prickly.

"I just can't believe you're going to let Mom down," he said, trying to make a joke out of it.

"Not nearly as much as you are, buddy boy," said Bobbie, laughing, arching her eyebrows, arching them right over the subject of me as Milo's bride. "Sorry, Charlotte," she said, as if she suddenly remembered I was there. "That was rude."

"Don't mention it," I said.

"No, but we have to mention it," she said, "don't we? Because you know everybody else will mention it."

"Fuck 'em," Milo said.

"Well, you know they may just fuck you first," Bobbie said. "In the mind."

"Yeah, yeah, yeah, we've talked about it," Milo said.

"Have you?" she said, real worry in her eyes. "I hope so. I really hope so." She came over and put her arms around her brother and kissed the top of his head. Her face as she smiled at me was rueful.

We went out. Richie Havens was at Sweetwater's. I have always liked Sweetwater's, the mix of Afro-Carib-Latino-Japanese-Euro jazzheads with their dreadlocks and black berets and Woodstock looks. But this night something was off. We arrived, and even though I was by Milo's side, the white hostess thought Milo was just with Bobbie. "Two?" she said, and smiled at them but not me.

"Three," said Milo, and pulled me in front, linking his arms around my waist.

"Oh, boy," said Bobbie. "This is your life."

"Charlotte handles it," said Milo—proudly. "She can deal."

What I could not handle was the remarks of a woman, a rather loud woman, and her friend, who were sitting behind us. We were eating dinner. Bobbie had excused herself to the ladies' room. I put my hand on Milo's. "I like your sister," I said.

He smiled, then leaned over and kissed me. "She likes you, too."

"That's right, kiss the mistress," somebody said, which made Milo pull back, look around. Over his shoulder I could see two black women, younger than us, staring. One was shaking her head in disgust so her big earrings bounced.

Milo turned back to me and said, "Pay no mind."

"Don't take the bait, don't take the bait," I said.

"Right," he said.

Now the one with earrings was getting up from her table and coming around toward ours. She glared at me but her beef was with Milo. She passed by, hissing "Some people don't remember who their mother was."

"Some people were raised by wolves," he said back to her calmly.

The woman huffed away but you could feel the rising hackles of Milo's discomfort, as she returned to her seat with her drinks and joked around with her friend. I was afraid to touch him, pulled my hand away. I wanted to leave. They kept it up. I snuck looks and saw the women were not more than twenty, both of them dressed up, probably hoping some guys would come and sit with them, I thought. You could see they had a bone to pick.

"The darker the berry, the sweeter the juice," said the one with the earrings, talking in our direction. The friend was laughing.

"Shit," Milo said, looking behind us. The louder woman had gotten out of her seat again and was talking to Bobbie, had accosted her on the way back from the rest rooms. Bobbie listened, then shrugged and smiled, gently touched the woman's shoulder as she left and came back to sit with us.

"God," she said to us. "Heaven help you."

Which is what my own sister said, too.

"What did she say to you?" Milo said.

"You can guess," Bobbie told him.

"I just wanted to go out and have a good time," Milo said.

"Me, too," she said, smiling. "Welcome to the party, Charlotte."

"Some party," said Milo. He was agitated, drumming on the table and jigging his leg. "In France I never got that. Germany maybe yeah, but not from—" Milo paused and shook his head as if his feelings were hurt.

Not from black people, I thought, is what he meant to say.

"I just thought that, you know: New York!" Milo said. "Honestly, all my life, I thought: New York is where I would finally find—"

He stopped.

"What?" Bobbie said.

"A place that could get it. That *got* it."

"The beloved community," Bobbie said patiently, as if she was talking to children. "Ha!"

"What?" Milo looked baffled. "You always said, 'Oh, you're missing so much, Milo.' So, I thought, New York was where I would find what I was missing, whatever that was. Where you could just be who you are, and not—"

"What?"

"Have to deal with this crap."

"Well good luck," she said.

Behind us, the two women started laughing hard. They had tears running down their faces. They hooted loudly and drank from their rum and cokes. They were really having a good time now, watching us.

"Let's get out of here," Bobbie said. She was fed up but it was hard to tell if it was with her brother or with the women or with me, the fact of me. There was pain in her face. We paid the bill while the women watched us, smirking.

"Could you believe them?" Milo said, when we got outside.

"It's not like they have no reasons to feel the way they feel," Bobbie said.

Milo turned sideways in the wind to look at her.

"That could've been me," she said. "I'd never say it, but I'd *think* it, if I saw you two. You've got to understand that."

"Is that what you *do* think?" Milo asked.

"No," she said sadly. "It goes way past thinking."

"Obviously," he said.

"It's a feeling you can't help," she said. "It just is."

"What is?" Milo said.

And Bobbie started muttering a list under her breath, which I couldn't properly hear, over the street noise: . . . *unemployment and prisons, drugs and history; the statistics, the ratios of something to something, emasculation and the heartbreak of the beauty standard,* all these words blowing out of her mouth in a frost and evaporating in the loud windy street.

"Why do you have to make everything be about politics?" Milo said, cutting her off finally.

"When it is," she snapped, "it is. You should know that by now."

We walked fast in the cold. There were no taxis. Milo had his hands in his pockets and did not touch me. Bobbie was storming along, her bangles rattling and her heels clacking on the sidewalk. Nobody spoke. The wind whipped our scarves and our hair, ripped tears out of my eyes. It was terrible. I was miserable and sorry for myself. I had made them fight.

Bobbie looked over at me and said: "Hey, Charlotte, lighten up."

That surprised me. She said it again. "Lighten up, okay?"

"That would be kind of difficult," I said. "I mean, I'm already so light you can hardly see me."

She laughed at that, and Milo did, too. We all did. As if a huge calcified deposit of Serious Problems had scraped off us. "Let's go get drunk," Bobbie said. "Forget this mess." She waved her hand in the air again the way she had before, as if clearing it. She took a deep breath and socked her brother on the arm so he smiled. She reached around him and grabbed my hand and said, "Come on, Charlotte, let's get Milo bombed." There were still no taxis so we got on the subway and went to a club, way downtown, with Brazilian music and rum.

Bobbie watched me that night, pretending she wasn't. She was just like her brother, I thought. That gaze. She was watching Milo, too, with his hand on mine, his smiles at me. She started enjoying herself, drinking dark rum and tonics. She wanted to stay out late! she said. Everybody was feeling better now. Milo got Bobbie out dancing, and I stayed back and watched. They were old partners, with old moves they had practiced to records in their living room all through junior high school. He was laughing. She was vamping around. When Milo took a break, Bobbie got me by the hands and took me out to the middle of the dance floor and we danced, too. I pretended to be some kind of debutante. I pretended to waltz with her. Not that I knew how to waltz. I picked her up and swung her around. People were staring at us. She laughed so hard we practically tipped over. We had a good time.

The next morning when Bobbie came into the kitchen, Milo was still asleep. I poured her coffee. "How did you sleep?" I asked.

"Better than usual," she said, "due to the fact that Marcus the Boyfriend is one of those men who sleeps by rolling around in the bed."

"Milo too. He drifts onto my side."

"I hate that," she said. "I like a night off. Chance to be by myself."

"Not me," I said. "I get lonely."

"Milo's good company," she said.

"He is for me," I said, shyly.

She smiled at that, and I could see her thinking about her brother keeping me company, precisely how I might get lonely for him.

"I was hoping you'd bring Marcus with you," I said, to change the subject. "I'd like to meet him."

She got a look on her face. "He has his doubts," Bobbie said bluntly, "about this match. I left him home with his doubts. He thinks black men should be with black women."

"And you?"

"I don't care," Bobbie said. "I just hope you know what you're in for."

"I'd rather not know," I said, "if it's bad."

"You're just like Milo," she said. "He'd rather not know, either."

I laughed because I knew that about him.

"We've had at least one white person in our family before, you know," she said suddenly, as if she'd been waiting to say it. "Our mother's great-grandfather was a white man."

"Oh," I said carefully. I waited to see what she would say next but she was quiet, so I said: "*My* mother's great-grandfather was a white man, too."

Bobbie laughed and looked at me like I'd surprised her. "He never told you that? He never told you where he got those eyes?"

"I never asked," I said.

"Jeez. No wonder he loves you," she said.

"He doesn't like questions."

"He certainly does not."

Bobbie told me how, when Milo was a child, people were always asking him: *Where'd ya get those green eyes?* And he always said just what his parents told him to say: *I got them from God.* But one day he asked his mother, Where did they come from, really? and she said, *My mother's grandmother, who had the same eyes, always said her father was a white man. Not that he was a member of the family.*

"Nighttime integration," Bobbie said, "was one name for it..." letting me supply the other name in my head.

People still asked Milo about his eyes. Sometimes they said, "Those are contacts?" Usually he didn't answer. *Where'd you get those eyes?* If he did answer he said, *Same place you got yours, pal.*

"Milo would just rather not bring any of that up," Bobbie said.

"I know," I said. "But that's okay with me. It's easier that way."

"I don't know," she said. "Is it?"

"If it's easier for him, then it is," I said.

Bobbie smiled at me. "You're okay," she said.

"He worships you," I told her. "He always talks about you."

"Does he? I've always believed he thinks I'm a big pain in the ass."

"No," I said, "he doesn't. He wants you to respect him."

"I do," she said. "Believe me."

Now we were quiet, looking out the window, steam coming off the tops of our coffee cups into the kitchen.

"Well, you'll be all right, then, the two of you," she said. "I think so."

18.

It was lovely. Nothing could change that. I was beaming all day, April 10, 1982. I got there early and stood smiling at the plain old church of St. Luke in the Field on Hudson Street, where Milo would marry me. Inside, the air was stained with colored light streaming through arched windows. It smelled of lilacs and dampness. I closed my eyes, alone at the end of the aisle, where soon I would march: *Dear God, please.* My lips moved when I prayed, standing there. A prayer for luck, hedging bets, praying out of superstition like throwing salt over the shoulder, picking up pins, wearing lucky socks, anything to ward off doubts: *What if they're right?* I prayed while waiting to promise such extreme promises. *Happily ever after, forever and ever, amen,* throwing the Brothers Grimm in there with the Lord's Prayer and whatever else I could think of.

My dress was white. My shoulders were bare. The back was cut down in a scoop almost to the small. Kevin did my hair the way I wanted it, twined with baby's breath. Claire, Diana, and Bobbie were the bridesmaids, wearing silk sheaths in shades of green: celery, leaf, jade.

We waited in the sacristy, a little secret anteroom where the ministers' vestments were hanging like bathrobes on hooks. It was crowded and bustling. Kevin was there doing maintenance on us girls. The Flower Lady was messing around with calla lilies. Bobbie was peeking at the ushers. "If that guy VD is the best man," she asked, "who is the worst man?"

Claire had many candidates.

She and Bobbie were cackling about that, making jokes at my expense, such as *Maybe the bride's a little chilly what with that dress cut down her backside, don't you think?* Kevin came over and adjusted my headpiece and kissed me, saying "I remember the day you walked in off the street, in your cow T-shirt, as if it were yesterday!" He kissed my mother and my sister and said: "Oh! You gorgeous Halsey women!" They both beamed and blushed and hugged Kevin back. And I wanted to tell them *You have just been kissed by a homosexual!! Was that so bad?* But I didn't. My mother was nervous and fidgety and having a grand time. In the end I believe she behaved because the wedding was a chance for her to get dressed up and have a title: Mother of the Bride. The Plaza Hotel awaited her with its red carpet and its crystal chandeliers. She would have a chance to meet the Couture King, the mayor, the Network anchorman, *People* magazine. She was thrilled. It was the allure of all this—Milo's fame and fortune and the fashion world glamour of it—that finally won her over, that found her now all caught up in the excitement and the jitters, gazing at me saying: "You look so beautiful, Charlotte, honey, like the angel you are."

Hypocrite, I thought, while kissing her and telling her she looked beautiful, too. "Like a goddess, Mother."

The buzz of the guests was getting louder out in the church, and the strings had started up with the flute. "Five more minutes, everyone," somebody said. Then outside, a siren careened up and stopped right out front: somebody arriving—the governor? The girls peeked out and said: The mayor! There were 300 people out there. Fashion Bigs and Network Wigs and the entire United States Ski Team.

Then my father appeared in the doorway of the little room, uncomfortable in his tux and in other, less obvious ways, but a good sport, considering his objections.

"Daddy," I said, and took his arm, played with the satin on his lapel. "Are you ready?"

"Ready as I'll ever be, Sunshine," he said, and hummed the song: *You are my sunshine, my only sunshine,* softly so only I could hear it. Which he hadn't done since I was small. His voice was low and out of tune. He was trying, bless his heart, for my sake, but he was all nervous tic, tucking his shirt, testing his hair, massaging his neck. He didn't seem to know where to park his eyes. It seemed to me then, in light of my new information, that he was wishing he had a drink. Would do anything for just a belt of it.

"It'll be okay, Dad," I said. "You'll see."

"I pray to the Lord you're right," he said.

We have the same prayer, I thought.

Then it was time. My mother put her arms around me, kissed me, left cheek, right cheek, a custom she adopted after visiting me in Paris. "Break a leg," she said mistily, what she used to say long ago, before my youth pageants. "Break a leg." She looked at me to see if I remembered. I was tempted to say *It's not some kind of show.* But there was something in the wings of her face, some apology, that stopped me. I hugged her. "I love you, Mommy," I said. She swallowed and smiled, left stoically for her entrance, escorted by my brother Sean, going to sit in the first pew.

Finally, out we went, me and Daddy. Down the middle, people stood up and craned to see, whispering *Isn't she lovely?* Somebody's kids said, *Hi, Charlotte.* All the Robicheaux cousins from Louisiana on the right and the Halsey relatives from the West Coast on the left, with me thinking *If only we'd thought to tell the ushers not to follow that particular seating custom.* Even in the midst of my wedding, I was arguing with myself: *But why? Who cares?*

Bride's side, groom's side. White side, black side.

Mix it up.

Shut up, Charlotte, shut up.

Up by the altar was my brother the Reverend Peter Halsey, acting as the guest minister, standing next to the groomsmen, my brother Sean and VD and Coach Winks.

And Milo, waiting for me. I never let my eyes go off him. Everything else was on the misty sidelines. He was beaming at me, pulling me toward him with his gaze. That look. Had we been alone it would have been the look before our clothes came off. That hooking smile, going up one side of his face. So handsome. The way his mouth revealed just a hint of red between the lips when he opened them to say something. My name. *Charlotte.* He was saying it as I walked. *Come here.* Gooseflesh rose on my bare arms, the flowers in my hands trembling as if they were still growing in a breezy field. I clamped my eyes on him and walked.

Claire took the bouquet from me, I think. I don't know. What I remember is, Milo took my hands and held them. Our knuckles were bloodless, we clenched so hard. Our palms were slippery and hot. In the pictures you can see my chest and arms are blotched red, big splotches of color mottling the skin with feelings I had never shown in front of a camera before. Still, we spoke out forcefully.

In sickness and in health. Till death us do part.

I do.

I do.

Milo found my fourth finger, pushed the ring hard over the knuckle. His eyes were watery when he spoke. *Take and keep this as a symbol of my love, wear it all the days of your life.*

I will, I said, and said the same words to him.

I will, he said. *You know I will.*

He reached to cup the back of my head. My arms slid forward around his waist, under the jacket, feeling suspenders crossed on his hard back. A long kiss, too long for in public. So what? We didn't care, kissing with our arms full around each other, eyes shut, so there was laughter, finally, and us breaking up for air. Milo turned and held our hands high above our heads, beaming, like we had won something.

The music came pealing out and everybody cheered as we passed, with more gusto than you'd expect at a wedding. They reached out to us from the pews, and waved, and dried their eyes. We got to the end of the aisle and I pulled Milo off to the side, down two steps into the little anteroom. I closed the door behind him and he pushed me against it. We were gripped together, out of breath, staring. We were married. I was crying. Milo was. He wasn't ashamed of it, he let tears run down his face. I brushed at them, collected them in my hands.

People think they cry at weddings because they are about happy hope and lovely love. All the materials involved are delicate as eggshell: lace and gauze, pearls and rice. But now I know weddings are really about terrible risks and gambles. They are about ends as much as beginnings; about the narrowing of possibilities, the putting of eggs all in one basket. To me it would make more sense if the ceremonial materials were steel and girder, masonry and cement. *The bride wore a Kevlar gown reinforced with carbon fibers, and the groom was nickel plated.*

My tears were because of the risky parts and the happy parts, both, but also because of the way Milo looked at me in that room. It reminded me of that day in the woods, that big deer, before it realized why we were there, how its eyes looked up with a routine question, then widened with one pulse of panic. It was only a flicker there in Milo's gaze, or maybe in how he swallowed.

"Wife?" he said.

Now we were laughing. Giddy. We were married. We couldn't get over it: *husband, wife*. The words suddenly seemed inane, relevant as *shoe, sock*. We heard people outside the door but we didn't want to go out and face them, not yet. The room smelled of elderly ladies, a cross of perfume and the spotted mold on hymnals. We straightened up and fixed Milo's tie and caught a look at ourselves in the mirror there. It was mottled where the silver backing had flaked. Our reflection was blurry and aged.

"That's what we'll look like in fifty years," Milo said. I loved that he said that. We watched ourselves kissing in the mirror, imagining our seventy-five-year-old lips, locked like now, all that time ahead of us.

We were married. We were off to the party. When we got out of the limo in front of the Plaza Hotel, all the men from the ski team lifted me up, lifted Milo, and carried us in.

The toasts were strange.

My brother Peter tapped his glass: "Milo, we'd like to welcome you to the Halsey family." Stiff as a steeple. "On behalf of my mom, dad, my sister Diana and my brother Sean. God bless. Three cheers for the happy couple!" And he led everybody in the cheer, made them say: *Hip hip hooray!* like British people, while under her breath, Claire was muttering to Bobbie, *He wouldn't know hip if a hippopotamus fell from the sky on his head.* Bobbie was choking back laughs behind her hand.

Milo's father stood then, serenely. "My son," he said. He perched his half-glasses on his nose and read notes off a napkin. "All your life you've skied your own trail. Sometimes into trees. (Laughter) Sometimes off cliffs. Though we often wondered where you were headed, you yourself have never had a question, and wherever you end up, it's always somewhere glorious. Your mother and I, we trust that this trail upon which you set out today will be no different in that respect than the others you've blazed, and we're proud of you, Milo. Congratulations to you and Charlotte on your wedding day."

I clapped and blew him a kiss. Then my father stood up.

"We always knew Charlotte would do something crazy—"

Nervous laughs and looks of alarm started going back and forth at our table. Milo reached for my hand.

"So that's why we're glad she found young Robicheaux here to keep her out of trouble." He raised his glass.

Relief bubbled up all around. Rick—VD—stood up, and everybody went: Uh-oh. There were groans coming from a table of skiers. VD said: "When Milo was at his peak—"

Hoots and razzes.

"I mean the peak of his downhill form."

"Oh yeah!"

"We used to call him Black Ice."

Milo shifted in his seat.

"Ice! Ice-man!"

"Now, for those of you who are not skiers, let me explain: Black ice is solid water, frozen sheer, under new snow. You can't see it, but when you hit it you are in trouble. You can't grab an edge or hold a tuck. You're f—...Sunk. Excuse me." (Jeers and hoots. Milo with a stiff smile on his lips.) "It's extremely dangerous. You can never win with black ice. And that was Milo. Dangerous. But, I have to say, and all of us agree, now that he's met the lovely Charlotte Halsey—"

Whoops. Wolf whistles.

"He's melted. The Ice is melted!"

Cheers. Applause. Blushing by me.

Now Milo stood up and raised his glass. "Those of you who know me know I like to go fast. So this won't be a long speech."

"Go Smilo!"

"When I found Charlotte, I knew by the speed of my heart racing that she was the one for me. To my wife," he said, "I love you." He pulled me to my feet and put a glass in my hand and linked our arms around so we drank to each other like that, twined. You couldn't have pried us apart for more than ten minutes that whole party, not with a crowbar or a bucket of cold water.

Everybody cooperated. It was etiquette that did it. Follow the proper procedures and you will be fine. Start with the outside fork. Scoop soup away from you. Bride dances with father. Groom cuts in by bowing. Mother of the bride dances with father of the groom, mother of the groom with father of the bride. Emily Post thought she could save the world with manners, and I see why.

They managed. They really did. The older generation was a little bit lost at sea, never having imagined it quite that way: Milton Robicheaux in a tuxedo, bowing to my coiffed mom in her gown modeled on the First Lady's shirred chiffon Inaugural Ball dress, the two of them doing a polite dancing school waltz. Then my handsome dad in his cummerbund, his shirt studs shaped like fish, the symbol of Christ, leading cool Hattie Robicheaux in her grape-colored dress and her dangling earrings. Chatting about nothing. *Certainly not about the grandchildren, who'd they take after?* All of us had to smile fondly at them later in the party, when the music got the better of everybody, and the Robicheauxs let fly with fancy steps, and the Halseys did an actual jitterbug, left over from their pre-Christian days, so you couldn't help but conjure them all up twenty-five years before, with dewy skin and doo-wop hair, never in their wildest dreams thinking of this night, not this version, all dancing at the same party, their children in each other's arms.

19.

How I feel now is undone, prised apart and strewn to the wind in drops of water like pieces of Charlotte raining down across the place, making no marks where they land. It's as if I am a mess of rain waiting to pelt out, bottled up in back of my face. I am sad.

Milo writes he is sad, too. He writes, *Please believe me.* Believe what? *I didn't hurt you.* You did, you did.

It hurts to be stabbed with betrayal and cut with lies, bloody with sorrow and jealous ache at the knowledge of what he did behind my back. How broken and angry I still am at him for it.

You should just never love anyone.

I loved him, Milo. Shallowly, at first, for his wisecracks and his celebrity and the way his eyes were green as chameleons, I loved him next for the way he peeled the neck of my T-shirt down my shoulder like the skin off a clementine and made random drawings around the hollow of my clavicle with his fingertip, his tongue, his breath. In between I loved him for stupid, sugar-pop reasons, like that he knew the words to Hendrix songs, the way he wore loafers with no socks and white tennis sweaters with a blue stripe at the V neck. But in the end, the whole time, I loved him for deep and complicated reasons, some of which had to do with me, what I needed.

Did he love me? Yes he did. He loved me first, he said, because he hated me, for not noticing him, and then because of my abandon in bars, dancing. He loved me next for the way he could see my photograph all over town. In between he loved me for my snide remarks, referring to various people as *skankballs, toadstools, rodents*. He loved me for refusing to flatter him, because I told him what he could do with his fame. He loved my refusal to be impressed.

But in truth I was impressed. And he knew that, too. He loved me finally because he knew I saw his ordinary American cheer was not cheer, but really bravery. I did not think his famous, talented life was a piece of cake, bowl of cherries, any kind of sweet food. He loved me because I respected his grace in the face of his experiences, his hometown, the police. He loved that I would listen to his stories.

Listening made me feel important. It was as if, by Milo telling me his life, I fixed something about him, and he fixed something about me, some feeling of worthlessness both of us, for utterly different reasons, had grown up with. Are these the "wrong" reasons people accuse us of? I don't think so.

When he heard I was with Milo, my old boyfriend Simon called me up. "So, you're with the dusky Moor?" he said.

"Si-mon," I said.

"But you have read it? *Othello*? You know he kills her, don't you?"

I hung up on him. But then of course I went and read it, worried that there was something about it everyone else knew, but not ignorant Charlotte, with my *blond education*, sneaking it so Milo would not catch me. Didn't much care for it, really, what with the thick language and the racist commentary! It was beyond me, clearly, I couldn't get through it. Still, there was a part I liked, where he, Othello the battle-scarred soldier, says: *She loved me for the dangers I had passed, and I loved her that she did pity them.* I did not pity Milo. Certainly I knew he hated any kind of pity. But I liked this part because it made me realize what it was that we loved in the other: Milo seeing himself in my eyes as a hero.

But as much as he tried, Milo did not know how to navigate his fame the way he could a downhill course or a New Hampshire town. When I met him again after college, Milo had already been famous for five years, but it was not until he got to New York that he learned why fame has been called a drug. Like some drugs, you can handle it in moderation. With the right doctors. But try it with the wrong ones, and the sky will surely fall on you, or an acorn that feels like the sky, so that pretty soon you are Chicken Little, your whole life a panic. What I am trying to say is: Like Chicken Little, the idea of the falling sky will so distract you, you will not notice that it's the Fox who is inviting you to take shelter in his lair.

In this story, Darryl Haynes is the fox.

Okay, he's not. Probably he's not. More like the goat. The scapegoat. I'm telling you I wish I could blame him. Anyone. God. Someone besides myself. Darryl is without shame. He is out there acting like what happened to me, this crime, is a spectacular spectacle, something to promote and profit from. Which he will, mark my words. He's taking out ads! Pages of newspapers. In the *L.A. Times* there was a double-page spread: one side with pictures of white cops standing over dead black men in pools of black blood, cops leading black men in handcuffs, mug shots of corrupt white cops; the other page had shots of handsome Milo shaking the hand of Ronald Reagan, Milo holding the Olympic medal aloft, Milo in his blue blazer from the Network's *Wild World of Sports*, Milo in his beloved role as "Cade, Rebel Fury," from the whole *Cade* series of action films. "Who do you believe?" goes Darryl's copy. "Them? or Him?" with an uppercase H, as if Milo were holy.

Mr. Top Agent Darryl is talking to everybody, all the press: *Milo Robicheaux would not hurt a flea.*

Well, he hurt me.

She says it's my child. Milo said this one night, sat me down and confessed: "Geneva says it's my son." Left me gasping like a goldfish dropped on the carpet. An ordinary Wednesday night. Hallie was in bed. We had finished up the dishes. "Come here," he said, "my darling. We have to talk." And he said: "She says it's my son."

So: Who am I to say, after that betrayal, that Milo is not also the one who did this? Who nearly severed the carotid artery in my neck? *Come here my darling we have to talk.* They say they found me in his arms.

The man came home and found his wife half dead, Darryl says. *And if it weren't for him, she'd be all the way dead. My client was trying to save the life of his wife, and he did.*

At the hospital they had the TV on in my room. I heard it playing in and out of morphine dreams. The private nurse turned up the sound, thinking I was sedated.

*Black Olympic skier Milo Robicheaux is still in jail tonight for resist-
ing arrest in the charge of assaulting his wife, former model Charlotte
Halsey, who lingers near death. Robicheaux, who assaulted a police officer, maintains his innocence.*

Some of the nurses, I could tell they hated me. The icy, quiet ones held my
wrist in their cold hands to feel my pulse, threaded IV tubes, checked my
wound, changed the dressing. The noisy ones flipped through the entertainment news and the gossip columns, each whispering her own pet theory.

Drug dealers obviously.

A jealous lover.

*Probably a botched suicide: She was a desperately unhappy woman
with her looks fading, and there's a black man in jail again.*

*You know there must have been a reason he had to run to the arms of
another woman, one of his own people who really could understand him,
wouldn't ruin his reputation like this model.*

Not to mention she's a drunk.

A thick-legged white one whispered out in the corridor: "That's what
happens when you sink down to their level, poor thing. I seen it before,
the way they treat their women."

A sloe-eyed dark nurse with her hair cut close to her head dropped my
wrist when she was done with the pulse and humphed out to the hall.
"That's the white wife," I heard her say to somebody out there.

That's me! White Wife!

There were some kind nurses, but I can't remember anything about
them except that they were kind.

Here at home now, my mother is careful not to leave the TV on. Because of
Hallie, she says. But I'm the one she wants in the dark. I demand to know,
turn on the radio, find the newspaper, the remote control. I don't care that
it makes me hysterical. It's my right to know what they are saying about
me, what the cops are saying, the hairdo-reporters, what Darryl says.

You know something? I was suckered in by Darryl for years. I always
enjoyed him, all the time I knew him. He was funny, teasing, cracking on
everyone. *Here comes your Barbie wife, Milo. Look how her feet stay up
in that high heel tiptoe. No really, check out those feet.* Half the time that
he was our friend, I wasn't even paying attention. I didn't *hear* what it was

he was actually telling Milo: *sun people, ice people*. That whites were evil, no exceptions. Sometimes I forgot, in a certain way, that I was white. *Melanin-deprived*, he called me, *ha ha ha*. The way he said it it was like a big joke between us. He had me going for the longest time.

Hey there, Miss Anne, how's the baby? He called me Miss Anne in what I know now is slang for snooty white girls, plantation mistresses.

Just fine, D., just fine. I called him "D." out of affection. He had me. Had Milo, too. Perhaps he still has Milo, who knows? As I say, I don't know what they talked about that night. The night in question.

I hate Darryl as much as I ever liked him. Hate. Call me whatever you want, call me cracker. Call me ofay. Get up there on your high horse and call me the big R word. You can believe whatever you want about me, but the truth is, I don't hate him because he's got brown skin. I hate him because he's a bad man. Because he had chances to be a good man. He had power and ideas. He had money and brains. I trusted him and agreed with him. He was our friend and we helped him. But he ruined everything. Everything that ever mattered to me. Milo. He took love and baffled it into hate. He took hope and ridiculed it down to despair. He knocked me out, me and Milo both, with sucker punches.

Or was that us?

Maybe Milo did that. Maybe I did. Probably it was my fault. Yes, I have my own big sins to confess. Who started it? Chicken or egg? Milo's betrayal or mine?

He got too famous. He believed what they said. The hype. None of this would have happened if we had just moved to a little house in the mountains somewhere, raised a family. I wish we had.

Milo! I am shouting at you. Do you hear me! Look! Look! Look! This is me getting old with you! This is our warm house and the dinner I made for you! This is our little girl! Come back here, listen to me. Hey! I am saying I love you.

I never did say any of that, not that way. My feelings were too hurt. I couldn't find the right voice. The one I found came out plaintive and rank. I said: "I don't believe you. I don't trust you." I had no faith. I said, "Where are you going tonight? Why aren't you ever home?" I said, "What about me? What about me?"

20.

The day I met Darryl Haynes was the first time I had ever been in a room full of black people. Let me tell you, your average white person has no idea how this feels until you feel it. Maybe you have never thought about your white self in a room full of another race. Say you're trying to imagine it now, walking into a big, high-ceilinged room and looking down marble steps at hundreds of elegantly dressed people who all seem to have known each other since childhood and who do not look anything like you. You might be thinking a range of things, depending on what kind of white person you are: *We don't belong in here, let's leave.* Or: *We oughta drop a bomb on all of them.* Or, to give you the benefit of the doubt, you might be the kind of white who thinks: *No big deal, what's the problem? I would feel just perfectly comfortable in a room full of black people; this is America.* That was what I thought, when Milo and I went to the party for the Dance Theatre of Harlem, which he was proud to say had invited him to sit on its board of directors. I was excited to go with him. He was my husband. That diamond the size of a molar flashed on my hand. We had been married half a year. If I was with him, I thought, no problem, I'd have the stamp of approval. Everyone there would know: *She's okay. She's one of the good ones.*

Well. It's almost poignant now, naïveté like that.

Milo was looking so fiercely handsome that night. He was such a beauty to me, more than ever. His hair was cut down close to his head, which was shaped so you wanted to hold it in your hands, to feel the planes of it, the rounding back lobe. He was looking warmly at me over his black tie, his narrow hard waist circled by the cummerbund, satin ribbon running down his pant legs. We left our coats in the cloakroom, and the gray-haired woman sitting there said: "Milo Robicheaux?" She was thrilled. "I just loved that story you had on the other night about that racehorse!"

"Thank you," said Milo. He put a ten-dollar tip in her hand and winked at her, took my arm. "You have a nice evening."

Going in to the party, I was relaxed and looking up at Milo, smiling here and there, but when we got to the top of the marble stairs leading down to the ballroom, the kind of stairs descended by Cinderella and Audrey Hepburn, I was unprepared. Walking down, it struck me how pale and unnatural my feet were, in their dark strapped heels, flashing from beneath the slit in my dress. You could count the other white people down there in the room like dots on a domino. The guests were embracing and talking, holding long-stemmed glasses, laughing in their tuxedos and bright cloth scarves, their glittering jewel-toned gowns and a few African robes threaded with silver and gold.

People nodded at Milo as we made our way across the room and smiled at me thinly, or just ignored me. I might as well have been made of Saran Wrap. I stuck close to Milo but suddenly was not comfortable touching him or whispering with my lips at his ear. He was having a fine time, but it was almost as if he was there without me. The people who came and introduced themselves nodded at me and then quickly went back to asking Milo questions. I didn't know what to say. I stood around with a glass in my hand.

"Hey, brother Robicheaux."

Milo turned and grinned, put his hand out to a light brown man in a tuxedo with a kente-cloth scarf draped around his thick neck.

"Darryl Haynes," Milo said. "How're you doin', man?"

"Who's your lady?" Darryl Haynes asked him.

"This is Charlotte Halsey," Milo said.

He did not say "my wife," I noticed. He wasn't in the habit yet. Neither of us was.

"Charlotte, this is Darryl Haynes. *The* Darryl Haynes, middleweight Olympic boxing champion of 1976."

"Nice to meet you," I said.

Milo explained how he'd recently tracked Darryl down and interviewed him for a series about former athletes called "Where Are
They Now?" "In the seventies, Darryl was an up-and-comer," Milo said.
"Olympic middleweight gold, going on world champion. We tracked him
down."

"Milo here was also Mr. Up-and-Coming," Darryl said, and raised his
eyebrows. "And he still is: still up, still coming."

They were grinning at each other as if they knew each other's secrets.

"Do you ever box anymore?" I asked.

"Nope, I don't," Darryl said. "I promote boxers, promote musicians, all
kinds of talent. Mostly sports talent. Why, do you have a talent?"

"Charlotte's a fashion model," Milo said.

"Ho-de-ho," Darryl said. "A fashion model!" He put his arm around
Milo, knuckled him on the head. He had a smile that showed perfect, perhaps fake, teeth. "Robicheaux, Robicheaux, Robicheaux," he said, and put
his arm around me, too. His arms were hard and big as tires. He hugged
us in by our necks so his tuxedo jacket lifted up and flapped out like wings
behind him. "So we have Barbie here, and Black America's Ken, out here
in Harlem on a date. Isn't that a beautiful thing?" He was laughing and
punching at Milo, winking at me. He was twinkly, with a habit of tilting
his head to the side in a question mark, just about irresistible, teasing
Milo like that. "A beautiful thing, right, Charlotte?"

"Not exactly a date," I said.

"Oh no? A business function?"

"No," I said. "I'm Milo's wife."

"Oh, Lord," said Darryl. "His wife now."

"Yeap," Milo said. "She got me." He pretended he was shot in the
heart.

"Then what you need is a drink," Darryl said. "Bring you back to life."

He asked if he could get me something, leaving me with the idea that
they were coming right back. But ten minutes later, Milo was still at the
bar talking, surrounded by people. When I wandered over to him, he
handed me my drink but didn't stop his conversation or pull me to his
side. I went off and made an elaborate inspection of the vegetable arrangements, went to the rest room, listened to the women in there talking
about the bank Goldman Sachs, which at first I got confused with Saks the
department store. When I went back out Milo had migrated to a different

room and was still drinking, laughing, talking, but not to me. I went back to the bar and took a long time to get wine.

In the end it was Darryl who rescued me. "So let me tell you about this party, Mrs. R.," he said, nodding at the circling crowd. "This is New York's Black Elite. There's the Boro President and Prominent Columnist, there's the man who sang Day-O, there's the Morning Show Host with the Elderly Author, there's the Fatcat Corporate Vice President and the Celebrated Defense Attorney standing with the Bigwig Law Professor. We have the brightest in here, and also the best, from the arts, law, politics, medicine. This is the crème de la crème—so to speak—of Black New York."

"And what about you?" I asked, gave him a sidelong glance. Darryl's neck was slightly too thick and it would be better, I thought, if he shaved his small mustache. He was not exactly handsome, but the way he listened with his whole face, the way his words were full of jokes—*fatcats and bigwigs*—made him attractive, relaxed you and made you laugh.

"The Elite," I said. "You must be included on that list?"

"Me?" said Darryl. "I am the man they all need to get to the top! Back to the top! Over the top! I am their agent. I am their *Black* agent. You are well acquainted, I'm sure, with the meaning of that word? Agent?"

"Oh, yes," I said.

He went on about himself. "I make demands my clients don't dare make. I can get whatever they want for them: money, power, houses, cars, film scripts, recording contracts, arena stages, the center ring, royalties, broadcast rights, attention." He was speaking grandly, as if addressing a large crowd, his hands expressive as a conductor's. "They want it, I can get it."

"How?" I asked him. "Just—?" I snapped my fingers.

He leaned in, as if divulging something. "Because what I do is not about money," he said. "It's not about fame. It's about history, and truth. It's about respect. And I have dedicated my life to winning respect for the people in this room." Darryl looked hard at me, and I noticed he had a pale scar above his left eyebrow. Old stitch marks were faintly threaded in the skin. When he turned his head to profile, I saw his ear was cauliflowered.

"That's God's truth," he said, "and I am not afraid to speak it. Wherever Darryl Haynes goes, Darryl Haynes wins his brothers and sisters their rightful honor. Their rightful place. You see what I'm saying?"

And I could see, in his eyes, hear the drop in his voice, that he was sincere. I nodded, listening hard.

"That's really great," I said. "It's wonderful." I meant it, too. *To be so dedicated, to stand for something, to have a noble purpose.* If I did any standing, it was on pieces of blank background paper, moving my head, arms, legs. My standing was not about history or truth, just about style, getting the right angles and light.

"Your man," Darryl said. "I want to talk to you about him."

I raised my eyebrows. I was afraid to say anything, since whenever my mouth opened, filler words came out of it like soap bubbles. *Really? You don't say? My, that's interesting.*

"The treatment of the black athlete in America," said Darryl, "is the moral equivalent of rape." He waited, watching me. "Rape. It's happening to Milo Robicheaux right this minute. I guarantee it. Did you know that?"

"Oh," I said carefully, trying not to picture it. "Milo's not a professional athlete anymore, though. He's a sportscaster, a sports reporter."

Darryl pulled his head back on his neck, like a turtle rearing into his shell. He looked at me with his hands open as if I had just said something ridiculous and obvious. "A sportscaster. Even worse," he said. "He's a piece of horseflesh. You oughta know that. What is a fashion model? Horseflesh. The question is simple: How much can they make offa your lovely behind? Same thing with Mr. Milo Robicheaux. He's fast, but I guarantee you no matter how fast he goes on snow, he is right now sucking the exhaust of the snow-job boys that own him."

"Oh," I said, thinking about Jed and Mark and how just the other day Milo had complained they did not return phone calls, had canceled a lunch.

"Charlotte, I can see you are a progressive, enlightened woman. Am I right?" Darryl said. "So, I want you to get a message to Milo Robicheaux. I want you to tell him: He needs to come home. To his community. I can understand him in a way his Midtown pinstripe boys can't. Darryl Haynes can get him what he is owed by this world, if he's willing to reach for it, you see what I mean? You can help your man. You can make him see."

I smiled and felt his flattery warming me the way a drink does. Right away he put me at ease. It seemed he respected me. *An enlightened woman, am I right?* That night, when he brought me around the room and introduced me to the people he knew, I thought he had simply noticed me feeling left out. I thought he was motivated by kindness.

"This is Charlotte Halsey," he announced. "Mrs. Milo Robicheaux. Just married. Still got the shaving cream on the rear window and the cans tied to the bumper." When he introduced me, people warmed up.

One man said, "The skiing brother!" and then did an imitation of Milo in a downhill tuck. "You'd have to be fast to catch a man like that, right?" he asked me.

A young woman came over then, in a conservative suit and strands of beads at her neck. She talked to Darryl awhile and then turned politely to me. Her name was Carla. She was a banker. "You look a lot like Princess Di," she said.

"Really?" I looked nothing remotely like that princess, with her short feathery haircut, her slightly too-close-together eyes.

"Your hair and all," said Carla.

"Oh," I said, "maybe." We talked about the Prince of Wales and the wedding, when the royals would have children.

"Charlotte just got married, too," Darryl said.

"Oh, really," Carla said. "Big wedding?"

"She's married to Milo Robicheaux," Darryl said, pointing. "The skier?"

"I know who he is," said Carla. I could see judgments passing on her face.

"This one," said Darryl, holding my arm a moment, "and Mr. Milo over there, don't they look like some kind of Dairy Queen accident, you know what I'm saying?" Carla laughed but then covered her mouth with her hand. She looked with feigned disapproval at Darryl, who was grinning at me.

"He's bad, this Darryl Haynes," she said to me. "You watch out for him." They were laughing. "A Dairy Queen accident," she said again, under her breath, shaking her head as she went in to dinner.

A Dairy Queen accident. I pictured the dropped sundae, dark sauce on vanilla, and it made me laugh, too. I went to tell Milo. He was across the room talking to a girl, a teenager really, tall as I was, in a dress the color of mangos.

"Charlotte," he said when I joined him. "This is—" he stopped.

"Geneva Johnson," she said, ducking her head, like a child. "Nice to meet you."

She had braces on her teeth. She had a yellow smiley-face on a necklace. She was an apprentice at the Dance Theatre of Harlem. She explained shyly how the founder wanted the young dancers to be here tonight to talk to people. They were supposed to be telling everyone how much young dancers like her appreciated the support. So she had come, and it was so exciting to be here, wasn't it?

Milo put his arm around me. "I know pretty much zero about ballet," he said, "but we'll do what we can." He looked at me when he said it, for the first time that evening. "Won't we, Charlotte?"

"Yes," I said, happy to have his arm around me where it belonged. But at dinner he sat across the table and was soon talking to the people on either side of him, a painter, or something, and a social worker. *My sister is a social worker*, I heard him say. He was going on happily for a long time about it. I stalled out talking to the man on my left, a businessman who ran a chain of restaurants. The lawyer on my right talked to him over my plate. I concentrated on my medallions of beef. Milo smiled at me occasionally from where he sat. We didn't dance.

"Did you have a good time?" he said, when we got home.

"I did," I said. My voice was small but he didn't notice. His eyes were shining like a boy's.

"That was some crowd," he said wonderingly. "Wasn't it?" He sat on the bed taking the studs out of his pintucked tuxedo shirt, not really watching me as I slithered out of my dress. "It's just so . . ." He was being careful. It was one of the times when he wasn't sure whether he could say something to me.

"What?" I said.

"It was fun." Which is not all of what he meant, I think. He meant: It was just so . . . great to be in a room full of people who were not white. A relief. A thrill. Not to be the sore thumb.

"You didn't talk to me," I said.

"I did," he said, too quickly.

"No, you didn't."

"Well, you always take care of yourself at parties," he said. "I saw you talking to Darryl Haynes."

"Yeah. Or anyway, he talked to me."

"See?" Milo said, and kissed me on the head. A smell of scotch and smoke came off him. He went in the bathroom to brush his teeth, talked through toothpaste and the open door. "They used to call him Hardhead Haynes. He knocked out the Panamanian Pedro Concepcion in '76 after two minutes."

"I don't like boxing."

"You know I was at that fight? The Concepcion fight? Montreal Olympics, 1976."

"No," I said.

"Amateurs fight with helmets and big fat gloves, and they're only in the ring for about three minutes. I'll never forget Darryl, though," Milo said. "He was amateur going on star."

Milo had won his own medals the winter of that year. He was twenty-two. He went to Montreal on a lark. It wasn't too far from New Hampshire, where he was visiting his parents, killing time before training camp in Chile. He had it in his mind, he said, to meet an American female track star he'd heard about named Gloria Parks. He met Darryl Haynes instead. Nineteen seventy-six was a boom year for American Olympic Boxing. Five Americans, including Sugar Ray Leonard, Leon and Michael Spinks, won medals. Darryl was the one they called the "Boxer with Brains," because unlike most other fighters of his rank, he had spent time in college. He was a Golden Gloves champ from South Orange, New Jersey, made the Olympic team after hard training with some legendary police officer in the local gymnasium.

Milo was all wound up that night, telling me about Darryl. "We went wild after Darryl got his medal. The two of us landed in some French-Canadian joint, drinking. Darryl speaks no French, right? So he gets me to teach him *Je suis le boxeur américain*, and he's waving his medal around in the air. *Voilà! voilà!* There was this waitress—oh, Jesus." He was about to tell me something, I could see the whole story going past his eyes. He shook his head, thought better of continuing. "Never mind. No. That man was wild."

"So why haven't I heard of him?" I had heard of Sugar Ray Leonard, both Spinkses, but not Darryl Haynes.

"He quit," Milo said. "Sometime after the '76 Games. Said it was because he wanted to finish his education...But I don't know." He looked skeptical when he said this, peeling off his socks. He hung up his tuxedo, put away his cuff links, talking and talking while I listened from the bed.

There were rumors. Maybe Haynes had fixed a fight, Milo said, thrown one right after his medal, in order to arrange a big comeback, big purse, big gate. Milo said he asked Darryl about it, in the "Where Are They Now?" interview, and Darryl had gotten so pissed he made the crew stop rolling tape. "That was a shitpack of lies then, same as it is now," he said. "And you even mention fight-fixing on your broadcast I will sue you all for libel." Darryl told Milo, "The people who run boxing are crooked as the pathways of Hell," and explained how a certain promoter had set him up to fight *a joke, a fake white hope, somebody without hands, and I'm not going to do that! Make a spectacle! So I quit! I quit in '77! Finished college!*" He would, he told Milo, make it with brains, not brawn. He then moved to Harlem and got a degree from City College, turned up just recently as Darryl Haynes, agent and sports promoter.

"He could have been a world champ," Milo said. "He really had fight."

"He seems to be making out well for himself."

"He's trying to make himself my agent," Milo said.

"He was telling me he understands you," I said, "in a way maybe your agents right now can't."

"Maybe," Milo said. "But understanding is not what you usually want in an agent. What you want is killer instinct."

"He was a professional fighter."

"So you think I should go with him?"

"Whatever you think."

"I think the guy's a hustler," Milo said.

"You know that kid?" he said later, in the dark.

"Kid?" I said.

"The one with the braces," he said. "You know what she told me?"

How handsome you are, how important, probably. "What?"

"She told me I was a big influence on her," he said.

I don't want to hear about her. Stop talking.

"Oh?"

"She said she remembers when I won. In '76. She was ten years old."

A lot of people remember that, Milo.

"Some Park Avenue ballet school had just told her black girls don't have the body type for ballet," he said. "Can you believe that?"

I do not want to hear any more right now about black people and what bad white people say to them and think about them. I am sick and tired of the subject and I just want you to pay attention to me.

"How stupid and not true," I said dutifully, down by the edge of my pillowcase.

"Anyway, her mother pointed me out to her—when I won. Told her: 'They said black people didn't ski, either, but Mr. Robicheaux right there on TV is proof they were wrong.' And now that kid—whatever her name is, Switzerland, or something, Geneva—is first in the troupe, or the corps, or whatever they call it. She wants to be a prima ballerina."

"All because of you," I said sarcastically. It was two o'clock in the morning. I wanted Milo to shut up. I wanted him to kiss me. I wanted him to get my hand and hold it.

"Not all because of me," he said. "She said I was an *influence*, and I just thought—"

You just thought you would keep on yammering about this till the sun comes up. I made sleeping noises, rustled the blankets around.

"It just means a lot to me that some kid like her noticed. At the time, I always wondered if anyone—noticed."

"Oh, they noticed."

"What's the matter with you?" he asked me abruptly.

"Just. Nothing."

"Something."

"You're completely ignoring me," I said, and rolled with my back toward him, hip rising like a wall.

He lay there quietly for the longest time. I was nearly gone, spinning into sleep, but waiting. Sulking. He was awake. He was rankling the bed-clothes. You could tell he was thinking. The way he breathed. Then all of a sudden, he got my hipbone like a handle and pulled, flattened me out and got up over me so I had to look at him in the dim dark, the outline of his head and his sleek shoulders.

"I am not ignoring you," he said.

He took my face in his hands and stared me down. He watched me even in the dark. He kissed me, got my mouth open. My lip was cut on his teeth. He reached down below the blankets, moving my legs out of the way without waiting, fast and pretending to be angry. *I'm not ignoring you*, he said, *I could never ignore you*, so I forgot everything, every hurt feeling. *I love you*, he said.

Why.

Because I do.

Say you do.

You know.

Tears. I remember them, the way the breath was caught in our chests and forced out by the weight of the other, the bones and the padding of muscle, how it felt when he pushed and I arched and pushed back. He said Lord. He kept me in his arms, under him. Milo, I said. Charlotte, he said.

I am telling you these things, these private intimacies, which are sacred. I'd rather not tell. But these moments are evidence, the tears and the breath and what we said, of how we were. We were not some taboo *liaison* or some other illicit idea you may have, one that proves I deserved what was coming or that he was capable of it. We did not love each other to make some point or to show off or tempt fate. We were married. *I love you*, he said. It was the simplest thing, the way we felt, and it made everything else so complicated.

21.

Maybe I should have seen caution lights blinking at that party up in Harlem, in the fact that Milo practically avoided me. Maybe I should have seen flags for trouble in the way Darryl's eyebrows raised and lowered, the way he registered the ring on my hand. Maybe the way Milo spoke about Geneva Johnson—his influence on her—should have rung alarms in my head. But they didn't. Maybe he was trying to tell me something: *how he always wondered if they noticed.* But I think I really did understand, even then, that Milo wanted to mean something to black people, wanted so badly to be appreciated as part of a struggle. Because he had struggled, no question. He was attracted to something in that room that I could not give him.

Still, it didn't worry me. I didn't doubt Milo. I wasn't jealous. Certainly not of a girl in a smiley-face necklace. I was glad she was a dancer! Glad Milo inspired her and that she proved something to the smug Park Avenue ballet mistress! Glad she was a happy young girl! We would never see her again. She was one of the many, many people we met who loved Milo, who remembered when he won, who thought he was just so wonderful. Milo smiled at them and signed his autograph and said, Thank you very much, you flatter me. Thank you.

Perhaps I should have been warned but I wasn't. None of it felt threatening.

It felt fun. Half the time I was giddy. Mrs. Milo Robicheaux. It cracked me up, to be Mrs. It sounded respectable and domesticated, as if I might abruptly begin canning tomatoes. Coming home from work, getting the mail, seeing that name on an envelope, I felt happy. All we thought about in those newlywed days was having fun. We thought about which party, which wine, what to wear. We thought about going to Wyoming versus going to Chamonix. We thought about our new duplex terraced loft on Mercer Street, which I loved so much it was embarrassing. *He that trusteth in his riches shall fall*, I know, but I couldn't help it. The carved old moldings, the tin ceilings, the way the light came in the windows in the morning full of golden dust. I loved coming home, putting my key in the lock, riding the elevator, the doors closing, pushing "3." It was only a number, but to me it had the beauty and significance of a beloved's name. Three.

Mrs. Milo Robicheaux. I didn't worry about Charlotte Halsey. She was fine. She was alive and well, modeling her head off. *The camera loves you*, they said. Everybody wanted to make pictures of Charlotte Halsey now: Scavullo and Avedon, Casablancas and Weber.

The camera loved Milo, too, all cameras did: film or video or still. He was headed somewhere, that's for sure, somewhere impressive and important. He was twenty-seven years old. Rumors went around: He wouldn't be a network sports guy much longer; he'd get his own show, maybe a film. Milo was interested in films. He had always done ads and commercials, of course. Cars, watches, stomach acid tablets, mint gum. He still did a lot of things with mint, since the Network let sports anchors sell pretty much anything but athletic equipment. Milo did a bunch of ads for a line of breath fresheners. He was always skiing in those ads, which he loved. *The minty freshness.* Swoosh. He'd ski up to the camera in a blitz of snow and hold the product. His teeth would flash.

At first Milo liked this. It was all a big adventure to him. He was good at it, you could see. He was easy to work with. Coachable, is what they said about him, a director's dream. They had said this about me, too, so I knew how it felt, for him to hear those words. Milo liked praise, but he wasn't surprised. He was used to being good at things.

A big chewing gum ad campaign featuring him began in late '82, I think, and right around that time, not long after we saw him at the Dance Theatre party, Darryl Haynes started calling Milo up. "Hey, Mint Man!" Darryl teased Milo mercilessly. "Where'd you get those teeth?" he'd say. "They just love those teeth of yours!"

And Milo would say, "You're just jealous, Hardhead, since you lost all of yours." Darryl had fake front teeth, since his had been knocked out boxing. But it bothered Milo, the teasing. One day he said *Fuck you* under his breath when he hung up the phone from talking to Darryl.

"What?" I said.

"Haynes," Milo said.

"What'd he say?" I said.

"He's on my case, wants to be my manager, my agent, says all this crap to me, you know, my teeth, doesn't like the gum ad, whatever."

"He's just teasing you," I said. "You don't like teasing, remember?"

"Not like that I don't."

"What else did he say?"

"He said my teeth made me look like—"

"What?"

Milo wouldn't say but I made him. He was really bugged by it, what Darryl said: *With those teeth you look just like Al Jolson in* The Jazz Singer.

I didn't know who that was. Claire told me later that Al Jolson was that white guy from sixty years ago who painted his face black and put big white lips around his mouth and went around singing happy slave songs.

"Jesus, Milo," I said. "He's just teasing you."

"The guy's out of control."

He changed the subject but I think it ate at him, Darryl's barb. Milo was under contract to do four more ads for the gum and he didn't want to do the last two. Around that time he would come home from work or meet me at a restaurant and he seemed . . . restless. Cooped up.

"This is just not what I had in mind," he said one night.

"Me?" I said. We were at some new gorgeous restaurant, for our first wedding anniversary. The air smelled of butter and wine. Milo was looking out of sorts. "The place?" I asked. "It's quiet, anyway."

"No, not the place," he said. "The job."

"The gum job?"

"Yeah," he said. "Dumb gum job."

"Why is it dumb?"

"What is *not* dumb about it? Hawking some product?" he said.

"Pays well."

"Like we're starving," he said. He poked his fork at the tower of seared scallops on his plate. It toppled. "Aaaagggghhhh," said Milo, making a sound effect for the falling food, another one for the crash: "Crrrrrghh!!!"

"Like you're dignified," I said. "What's the matter?"

"I just spent a day skiing down the same fucking fake slope, saying 'Taste the minty freshness.' It wasn't even real snow! It was a hill in New Jersey!" He was piling up his scallops again into a tower, concentrating. "*Taste the minty freshness*. Fuck the minty freshness," he said.

He was sick of the ads, sick of sportscasting, too. "The athletes are all having more fun than I am," he said. "Out there playing, running, crossing the finish line, diving, jumping. All I'm doing is interrogating them about it, the thrill of victory! The agony of defeat! Same story everywhere you look." He didn't like sitting in the dark, editing tape. It sucked, he said. It was dark and hot and smelled stale.

And there was something else I couldn't put my finger on. Maybe it was that Milo had no friends in town. He really didn't. I mean, except me. Which I liked. But what I mean is, no one else. We went out all the time. We hung out with models and their boyfriends. Glenda, the one from Trinidad, had this white boyfriend now, Etienne, who was Belgian, and we made jokes about *what we had in common*, but it wasn't true, because really, they were both . . . European, somehow. They didn't get our jokes. We hung out with Claire and her nice new flame, named Tim. We were on lists, went to events where we sat next to celebrities, soap opera actors, society Hairdos and Neckties. Milo was a master of talking to them. He had his smile, his aloof reserve that turned brilliantly charming. He got along with everybody. But they weren't friends, not like Milo was used to: VD, Winksie and the guys.

"What about the guys at work?" I asked him. "You like them?"

"Buncha fatsos," he said. "Even the skinny ones. Buncha dweebs. Never broke a sweat in their lives. Hitting the search button on the raw tape is exercise for these people. They get their thrills *watching*, you know? Not me." He was sorry, he said. He didn't mean to complain.

"I don't want to *talk about* other people doing things," he said. "I want to be the one doing them."

"Maybe," I suggested, "we should just go up in the mountains and live."

"I've lived in boondocks," he said. "I'm not interested in boondocks."

People told him he should do films. He thought it would be fun to try, anyway. He had meetings with Jed and Mark. They took their time about it, but finally Jed, the one I used to always call Ted, just to annoy him, got Milo a part in a movie.

It was 1983. The film was called *Slope!* (Don't ask, it sank like a stone.) It was a comedy about an American ski team sabotaged by Soviet spies. As far as I could tell it was a spoof of *Help!*, the Beatles film, only bad. But from the beginning, Milo was excited. Mr. Positive Attitude. "It's small, but it's still a start. It's a film anyway," he said. "Not an ad." Just to be skiing, to get six weeks' leave from the Network, to be up in the real mountains where he was happiest. "Beats hawking gum," he said. He liked that he got to do some of his own stunts, which involved flipping off cliffs on skis with a fake submachine gun strapped to his waist. He liked that he was the hero of the movie. Or rather one of the heroes. There were two. Milo and this other guy, named Revo, an actor with shaggy blond hair and multiple pairs of mirrored sunglasses. In the film, Revo got the girl, of course.

"I *have* the lead," Milo said to Darryl, on the phone. "I play the lead guy." (Pause) "No no no, Haynes." (Pause) "Of course I had my own trailer. Yes, they paid me. None of your business how much." Milo was shaking his head, exasperated. "Haynes, you're not going to *beat* the system. You've got to *use* the system." Whatever Darryl said next got him, though. He cracked up laughing. I started to see that Milo was sort of fascinated by Darryl, wouldn't mind having him for a friend.

But Darryl seemed to have other ideas. He wanted to be Milo's manager. He wouldn't give up. *You need me, I need you.* He took Milo to lunch and invited us to performances and events he promoted: the Track and Field All Star Event, the New York City Playground Ball Championship, Double Dutch tournaments and boxing matches. He kept inviting us to the fights. The whole idea of boxing automatically made me cringe, but Milo wanted to go.

"You're wrong about boxing," he said. "It's pure. It's about one lone athlete against another." Milo admired boxers. You had to be in amazing shape to be a fighter, he said, and he respected that. So finally, one night, we went to the fights with Darryl.

The Garden was full of men, smelled heavily of men, too: smoke and beer and sweat mingled with deodorant. What women there were all dolled up with makeup and tight pants. Our seats were ringside. "The better to get spattered with blood," I said.

"Don't laugh," Darryl said. "There may *be* blood. Always was when I was fighting."

"Yeah and not on you, either," Milo said, laughing, but I didn't think it was funny, men pounding each other like they were tenderizing steak.

Darryl told us a guy named El Gallo and another one called the King would be fighting first.

"Didn't you have some nickname, too?" I asked him.

"Hardhead," he said, knocking on his skull. "Hardhead Haynes, the Boxer with Brains." He winked at me. Three women in matching long chiffon gowns climbed into the ring, their hair piled high.

"It's a bridesmaid fight," I said. "They're gonna rip each other's hairdos off."

"Ha. I'd promote *that*," Darryl said.

The announcer told us all to rise. The bridesmaids began to sing "The Star-Spangled Banner," and Milo and I stood with our hands on our hearts automatically, singing along. The song always reminded Milo of his Olympic medals, standing on the podium with the flags of the winning countries rising up and fluttering, everyone silent. I noticed Darryl was still sitting. He was tapping his heel and bouncing his knee. Milo moved his head at Darryl, like *Stand up!* But Darryl put his middle finger up and saluted the flag with it, wagged his eyebrows in disdain. Milo shrugged and kept singing.

"You respect that song?" Darryl asked Milo when we sat down. "That rag, I mean flag?"

"Yeah, I guess," Milo said, shrugged again. "Never thought much about it."

"Won't catch me standing for that shit," Darryl said loudly. Several people turned around. A couple of them smiled.

"Hey, Haynes," one man waved.

"Land of the free nothin'," Darryl grumped. "Man making a buck offa few guys they pick out of the garbage. Home of the brave, my ass. Home of the knave, you ask me."

"You're making a buck offa few people yourself," Milo said.

"Like to make a buck offa you," Darryl said. "Oh, please say yes, Mr. Robicheaux!" He looked at Milo and beamed.

Milo was shaking his head. "Not a chance, Haynes," he said, but he was laughing, covering his eyes so he wouldn't see Darryl mugging and beseeching him, hands folded like a supplicant.

The fighters made their entrance and quickly got down to their jobs of bopping each other on the head. I hated the fight. I kept covering my eyes. "The poor things," I said, watching the fighters wincing and darting. They hugged each other constantly in exhaustion. "Poor guys."

"Shh," Milo said. I was bugging him.

"They are poor things," Darryl said. "I oughta know. Every kid who gets in that ring got nothin' but dues to pay."

For me it was impossible to tell who was the better fighter. Both men ended up bleeding. El Gallo did win. They put a big belt on him, with a medallion on it, something a Marvel Comic Hero-Man would wear. Darryl was disgusted, muttering about the phony score, just a point apart.

When the fight ended a man came over to Darryl with a boy, about ten years old. "Haynes," the man said, "my son here wants to know when's my next bout?" He was a small dark brown man with a shaved head. A welterweight, Milo told me.

"Milo and Charlotte," Darryl said. "This is my client, Bones Rankel."

"John Rankel, ma'am," Bones said formally. "Nice to meet you."

We shook hands and Milo talked to the boy while Bones pushed Darryl for a match, a date in the ring, anything. He looked hungry and angry.

"Bones," Darryl said, with his arm around the man, "the Garden. Vegas. Closed circuit. You name it. It's yours." He was showing off for Milo's benefit, offering Bones a hired car home that very evening, peeling fifties off a big roll of money. "Don't give up now," Darryl said.

But later, in a restaurant high over Times Square, Darryl told me and Milo that he was the one giving up. "I'm getting out of boxing," Darryl said. "It's a fuckin' nest of vipers, hornet nest, barnyard epithet of scum and criminals."

"You love it," I said.

"Of course I love it," he said. "Got me where I am now. But it turned out to be all a big joke. All these joke matches. They make you fight a ham sandwich, or any white club fighter without a main event on his ticket." His voice hushed. "And the hurtin' part of it is, all my idealistic dreams of a pure fight went up in smoke, because of what a travesty the whole sport has become."

Darryl looked tired, his twinkling eyes not so twinkly right then. "I'm quitting it. I'm moving on. I'm going to do movies," he said. "With you, Robicheaux." Again he asked Milo to sign with him, but Milo said no in polite clichés. *If it ain't broke don't fix it.* He was doing well, he thought, he was on the brink of bigger things.

"Too bad about Darryl," I said, when we got home that night.

"Yeah, but he's deluded," Milo said.

"He wants to work with you."

"That's not how it works," Milo said.

"What?"

"He thinks it's all politics, it's all that radical stuff with him."

"How does it work then?"

"It's who you know, you know?"

"He knows you," I said. "You're who he knows."

"He doesn't know me all that well," Milo said.

"Like Ted and Mack?"

"Jed and Mark."

"Right," I said. "They know you like this." With my fingers twined.

A lot of people wanted Milo. Darryl was not the only one.

Maybe that should have bothered me. Maybe I should have been jealous of Mr. Important Celebrity Milo back then, instead of later. But that's not how he seemed to me. Yes, he was the handsome recognizable husband by my side, but he was also the concerned husband who was good at giving aspirin to a wife with a headache, he was the annoying husband who left his rotten socks on the floor, who forgot to rinse the stubble from the sink after shaving; the husband who demanded stone cold silence during televised sporting events, especially one that included him. He was studying the sportscasters, the way they bantered and spouted facts, compared to the way he did. "Shh, please, quiet please." I mimicked him and teased him, *Ooh, he hears the voice of God,* but soon learned that if I did that stuff, I was in for it. "Shut the fuck up" is what he said sometimes. Once he threw a magazine at me to make me stop talking on the phone. At the time I thought: *That's just Milo. Just his temper.* It was one of the things I hated about him, how set he was in his ways, how his ways were the ways we had to have. Mostly, though, I was happy for him. I liked his ways. This is how he must have been as a child, I thought, obsessively learning to win. I was rooting for him, the cheerleader at the finish line.

To tell you the truth, I was preoccupied with something else. I didn't tell Milo, really, or anyone how obsessed I'd become. How for the better part of the last year, I could not pass a pregnant woman in the street without fumes of jealousy and longing following me in her wake. How I avoided store windows if there was any chance they might display wee little clothes or a baby bonnet. We hadn't mentioned children, since our phantom baby had come and gone, a year before. Milo had forgotten the whole subject in the excitement of the wedding, his movie, the new apartment. I thought he had changed his mind, was not ready. He was young, only twenty-seven. But I was old. I was twenty-seven, too.

Then one morning we left our building together and there was a woman holding a newborn infant no bigger than a heartbeat. Its thin bare arms hung over its mother's shoulder as she stood talking in the sunlight to a shopkeeper. The fingers looked ancient and translucent and just as we passed, the child bleated, a cry so tentative and blind that it broke my heart.

"Ohhh," I said, stricken.

Milo turned to see why my voice was strange.

"Let's have a baby now," I said. "Let's just have one."

He stopped walking and checked my face. "Okay," he said. He kissed me on the head and took my hand so I wondered why I had ever worried, or thought I couldn't tell him.

"Scary to think about," he said later. "That's why."

It scared us both, the idea, that we could make a person, then have to be responsible for it. "I'm afraid I'd drop it," Milo said. Me, I was afraid of the fat. I had creeps about fat the way some people do about mice. The thought of pregnancy made me picture some instant sprouting of an enormous abdominal pod, like a snap-on unit.

As if fat was the half of it. Jesus.

I had another miscarriage in the middle of that year. "We don't know why this happens," the first specialist told me and Milo. He was an old white man with moles on his eyelids. "Sometimes," he said, "the partners' cells are not compatible," and explained how one person's cells kill the other person's, or something like that. About the previous so-called chemical pregnancy, he had this to say: "It usually means that something was wrong with the child, and it was *nature's way* of taking care of it." He looked like he thought it was for the best. That nature, in our case, was doing its job with our incompatible cells. Maybe this was true. But maybe he was a flaming fuck. We got out of there and Milo was furious. Veins stood out on his temples. "You get a new doctor!" he said, pointing his finger at me. Practically shouting till he saw my face.

We were so sad. We could barely speak of it.

"I got a new doctor," I told him that night.

He nodded. "Good," he said. He was still upset, shaking his head. We sat on the couch and I leaned against him. "Don't worry, sugarfoot," he said. "It'll be okay." He kept me near him and treated me gingerly, as if I were breakable. There was nothing to say. *What if we never had a child?* Not out loud. *Our cells were killing each other.* We drank a bottle of wine down to the end. Milo poured till the last drips fell into his glass. He fingered the depression in the bottom of the bottle and showed me the way the glass rose up inside, like a hill.

"In French this part is called *le mont de désespoir*," he said, and didn't need to translate. "Don't despair," he said. "There's plenty more." He opened another bottle and tried to cheer me up.

It was harder for me than it was for him. For him it was all sort of... not real. He was always Mr. Optimist. He just went ahead with his days, making *Slope!*, doing his ads, his sports commentary.

Me, I spent all my time in the waiting room. Hours and hours of many days in doctors' offices lying on cold tables. I tell you, it's not romantic. It reminds you of how you are a mammal. All the tests were on me, all the unmentionable exploration. I was a good sport about it. I modeled the paper gowns. I said the blood pressure cuff would make a high-fashion accessory. I was a trouper. Milo said so. "Hey, Champ, we'll win this one, too, you'll see." He kept my spirits up. He coached me along, made me feel safe and sound. We were happy, weren't we? he said. We were together. That was what mattered. The reason it was taking so long, he liked to say, was because we were making a deluxe model child. When our baby finally got here it would be perfect. But other times he got sick of the whole subject. He'd go out of town on crucial days, or leave the room when I started crying, go watch TV. "Jeez, Charlotte, you're becoming such a mope," he said once. "You're so gloomy half the time."

He'll go get a happy fruitful new wife, I thought.

He did his best, I guess. I don't know how to weight the good parts and the bad parts. He had his own challenges during that time. Darryl, for example, really gave Milo the hard-sell treatment. Not to mention headaches, and food for thought. Also a new career. That was thanks to Darryl, too.

We were trying for a baby, but I think maybe something else had to be born first. Namely: *Cade, Rebel Fury.*

22.

"Charlotte! C'mon and have coffee with me." This was Darryl one spring morning, coming up behind me on the street as I was walking home from the gym, taking my sweaty elbow. "Whattya say? C'mon, let's go have a chat. A business chat."

"Sure, okay," I said.

"Quack," said Darryl, behind me. He was copying my walk, which is splay-footed, like a duck, with the shoulders back. "Quack, quack."

"Darryl, cut it out!" He made me laugh.

"Quack, quack," he said, toes out and waddling. We walked like ducks into a narrow coffee shop run by old Greek men with no time for words that are not on the menu.

"What?" the counterman said.

"Coffee light, extra sugar," said Darryl.

"Black," I said.

Darryl looked hard at me when I said that, a little grin on his face. Even coffee was a race joke to Darryl. When we sat down, he said: "Are you ready?"

"For what?"

"I got a deal for Milo he can't resist."

"Why are you talking to me, then?" I said. "Talk to him."

"Because," Darryl told me, "unlike your husband, I know you will give the black man a hearing."

"That's not fair."

"Aw, c'mon, Charlotte, allow a little levity," he said.

Darryl had a movie he wanted Milo for. He started telling me about it, painting the air with his hands, framing words with his arms like a big screen. "A rebel leader, okay?" he said. "Cade. He's a human from another time, the future, right?" Darryl told me the whole plot: alien masters, human slaves, fiery battles. It sounded far-fetched to me, but his excitement was contagious.

"Have you got anything on paper?"

"Yeah." He reached into the breast pocket of his jacket, pulled out an envelope, and handed it to me.

"I'll give it to him," I said.

"Thank you, Miss Scarlett. I mean: Charlotte." He batted his eyelashes at me. "Rhymes," he said coquettishly, and paid the bill.

Milo and I were eating dinner that night when I told him about it. "Darryl gave me something for you to look at. He has a deal you can't resist." I started to give him the envelope, but Milo put his fork down on his plate. He looked at me, chewing. He didn't seem to be swallowing. He bounced his head in a way I now recognized as a prelude to fury.

"What," he said, chopping his sentences, "are you doing. Trying to tamper around. With my professional life?"

"No, I—"

"I don't go telling you your agency is lousy or that your bookers are incompetent. Do I?"

"But Darryl is—"

"I don't want to hear about 'Darryl this, or Darryl that,'" he said. "Darryl is not what you would call bona fide." He pushed back his chair.

"Look. I'm really sorry," I said.

He sat back and calmed down. "Listen, forget Darryl," Milo said. "He's a smart guy. But he's not part of the system and he never will be."

"Why?"

"Because he refuses to play the game."

"Which game are you talking about?" I asked him.

"You cannot refuse to stand when they play 'The Star-Spangled Banner,' for starters," Milo said. "You don't give the finger to the flag. You don't get anywhere by sticking it to the powers that be." Then he said, "Much as you might like to."

"Would you like to?"

"Let's just say I never would've gotten anywhere if I stuck it to half the people who pissed me off," Milo said. He stood up and cleared his plate, then he picked up the envelope from Darryl and threw it in the garbage. But the next day, tidying some papers, I noticed that he had fished it out and opened it.

Still, whatever was in that envelope did not change his mind. What changed it, just six months later, had to do with *Slope!* and the way in which it bombed.

That movie was terrible. A disaster. We burned the reviews, but I remember them, one in particular. "In the course of this embarrassing film, Johnny Miller, a stumblebum skier (Milo Robicheaux) who wins gold medals by accident, tries to help the members of the Soviet Winter Olympics team escape to freedom in the West, pursued by the KGB down every ski slope in Europe. The fine, real-life Olympian Milo Robicheaux is not memorable in the role."

Poor Milo. It was the worst time. The only lucky thing was that nobody—nobody in *the public*—seemed to notice. Or care. Hardly anybody got a chance to see the movie, which closed in a week, or even remember it had anything to do with Milo.

Except Darryl. He was there right from the minute the credits faded out in the screening room high above Columbus Circle, and the house-lights came up to reveal a polite group of studio suits and distributors, and—luckily—nobody else we knew. How he found out about the screening, which was private, or got himself invited, I never discovered, but there he was, coming over to us through the crowd, with the sympathy of a funeral director on his face. "Say hey, my brother."

We got out of there, Darryl shaking his head in pity the entire elevator ride down.

"This is a travesty, Robicheaux!" he said, as soon as we were on the street. "This cannot happen! I will not allow them to bring you down. Because they have tried. Tried to make you a laughingstock."

"Which would be an accurate description," said Milo, sunk into himself, not looking at us.

"A buffoon!"

"Also right on point."

"A turkey! They made you look like a turkey! And that's one thing you are not!"

"Don't put any money on that," Milo said bitterly. "Check at Thanksgiving to see am I still around." He was furious, walking fast. We passed a parking sign and he whacked it violently with the flat of his palm.

"That's right," said Darryl, "that's right. You got a right to feel that way."

Milo cursed.

"I'm with you," Darryl said. "I'm on your side."

I was keeping quiet. I knew Milo better now than to talk. Darryl was between us. At some point he got me by one arm and Milo by the other, taking up the whole sidewalk, as if we were his pontoons, and told Milo his present agents were charlatans. That the whole talent management establishment was run by *those slave traders and those albino demons in stuffed suits*; that they never would find a role suitable for a great black talent like Milo; that they wouldn't think of putting him up for great parts.

"They don't think about the black man as a leading man!"

"Apparently not."

"They think of us as dopes and dope fiends. Houseboys and homeboys."

Milo laughed but it was still a bitter laugh. Darryl talked and preached: *They will not aggressively fight for you to be a leading man! No! But I will! Darryl Haynes will fight!*

He was right, I thought. I was rooting for him.

Milo was listening, too. He had started out grim and embarrassed, hands deep in his pockets, jaw hard. But as Darryl talked, Milo began to loosen up, murmuring *Yeah, I know. I see what you're saying.* We left Columbus Circle far behind us, walked all the way up Broadway till I thought my feet would be pounded up through my legs into the bones of my spine, they hurt so much in their spike heels. I wanted to say *Let's stop somewhere and get a drink.* I wanted to sit down. I was on the far side of the conversation now. Darryl had his body turned to Milo in such a way, walking, that I was shut out.

"Unless something drastic happens," Darryl was saying, "Milo Robicheaux will be doomed to a career full of movies like *Slope!* and *Nope!* and *Can't Cope!* and *Ain't I a Nobody?*"

That got Milo. His real laugh was back. He started swapping bad movie titles with Darryl.

"I Shot the Pope!"

"I Ain't No Mope!"

"Girls I Have Groped!"

"Dopes on Dope!"

Everybody was laughing now. Milo was half giddy, almost relieved.

"You need somebody who knows the ropes!" Darryl said. "And no fighter alive knows the ropes like Darryl Haynes, the Boxer with Brains."

"Look, Haynes," Milo said, "what I don't understand is—"

"Hey, now you look, Robicheaux," said Darryl. "Open your eyes: You can stick with White and Company and see what gorilla monkey suit they got for you next—or: You can come home to your black brother." He opened his arms wide to Milo, and Milo laughed. But then Darryl got that undertaker look on his face again. "I hate to say this, Milo," he said, "and maybe I shouldn't: But what, exactly, have you done to uplift the race since you got your fame? And I don't mean little sports clinic here, little black-tie thing there, I mean payback time. To the community. Buy Black. Hire Black. That's something we all have to do. It's a stone responsibility."

Milo stopped walking. He turned and looked at Darryl. "Why is it more my responsibility than, say, hers?" he said, pointing at me.

"You got a point. You got ten points," said Darryl. "But I don't worry about the white male, the white female. With all respect to your wife. I am not about that." He looked right at me then, smiling.

Milo checked my face. I left it neutral, since this was between him and Darryl, I thought, had nothing to do with me.

"My point is about payback time," Darryl said. "And you're the one who's gonna get paid, in the end, you'll see." He got Milo around the neck again, in the brotherly embrace. "Wake up! It's 1983, and Hollywood has not shot a film by a black man since *Shaft*. Since 1971! Twelve years! You can change that. I already have a part eyed out for you. Not some *Negro* part but a real gig. A gig to make you bigger than big. Bigger than Sidney Poitier. Big as Arnold. Big as Sly and Clint. You say the word and it's yours."

"You don't have any such thing," said Milo.

"Right here in this pocket," said Darryl, patting his back flank. "And in my other pocket, I have backers already." He named a big boxing promoter and a soul singer, household words, both of them.

"You got those guys?" asked Milo.

"In the palm of my hand. Like a moth to flame," Darryl said solemnly. "On the end of the hook."

"Long as I'm not the worm," Milo said.

"You *are* the worm! You're the worm and you're the flame! You're it! You're whatever you want to be! Can't you see that?" Darryl pulled Milo onto a bench right in the center divider of Broadway. We sat there with cars roaring around us and I have to say I was rooting for Darryl. I thought he was right. "They have put you in the jock box!" Darryl said. "You have two choices with the man: the jock box or the lock box. Now, what you may not realize is: Half the time, the jock box *is* a lock box."

"But I'm an athlete," Milo said.

"You *were* an athlete," Darryl said. "But that's just a trampoline to spring you to something else, to Mr. Movie Star. If they haven't gotten that across to you, then you need me to do their job."

"I'll think about it," said Milo.

"Look, Robicheaux, you have a white wife, the least you can do is get yourself a black handler. Right, Charlotte?" Darryl winked at me.

Milo laughed, but he did not know what to think about what Darryl said. The jock box. The lock box. The black man as the leading man. At home, later, he said, "Maybe I'm not an actor."

"Believe me," I told him, "you are."

"Jed and Mark have always seemed fine to me."

"Since when was just fine good enough for you, Milo?"

He thought about that. Milo did not like to say anything bad about people he knew. Not Jed and Mark. Not Darryl now, either. He was sweet as pie to everybody, which is the way he was raised.

Bobbie Robicheaux, raised the same way, had no such qualms. She thought Jed and Mark were fools. That was her word. "Any agent that can't find classier work for you than a chewing gum ad is a first-class fool," she said. "You're better than that junk, Milo." She had come to visit

us, and this time, she brought Marcus. I'd never met him; he hadn't come
to the wedding. "I dumped him, for a while," Bobbie said. "We weren't
getting along." They were back together now and seemed to be getting
along just fine, the weekend they stayed with us, holding hands at dinner,
at the café where we had breakfast.

Marcus was a slight dark man with horn-rimmed glasses and a thin
beard trimmed close to his face. He looked owly and didn't say much, but
when Bobbie spoke he smiled and nodded, watching her intently.

They were talking about Darryl, how he wanted Milo for a client.

"So why wouldn't you give a guy like that a chance?" Bobbie said to
Milo.

"Because he's got no track record," he said.

"Someone gave you a chance once upon a time," Bobbie said.

"That's sports. There's a hard cold time trial you can't argue with,"
Milo said. "And anyway, why should I cast my lot with this guy because
he's black and I'm black—"

"That's not our point," Bobbie said.

"It's Haynes's point, then," Milo said. "Why is that a reason?"

"Why don't you find out for yourself?" Marcus said quietly.

The three of us looked at him. He was smoking, leaning back with
his elbows up against the back of the booth where we sat. "It's not
like you have to bail out of your gig with these other guys, the establishment guys," he said. "Stick with them, moonlight with this Darryl
fellow."

"Agents don't like a two-timer," I said. "I know someone who tried it."

"You'd better not try it. Not on me," Milo said, joking around. "Better
not."

"What I'm trying to say," said Marcus, in his slow voice, "is Milo here
needs one agent to represent his interests in one world and another agent
for his interests in another. Nothing wrong with that."

"Two worlds is what's wrong," I piped up, Miss Righteous.

"I hear that," Marcus said, as if he'd heard it one time too many. Bobbie
smiled at me, though, and I felt complimented, like an A student.

"Marcus is right," Bobbie said. "Darryl is your man."

"I don't know," Milo said. I could see he wanted badly to please his sister, but he thought she was motivated by politics. "They operate in a different world," he said, when she and Marcus left. "Prisons, teenage

mothers. All that. They don't get what it's like." He thought that was Darryl's problem, too. Milo really didn't know what to do about Darryl, about Jed and Mark, his future. Bobbie and Marcus had powers to influence him, I saw. What he said was: "If my sister thinks me in a gum ad is bad, wait till she sees *Slope!*"

She did see the picture, that first week. "Lucky nobody reads reviews," she said. But Milo read them. *This embarrassing film.* It was those words on top of his sister's that carried him into the arms of Darryl Haynes. Sometimes in my more paranoid moments I have even wondered whether Darryl didn't write the reviews himself, for that reason. Still, the critics were right. *Slope!* was a dog.

Cade: Rebel Fury, on the other hand, was a sci-fi thriller blockbuster. *Rebel Fury* was Milo's next movie. He played Cade, the alien fighter, and has played that character in sequels ever since. You will remember Cade, the defiant captive held on the planet Cryos, working at hard labor, mining the Ore. The Ore was the source of power for the alien Cryotrons; it gave them strength and brilliance. They drank it in liquid form, dissolved in a glowing blue solution. The Ore could only be melted at the human body temperature of 98.6. Since the Cryotrons had no heat source of their own, being bloodless, they depended on slaves—human beings captured from Earth—to mine it.

People often tell us, with total recall, of the first time they saw Milo as Cade, his noble face ashed and sweating, melting the blue Ore with the sheer warmth of his hands. The most famous scene, of course, is the one where Milo as Cade picks up a stolen goblet of liquid cryonite and drinks it, only to discover that the Ore does nothing. It has no intrinsic power at all but is addictive and narcotic for the Cryotrons. With this discovery, Cade becomes a rebel and leads the captive miners to escape and, ultimately, to victory.

Cade: Rebel Fury was born from that deal in Darryl's pocket, the one that spent time in our wastebasket. It was a treatment for a script supposedly written by one of Darryl's clients, a kid Darryl had met years before at City College, who was, unfortunately (allegedly), now dead from a drug problem. I always wondered if the kid was actually Darryl. But

Darryl said no, it was a kid with a wish to see Cade live on film. He got his wish, but not a credit, I noticed.

How Darryl ever put the whole thing together I don't know. He wasn't just brokering between parties. He was the whole party. He got writers, he got the script, he got Milo for the lead, and he got the money. The story is that he was telling the Soul Singer that he had money from the Boxing Promoter, and vice versa. Telling them he had Milo, and telling Milo he had them, when, in fact, he had neither. The minute the Business Suits showed any reluctance, Darryl would say: *What's the matter, don't you deal with black people?*

Milo fired his agents and hired Darryl, who got to work right away. He got Milo a freelance contract with the Network, so Milo could do a story a month, and keep an office. We could easily afford it, what with our savings, and my paychecks. I don't know what Darryl lived off, that year, unless it was Milo. The two of them lived and breathed that movie. Milo was helping with the script, with raising money, with choosing locations. He took acting classes. Jesus. I had to listen to him practice. Milo as Hamlet. Milo as Stanley Kowalski. He went around saying *Get thee to a nunnery*. It was funny. Milo in the kitchen with his hand on his heart. But he was good; he really had something. It was unsettling, how completely he could change himself, menacing and bellowing *Stella!* or saying his lines from Cade: *I will spare your life, Cold King, but not your power.* He would rearrange his face. "Look," he said, "my mask of fury," and he'd harden his mouth and narrow his eyes, so you got chills. And then he'd be right back to Milo in the kitchen, smiling at me. You could see him learning, working at it, making himself up as he went along. What bothers me now is this: If he was born to it, as the critics said, how do I know what was Milo acting and what was just Milo, all these years? They said he had a natural gift.

23.

When I knew I was pregnant I kept it a secret. Even from Milo. I held the news to myself the way you hold some complicated food in your mouth, deciphering the flavors. I was afraid and full of hope. I was sleepy but couldn't sleep. It had taken so long, two years; telling would jinx it, I was sure.

The day I finally told him, I was six weeks gone, twenty-nine years old. We were surrounded by packing boxes and the maelstrom of moving. The plan was: go to L.A. for the shooting of *Cade*, see how we liked it, keep the place in New York. We were sorting through our things, to see what to take from nearly three years of living there and what to leave. Milo was sitting exhausted on the couch with his feet resting on a stack of magazines. I went to sit next to him.

"I'm still not really sure about this move," I said.

"We'll see," he said. "I think you'll like L.A."

"I never liked it," I said.

He twisted my hair around two fingers. "It'll be a good change," he said, and lowered his voice, peering over his nose at me, imitating his father: *Change is good! Change is progress! You gotta grow and expand and live!*

"There are going to be a lot of changes," I told him. "A lot of growing and expanding."

"Yeah." He smiled at me. "In L.A. I'm going to take up surfing. I am going to say 'dudes' constantly."

"I mean, sometimes ten changes a day."

"What?"

"From what I know," I said, sitting up, "you have to change them ten, twenty times a day, for like, two years."

"What!?" He was afraid to jump to conclusions, trying to make me say the words. When I said them—*It's true. I am. Six weeks along*—he closed his eyes and put his face in his hands. Then he looked at me through his fingers, smiling. "Really?"

Neither of us could discuss it, not until the top button of my slacks safely refused to close anymore. We were superstitious. Once, walking past a shop with rocking chairs and tiny socks and shoes in the window, Milo put his hands to my eyes like horse-blinders, so I wouldn't see. "Don't look," he said.

I was dying to look. Milo, too. We steeled ourselves and hustled by.

But then we were safe. The doctor said so. We went into a dark room with her and I lay down on yet another table, and she hooked me up to a kind of television to show us: a tiny jumping creature on the black-and-white screen.

"Look," Milo said, hardly breathing. "Oh, will you look at that."

There Hallie was, like a fish, like a bungee jumper, like a pearl floating. Her spine was a chain of tiny bone beads. Head bulging, belly bulging. We couldn't get enough of looking at her, listening through the stethoscope to the wet echo of her heart beating under mine.

Milo couldn't get over it. He told everybody he saw, tollbooth attendants and waiters. He couldn't stop handling me around the belly, polishing the rounding-out part. *Hello in there!* he said to my middle. *It's your dad! You listen to me now!* It was funny. I was constantly breaking down in a mess of giggles. Milo would put his lips to my belly and call: "Hey! Kid! Bend those knees! We're gonna have you on skis by the time you're weaned, you hear me?! You just hold that tuck, kid. Don't forget!" It was so funny and darling. Most of the pregnancy, Milo was working on *Cade*, but in between takes, he'd go to his trailer and call me on the phone. *Charlotte? How're you doing, babe? Are you feeling okay? Are you resting?* Or he'd ask me to come with him to the set. I'd sit there and watch and chat up the crew. I even have a small part in the first *Cade* film myself. You can see me in the mine scenes, an extra captive heating the Ore, my hair stringy around my face. I accused Darryl of making me look bad on purpose. "You're a slave," he said. "It's not a glamorous job."

I watched Darryl on the set one day. He was always there for Milo, like a trainer in his fighter's corner. They were shooting the scene where Cade is thrown in an underground cell—an *oubliette*, they called it—by the evil Emperor. Guards toss him food and water. Just a few rays of light come down to illuminate Cade's troubled face. Before the first take Darryl got Milo off away from the set. He had a big white towel around Milo's neck. He massaged his shoulders, gave him drinks from a water bottle, squatted down on his haunches in front of him, talking to him. I was sitting right there and I heard him.

"Listen to me, listen to me now," Darryl said to Milo. "Think about Dr. King in the Birmingham jail. You think of that, you hear me? What he said. How he felt. Did you read that? What I gave you? The letter from Birmingham?"

Milo nodded.

"Think about him, let's see that on your face, what King wrote: 'The question is not whether we will be extremists but what kind of extremists will we be?' Remember that part? Cade's an *extremist*. Right? He's gonna bust out. You put that in your face, you feel it down there in that jail."

Milo listened. He kept his eyes averted but he nodded. When they called action Milo jumped up and got ready. He sat in the dark like a coiled snake with a blue half-light on his face from above, a leak of sky coming in, and water dripping down stones behind him. The camera stayed on his face for a long time. In that shot, watching later, I saw things about Milo. Desperation and rage and resolve. It didn't seem to be acting. He didn't talk. He just sat, swallowed. He was sweating and his fingers worked the flesh of his face. But not too much. He was subtle; riveting, really.

And then he burst out with a roar. Cade broke through the top of the cage and that was the end of that sequence. They said cut and Darryl was right there, pounding Milo's back, saying "You did it, you aced it, you got it," collaring his neck.

Milo always had a coach. He had these talents—skiing, and now acting, too—but he needed somebody to tell him techniques, things he wanted to learn. Right now Darryl was Milo's coach. He was always around, always calling Milo and sending stuff—books and tapes and documents. The piles in the bedroom, in the study, by the TV, were getting higher. Malcolm X and Eldridge Cleaver and biographies of King and W.E.B. Du Bois. Milo didn't spend too much time with it that I could tell, not then, anyway. The two of them were thick as thieves, obsessed with the movie. It was good for Milo, I thought, to have a friend like Darryl.

I was too tired all the time to pay much attention to *Cade*. I napped in Milo's trailer, not noticing that I was gradually becoming nothing but an incubator. I couldn't work as a model, not after showing in the third month. I developed a habit of standing with my back swayed and my stomach stuck forward so nobody would think I was merely fat, which is how it looked to me. It wore me out, all that bulk, that napping, waiting for Milo, waiting for lunch, waiting for dinner, waiting for nine months to be up. I missed Claire.

"Hello, Claire, it's me, the Incubator."

"Yes?" Claire said, in her office voice, then whispering, "I can't talk. I'll call you back." She was busy being a lawyer, a prosecutor in the D.A.'s office, and was married now, to her boyfriend, Tim, who had always reminded me of myself in one major way—how much he loved Claire, and depended on her. I liked Tim, but he was always around, cramping her conversation. It wasn't the same.

I filled up my time reading books that described the formation of a human being, week by week. In the twelfth and thirteenth weeks, I picked out carpeting for the living room of our marvelous new Malibu manse, while somewhere down in central Charlotte, ears were growing, buds of fingers and toes. In the twentieth week, when the pictures in my book showed that what I carried was a luminous alien in a gossamer sac, I glued glow-stars to the ceiling of the baby's room. In the twenty-eighth week, I tried to remember how to knit, laboring over a microscopic white sweater till the wool turned gray. When it was time, in week 30, for hair follicles to form and sprout, I was going to classes to learn the special breathing, closing my eyes and thinking of eyelashes, wishing them long and luxurious, like Milo's.

All along, my dreams were strange, every night teeming with weird life: babies being born from the top of my head; or the foot of the baby sticking straight up from my middle and then turning into a submarine periscope, spying on me; or Milo delivering the baby instead of me. Ha. Even I knew my unspoken panic when I dreamed it. That no one would recognize me as the mother, that I would not recognize myself. I never said any of this or told anyone. Which is a good idea, sometimes, to just shut up and keep your thoughts to yourself. I wish I'd learned that then, since, as soon as I saw her, I knew she was mine, and I was hers.

Halsey Jane Robicheaux, called Hallie, was born in Cedars-Sinai Hospital on March 12, 1985. *Funny-looking as a bald squirrel*, Milo said, shy to admit she was beautiful as nothing else in this world, with eyes dark blue as the sky at night, pricks of light in their centers. We loved her so much, Hallie, Up to here, as she herself now says about love, up to the universe and back. She was breathtaking. The smell of her could break your heart.

All I ever wanted, I thought.

Milo took the baby from the nurse. He was there in the delivery room. He was the first one of us to hold her. He knew how right away. She fit in his hands like a bird. His face was full of wonder and raw feeling. He couldn't swallow. Couldn't stop smiling. We got her home and he lay her on the bed, stretched out alongside her, this big man gazing down. She yawned with her mouth in an O.

"You sleepy girl," he said. "You tired peanut." She closed her eyes and he put his face right down next to hers. "Shhhh," he said. "That's right."

We stared down at her sleeping in her pink and white bed, her tiny heart of a mouth sucking milk in dreams. I picked her up and her arms flew out like wings. Her head rested in the crook of my neck, the crook of my elbow, the circle of my arm while I lay feeding her. Milo sat with her sleeping on his chest, her wrinkly, newborn fist tight around one of his fingers. She was the gold color of good bread. Her hair was black and fine. I whorled it around with my free hand while I fed her. I fed her constantly. I was a human restaurant. I was up with her nursing in the dark, walking her up and down the halls, singing lullabies whose words I somehow knew. *When you wake, you shall have, all the pretty little horses.*

I seemed to know a lot of things. Lullabies. How to nurse. It was the best feeling. Sexual, practically. I could get arrested for saying so, but it's true; I don't know what else to say it comes close to. How that baby roots and latches on ferociously, desperate. The pull of that suck goes right down through you and you feel it like you feel your own desire, in all the same places. The heart especially. I loved it. I loved her. Her hand, with its pink chips of fingernail, reached and held on, kneading my skin. She was ecstatic, swallowing and murmuring and falling asleep with crooked smiles on her milky lips. She was drunken. She was smitten. She was gorgeous. Love was welling up and choking me. I leaked milk just thinking of her. Really. I'd be in the kitchen and she'd be off in her crib and I'd have a thought of her and right away my shirt would be soaked. It was beyond my control. My daughter. God, Hallie. If you knew how much your mother loves you.

And your father.

He got tears in his eyes all the time, looking at Hallie. He gave her so many names, endearments. Miss Lady, Sweetcake, Hallie Ballie Bee. He gave her one of his fingers to hold. "She likes me," he said. When she got colicky, he carried her up and down, talking to her, telling her things.

One night he showed her the stars. "Look up there," he said, standing with her at the window. "Planets." He said all their nine names, Mars to Pluto. "The way you remember them, is by this: My Very Educated Mother Just Served Us Nine Peanuts." I swear Hallie was listening to him, four weeks old, not crying as long as he talked, kept walking. "You say it now. Thatta girl." *My Very Educated Mother Just Served Us Nine Peanuts.* "My own educated mother taught me that. Your grandma."

Milo's parents came when we were just home from the hospital. Hattie couldn't wait, she said, she was trembling. She put her arms around me, first thing, before she even looked at the baby, and she said, "Charlotte, honey. We're so proud of you."

I felt proud, because of the way she said it. I don't know why. Women have babies all day long. Big deal. But it was, it felt big to me, like an accomplishment. And the way Hattie hugged me made me think: *Maybe she could even love me, someday.*

Hattie was a wreck over that baby. With Hallie in her arms, her face had no reserve, no guard up. She never quite recovered the annoyed way she used to have with me. *Sit sit sit, sit now, I'll do it.* She was always making a fool of herself baby-talking and going through the repertoire of singsongs that she had: *skinamarink a dink* and *maresey doats.* Nonsense like that.

Mr. Robicheaux, too. Milton. But not in public. Not at first. He was formal. He said he thought he'd like to be called Grandfather, not Pa or Gramps. But one morning I started into Hallie's room and saw him looking at her. He didn't know I was watching. He picked her up with two fingers behind her head, her small form lying the length of his forearms. He was whispering to her: *Yes, ma'am. Yessir. Yes, ma'am, yes.* I got my camera and came back. He didn't hear me. I took his picture. As soon as he heard the shutter click, he straightened up, put Hallie back in the crib, pushed his glasses back, cleared his throat. "Very cute, very cute," he said, as if I'd caught him at something secret. We have the picture. It shows his face in profile with hers, both of them wrinkly, old and new. I'm always struck by the lovesick look on Milton's face, when I see that picture. Those Robicheaux men, you know. Softies for a baby.

They stayed two weeks. Hattie taught me everything she knew about germ prevention and swaddling. She pampered me with naps and praised me for no reason. "Look at her, Milo, look how Charlotte changes that didie." It started to get to me after a while, the lispy baby-talk way she had with Hallie, but I was sorry when she left. It was right around that time that I started to love her. More than my own mother. I'm not sorry to say it.

After three months, Barbara and Arthur had not come to meet Hallie. Conestoga was a two-hour plane ride, but they couldn't get to L.A. Because, Barbara said, "I don't know if I'm, I'm not sure I'm really *ready,* and you know the first weeks are very trying, tiring, I mean, and..."

Ready for what? She hurt me.

After five months, after Diana shamed her into using one of the tickets I sent, my mother finally met Hallie. My father, she said, had thrown his back out and couldn't come after all. His back apparently remained out for about a year, since that's how old Hallie was when they finally met.

"I'm so surprised," Barbara whispered. "She's very, she's almost, she's pink." I did not say *she will darken with age, like cherry wood.* I did not say *Wait until the melanin kicks in.* I watched her. She gazed down at her perfect, black-haired granddaughter and traced her salmon-colored fingernail gently down Hallie's cheek. She picked her up and held her tenderly, hummed, "Swing Low, Sweet Chariot." Hallie looked up at her with big eyes dark as a seal's.

"Mom," I said, "don't sing that."

"Why?"

"Just . . . I can't explain." I shook my head. I hurt her feelings so she had to leave the room for a minute. I shouldn't have been so critical of her. She meant well, she really did, and she loved Hallie, I could see it in her face. But I didn't want her around. She brought miniature T-shirts from her church that said "Little Lamb of God" on them. She sang "Jesus Loves the Little Children." *Red and yellow black and white, they are precious in His sight, Jesus loves the little children of the world.*

I took Hallie from her, into another room.

"Well, I was just trying to be helpful," she said, following me with her furious smile on.

"It's time to feed her," I said, though it wasn't.

She watched me nurse. It was excruciating. She averted her eyes and said, "I never did that, you know, with you children. It wasn't considered sanitary."

"I could boil my breasts," I said. "That would be sanitary."

This was not funny to her at all. She looked disgusted. Just the word "breasts" was a shock for her to hear, but I didn't care. *Breasts breasts breasts.* I could say it as much as I wanted now. *Intercourse!* I was married and a mother. She left after only a couple of days, and went back up to Conestoga to report to my father on their surprisingly pink new granddaughter.

24.

We had a baby now. This changes everything. No one realizes. They tell you about the afterbirth but not about the aftermath. Not about how the sneaky baby rearranges you thoroughly, like snow in the night, transforming everything familiar, every twig and blade of grass. This is what happened to us when Hallie was born. She snowed us in. And right at the same time, Milo became Cade. He was captive of evil bloodless aliens, and I was captive of a tiny honey baby. Everything changed at once. It all whacked out at once.

Hallie was born, and *Cade* opened two months later. It was nonstop *Milomania*. The *Hollywood Reporter* coined the term, Milomania. You could not find a single freeway without a *Cade* billboard. You could not turn on the TV without seeing my husband on some morning show, some afternoon show. Milo became Cade, and everybody knows that story.

What was so brilliant about the movie was that it was science fiction. The slaves were played by all races and ages of people. But by casting Milo as the rebel leader, and Klaus Krieger, a man white as teeth, in the role of the Cryotron Emperor, the story of *Cade, Rebel Fury* took on significance much closer to home than a galaxy far, far away.

Even Milo didn't see how powerful it was, not until the day after the opening when we went downtown to watch the movie in a real city theater, anonymously. It was Milo's idea. He put on a baseball cap and sunglasses. We went at lunchtime with Hallie, eight weeks old. She slept through the whole thing. It was during the part where the rebels are fighting, smashing the aliens with chunks of Ore and pickaxes, that we heard the murmurs in the audience: *Yeah, brother! Kill that white son of a bitch!* And in the scene where the rebels got the Ore, some in the audience shouted: *Drink it down, brothers! Get the power!* When the glowing blue liquid did nothing, when all that superior strength and brainpower was found to be a charade, a silence came over the people watching. *Uh-huh,* somebody said. *That's the truth.*

We walked out of the theater before the lights came up and blinked. "Holy shit," Milo said. He kept saying that. "Holy shit."

"What?"

"Darryl was right," he said finally.

"About what?"

"He said it's more than a movie." Milo was shaking his head.

"What does he say it is, then?"

"A bombshell."

After the first weekend, in Los Angeles and Detroit, Chicago and New York, police details were posted outside theaters in black neighborhoods where the movie was playing. Disturbances were anticipated. (They *should* be disturbed, Darryl said.) People stayed peaceful, but they were not calm. They lined up around the block for *Cade.* White teenagers were some of Cade's biggest fans. When asked by a reporter for the *Times* why Cade was a hero, a white kid said: "He's a *rebel*, man. A human rebel." Whereas the black kids who were interviewed all said something along the lines of: "He's a great black leader." The movie was not what anybody would call a critical smash ("This heavy-handed allegory stars the magnetic black Olympian Milo Robicheaux..." one said), but it made $168.2 million and, for a few years, a hero out of my husband. From *Cade, Rebel Fury* was born Milo Robicheaux, the New Black Messiah. Or so some people seemed to believe.

"What's next for you, Milo?"

From the living room couch Hallie and I watched Milo on TV, fielding questions from a daytime talk-show host. "What's next for this new star? He's an athlete, a screen artist, a born crossover crowd-pleaser," the woman said. "Can politics be far behind?" *There's Daddy*, I whispered to Hallie, made her wave her little hand at him. She seemed to recognize him, honestly, she did. I told him later how her eyes got big and she bi-cycled her legs when she heard him answer.

"Well, gee, Marsha, I don't rule anything out," Milo said. "Certainly it would be an honor to be involved in public service. At the moment, I'm concentrating on my career as an actor—"

"But just tell us, what are the issues that most concern you?" The host was a black woman named Marsha Mays, and she leaned toward Milo with great expectations in her eyes.

"I'd have to say, Marsha—and this is just hypothetical, of course—that I'd be interested in the health and well-being of all people, and of course, as Cade says in the movie: *justice*." Milo raised his eyebrows and smiled at the camera, as if all the audience knew exactly what he meant by that line.

"Justice," Marsha repeated solemnly.

It was in this way that people began to look at Milo not as some nov-elty skier or B-movie actor but as somebody who might be the answer to their prayers. And it was in this way that Milo was set up to think he was hearing prayers for all the usual reasons: deity. Power of the genie-in-a-bottle kind. If people like Marsha Mays and kids on the street think you're a god, or a savior, how long does it take before you believe them?

Darryl hired Milo a staff. A manager, a secretary, an accountant, a travel agent, a driver, a publicist. He offered to hire us a baby nurse but we didn't want one. *We're Hallie's parents*, we said. *We'll take care of her*. He got people to hire us baby-sitters when we needed them. He hired Milo a bodyguard. Every single one of the staff was a black person. *We're black owned and operated!* Darryl said, and we were all proud of that fact, me included. The publicist was part of an exclusive company called the Ray Group, headed by a woman named Liz Ray. Milo affectionately called her Lizard, and I spoke to her on the phone all the time. She was always working two or three phones simultaneously and talking about Milo's needs. *He'll need his driver at six* A.M. *He'll need to be out of there by two-fifteen because he needs to meet his trainer at two-thirty. He'll need you to respect his private life. Absolutely not. He'll need to see the ques-tions in advance.* She booked Milo everywhere. On the daytime shows, on radio, on sitcoms. He was on Johnny Carson, then on Cosby, playing him-self. Milo was thrilled by it, so excited. He never acted as if it were ordinary, all that press attention. He was still normal, I thought, not some Hollywood slicko. "I'm so happy for you," I said. "Isn't it great?"

But actually, it wasn't, entirely. I was having a hard time. We had a new baby. We had a bodyguard. We couldn't go anywhere or have any privacy because Milo was famous, and I was—threatened, if you want to know the truth. The more you saw Milo, the harder it was to see me. I felt transparent as the wings of a housefly.

"You don't want anyone to know about me," I said one night, after nearly three weeks of Milomania. I was reading about Milo in a magazine, looking for some mention of *his wife, Charlotte Halsey.* Just a hint of a family. His parents were in there, with quotes. *His mother, Hattie, said her son was always something of a showman.* His sister was quoted, too. But there was nothing about me, or Hallie. "You want everyone to think you're a bachelor," I said.

"Not me," said Milo.

"Who then?"

"The handlers," he said.

What was that supposed to mean? I asked him.

He came over and scooped his arms around me where I sat feeding Hallie with the movie magazine folded and balanced on a pillow. He told me what Darryl and the Ray Group had explained to him, how *publicity-wise* it was just not smart, *careerwise,* for the Wife and Child to appear with Milo. There would be marketing problems for Milo's movies, especially in the South, *If it were known about the interracial nature of his marriage.* Advertisers would pull out of magazines or TV shows if there was any hint of, you know what: miscegenation, a word that always makes me think of mangling and vegetation, for some reason, like it couldn't possibly be a word that meant anything.

"Darryl says it could wreck my career."

"Oh, come on," I said.

"Maybe not wreck, Darryl says. But hurt."

"This is not 1955," I said.

"Nineteen fifty-five, 1985. Can't do it," said the savvy new media-guy Milo. "For example, you know what surprised me?"

"No," I said. "What?"

"No black person, except maybe my mother, will even listen to a Harry Belafonte record," said Milo. "Not since he dumped his black wife for a white one."

No black person, Milo said, like words handed down from the top of the Mount on a tablet. Like there was a test you could pass, with final authorities.

"Who told you that?"

"It's true. It's not done. The Ray Group says Quincy Jones never appears in photographs with his wife. Or Sidney Poitier, either."

"Why can't Quincy appear with Sidney?" I asked.

"It's not funny," Milo said. "Too many nutjobs and wackos and stalkers and sickos. From now on we say: 'Mr. Robicheaux is reticent about his private life.' Period." Nobody was even permitted to ask Milo about me or Hallie, or he'd refuse the interview.

"It's not safe," Milo said. "Look what happened to Vernon Jordan."

I waited for him to tell me who Vernon was and what happened.

"Shot. He's head of the NAACP. Shot. Just for getting a ride in a car with a white woman. We have to be careful." He turned my face to him by crooking my chin with his finger. "We do."

I put my head on his shoulder. Hallie had fallen asleep. Milo now gently moved her aside and kissed me. We kissed over our sleeping baby until the magazine I'd been reading fell on the floor, open to the picture of Milo with his shirt unbuttoned almost to the navel, a hint of oiled chest showing and a gleam in his eye. I stopped.

"They want everyone to think you're available," I said.

"Yeah," he said, "but I'm not." He kissed me some more but I was distracted. "I am a Family Man!" he said, pushing his lips at my ear, whispering. "I'm not available, am I?"

"Aren't you?" I said.

It came out wrong. I couldn't help it. My voice was like a balloon leak. I was having a hard time coping; a hard time squaring how I felt with how I was supposed to feel.

Isn't it great? You must be so happy!

Look at you, Charlotte!

Will you look at her?

God, look at her. Just had a baby and more gorgeous than ever.

People said these things to me, but I didn't trust them. Maybe I didn't look different to *them*, but I felt different. I was a mother! It changed me. I'd be waiting in the dark with Hallie when Milo came in late. He'd be happy because he was always so happy during that time, with his new darling baby, and *Cade* doing so well. He'd be a little drunk, full of some story, some new deal, and he'd take me up in his arms and say, *Isn't it wonderful?* his lips at my sour milk-smelling neck, his hands on the hard torpedoes of my chest, streaks of pain making me leap back away from him. And he'd say: *Oh, I see how it is.*

No— I'd start to explain. *I'm so tired.*

Rest, Milo would say, and pull my head on his shoulder, as if I would soon revive, stroking my hair until I pulled away. I was the one who pulled away. It was me. This happened more than once during those early days. He was tender. He didn't understand because I couldn't explain: how it was different, how I was exhausted, how I was afraid of him—*the famous one with the oiled chest*, afraid of how he saw me now, *a mother*, and what he would think if his hands traveled down my ribs, looked for my waist and couldn't find it, couldn't find me, the muscles and flat planes of his memory. And my memory, too. *That used to be me*, I thought, *the one in the pictures.*

Aren't you? I asked him. *Aren't you available?*

"Charlotte," Milo said, sick of me, "for Chrissakes. You don't need to ask that." He got me off his lap and got up. "You don't. That's. That's—" He couldn't say. He was mad. He shook his head and left the room.

But any woman would wonder, would ask. There was never any mention of *his wife*. He was out all the time, being famous. When I went with him—and I did, once or twice a week—I saw the candy box of girls at those parties. Chinese Cherokee African Caucasian Latin hyphen American, wearing whatever you can dream. Marabou. Spangles. Hanging all over Milo and kissing him. He kissed them back, winked at me and gave me a look like *Help!* and kissed them again. He made a point to look at me, I thought, he always had.

You don't need to ask that. I had to believe him. He looked at me over the heads of those party girls and didn't seem interested in them. His gaze followed me. We went home and as far as I could tell he was the same Milo. He still ate cereal directly out of the box, drank milk straight from the carton, ran eight miles a day. He kissed me over our sleeping baby. He wanted us to be safe, wouldn't do anything to risk his family. He was the same Milo as ever, only right now he was the guy of the hour. Girls were after him. Of course they were. It was part of the celebrity package.

I hung in there, but that doesn't mean I handled it. Motherhood is a hard enough road, without celebrity and race and money piled across it, flaming like barricades of burning tires. Sometimes I think our days have been like that, our family driving along in one of those outlaw countries where desperadoes stop you, waving machetes, speaking some language I wasn't equipped to speak.

Milo came home after dinner one Thursday night, early for him. It was May. Hallie was about three months old and so colicky. Crying, crying, crying. You have no idea. That sound. Rage and pain boiled into a teapot scream. At first you say *there there baby sweet lovey shhhh*, and you are scared. You think there is internal bleeding. A pin sticking her somewhere. You say *shhh shhh shhh, there there there* for an hour, four hours. You try all the remedies and nothing works. *Colic is a mystery!* the doctors say. *It will go away*. She screamed every night without relenting and what was a mystery to me was how much I loved her anyway. It was Milo I resented, for being out.

He burst in the door around nine o'clock, so excited. "Hey! Where're my girls!?" He'd been interviewed again and he was beaming. I was on the couch, still in my nightgown from the morning.

"Hey, babe. Hey, darlin'."

"Take this fucking baby," I said.

"Jesus, Charlotte, control yourself."

He took Hallie from me. "Aww, sweetcake, Daddy's home." I ran to the bathroom and shut the door and cried and took a shower, crying in there. A failure. A shrew. Take this fucking baby, I said, of my own daughter, my darling. I loved her. She was all I ever wanted. I said fucking baby.

I cleaned myself up and put on perfume and lipstick. Everything was fine! I was a happy mommy. Happy, happy, happy. When I went out again Hallie lay quietly on Milo's chest, as he hummed some soft song to her.

"Hi."

"Look who's got the touch," Milo said smugly.

I burst back into tears.

"Jesus, you're a mess," he said. "Just hire someone."

He patted my head with his free hand while deftly maneuvering the baby down into the crook of his arm. Everything he did, he did with athletic grace and efficiency. *Everything's easy for Milo*, I thought.

"Get someone to live in," he said. "Would you please?"

I didn't want someone. I wanted him. He was the father. We had talked about it even before she was born, how our baby would not be like those other babies, the bonneted ones we saw around Beverly Hills, pushed by people in uniforms. It's true we had not really understood how hard it would be, but we had said we would raise her, the two of us together. Now here was Milo barely three months later saying *Get someone to live in*.

"What about you?" I said. "Why don't *you* live in a little? Instead of out?"

"Someone has to work around here," Milo said.

As if shooting movies is work, I thought. *As if we're starving.*

"As if I'm sitting by the pool eating chocolate-covered cherries," I said.

That was when, I think, my voice got that whine. I heard it, but couldn't help it. Milo never said anything about the twelve diapers a day, the ten feedings, the bath, the no sleep, the hours of colic, the trips to the market, the staying home and organizing all those pool cleaners and hedge clippers, house cleaners and drivers, the swarm of smiling silent illegal guys who came to cut the grass. What I did all day did not count. I knew complaining was unseemly, surrounded by this life, but Milo went out in the world, where *Cade* had opened to huge crowds in Europe, Canada, Mexico; he went to meetings and parties, was already planning for *Cade II*, while I was tacked to the feeding chair like a butterfly on a pin.

Someone has to work, he said, meaning *You're too fat to work*. Is that what he meant?

"As if anyone would hire me right now," I said.

"Charlotte," Milo said, "snap out of it."

I went in the kitchen to steady my nerves. Milo followed me and said nothing when he saw the glass in my hand. But he looked. As he poured for himself, he looked, raised his eyebrow. They say consumption of alcohol encourages something called the letdown reflex in a nursing mother, eases the flow of milk. That's what I told him. "I'm encouraging the letdown reflex."

He said, "I'm worried about you." He was. His eyes were steady with worry.

"We just had a baby," I said. "You're always out."

"Just for work."

"You're never home. I never see you."

"See me now, don't you?" Big grin, big arms open wide.

"Every week you're somewhere: Paris, Montreal, New York."

"So come with me!"

"We have a new baby."

"Baby-sitters!" he said. He spelled it out for me. B-a-b-y-s-i-t-t-e-r-s.

"We have a tiny new infant, Milo."

"Charlotte. This could all be solved if you would hire someone."

"That's not the point. Hiring someone is not the point."

"What, then?"

He was frustrated. Men hate it when they can't fix something. You know why Jesus was a carpenter. "Get a grip," he said. He went out of the room and I heard him rummaging around the garage. When he came back he had a flashlight and a small night-light. "Look," he said. "I thought of these."

This was his solution: a night-light for me. So I wouldn't have to turn the lights on when I did the 4 A.M. feed. He was really very sweet, a boyish look on his face.

"Oh, thanks," I said meanly. "So I won't wake you up? So you can get your rest? How thoughtful." I practically threw the lights back in his face.

He stood there smoldering. He picked Hallie up and carried her upstairs. A few minutes later I could hear water running and Milo singing Bob Marley, *Three little birds sittin' roun' my doorstep, singing sweet songs, a melody pure and true* . . . When I went up he was bathing Hallie, washing her small heart of a face, the book about how to do it propped on the sink, singing at the top of his lungs.

I admit I was the whiny one. The winey one. I can't say that I quote unquote started really drinking then, because I've always had a taste for it. And no more or less than our friend Milo. You can go ahead and say I had a problem. But look: It was the stress and the jealousy. My drinking gets bad when everything else gets bad. I could've quit anytime. Later I did quit, often. I didn't need it, but I wanted it. I'd have my bottle and Hallie'd have hers, each with our own formula. It got me through the nights.

. . .

"Are you okay?" Claire asked me on the phone. "You sound a little loony." Hallie was four months old then.

"I miss you." I hadn't seen Claire in almost a year.

"You must be so happy," she said. "You're so lucky." She wanted her own baby, I knew.

"Yes," I said. "Oh, yes, of course."

"You seem—" She stopped.

"No, I am, I am." I couldn't explain to her. What did I have to complain about? I loved being a mother. I was getting better at it. When Hallie looked up at me her eyes were full of . . . gifts, what we used to call gifts, of the spirit, of prophecy and tongues and healing. She loved me. It brimmed out all over her face. She saw me and smiled. Even when she cried now, I knew what she wanted. Me. She turned her head to the sound of my voice the way a sunflower follows the path of the sun all day. Her noises—her coos and raspy bird sounds, how she laughed—got me in the heart so I could feel it swelling up. "Half the time I just want to cry," I said to Claire. "I do cry."

"Oh, Charlotte, you're sad?"

"No! It's out of love," I said. "Unbearable love."

"But, what?" she asked, her voice sharp with suspicion. "Is Milo behaving?"

"As far as I can tell," I said. "But lately we can't even go for a walk without people surrounding us, trying to get near him. It's creepy."

"Oh, the Price of Fame," Claire intoned, rolling her *rs*. "The Terr-rr-ible Prr-rrice."

I wasn't going to get any sympathy out of her. She thought I should be enjoying myself. *She* would be, she said. "Are you two getting along?" she asked.

"We argue a lot," I said. "All the time."

I was exaggerating for her benefit. I knew how she imagined my life, as a spangled starry ball. It would make her feel better if I told her something she didn't have to envy.

"Sometimes I think Milo just—doesn't want me around," I said.

"Oh, honey, really?" Now she was paying attention. Claire is happier when she is comforting me.

"I'm just jealous, probably," I told her. "Plus all these hormones, and I'm exhausted, and this matronly shape I've assumed." I put my hands on my waist as if she could see me.

"Jesus, Charlotte," Claire said. "You know what you need?" Since I was pouring wine again I thought she was going to tell me long-distance to stop drinking, but she said, "Work."

"Whoever heard of a mother who was a fashion model?" I said.

"Oh, shut up," she said wearily. "Your face is probably even better now, right? With tiny hints of experience and character in it."

"*Age*, you mean."

"If you want to call it that," she said, disgusted. "We're barely thirty."

After we hung up, I looked hard at myself in the mirror. I did not see lines, exactly, but something different. Some weariness around the eyes. Like Milo's mother had, maybe. Like a mother. That's how I saw myself now.

We all know we will grow up and grow old. That knowledge is what makes us different from other animals, who just plod along contentedly on four legs until they die under a tree. They don't know what's coming. But we do, supposedly. Then it comes, and still we are shocked! Shocked at the broken veins in the leg! The liver spots on the cheek! Apparently, until I became a mother I had not believed any of that would happen to me. I was "beautiful," had been told that since I could make sense of speech, and all that time, I was a scoffing young girl, wondering if *beauty* even mattered. But now, glimpsing that weariness in my face, I realized I had bought the whole line about beauty like I bought the blusher, the concealer. That it was truth. Apparently it had mattered quite a bit to me, because I was chumped now, wrinkled. Grown-up. Someone's mother, never a glamorous role.

Oh, yeah, yeah, woe for the loneliness and sad trials of the fashion model. What a joke. No one will feel sorry for you. So grow up and get over it, Charlotte.

I tried to get over it, but I'm not sure I ever did, really.

25.

Darryl had a party. He had lots of parties. The blowout biggest one was the housewarming in June, after *Cade* had been filling theaters for four months. Thanks to *Cade*, Darryl had bought a big Hollywood mansion with a ballroom. He loved that it had a ballroom, and to fill it up for the party, he invited everyone he knew or wanted to know. He hired a serious funk band and a DJ. The studio was sending ice sculptures.

"Charlotte! You gonna get yourself back in your Barbie doll shoes for this bash?" Darryl said. He had arrived at our house one morning to drop off some mail, and an invitation. His party was a week away.

"Charlotte hasn't been getting out much," Milo said.

"She needs to get out!" Darryl said. He smiled his cheeky smile at me. "You coming?"

"She's been staying home with Hallie," Milo said.

He doesn't want me to go, I thought.

"That's a good mama, staying home," said Darryl.

"Yeah, she is," said Milo, roping me in by the neck. It made me feel safe when he did that. Usually. "We'll miss her," he said. "Won't we?"

Doesn't want me.

"I wouldn't miss it!" I said. "Darryl's going to dance with me."

"Oooooh, Pink, I don't know about that," Darryl said, sucking air through the space between his teeth. "Get myself a reputation like Robi-boy here. Mr. Robi-show."

"What reputation is that?" I said, teasing.

"Just kidding, Pink," he said.

"Hey!" said Milo. He shadowboxed Darryl. "Nobody's dancing with my wife but me! Right?"

He doesn't want me to come. It haunted me all week.

"You sure you're not too tired?" Milo said, while we got dressed to go.

"You're the one who said I should get out more," I said.

"And you should," he said quickly. He was attentive. He complimented me. *You look beautiful. Put your hair up. Yes, like that. No, not the satin pants, the others. What about those smaller earrings? Not the diamond ones. There,* he said, *perfect.* But I couldn't shake the feeling he wished I wasn't coming, wished I was someone different, someone with her hair up.

Arriving, we saw cars parked for blocks around Darryl's new house. There were valet parking guys in uniforms and torches lining the driveway.

"Hey, hey, hey," Darryl said, opening the front door. "It's Cade himself! Charlotte! Hey! Come right on in!" He bearhugged Milo, kissed me, said, "Make yourself at home."

It was the first time I'd been to Darryl's new house. He'd been living in hotels for months and had just finished renovating this big palazzo up in the Canyon, a California mission-style place, with Mexican tile floors and arched doorways, a sunken living room. It was dark and the music was loud, with the bass line so heavy it throbbed in your rib cage. "Hey," I said in Milo's ear, "there's dancing. Let's dance."

"Not drunk enough," he said.

"Who, me?" because truth be told, I was the smallest bit drunk already, having started at home.

"No," Milo said, "me." He was wearing his sunglasses indoors, a new habit of his, and I wondered how much he could see, looking for the bar in the boom-boom-boom of the music.

A jheri-curled man I didn't know pulled him off by the elbow. "Hey, Charlotte," Milo called over his shoulder, "excuse me a minute." He and the guy disappeared toward the pool, leaving me wandering around by myself. The rooms smelled of reefer and incense and perfume. Candles and oil lamps burned inside, lanterns and torches out by the pool. The place was opulent with tile and carpeting and crystal and chrome. TVs took up whole walls. A painting of a reclining nude, red-tinged nipples on brown breasts, hung over a desk in an office, where the shelves were full of books and the file cabinets bursting with paper. I was tempted to open them, see what was inside.

I was one of maybe ten white people at this party, which was not such a big deal for me anymore, certainly not as much as the fact that I was probably the only mother, the only one not fumigating myself with spleefs and blunts and bones of weed and tobacco, the only one drinking guiltily, alone, turning champagne into mother's milk while Hallie slept at home with a baby-sitter. The music now was softer and older, Al Green or Isaac Hayes. Nobody talked to me. I was shy to start, myself, and just sat on a couch, watching and drinking.

Finally, a tall woman with elaborate hair extensions said, "Hey." She sat down next to me. "I'm Khelli." She had purple lipstick and triple-pierced ears, many rings on her hands, and a strapless red top. She was all of eighteen years old, it seemed to me.

"I'm Charlotte," I said.

"Yeah, everybody knows that," she said. "You're Cade's wife."

"So far," I said. Who knows why I said that? It had something to do with the self-conscious feeling I had whenever I was the only white person in a new place: that I should signal I didn't take anything for granted, demonstrate I was not unaware of the complexities. "So far."

Khelli hooded her eyes and smiled in a way that meant something mysterious I didn't care to ask her about. "I for one was not shocked to find he had a white wife," she said.

"Oh," I said. *Do go on.* "Why not?"

"Because"—she shrugged—"you take a man like him, you know, raised like that among white people, doing what they do, skiing and that, then you know he's not really black, down deep, right? So unlike some other people I was not shocked."

Black down deep.

I tried to think what to say, but all I could imagine was guts, the organs all black like rotten bananas. *Better not mention anything like that,* I decided.

Luckily, Darryl came over to us then, sat on the coffee table, and kissed Khelli smack on the lips. "Is this not the most beautiful woman you ever saw?" he said to me, pointing to her.

"She sure is," I said. "Gorgeous."

"Gorgeous," Darryl said to Khelli. "That's a good name for you."

Khelli beamed.

"What *is* your name?" Darryl asked her.

"Khelli."

"Sheee-it," Darryl said, laughing. "Name like that you'd think you were some kinda colleen, right? Little shamrocks, little rainbow, little pot of gold."

"Khelli with an *i*," she said. "And a *k-h*."

"I'm gonna call you Gorgeous."

"You can call me Gorgeous when I say," she said. She was trying to be tough but she was dimpled up with pleasure and the flattery of his attention.

"You an actress? A singer?"

"A singer."

"Maybe you need an agent?"

"I do," she said. "I've heard you might know somebody."

"Darryl Haynes," said Darryl, extending his hand, "Super Agent. You call me in the morning." He drummed his fingertips together and raised his eyebrows at us to show he didn't take himself too seriously. "Charlotte is not—obviously—one of my clients," he said to Khelli, laughing. "But her husband is my Number-One Man. You know Cade?"

Darryl had used *Cade* and Milo to make himself into *Super Agent*. Now he had a big crop of new talents. Khelli would soon be among them, I could see, one way or another. I got tired of her wide-eyed questions to Darryl about demo tapes and studio musicians and record labels. So I excused myself and strolled through the crowd out to the pool. Torches were planted all around, and people were dancing on the terrace. I saw Milo across a glowing blue lilypad of pool water. He was standing with a group, laughing, his sunglasses still on. They looked good on him. I still get a knot in my stomach, thinking of his looks. That night he had on a black sport jacket with a pale green shirt. No tie. The Italian pants I picked for him showed off the taper of his waist. I went over and touched his arm. He was talking to a very tall man with short dreads and a round face, round glasses with black frames. The woman standing next to him was laughing at what Milo said. She had short finger waves and a wide mouth that she covered with her hand sideways when she laughed. They stopped talking when they saw me.

"Charlotte Halsey," Milo said, introducing me.

"His wife," I said, and what with my right hand holding a drink, stuck out my left hand with its flashing diamond, so the man with glasses had no choice but to take it. "Hi," I said. The woman looked at me and then at Milo and back to me. Even with his sunglasses on, Milo looked sheepish.

If I could change myself into a bird, I thought. *If I could airbrush myself out of the picture. If I could be a brownskin person. I wish I were.*

I had never wished for that before. Not that I would trade.

"Excuse me," Milo said. He turned away from the group and steered me across the terrace.

"More champagne!" I said gaily.

"Haven't you had enough of that, Mother?"

"I am not your mother," I said, wheeling past him into the house.

It was a hairy ride home, both of us under various influences, not all of them chemical. It was two in the morning. Milo tapped his ring on the wheel and I had the idea he was trying to apologize, watching me across the front seat. He reached a hangdog hand over and touched my knee. I pretended to be asleep.

Hallie woke up the minute the baby-sitter left, screaming for a feed. *There, Hallie, there you go,* I said, glad to see her. We lay on the bed, our small family, Hallie drinking and the carousel room circling.

"Where did you go?" Milo said after a while. "I tried to find you."

You did not, liar. You stayed out on the patio.

"Where did you go?"

"Inside."

"Who'd you talk to?"

"Khelli."

"Khelli?"

I said some stuff to describe Khelli while thinking: *She's the one who said that, unlike some others, she was not surprised to find out you have a white wife.* I was not going to say that part.

But then I did. I said it anyway.

"Why was she not surprised?" he asked.

"Because. Never mind."

"Why?"

"Never mind."

"Tell me," he said.

Well, I was drunk enough to say anything. "She says you're not really black, you know, deep down, so it's not surprising your wife is white."

"Plgggghh," Milo said. He blew air so his cheeks made noise like a winded horse. He turned in the bed away from me. Fuck her, he said. He got up and went in the bathroom and ran the water and dropped something that clattered. Another curse.

"Milo?"

Another crash. Hallie startled. I could tell by the cascading sound of glass breaking that Milo had just swept everything off the vanity onto the floor. A bottle of aspirin, cakes of blusher, hand mirror, whatever else was by the sink. He swore and slammed cabinets. "Shh, honey." I covered Hallie's ear with my free hand. "It's okay now." I lay there waiting for it to be over.

Milo felt better, smashing that stuff. He calmed down and took a shower, cleaned everything up and came back to bed like it was an ordinary night at our house. He spooned around me where I lay feeding.

"I hate that you're so guilty to be with me," I said after a while.

"Shee-it. I'm not, I'm not," Milo said. He kissed the back of my neck.

Shee-it. He said that now, sometimes. He said *my man, my brutha. That's solid, that's phat.* He dropped his *g*s.

"You know, excuse me for noticing this, Milo," I said thickly, "but whenever you're around Darryl you talk like him."

"Hmmmm. Well: when in Rome." He closed his eyes, fingers twisted in my hair.

"I'm just wondering," I said in a small voice, "which is Rome for you? When you're with me? Or with him? Which is Rome and which is home?"

"Maybe they're both Rome," he said. "Maybe there is no home, somebody like me."

I brooded about it. I couldn't sleep and lay there with a headache. *Maybe they're both Rome.*

Milo was awake, too. He was up and down that night, checking Hallie in her crib, in the den with the light on, reading. He was leafing around in all those books Darryl gave him. *Invisible Man. No Name in the Street.*

■ ■ ■

In the morning I saw them open by his big chair. They threatened me, those books. It seemed to me Milo was looking for answers in them the way I looked for fortunes in the Bible, and that the answer he found was that he should be ashamed of me now, because he was Cade, the Rebel Fury. Rebel Furies couldn't have white wives.

If I had known any better, if I had not been so tired, if I was not such an ignorant person or such a selfish one, maybe I would have understood that Milo had his own growing pains. But we didn't talk about what those pains were, or what was going on between us. Milo wouldn't. I couldn't.

People watched him more than ever. Strangers thought he was fair game, and Milo was having trouble accepting the fact that we couldn't walk around anymore without paying *the price of fame*, as Claire called it, *the terrible price*.

One Saturday morning in July we went to Venice Beach and walked the Strand with Hallie in her carriage, Milo in his cap and dark glasses. I sat on a bench in the shade, and Milo went to get iced tea for us. A woman in a wetsuit, not younger than sixty-five, sat down next to me and looked at Hallie, looked at me. "So beautiful," she said, smiling. She picked up Hallie's hand. "Aw," said the woman, "I really really believe in adoption."

I must've made a face.

"She is adopted, isn't she?"

Milo came back then. The lady smiled at him and fled.

"Don't take it personally," Milo said, when I told him. He handed me iced tea and took Hallie, fed her a bottle. We soon had some fans around. Girls. "Oooo, Cade," said the one with the pierced eyebrow, "what a good daddy."

He is a wonderful father. I wouldn't take that away from him, or his success, which he deserved. He worked hard and he had gifts. For him the problem was everybody telling him that all the time. Milomania. The girls at the beach. We had to leave and even so they followed us. "I can't get away from it," he said that day. "I'm not complaining. But I can't get away."

"What about home?" I said.

"That's the only place," he said, and he smiled at me. "Home with you and this girl." Then he leaned down and whispered to Hallie, "Except your mother here is crabby half the day. She's not the feisty Charlotte of yore."

I knew he was trying to tell me something, talking through Hallie. I stewed over it the whole afternoon and all through the small but well-integrated dinner party that night in Beverly Hills, where I tried to be feisty as hell, wearing a tiny black cocktail dress with a rhinestone zipper up the front that constantly threatened to unzip. Milo watched me across the table. I laughed for his benefit and ate almost nothing, drinking champagne and flirting with an elderly white screenwriter next to me, who kept talking about the *blacklists* of the 1950s.

"Don't say *black*list!" I said, teasing the guy even though he didn't get my stupid joke. Milo heard me and I saw him trying not to smile. "Don't say *dark forces* of McCarthyism." The poor guy kept trying to explain about rats who named names. "And what were the rats' names?" I said, giddy and laughing with very little idea of what the guy was talking about, HUAC and the Hollywood Ten, movie stars accused of being *commie pinkos*, as my Uncle Paul used to call them.

"You were having fun," Milo said, after we got home.

"Yes." *Was he, maybe, jealous? Yes! And of an old man!*

"I've been worried about you."

"Have you?"

"You haven't been yourself."

"You mean not the feisty Charlotte of yore?" I said. Then, quietly: "Of your what?"

He laughed.

"Your dreams? Your heart's desire? Your requirements?"

My tone was supposed to be the flirty one of the dinner party, but it came out tinged with vinegar, the champagne bubbles turning now. I had drunk a lot. Both of us had. We were lying on our bed but Milo couldn't see me. I had my back toward him.

"What's the matter?" he said carefully, after a minute.

"Nothing." I had wanted him to ask but now that he had, I didn't want to explain. He should just *know* what was bothering me, just *see* it.

"Hey," he said, propping himself up on his elbow. He put his hand on my face and felt the wet spill from the corners of my eyes. "Aww, honey." He lay still a while and then he said something that surprised me. "I'm sorry. I know I've been distracted." He took my hand suddenly, held it too hard. "Listen, I've been having trouble sleeping. I can't sleep without you in the bed, up and down all night with the baby, and thinking of everything that's happened. All this, this..."

He waved his hand vaguely in the air, curling up the fingers as if trying to grasp something. "All this." He felt, he said, as if I was angry with him now. As if people expected things from him and loved him for reasons that had nothing to do with him. And that I hated him for reasons that had nothing to do with him, either. "I can't go out in the world and handle it all and then come back here and you're—you're miserable."

"I'm not miserable," I said.

He was under so much pressure, did I know that? "You think it's easy," he said, "but it's not." He talked and I listened.

"It feels as if Hallie is your baby," Milo said, "not mine. It's like you're soldered together."

"No!" I said. "It feels like she's yours. When we go out no one knows I'm her mother."

"Forget it," he said. "She looks just like you. To me she does. She wants you, looks for you. She won't smile at me. Cries when I hold her. I think she's scared of me, the big dark daddy, after looking at you all day."

"Milo!" I said. "All babies are that way. Don't say that."

"I can't help it," he said. "Sometimes I think these things."

"Well, stop," I said.

"Want to know something strange?" Milo asked, after awhile. "Used to be, if I couldn't sleep, what I'd do is run courses in my head, run the downhills at Lake Louise, or Cortina, hit the compressions, the meadow, jump the camels, hug the tower turns, you know? And I'd ski them all in my head. Take the mental chairlift and I'd fall asleep like that." Milo turned now under the sheets and put his arms around me. "It doesn't work anymore, though," he said. "It's the strangest thing. I can't remember the courses. It's like I never was a skier who could do that."

"Funny," I said. "Same with me. I look at my book and see all the tear sheets and those contacts and the headshots and I say, 'That's not me. I never did that, wore that, stood like that.'"

"Yeah, you did," Milo said. "That's you. And this is you." He ran his hand over the safe cotton of my nightgown, down my side, down the ribs and over the hipbone, along the flank to the calf.

You're beautiful, he said. *More than ever.*

When he held my shoulders and pulled back the strap of the nightgown that I never used to wear but wore now, every night, his hands on my skin and his words in my ears were warm as lanterns. He sat me up. He lifted the whole dress over my head and looked at me in the dim light, naked. I shivered, pulled the sheets over me. He pulled them off.

Charlotte, he whispered, *come back here.*

I was at his mercy. It was up to him.

He touched my shoulder. He ran his hand down my arm, up my rib cage, placed the flat of his palm against my cheek. He took my hand then and put it on his face. He pulled it down along his ribs, his flanks, down along his long folded length, the muscles of his legs, the knots of his knees and his elegant feet. He left my hand to wander back where it would. And it did. I felt how he was the same; mine. His eyes stayed on my eyes. *Look at me*, he said in the dark. He sank me down on the pillows. He was shaking. *I missed you*, he said. *Where've you been?* as if it was me who'd been gone.

Nowhere, I said. *Right here.*

He said, *Sorry sorry sorry.*

I said, *No, I'm sorry. I am.*

We fell asleep and slept till morning. We didn't hear the baby cry, if she cried, and we didn't have dreams. When I woke, Milo woke at the same time. I felt him stirring, the skin of my face stuck to the skin of his shoulder where I was lying on it. We pulled apart and I saw the imprint of my weight on his flesh, dents and lines in a creased pattern.

"Morning," he said, and the wrinkles at the corners of his eyes from smiling at me made him look like the best man ever, the best one I knew, or could imagine.

It was something we weathered. The Aftermath. I thought so. We grew accustomed to all the new things we were: mother, father, Californians, Famous and Mrs. Famous. What helped me was the feeling I had from that night, that Milo loved me because he needed me, beyond what he could see, touch, take to a party. Milo loved me. Maybe I hadn't really believed it till then, because I did believe it.

26.

Marcy Aquino came to work for us. A nanny. She had straight black hair with bangs cut across her brow, and her bones were small, like a hummingbird's. She was some kind of Zodiac practitioner from the Philippines, about thirty, like me. Marcy moved into the guest house above our garage when Hallie was six months old. On weekends, she went home to East L.A. She arrived with just a suitcase, her zodiac books, and six pots of geraniums for her room. She was gentle and practically a lunatic, I thought. According to her, everything about Hallie could be attributed to the fact that Saturn was crawling backward into her twelfth house.

"Pisces. Overemotional," said Marcy, when Hallie cried.

"She still has a touch of colic," I said.

"Tcch," she told me. "Because Pluto is opposing her sun. Give a little sugar water."

Marcy talked to me while I was feeding Hallie, while I was playing with her, when I was trying to talk on the phone. I was too shy to tell her to go away. I wasn't a good boss. She told me all about her horrible childhood in Manila, how her father was a veteran of the war. (Which war? I wondered. Where were the Philippines, anyway?) The father was an amputee and Marcy's eight siblings sometimes found food by scavenging outside restaurants, and if it weren't for the nuns she'd never have bettered herself. I hid the bills and took the price tags off what I bought so she wouldn't see how much I spent. Thirty dollars on a pair of knit booties. A hundred for an off-white baby Dior fleece coat that never even got worn.

"You're lucky." Marcy said this often. "Your husband takes care of you."

I was lucky! I wasn't complaining. I was bench-pressing 120 pounds now, more than ever, swimming laps three times a week, running with Milo the way we used to run, on Tuesday and Thursday mornings. I was thinking about maybe working a little bit. I was learning my way around Los Angeles. I was learning not to take things personally, I hoped.

Hallie loved Marcy, who had a musical laugh and got right down on the floor and played. Hallie would be fine with her, I thought, but wistfully. Sometimes when we went out together people assumed Marcy was Hallie's mother. *Don't take it personally*, Milo said all the time. I tried not to, and felt more and more worried that I had to do something with my days now besides shopping, running, and listening to Marcy call the hot-line for our horoscopes. Sagittarius for her, Leo for me. I only remember one of them, the day when hers said *You may look forward to a prolonged period of prosperity*, and mine said *Plan ahead for retirement.*

That horoscope made me return Kevin's call as soon as I got it. I had not spoken to him since before Hallie was born.

"Charlotte!" he said. "Are you surfacing?"

"I don't know," I said. "Maybe."

I wanted him to talk me into it. He said he was just dying to see me.

"You just want to see if I'm fat," I said.

"I will love you even if you are," he said. "I have a project for you."

A week later, he came to L.A. just for me and I took him to lunch. He was so pale. He was wearing a Brooks Brothers suit, but with some creative necktie made from strips of old porn film knotted around his neck.

"I hate my job," he said.

"Which is what again now?"

"I am a style editor for people with repulsive style," he explained. "It's all so sickening, the whole fucking fashion kingdom. It's a charade." He said he was quitting. He had nothing but disgust for all the big glossies. "They're only about money and lies and contempt for others disguised as fantasy."

"Whoa," I said, shocked, really. "What happened to you?"

What happened to him, he explained bitterly, was that six people, five friends of his and the man he loved beyond belief, were dead of AIDS in just the last year. When he said that part, *loved beyond belief*, his eyes filled up with tears. "His name was Douglas," Kevin said. "He was only twenty-eight."

I put my hand across the table toward him.

"Don't," he said. "It makes it worse."

He drank back an entire bottle of mineral water, put his napkin to his eyes briefly, and shook himself. "Okay, now," he said, too brightly. "So I've changed! Now I see life in a whole new light!"

"What light is that?"

"Oh," he said, "the harsh light of death! It's a fuck-it-all light."

He worried me a little. He was joking but he seemed so tired. He didn't ask about Hallie or Milo; he only talked about his new project, a magazine called *Edge*. It was going to be a downtown, avant-garde, high-end, totally new kind of glossy. Kevin and this former *Voice* editor named Lucy were working on it, raising capital to start it up. They were shooting the mock-up for investors and advertisers in a couple of weeks. "It has to be real and dramatic and startling," he said. "It's about fashion, but not fashion the way we're used to it." He was thinking of me as the Face of *Edge*.

"I need you," he said, his eyes burning and lively. "Your experience, your so-called American look. Because believe me, what we want to do is take that look apart completely and comment on it in a way that hasn't been seen before." He wanted me to be like a character in a story, recurring in the different issues, having different adventures. Everything would be on location. No studio stuff. "You're interested, right?"

"Of course," I said. I liked the sound of the adventures, of being a character in a story.

"You'll have the first cover," he said. "But I need more than just your face, Charlotte. I need your help." He wanted me and Milo to invest. He explained he needed individuals with a high profile. "You and Milo are exactly right," he said. "You'll be part of our publishing consortium."

"Well, sure," I said again, because every time I did, Kevin looked more cheerful. If only I hadn't said it. If only I wasn't such a sucker for a cover, for flattery, the fancy sound of the word *consortium*.

I signed to do six issues a year with *Edge*. Milo agreed to a 25 percent stake in the magazine, which was a pittance for him, considering what he was paid to sign for *Cade II*, called *Beyond Fury*. We flew to New York with Hallie and Marcy in early April and put Marcy up in a hotel, which she loved. Every night, she explained, someone came and left chocolate on her pillow. We stayed in our Mercer Street apartment. When we opened the door, there was the loft sweeping out in front of us, with those huge sunlit windows at either end, and the six-winged Indonesian goddess sculpture we bought years before in the Village, welcoming us by the front door. Still, it felt odd somehow, to be on Mercer Street with Hallie. There was no trace of her there yet, no sign of how she had transformed us.

The first shoot was on a Monday, in the meat district by the Hudson River, under the old elevated highway. It was a neighborhood of trucks and stench and hookers. We would be working in a meatpacking warehouse, rented for the day. "It's gonna be a real trip," Kevin had said, "so be ready. It won't be like any shoot you ever did before, Charlotte."

I have to say, I was shocked. A meatpacking plant! The smell alone was enough to knock you flat. One of the three other girls, Didi, left right away. She was a vegetarian, and nearly threw up. Frankly, I wanted to leave with her, after seeing the pale, skinned cows hanging in a row, marbled with blood and headless. But I'd done shoots in missile silos and junkyards, on lobster boats and factories, working with extreme photographers who were always thinking up outrageous things for us to do. You were good only if you could give them what they wanted, so I did. I was happy to be back at work. My job was not to have my own vision but to mold myself to fit theirs.

This time my job was to stand in the big freezers next to the cow carcasses and the sides of meat and the big steel hooks hanging from the ceiling, wearing the clothes. I went first. Kevin had me walk down a conveyor belt wearing a spring shift, shocking pink silk, with spike-heeled mules of the same color. "Oh, my God, Kevin," I kept saying, as his photographer snapped away, "this is so obvious!"

"It's great!" he said. "We can see the meat behind you!"

"I'm supposed to be meat, too, right?" The place was freezing.

"Right!" he said; he was laughing. "The first issue of *Edge* is called Off the Rack! Isn't that great?"

"It's disgusting!" I said. "I feel sick!" The smell was strong and raw. But I put all thoughts of where I was out of my mind and walked the conveyor belt as if it were a Paris runway.

"As of right now," I said to Milo at the restaurant that night, "I'm a vegetarian." I ordered some salad made of cracked wheat and told him all about the day.

"A meat shoot!" Milo kept calling it that. He kept laughing and shaking his head. "That's wild," he said. "That's great. It sounds really rank." He seemed impressed and proud of me. "I have to say, you seem like your old self."

"I have to say. So do you."

After dinner we walked down Prince Street, looking in the windows of the bars and the dark galleries. We turned onto our old familiar block and went upstairs to our lofty apartment, packing Marcy off to the chocolates on her pillow. We checked Hallie and took turns brushing our teeth. Milo closed the bathroom door and I could hear him in there, gargling and spitting and listening to the radio. I went to sleep to the ordinary sound of it. I felt safe. I always felt safe with him in our house.

Edge got a reputation fast. The magazine was hot and hip and the launch party was one of the best times I ever had, high up in Soho, in the Puck building, dancing barefoot to Haitian compas, and Milo feeding me oysters directly out of the shell, flashbulbs going off like it was a wedding or some historic moment, not that we noticed the flashbulbs. For once, we didn't. We were having too much fun. We were among friends. It's a shame, but that was the last time we could afford not to notice, since that was the year the phone calls got ugly and the mail got chilling.

"Charlotte Robicheaux?"

It was a man's voice that summer, on the phone in the Malibu house. White-sounding.

"White slut," he said.

I ripped the plug out. I was shaking.

He called several times. The same one. I recognized the voice. We got other calls of that nature, all of them from white people. Or at least white-sounding. We unlisted all our numbers and still had to change them, often. But it was hard to avoid the mail.

You are nothing but animals, dogs, making a mongrel race like monkeys.

That letter came with the picture of us, the one of Milo feeding me oysters, that had been on Page Six of the *New York Post*. This was the first published picture of us together since Milo had become Cade. Clipped to it was another one of our family, that somebody—who knows who?—had taken at LAX airport. There was a big X inked over Hallie's face, a noose drawn in dark ink around Milo's neck, a gun drawn pointed at my head.

It made us ill. Because of Hallie. That was the worst one. Thinking of it still fills me with panic. We took it to the police, along with some others, such as the one that arrived addressed to me. "Dear Traitor," it read. "In the coming White Rage War, Race Traitors like you will be the first to die." It had a letterhead with a little motto on it that said: "Your skin is your uniform! Wear it with pride!"

Milo got very quiet over that mail. It just made him grim. All the small muscles in his face flexed and stayed taut while he read it, and then he crumpled the paper like he was killing something. Fuckers, he always said. Cracker fuckers. He tried to tell me it was nothing new, and it's true he'd gotten this kind of thing before. But never so much. And never involving Hallie.

The worst of it happened that summer, when Milo was promoting *Beyond Fury* at various locations around New York and Los Angeles, and I was traveling a lot for *Edge*. Darryl hired extra security for us whenever we went out in public. "You take this seriously," he said.

"I do up to a point," Milo replied. "But: sticks and stones."

"Break your bones," said Darryl. "This is America. There's some sick people."

"It's a free country," Milo said.

"It's a sick country," Darryl said. "You watch out."

"But at a certain point you gotta live your life," Milo said.

"It's my job to protect you," Darryl told him.

"Whattya gonna do, Hardhead, box 'em?" Milo laughed. "Pow pow! don't write them mean letters no more to my buddy Milo or I'll bust your head."

"Milo," I said, "Darryl is serious. You listen to him."

"I'm listening," said Milo.

We bought the apartment downstairs from us in New York and installed twenty-four-hour security guys in it. In L.A. we had big gates put in front of the house, with intercoms and buzzers. The neighborhood was secure, we thought. A private security guard patrolled in a car twenty-four hours a day. We had sensors and alarms and big lights around our property, but still, they didn't stop the hate mail.

Milo got other kinds of letters during that time. People asked him to marry them. They asked for pictures to put on the walls of their hospital rooms, their prison cells. They asked for money to get them off the streets, into college; to buy their babies' diapers or their medicine.

Just 15 dollars a week would buy Pampers for my son for the entire year.

If you would contact a lawyer specializing in Death Penalty cases I'm sure your influence would make a difference on my behalf.

These letters weighed on him. On me, too. They were overwhelming. Milo was nothing but an actor, a celebrity, not some institution with power. He was not a Supernatural Being, though I wondered if he had started to believe he was. *I could make a real difference,* he said, often now. We gave our money away, lots of it, but we kept lots, too. Crunchy the accountant and Pepe the financial advisor set up all these accounts for Milo, bonds and trusts and funds and stocks. Darryl liked to call himself Milo's *Minister of Portfolio,* or the *Secretary,* since he came by about once a week, with stacks of things for Milo to sign, deals and ideas for deals, scripts and ideas for scripts, and all his fan mail.

One of those days, a Wednesday morning around nine o'clock, Darryl arrived at our house in Malibu. "Hey, Snowflake!" said his voice on the intercom. "It's D.!" I buzzed him in and opened the front door with Hallie in my arms. There was Darryl, balancing a cardboard coffee tray, his arms full of bags.

"Hey, Pink!" he said. "I brought breakfast! Where's the Snowflake?"

"Asleep." Milo had been out late at a party the night before.

Darryl put his packages down and headed up the stairs.

"Hey," I said. "He's asleep!"

But Darryl kept going, went straight into our room and dove next to Milo in bed. "Wake up, Snow! Wake up! We got work to do!"

"Fuck out of here, Haynes," Milo said. "Out, you motherfucker."

Darryl mocked him, saying "Out, you muth-err fuck-err," with a hard pronunciation of the *r*s, like a choirboy trying to curse.

I could hear them. I handed Hallie off to Marcy and was coming up the stairs, padding down the carpeted hall in my bare feet. I stopped to listen, waiting just outside the door of our room.

"So," Darryl was saying, "this is where you do your dalmatian love thing. You know, 'flake, I was surprised you didn't have a cute little dalmatian baby, spotty black and white! Robicheaux! Wake up! I'm talking to you! When you gonna get yourself some brown sugar!? Instead of chasing this vanilla frosting shit. Why you gotta have that silk? when I got a hundred chocolate foxes just dying for your ass."

"Shut up with that rap, Haynes," Milo said. "This is my goddamn bedroom."

"Eau, eau, eau," Darryl said, with a British accent. "Your goddamn bedroom! Don't get bent outta shape on me. You know I love you. You know it, Robicheaux! I love you! We got work today! Big plans! I got contracts for you! Deals!"

"Darryl, get the hell out of my bedroom," Milo said, but I could hear he was laughing, and when I showed up in the doorway just then, I could see Milo pounding a pillow on Darryl's head.

"The lovely Mrs. Robicheaux," Darryl said when he saw me. He put his arms behind his head on my side of the bed, his legs stretching down next to Milo's. "Your wife is very beautiful, Milo, for a white woman."

I looked at him, and part of me, the trained seal part, wanted to say *Thank you so much,* and the other part wanted to say *Just get out of here.* Of course I said nothing at all. Darryl got up, came over to me, and charmed me completely, saying "Nothin' personal, Pink, you know that, right?" holding his arms to display me like a game show hostess. "Right? You are more than beautiful! You're fabulous! Plus, you're SuperMom! SuperMom!" Darryl sang it to the Superman theme song. It would have been embarrassing, him flying around the room, singing, with his jacket flapping out like a cape, if it hadn't been so funny. He was fired up with a new idea. He roused Milo out of bed, sat us down at our kitchen table, and told us all about it: the Cade Action Figure, the Cade Game and possible Cade cartoon series.

When *Beyond Fury* opened at Christmastime, Darryl explained, spin-offs of the movie were going to make us multimillionaires. He showed Milo an agreement he would have to sign with a toy company. "Definite options for other products," Darryl said. "Underwear! Toothpaste! Candy bars!" Darryl was so excited. He'd been negotiating for months. "It's worth three point six *million* dollars, up front, and much more down the track."

"Shee-it," Milo said. "That's a pile of dough."

"All for you and your loved ones," Darryl said.

"I don't need all that money," Milo said. "I don't even know if I want it."

"You do too need it," Darryl told him. "You know you want it."

"Actually, Milo really has been thinking," I said.

"Right, that's right, Charlotte, you're right," Milo said.

"Right about what?" Darryl wanted to know.

"Time to do unto others," Milo said.

"We get all this mail," I explained.

"All these desperate people," Milo said.

"He would like to do something," I said.

"Really?" Darryl looked interested.

"Maybe a scholarship fund," Milo said. "Something like that."

Darryl got really excited then. He jumped up from his chair. "That's a great idea," he kept saying. You could see him thinking. "Look," he said, "we'll call it the Robicheaux Foundation for Black Youth."

"Okay," said Milo.

"See," Darryl said, "what you're gonna do now is you're gonna give loans. No, grants. Wait wait wait—" He went and got the sack of mail he'd brought from his office. "Look here, look here: to people like this." He fished around in the pile, found a letter and tossed it to Milo. "A promising black kid like that, like maybe I was, long time ago, nobody to help me out, or like this one here, or this—"

He tossed letters to me and Milo. In my pile was one from a dancer who wanted to become the first black prima ballerina of the New York City Ballet and needed tuition money for dance classes while helping to pay the rent on her infirm mother's apartment.

Dear Mr. Robicheaux,

I know you will understand when I say that in 1987 nobody thinks a black woman can be a prima ballerina. Just as nobody thought black people were skiers, until you, that is. So, apart from the fact that you may recall meeting me several years ago, I thought I might ask you for a tuition loan, due to the fact that I would like to break down certain stereotypes and barriers just like you.

The name Geneva Johnson was vaguely familiar, and after we read through piles of letters for an hour, talking, and when I reminded Milo of the benefit we'd gone to, *Where we met Darryl! Remember?* we all agreed, with great excitement, that this young dancer should be the first recipient of a grant from the Robicheaux Foundation for Youth, which was born that very morning.

"This is a dream you're giving," Darryl said solemnly. "And this gift of a dream will roll like water in a dry riverbed, lifting the boats of others on the swells of hope! It's a dream like the dream you had!" His voice was an intense whisper. "Like I had."

It was so quiet you could hear the ice in the automatic ice maker fall into the tray. He pointed to the famous snapshot, on the refrigerator door, of Milo in his striped pajamas and his ski boots on Christmas morning, 1961.

"Remember?" Darryl whispered. "When you were that little boy? How you wanted to be great? Your parents had means, but *still* you had to fight!" Darryl was so eloquent, holding the back of a chair like a pulpit. "Didn't they say no black man could be an Olympic skier? Didn't they laugh at you? So many today have needs! while so many with means turn a blind eye! We know the real definition of the word 'color-blind,' which is: if it's colored, then they are blind, and cannot see it. This Robicheaux Foundation will open eyes, open minds."

At the moment it was Milo's mouth that was open, impressed at Darryl's heroic version of his life. Milo's own version was mostly about a little kid who just wanted to ski, so he was rapt, caught up in it. Me, too. Holding Hallie in my lap, I felt warm in the heart, as if the future was indeed a brighter day, and we could make it so.

Beyond Fury opened and there were Cade action figures in all the toy stores. Milo traveled around doing appearances and promotions, and started work on the script for *Cade 3, Truth to Power.* And in the spring of '87, he presented a check to Geneva Johnson at a press conference held by Darryl in New York. I wasn't there. I couldn't just up and fly all over the place, dragging a two-year-old along, every time Milo went away for a night. I stayed in L.A. with Hallie. But in the photo opportunity picture I saw the young dancer—was she eighteen?—dressed in her Sunday best, with the lace collar, cross of gold now at the throat, hand clasped in a shake with Milo's across a replica of the ten-thousand-dollar check, blown up—now that I think of it—to the size of a queen-size bed. When he got home he said, "She's a very nice kid." She reminded him of himself, when he was her age, ambitious and determined.

It didn't happen then.

Milo swears. He said it happened later, after I opened my mouth and all that dynamite and rubble rained down on us, and we got lost in the fall-out of what I said.

That time . . . no, he said. *It was nothing but formalities.*

I remember he missed me. He called home from Mercer Street. "It's empty here," he said. "Hallie's jacket is here and it smells like her."

"Come home," I said.

There was nothing in his voice but missing me. Nothing that I remember like guilt. I didn't think, *Oh, you know, but he's a natural-born actor.* I thought, *He misses me.* I still think he did then. Does now. No matter what.

27.

Now that I need to speak, I can't.

Back when I should have been quiet, when I knew nothing, that's when I did all my talking. If only I had kept my mouth shut, zippered up my lipstick lips, politely declined to answer the question, maybe I'd be talking to you now, actually making sound leave my throat.

Please excuse me but I am reticent about my private life.

That's what I should have said.

What the fuck was I doing? What was I thinking?

Apparently there was precious little thinking going on at all.

How the trouble began was with a telephone call. It was only Kevin. Not Satan, not some mustachioed swindler or polyester used-car salesman. Just good old Kevin, calling to talk about my next *Edge* assignment. A shoot in April.

"This time I want to juxtapose violence and fun," Kevin explained, excited. It was for an issue called Bombshells. Even after two years of *Edge*, Kevin was still coming up with extreme ideas. "I want it to have the look of urban ruin," he said. "I want burned-out building shells and desolation." He was scouting locations in the South Bronx and New Jersey; he was after "the look and feel of a war zone," but American. "I want to show the American idea that the party continues, no matter what. That creepy eighties Zeitgeist. You know what I mean, right?"

"Whatever you say," I said, happy to keep working exclusively on *Edge*, to be in an issue called Bombshells. The title reminded me of a caption someone had once written: "Charlotte Halsey, a bombshell on non-stop legs." But it turns out Charlotte Halsey was actually a bomb, a time bomb that finally exploded, wrecking everything, spreading shrapnel all over the place.

That day of the shoot, the April sun came pouring in the kitchen window of our Mercer Street loft and the swatch of sky over the rooftops was Popsicle blue. Hallie cruised around my feet while I made coffee. *Pick me up, pick me up.* She said this all day long, sometimes singing it: *Carry me, carry me.* I got her on one of my hips where she fit like a clamp, and let her put the scoops of coffee in the machine. Never let them do this. Three-year-olds have their own ideas about scooping.

Coffee went raining and crunching all over the floor.

"Hallie!"

"Yippee," she said with determination, as if it were a statement.

I laughed, because she enjoyed so much the way the whole mountain of grounds looked, toppled out of the can onto the counter. We had to brush it into a pile, and then we had to track some around the kitchen and get the miniature vacuum to suck up all the coffee bits so Marcy wouldn't have to, and then we had to do it again and push the "on" button twenty-six times. Finally I got to drink some, spooning a taste into Hallie's mouth, too. She was a baby bird now. "Cheep, cheep," I said. "Eat up these tasty worms." We flapped our wings and flew into the bedroom where Milo was sleeping, still on Pacific Coast time.

"I have to get to work," I said. "Tell Daddy time to wake up."

"Daddy," Hallie piped. "Hello in there!" She was gently trying to pick up his eyelids, as if they were flaps on one of her lift-the-flap books. "Get up, ya darn lazyhead," she whispered.

"C'mon, birdie," Milo said sleepily. He raised his arm like a wing, holding up the covers. Hallie scrambled under, cheeping. He made a nest for her with pillows and groped around for her small box of cereal Os on the bedside table. She ate them right out of his hand, the way she did every morning, so that half the time the bed was full of crumbs. "Cheep, cheep," Milo said. "Here, birdie."

When I got out of the shower and was dressed, I kissed Hallie's hand, leaving a big lipstick print on the back of it. "There's a kiss for you all day," I said. She examined it, smiling happily up into my eyes, in love with me. "Oh, Mommy," she said. "Mommy, you stay." Lately Hallie ordered everyone around like a dog obedience trainer. No. Stay. Give it. Read it. Get it. "Stay," she said, pulling my jacket plaintively. Her seal eyes glassed over with tears. "Stay!"

If only I had listened to her. "I can't, trinket," I said. I gave her another lipstick kiss, found Milo's hand, gave him a kiss, too, a red-lip shape right on the palm. "There's one for you, too, sailor," I said in a Mae West voice, folding his fingers around it while he laughed.

Outside, a waxy black limousine was waiting. Kevin was in it, and Lucy, the editor of *Edge*. "Charlotte," she said, "how lovely to finally meet you." She was a pale Englishwoman in her fifties, with blunt-cut brown hair and shoulder pads. She studied me. "So absolutely blond!" she said. "Just dazzling! I hadn't realized!" *Re-ah-lyzed*.

"Charlotte's practically an albino," Kevin said, and Lucy laughed.

We stopped at a hotel on Fifty-seventh Street where Kevin said there was a surprise for me. He went in the lobby and came back with a light-brown-skinned woman with sunglasses and an angular haircut who turned out to be Glenda. We shrieked when we saw each other, the two of us going off like car alarms, hugging.

"Look at you," she said. "I thought you had a baby! I thought you quit!"

I showed her pictures of Hallie and asked, "What about you?"

"Oh, I could never have a baby," she said, and shuddered. She joked that Etienne the boyfriend was her baby, anyway. "A big Belgian child."

We stopped again and picked up a girl named Honey, younger than us. She was lanky and Asian-American, with a cropped bowl of black hair and an agitated manner. "I'm so nervous," she said, biting her nails. "I couldn't sleep."

"That's okay," said Kevin. "We need that fabulous new nail-bitten look! It goes with our bombshell war-zone party theme."

I was a little nervous, too. Kevin had explained that we'd be shooting in New Jersey. "Newark!" he said. "The perfect ruin." It seemed the city government was demolishing a bunch of empty buildings, housing projects. Kevin had scouted the location and was *thrilled* at the possibilities. We were going to model stuff amid the rubble. What scared me was that we were also planning to use an actual explosion! that very day! as a backdrop.

"It will be spectacular," Lucy said, in her English accent. "Have you ever seen it done? Demolition?" No one had.

"I've never been to Newark," I said. "Except for the airport."

"You don't want to go there," Kevin said. "It's a wasteland. Trust me."

Lucy knew all about it. She had been a stringer for a British tabloid in the late '60s, she said, when there were riots and looting, and the whole city burned. Now it was desolate. Today's demolition was part of a big urban renewal project. "Things are looking up!" she said brightly.

By the time the limo turned off the turnpike onto a big road circling the city, we were all keyed up, talking. Silvery office buildings pierced up into the blue sky. The glass and the chrome sparkled like money. We left these behind though, came around a bend, and saw hulking apartments made of dark brick. They were so close to the elevated road you could see in the windows as you passed, glimpses of plants and faces, the blue light from televisions in living rooms.

"That's where we're going." Lucy pointed. "They're blowing up that one, over there, see? They move everyone out to a new home, and then: Boom!" She was full of pep. "Look! There's the one they already took down."

"Why again, exactly?" I asked.

"They were full of drug dealers and addicts and criminals," Lucy said.

"Oh," I said, as if she had explained. They were called the Hughes Homes, according to a sign we passed. Named, I thought, after a writer?

"Langston, right?" Lucy asked. "I don't know the American poets, do you?"

"*Raisin in the Sun,*" Kevin said. "Something like that."

Most of the buildings were abandoned, we saw, standing gloomily in the bright morning light. The road took us through the long shadows they cast, then past an enormous pile of cement and twisted metal. BUILD-ING FOUR said a sign, with an arrow pointing to its remains.

"That's the one that's already been demolished," said Lucy. "Brilliant! I've never seen anything like it. Just brilliant. Look at that wreckage!"

"We'll be shooting there first," Kevin said. "That's the bombshell!"

We drove by the rubble for the length of a city block and pulled into the Hughes Homes parking lot where we could see our dressing room

trailer, a few cars, and a bunch of police cruisers. Crabgrass pushed up between the cracks in the pavement. The wind floated a plastic bag languidly
through the air. The few wisps of trees had bags just like it twisted in their
branches. The Hughes Homes themselves were arranged around an enormous dirt courtyard. Only one building still had people living in it. Music
piped around curtains billowing from its windows; women hung over
sills, calling down to kids playing in the dirt; men were coming and going,
sitting on steps, leaning on a broken railing. Just about all of the people
were black people.

"I'm not getting out," said Honey.

"You'll be fine," Lucy said, scolding. "They're going to love this! And
so will you!"

Glenda flexed her eyebrows skeptically, shook her head.

"This is just like a show for these folks!" Lucy said. "And look at all the
cops."

The idea of cops was never exactly comforting to me anymore, and I
knew this was not a show, for the residents. *This is the kind of place
Bobbie finds her teenage clients,* I thought sadly, but then banished that
thought, tried to keep my mind on my professional responsibilities. Far
across the courtyard I saw a fence of blue sawhorses festooned with yellow tape, police officers posted around it, circling the doomed, about-to-
be-blown-up Building Three, whose twenty stories of windows were
empty holes. Oddly, in the middle of the courtyard, a wooden platform
stood draped with red, white, and blue bunting. The mayor was coming,
Lucy explained, and the older woman senator, and possibly the governor.
They would announce all the new housing that would replace these apartments. Townhouses, supposedly, going up in some other part of town. The
platform and the fluttering police tape looked festive, like a Fourth of July
bandstand, with chairs facing a microphone.

As we piled out of the car, a van from a television station pulled in beside us and three guys climbed out with equipment. "Hey-ey-ey-ey, models!" one of them said. The one in the safari jacket was the reporter. His
hair looked wet. He ran his fingers through it and winked when we smiled
at him.

Lucy was excited to see the TV crew. "Hello there," she said as the rest
of us crossed the parking lot toward our trailer. She stayed behind to talk
to Safari Jacket, a guy named Marv. "He's going to do a feature about

Edge," she announced happily when she stepped into the trailer. "He's already calling it the cutting edge of *Edge*." Hair and Makeup got to work on us, while Lucy and Kevin and the rep from the designer talked us through how they would be styling the Bombshell shoot.

"It should look," Kevin said, "as if you are socialites who got lost in a war, a concrete nightmare."

"You mean hookers," I said. "I know you, that's what you're after."

"Charlotte," Kevin said, smirking at me, "this is about party animals. A creature you ought to know well."

I spritzed him with water from the stylist's bottle. I was starting to relax. Being in the trailer with someone brushing my hair always felt safe to me; the soft sable bristles, the sharp pain of the tweezers, the asphyxiating smell of the hair spray and the nail polish were comforting somehow. I felt at home and unguarded.

By the time we stepped out of our trailer, with white robes over our extreme clothes, our hair ratted up dramatically and makeup raccooned around our eyes, a little crowd had gathered to watch us. We were all pumped up. Vendors were selling hot dogs and little pies from carts, and the ice cream truck was playing "Pop Goes the Weasel." We got back in our limo, waving, for the quick ride around to the heap of Building Four rubble, where a photographer named Michael and two of his assistants were messing with lights. Kevin got us to stand on some cement steps that led to a broken door with nothing behind it but sky. *Don't you love this?* he said to me. *Stairs to nowhere.*

The first piece I modeled was a one-shoulder job, gathered tight across the chest, with a tulle apron tied over a skirt, slit up the east and slit up the west. Aqua. It was gorgeous, really, and I hoped I'd get to keep it. The Italian heels with it had straps like webs. Glenda and Honey were in the same dress, only Glenda's was tangerine, Honey's was magenta. We were wearing baubly earrings, teardrop necklaces. We were gaudy as parrots except for our nightmare hair and makeup.

"Okay," said Michael. "Ready"—lowering his eye to the viewfinder.

I lifted my arm and leaned on the doorframe. Honey put her weight on her front foot and her hands on her hips. Glenda rested against me, and we vamped and posed as usual. When they were done shooting on the steps we climbed over the broken building on slabs of concrete in our nail-spike heels, holding the hands of Kevin and Keith and Bonni, Michael's assistants. The air smelled of wet cement. Where we were posing now had been somebody's apartment. The green paint on one of the standing walls was faded except where the people who lived there had hung things. You could see a blue patch where someone had simply painted green around a picture, without bothering to take it off the hook. Mixed into all the debris were buggies and dishes, chairs and clothes, toys and magazines. *People were certainly moved out in a hurry*, I thought. I was distracted by one small sock the size of Hallie's. I bent and picked up a piece of paper that turned out to be the sixth-grade report card of a girl named Latisha Harris. She had mostly Bs that first semester of 1986 at Our Lady of Sorrows Academy on Broad Street.

"C'mon, Charlotte, get into it," Michael the photographer said. He sounded annoyed. "There's a girl, that's it."

I was having a little trouble. I knew it. We were posing in a wreck of metal and cement where someone had lived. That crowd was watching, a circle of children pointing, teenage boys on bikes, girls smoking cigarettes and pushing strollers, an old lady with a walker, guys with brown paper bags around their cans. It made me embarrassed, which is always deadly in pictures. I moved halfheartedly, distracted and self-conscious.

"Charlotte!" Kevin said. "To the camera, please. Remember, it's a party."

We leaned on the one standing wall, put our bare legs up on blocks of concrete. I looked at Glenda to see what she thought, but she was working, concentrating. She smiled into my eyes while Michael clicked away.

The crowd watching us was getting bigger and noisier.

Hey! Hey you! Could I be a model? I got the look, right? I got it? How you get to do that? I wanta be a star! Make me a star. They started clowning around, imitating us. *Look how she do that! Look how she lie on the other one, how they stick the butts out.* Then a girl about eighteen years old started singing, in a big gospel voice. She sang a few bars of "Amazing Grace" and then did a sweeping, perfect curtsy. *Make me famous, y'all!* she called, and there was clapping.

We drove back to the trailer to change for the next series of pictures, looking out of the windows like tourists. Garbage was stacked in hills along the sidewalks. Knots of men sat on benches drinking. A hairy black tangle of spray-painted graffiti covered all the low walls, the sides of trucks and dumpsters.

"Look at this place," I said. "God." It was hard to believe it was American.

"They should blow it up," Glenda said. "Looks like Hell. It is Hell."

"I guess," I said. "Seems like a waste, all those apartments. Maybe they could fix them up."

"Would *you* live here?" she asked. Sarcastically, I thought.

"No," I said. "Of course not. Neither would you."

"Got that right," she said, shuddering again. "They should level the whole place. Horrible."

Maybe she was right, but it was not the time to discuss it. I had to keep my mind on working, on the party mood Kevin wanted. If I didn't, he would bark at me again; inhibition and doubt would show up in the pictures.

For the demolition shots Kevin had us change into what he called our urban combat gear. Glenda was in a red suede trench coat over a black brassiere top, narrow satin pants. I was in a black leather flak vest, open over a purple satin teddy, short leather skirt, thigh boots with crêpe heels. Honey had a leather camouflage-pattern dress that was unzipped to the navel, with thick army-style boots and bare knees. It was crowded in the one trailer and we were all cranky and hot. Nobody was enjoying this shoot now except maybe Kevin. Maybe Lucy, who was unredeemably cheerful. "This is brilliant," she kept saying. "You girls are fantastic."

Well, it was not brilliant. It was nerve-wracking. We were not fantastic, we were jumpy. Blastoff was in thirty minutes. A siren kept sounding, big whoops of alarm. "They're warning everyone away from the building," Lucy said. "They're sweeping it now." Every time the siren went off we jumped and shrieked like women in cartoons who have seen mice.

"Okay, get set," Kevin called us. "Let's go."

When we came out of our trailer this time, the parking lot was full of commotion. Police cars stood by, lights flashing. We somehow had to get to our own "set," a space roped off far to the side of the official platform with the bunting and the dignitaries on it. We trooped in our robes over the hardpack of the courtyard, over the glitter of broken bottles and stubs of cigarettes and colored crack vial stoppers. A straggle of people followed us, watched as we climbed onto a wooden stage where seven photographers, all hired by *Edge*, had cameras trained on us from various angles, high and low, on tripods and handheld.

"About fifteen minutes," Kevin said.

"Hey, cocoa." A man in a black beret and dark-framed glasses had followed our little party as we walked. "Hey, yellowbone." He was talking to Glenda, staring up at her from the edge of the platform. "Hey, cocoa."

"Get the guy away," Glenda asked Lucy.

"What're you coming in here for?" the man shouted suddenly. "What you white people want coming in here taking pictures for?"

"Oh boy," Glenda said.

"You people always coming around sticking your cameras in our face," the man said. "Doing your news, doing your photography, doing your questions! Stick it in your own face! That's what I say! In your face! Hey, you, cocoa, what you doing in with them?"

A nearby police officer took the man by the elbow and led him away. As he left we heard him, shouting. "Go turn the camera on your own self! Look in your own house! Look who's the one with the dynamite!"

"Kevin," I said. I wanted to leave.

"Shhh!" he said.

The mayor was making a speech at the far end of the courtyard. The mike squealed with feedback sound that echoed around the buildings. He said some things about failure and dreams. Crime and time. As he talked, we rolled our necks and limbered our backs. He talked about cleanup, renewal, and hope. The three of us girls stretched, and he mentioned the new *replacement units;* he mentioned the Phoenix, *a glorious bird rising up from ashes.* Kevin signaled us and we took off our robes. The men in the group watching us let out a little cheer, which coincided with the mayor's introduction of a tiny old woman named Beulah Reynolds, a former tenant of the project, the one who was going to press the trigger to blow up her former home. She stood on a plastic crate to reach the microphone. *Good-bye and good riddance,* she said.

Some official began counting backward, and the small crowd joined in. *Ten, nine, eight . . .*

Lucy said, "Start, girls."

The cameras clicked and whirred. We began a choreography of poses, slouching and crouching as if we were under fire. Glenda threw her head back in fear and Honey closed her eyes in a spasm meant to look mysterious—ecstatic or petrified, however you wanted to read it. I covered my head in defense but made sure my face was open to the camera, panicking and terrified.

There was a quick series of booms, like backfiring trucks. Then a tearing rumbling that shook our small platform so it was difficult to keep steady. Behind us, the noise built and the crowd burst into bloodlust cheers and wild clapping. We couldn't turn to look, though. We were working. We moved slowly. Kevin sounded like he was whispering but he must have been speaking loudly over the noise. *Great, beautiful, wonderful girls.* Maybe it lasted sixty seconds? Two minutes? *More fear,* Michael said. *More, more.* The rumbling faded. We kept going till Lucy said *Okay, enough.* We relaxed and turned, expecting to see the building falling behind us, but there was only a choking puff of rising dark dust.

We scrambled shakily off the platform. Kevin and Lucy were ecstatic. The Polaroids were excellent. "This is going to be radical," Kevin kept saying. "Astonishing." We walked across the courtyard with everybody hugging and giddy. Me too. I was so happy it was over. That band of kids and the TV crew were following us back to our trailer. Safari Jacket was hustling along trying to keep his microphone wires clear.

"So, ladies, hang on, hang on," he said to us.

Lucy said we'd talk to him after we changed.

I was just so glad to have that leather vest off. It was over. Done. I could go home and take a shower. Go home and not come back. The air had a smell of cement dust and singe. I sat on the bumper of the limousine drinking seltzer water and waiting for Lucy and Glenda and Honey to finish talking to the news team about our fabulous weird magazine. Then it was my turn, and Honey lingered while the tech took her mike off. Another guy wired me up while Marv chattered away.

Marv: *Name?*
Me: *Charlotte.*
Marv: *Charlotte...?*
Me: *Halsey.*

Honey said, "Robicheaux," just casually over her shoulder as she left, like an afterthought. I smiled and said that I preferred to go by Halsey, and Honey said, "Ooops, sorry."

But Marv perked up. "Cade's wife? Milo Robicheaux's wife, right?"

What was I supposed to say? No? I was his wife. Am his wife. I don't hide it. Why would I?

"I wondered," Marv said. "I thought so." He got extra charming then. He asked me, how was Cade doing? When would the next sequel be released? What did I think the box office would do? They were not rolling tape that I could tell so I just answered him. Soon Marv did a white balance for the cameraman, holding up a sheet of blank paper, and started asking me questions.

Marv: *So why'd ya pick this location for your fashion spread?*

Me: *Well, I'm not the editor, I'm just the clotheshorse, but I'd say we picked it because we always try to show off the clothes in a new way, grab your attention with an exotic location like this, and of course anything dramatic, like an explosion, would tend to be a real eye-catching backdrop for a fashion shoot.*

Marv: *Would you say this event here today is a sign of the failure of public housing?*

Me: *Well, again, I'm a fashion model, so I don't know.*

Marv: *What's your feeling about this demolition?*

Me: *My feeling?*

My feeling was of being out of my depth. I just knew what Lucy said. What Kevin and Glenda and the mayor said. *The perfect ruin, full of drug dealers, looks like hell, urban renewal, new townhouses.* Everyone around me was giddy with the celebratory mood of the speeches and the shoot, the sun shining. I heard people saying *Congratulations, it all went so well.* I was caught up in the mood of it, distracted and still kicking myself for losing my concentration earlier, eager to please, so I said in this chirpy uneasy voice, sort of shrugging:

Me: *I don't know. All I know is that I've heard all the buildings were full of drug dealers and criminals, or something. It's supposed to be Hell.*

It came out wrong, the way I said it. Marv just looked at me blankly like he wanted some elaboration and combed his hair with his fingernails.

Which were polished! with clear lacquer. He just kept looking at me, and I got more flustered, distracted by his polished nails.

> Marv: *With all the homelessness we have in the eighties, why blow up buildings? Why not renovate?*
> Me: *Gosh, I don't know. But maybe no one should have to live in a place that's not, you know, nice, so they should be blown up, I guess.*

Isn't that what the mayor said? I pictured rows of newly built town-houses with neat lawns, carpeted hallways.

> Me: *You'd really have to ask the people who live here. I don't know. I live in California.*
> Marv: *Is your husband a supporter of your work in this magazine?*
> Me: *Well, of course he is! We're investors in* Edge *and have been since it started up a year or so ago. It's doing very well, you know, it's a wonderful magazine and the new issue will be the greatest ever. It's called Bombshells!*

I said this last part in my best girlish advertising voice, with a little wink. I was glad to push *Edge*, for Kevin's sake. He was my friend and he had certainly helped me, so I would do anything I could for him.

> Marv: *Thank you.*
> Me: *No, thank* you.

28.

We had dinner late that night. Hallie was still on West Coast time, and it took us forever to get her to sleep. By the time I got downstairs from her room, it was nearly ten o'clock. Milo had Sade on the sound system, singing "Diamond Life," and we started cooking in the kitchen, feeling happy, as if the song was about us.

"So," Milo said, "tell me." He was pouring tequila into triple sec.

"I don't know, sweetie," I said. "It was even weirder than the meat shoot."

"Not possible," he said. "Not possible to be weirder than the meat shoot."

I explained the whole thing to him, about the building blowing up, and the mayor and having to climb around a wreck in heels. He was impressed. He kept rearing his head back on his neck in surprise. "Sounds wild," he said.

"Maybe it will be on the news," I said. "Reporters were there."

We turned the kitchen TV on without sound to the ten o'clock news.

"That's it!" I said. A freeze frame of the derelict projects lingered over the anchorman's shoulder.

"Lead story?" said Milo.

"That's where we were."

"Jesus," Milo said, turning the sound up and listening.

Boom!

We watched the building collapse in on itself like a falling cake. Marv was talking on the voice-over.

It took tons of dynamite and just about 120 seconds to demolish this urban jungle today, when the Newark, New Jersey, Housing Authority blew up the second building in its long effort to dismantle the thirty-five-year-old Hughes Homes.

"Great footage," Milo said.

Marv rattled on about vacancies, maintenance problems. He said *drug-infested and crime-plagued,* voicing over pictures of the men drinking from brown bags and women leaning out of windows.

Next we saw Beulah Reynolds, with "Former Resident" supered underneath her, saying *Good-bye and good riddance.* They showed the building going down again, in slow motion.

And then there was Charlotte and Honey and Glenda, all of us parading around the wreckage, and Michael snapping away. Marv was voicing over us, too. *Unbelievably, a group of models showed up at the demolition ceremonies, shooting a fashion spread. And they touched off dynamite of another kind.*

The piece cut to the guy in the beret who'd been bothering Glenda, ranting to Marv, too, now: *Why are you here? Why are they here? Why don't all you people take your TV cameras and check out of here?* "Taj, Activist" was supered underneath his picture.

There was more footage of me and Honey and Glenda, vamping around the rubble. Then came a picture of just me and a cover of *Edge* magazine.

"Jesus," Milo said.

One of the models, Charlotte Robicheaux, is married to the actor Milo Robicheaux, said Marv, over a clip from *Cade, Rebel Fury. Robicheaux, the first black man to win a Winter Olympics medal, and star of the popular* Cade *films, is a financial backer of the magazine. His wife says they chose today's demolition for its visual potential.*

Then there I was again, brushing my hair off my face, opening my mouth, and speaking: *We try to show off the clothes, grab your attention with an exotic location like this,* I said. *Anything dramatic, like an explosion, would tend to be an eye-catching backdrop for a fashion shoot.*

"Whoa," said Milo. "What—"

Marv's voice-over again: *Robicheaux said it was a good thing the projects were being destroyed.*

Back to Charlotte, saying: *The buildings were full of drug dealers and criminals, so, they should be blown up.*

There was a little more: a bit from the mayor's speech, some shots of the dust rising up, people saying it was a blessing, people saying it was a shame and a waste and those new houses would never get built. And then Marv, signing off. *Reporting from Newark, I'm Marv James.*

I remember it was suddenly hard to swallow. All the regular noises of the kitchen were dulled down; the hum of the refrigerator, the anchorwoman reading more news, the scratch of the phonograph needle picking up off the record, all dropped into the background of one tiny sound, which I heard the way a field mouse hears owl wings in the night. It was the sound of Milo breathing.

His breath was shallow. "Whoa," he said. He rubbed the ridges on his forehead and blew air through his cheeks. "Jesus."

"I had no idea," I said.

"That what?"

"That, you know, this, that they would—"

"That was you, talking to the guy, wasn't it?" he said.

"Yeah, but—"

"Jesus, Charlotte." He stopped.

"What were you thinking?" He tried again but stopped again and walked away, the whole length of the loft to the front window, where he stood looking out at the street. From the kitchen counter I could see his shoulders going up and down with his deep breaths and the size of the hard swallows he took from his glass. The juice of the lime in my hand dripped into a cut on my finger, searing and stinging, but I didn't care. I felt ill. Milo didn't say anything for a long time. Then he walked back toward me, to the kitchen. It seemed to take him forever and it seemed to me that he got bigger as he got closer.

"I'm sorry," I said, "I—"

He stared hard at me, as if he could find out something by looking at me, and then the phone rang. Milo was still watching as I picked it up. "Hello?"

"Is he there?" said Darryl. His voice was serious and flat.

I handed the phone to Milo.

"Hey, Haynes." Milo took the phone and walked toward the window again, his face flexed and furrowed up. "I saw it," he said. "Just now." He didn't look at me. He was pacing and nodding his head, speaking in a voice so low I could only make out some of the words.

"Yeah," he kept saying grimly, "I know, I know."

It was as if he was hearing news of someone's death.

He hung up.

"Milo?" I said, and started over toward him.

"Darryl has gotten eighty phone calls."

"Milo—"

"Eighty phone calls! Since six o'clock! He was out and comes back to find eighty calls! Since the six o'clock news!"

"Who—about what?"

"You don't know?" he said. "If you don't know, that's a problem."

"I was just—"

"What the fuck did you mean by that? Charlotte?"

"I was just—"

"They're full of drug dealers and criminals? You said that!"

"They edited it! They changed it!"

Which was only partly true. I knew that. He did, too.

"They're blowing up somebody's fucking houses and you're out there talking about fashion and clothes and how you're my wife!"

"I said nothing about you!"

"Well, who did? Darryl says it's all over the radio, everybody calling in, outrage this and that, and that *he's* married to her!"

I was *her* now, to him, all of a sudden.

"I said Halsey. Charlotte Halsey."

"You said drug dealers and criminals."

"That was Lucy—" I said. "That was the mayor. I—"

"That was *you*. I saw it."

It was me. He was right. I couldn't think of what to say now. And what's funny is that, standing there, I had the feeling that I'd been expecting this moment all along, that I was caught. Had always known I would be caught. Somehow, I think, Milo was expecting it, too.

"What the hell were you even doing there?" he said.

"I was on assignment," I said plaintively. "I was working."

"As if you need the money," he said, and turned away, opened the door, heading out, his jacket over his shoulder. He hit the elevator button, but then when he saw me standing there he turned and started down the stairs.

"Milo—" I said, but he was gone.

I closed the door and leaned against it, shaking. Our apartment seemed empty, stripped, even though the lamplight was warm, the water for rice was boiling on the stove. The TV was dark and quiet and the phone squatted on the countertop, out of its cradle. *Eighty phone calls.* The ice made a fairy tinkling sound in my drink. The tequila burned my throat on the way down and made me shake, the quick shiver of a person touched by some sightless creature, a slug or a clam, trying to get the feel of it off her skin.

I was crying, walking around trying to think what to do. I thought of calling Darryl, asking him what he said to Milo on the phone. But Darryl wouldn't tell me anything now. *Eighty phone calls.* From who? What did they say, the callers? It was dire, whatever it was. I knew that. I drank tequila till I was weaving. I picked up the phone and put it down. Who could I call? Kevin? Claire? Glenda? No. What would I say? That I was having a breakdown? I had no idea where Milo was, or if he was coming back. It was midnight. Then 2 A.M. The lights were off in all the other buildings. Milo was still out.

I checked Hallie. Her room was dim and smelled of lotion and dried bathwater. She was sweating in her sleep like she always did, with little tendrils of hair sticking to her face. I pushed them back. I leaned and kissed her and could smell the tequila on my breath coming back at me. She had kicked her covers off so I pulled them over her again. She stirred and I lay down on her small bed, curled myself around her. Her breathing was even and steady, and I fell asleep to the sound of it.

"Mom," she said, at six in the morning when she saw me there next to her. "Wake up. It's a brand-new day." *Bwand new day.*

Huh. She was right. It was a bloody brand-new day.

When we came downstairs Milo wasn't there. I put the TV on for

Hallie, avoiding the news channels. I made coffee and when I had drunk three cups I went to get the newspapers. Just opening the apartment door and seeing them sitting on the mat made me dizzy. I sat at the kitchen table and opened the *Times* first, searching for what I knew would be there. Buried in the part of the paper no one reads was a small article, half the space above the fold. "Newark Public Housing Demolished." There was a picture but no reference to us, nothing at all about what I said. The tabloids, I was hoping, would not find it newsworthy, either.

I waited for my hand to stop its tremor. With great effort I stood up and looked in the cabinet for something to help me, and found a bottle of Cointreau, that orange-flavored liqueur, which seemed somehow appropriate for morning. I poured it in my coffee and drank it gratefully. I lifted the *Times* now, looked underneath it at the *Post,* which had pictures.

The story took up Page 4 and Page 5. The photos were big. Photo One showed the building at the moment of implosion, gray newsprint puffs of dust. Photo Two was us three models posing with a spray of explosion in the background. I recognized it as one of the Polaroids Michael's assistant had taken. Probably Lucy just handed it over. Photo Three was taken off the TV news, a freeze frame of me with sunglasses on top of my head and a strand of hair blowing across my face. Photo Four was a shot of Milo at the Oscars in a tux, smiling and waving.

I leaned in and read the captions.

Bombshell Models at Explosion Site. Model Charlotte Robicheaux (Yes! If the name's familiar that's because she's HIS wife!) says housing projects "full of criminals and drug addicts...should be destroyed." Robicheaux was shooting a fashion spread in Newark for her hubby's new magazine Edge.

I began to cry. I couldn't help it.

"Mommy!" Hallie said in a rage. "It's over."

She meant the show, of course.

"Change it!" she ordered.

I drank the rest of my orange-flavor coffee, changed the channel to some cartoon, and just as I had worked my way back to the kitchen table Milo came in. He sized up me and the papers and the Cointreau bottle with one glance. "Hallie girl," he said.

"Daddy!" Hallie went running to him.

He swung her around and held her. His voice to her was warm but his eyes were flat, looking at me over the top of her head. I tried to look back but he avoided my eyes.

"I'll be back in a sec," he said to Hallie, and climbed the stairs. She settled herself again by the television and I waited. But for twenty minutes Milo did not come down, so I climbed the stairs to find him. "Hello?" I said, on the landing. He didn't answer. In our bedroom I saw the bathroom door was closed. He was in there with the radio on. I put my ear to the door and listened.

Caller Didi, from the Bronx?

Didi: *I was shocked! I mean, please, on top of these fashion people talking about us as an exotic location! The fact that he's married to her is— We have enough problems in the community without his kind of role model, self-hating black man deserting the race kind of thing.*

A man: *I agree it's the leaders like Cade, like this guy Robicheaux, excuse me, who need to come and give back to the community instead of being an owner or investor in some magazine which tries to exploit us, with his wife, you know, and I don't know about you but why is every black athlete or movie star with a white woman? Am I right? Why is that?*

Host: *We're taking your calls this morning.*

Another woman: *On top of the prison system, it is the white girls who are taking the strong black men from communities, too, because of some kind of fascination they have with it, and all that.*

Host: *Professor Harvey Grant of Harvard University is here in the studio today. Professor, your thoughts?*

Professor Grant: *I think first this incident reflects an interesting phenomenon which we've started to see in our society, which is that Robicheaux is not, in fact, actually black, he's famous. Fame changes the racial dynamic, so a white woman like his wife, this fashion model, a woman of that background, would find it acceptable to marry him, to have a family with him, whereas if he had been an electrical worker, say, or even a banker, instead of a world-famous athlete and media star, there would not have been the willingness on her part to see him as a*

man, as a human being—if in fact she does see him that way—
and certainly not as a potential partner in marriage.
Woman caller: *I'd just like to say I think that unless, you know,*
this Robicheaux and his wife can apologize for what she said or
remove themselves from either this whole magazine thing, then
maybe we don't go see his films. Am I right?
Host: *Are you calling for a boycott, Aisha from Brooklyn?*
Woman caller: *I am. I have to say we need to blend together*
economically and get behind those who are behind us at the
same time we stand smack in front of those who are not, and
I'm wondering, is Cade behind us? or in front?

Behind or in front, which was it? In front of me was this door and these voices and behind me was nothing but this big mistake and I was upside down and sick from the sound of those people talking on the radio. They were loud and smart and mad. They were talking about us. Milo was listening to them. I wanted to stopper his ears, go in there, get him away from them. I reached for the doorknob and was sure it would be locked, but it wasn't.

At first I didn't see him with just the night-light burning low by the floor; it's a big room, for a bathroom especially, and he didn't have the lights on. But then he moved, looked up from the chair where he was sitting by the vanity. He startled, seeing me there.

"Milo," I said, his name breaking in my throat.

Sharp radio voices overlapped what he said back to me, which was: "Isn't there anywhere, one spot on Earth, that I can go to get away from you, even for one goddamn minute?"

29.

He was so furious. When he finally came out of the bathroom that morning, he was too furious to talk to me. He went back downstairs and when I followed him, sadly, he was on his way out with an attaché case of papers.

Marcy came in at nine and I went back to bed. When I woke again, in the late afternoon, Milo was still gone. He was off with Darryl somewhere, I was sure. They were having meetings, strategizing what to do with me: stuff my mouth with rags. Darryl would be going on about *the hundred chocolate foxes*, calling Milo Snow. Calling him Ice. Calling him Flake. Calling me Pink.

Milo didn't call and didn't come back. Lucy called twice. So did Kevin. Also my booker. I let the machine answer.

"G'night, Marcy," I said, at 6 P.M. "Have a good weekend."

I was glad she was gone so now I could drink.

I went straight to the refrigerator, where, lined up in rows, were many tall bottles of pale green glass, with miniature rivers meandering down the mist on their sides, each bottle a cool and peaceful vacation. I poured a glass of wine and fed Hallie her dinner and poured another.

"Where's Daddy?"

"At work?"

"Not home!"

"Nope, not home."

"Soon," Hallie said, with confidence.

When Milo did come back she was asleep.

I was on the couch, just drinking and waiting for hours now. It was past midnight. I did not feel exactly drunk because I was sitting down. I was quiet and sad. But then I heard his key in the lock and right away panic made me stand up, sit down, stand up again, swaying. He came in and saw me, locked the door behind him, put his coat on the coat hook. It was so still. The air of the room felt thick with dust, as if walls and windows that had been standing just the day before were now not standing; as if actual rubble and debris was all around us.

"Charlotte," Milo said. He sounded wooden.

I began to cry.

"Don't fucking cry. Listen. Shut up. Listen."

"What."

He walked over to the bar and poured himself a drink. He sipped deeply and crossed the room to stand in front of me. "People are in an uproar over this," he said in a dead, controlled voice.

"I heard the radio," I said.

"It's worse than that."

"What?" I said. "Tell me."

"Just, you know, don't keep fucking crying, Charlotte, because I don't feel sorry for you," he said, barely calm. "At all."

But I did. I couldn't help it.

He raised his finger now and pointed it at me. "One thing," he said. "I am not an investor in that magazine, that so-called magazine, from this minute on, is that clear? I am not a financial backer. Or any kind of backer."

I nodded.

"Do you understand me?" His finger jabbed the air in front of my face, once, twice, as if he would really like to jam it deeply into my eyes, or poke me in the sternum, jabbing it on the bone to bruise it, or maybe have it go right through bone to the heart.

"And you will never, never, never talk to another fucking media person again or use my name, is that clear?"

"Okay but—"

"Stop fucking crying."

"You don't want to know my side—"

"You're right I don't."

"Wait. Listen—"

"Don't. You. Say. Anything," he said. "Not. Another. Word."

He was right up close to me now, his finger under my chin. His teeth were having a hard time not gnashing and clenching. That finger, threatening and angry. It made me stop crying. It made me want to do something extreme, lash out, maybe rake him across the face with my nails drawing blood in claw marks right down his face, I was that mad and stoked up with alcohol and regret and fear.

"Understand?" he said, like I was some delinquent child.

And that did it right there. "Oh, sorry, Milo darling!" I said, wheeling away from him. "Too late! There was a reporter here just now! A whole pack of them. I let them in! They set up their lights! Sorry. Whoops!" I clapped my hand over my mouth. I was shaking my hair and vamping around. "I told a whole bank of TV cameras how I was your wife!" I said. "And how you were my husband!"

"Shut up."

"I said: We have had sex! We have a child! I revealed the secret that Milo Robicheaux is my husband."

"Shut up now."

"Since you won't talk to me, I talked to them!"

"I told you not to—"

I made a kiss with my lips and kissed it right at him. I kept on going, kept right on making this stuff up, knowing exactly what to say that would get him. I was on a tear.

"One was such a nice reporter, too!"

"Charlotte."

"From the *Amsterdam News*, which, in case you don't know, honey, is the African American newspaper here in New York, and I showed him our wedding album and gave him that roll of film from our last vacation in Switzerland! And I thought you would be so glad, you know, for the publicity, for the Milomania, you being such a media hound—"

He hit me.

He backhanded me across the face and floored me.

I went down. *Good*, I thought. *He hit me. Now I know. Now I know.*

He stood over me, looking at me. I was down, holding my cheek. On the floor. On our carpet. The 200-hundred-year-old Persian one, hand-

loomed by serfs or children probably, that we picked out at a private
showroom for exclusive customers. Years ago. Ages. We had fallen in love
with it, one rainy afternoon, with its rich reds and burnt ochres, the deep
blue of the border, and the pattern of peacocks and flowers, and now here
I was, curled among them crying, the scratchy wool pile hurting my
cheek, my struck and throbbing cheek.

Milo stood over me looking down. I thought he would kick me. He was
breathing in a shaky way. His cheek twitched so he seemed to be smiling.
Like he might do it again. Like any moment he might pull me up and flat-
ten me again for the fun of it.

He stalked away upstairs.

I stayed down on the carpet. I noticed dust balls under the couch. Also
some magnet letters of Hallie's that belonged on the refrigerator, an old
dried-up apple core. It was safe there, in an odd way. To be down already,
to be curled up. *He hit me*. I had asked for it. I had pushed him and pushed
him, tested him and tested. I could feel my cheek swelling, a blue rising
on the bone, puffy and welted up. Maybe my teeth were loose. I checked
them and tasted blood from where I had bitten my tongue. If only I had
bitten it—straight through. The strongest muscle in the human body, the
tongue. If only I had shut up. Taunting him like that! I was just asking for
it, and feeling so bad now, like I deserved it. Pow. You couldn't recover
from something like this, I thought, no matter how much you loved
someone, or someone loved you, before. Could you recover?

I could hear Milo upstairs, the floors creaking as he walked back and
forth. I lay on the carpet listening and waiting. When he came down the
stairs with his bag packed, I didn't get up and go to him. I didn't apologize
or try to make him listen to my side of the story. *You know damn well I
don't really think all the people in those buildings were drug dealers and
criminals. Don't you see I just repeated what everybody else said that
day? That I was distracted and trying to say the right thing so I said
the wrong thing. You know how I get.* I didn't say any of that because
it was not an explanation or an excuse. It wasn't good enough. Nothing
was. I lay there curled up on the carpet, resting my head on my folded
elbow.

"You hit me," I said. I knew he saw the bruise.

"I'm sorry," he said, hard and grim as Judgment Day.

"No, I'm the one."

He began to help me up off the floor.

"I'm sorry." I kept saying it. "It was my fault. I deserved it. I never, I should have—please. I'm sorry."

"Here, get up," he said, and pulled me.

I stood there swaying.

"What are we going to do?" I said after a while.

"Do?"

"About how angry you are with me."

He looked at me and brushed the hair out of my face. His eyes went to my bruise, and he touched it gently. He winced and swallowed and looked away.

"Also, I love you," I said, crying again.

I was tottering a little, and fell against him so he was holding me up like he was wishing he didn't have to, like he was a post that happened to be there, with his chin resting on the top of my head.

"I don't know what to do," he said. "I don't know." Then he held me away from him and let go, the way you try to balance a lamp that is unsteady. He saw my bruise again, looked away quickly and sat me down on the couch.

"I'll tell you something," he said, picking up his stuff.

I waited.

"All my life—" he stopped. He was having trouble. His eyes flicked over me and away and he couldn't decide whether to say it but he did. He said: "Darryl told me just you wait, you know, sooner or later, every one of 'em has his day. He said, You'll see. And I said for him to go fuck himself. Because I was not raised like that, to believe that. So I never listened to Darryl. Not about you. Darryl said, You'll see. And I said, Yeah but not her. And then—"

"Milo, I'm sorry I said it," I said.

But Milo knew my side already. Knew it all too well. Somewhere in there I realized that the time for explaining was over. It was going to be up to him to decide, up to him to take it or leave it, and right now he was leaving it. He was packed up, he said, and was going out to the beach for a couple of days. He needed some time to think. While he got his keys and his wallet organized, and even while I waited with him out by the elevator, he refused to meet my gaze. He said nothing. The door shutting and

the lurch of machinery carrying him down to the street was all the good-
bye he said to me.

I had a bad night. I could not sleep. My cheek hurt, cut and swollen up
over the bone, blue as plums with a lick of red in one eye from some broken thing in there. I tossed in the bed and the room spun. I got up and
walked around. I made calls—to Claire and Diana—but hung up without
speaking. The touchtone buttons played tunes. I hung up twice on Bobbie,
and then the third time, I spoke.

"Oh, God is everything okay?" she said, from Cambridge.

"Sure!" I was managing not to cry.

"It's two in the morning," she said. "Where are you? Where's Milo?
Charlotte?"

"He's very mad at me, Bobbie. See—" And then I lost it, tears starting.
"I just have to—"

"Oh, boy," Bobbie said. "Slow down." I could tell she knew I was
drunk.

"Maybe you should talk to him," I said. My voice was very small.
"Or me."

"But nobody's hurt, right? Hallie is fine and you are fine and Milo?"

"Yes," I said. "Mostly."

"Okay. Where is he?"

"Montauk?"

"Can you give me any more information?"

"The phone number but he doesn't answer there yet," I said, really
struggling to tell her, to say the numbers. "Just—we had an argument, but
can you talk to him?"

"I can talk to him," Bobbie said. "But maybe it's you that should."

"I tried, I can't, he—" I was losing it too much.

"I'll drive down there to New York," she said. "You want me to come?"

"It's okay. Just—talk to Milo."

"Okay, okay, sure, but hang in there now," she said, a familiar tenderness in her voice, coaching me like Milo did. "Charlotte? Hear me?"

"Okay." I hung up, comforted a little, and slept finally, having sounded
the alarm. Bobbie would take care of it. She would find Milo and talk. And
then we'd see. We'd know what to do.

. . .

In the morning, Hallie came in early. The darling girl. So good. She didn't try to wake me. Eventually I just noticed her next to me, humming and whispering to herself. She had two small dolls with her, making them talk, walking them around the covers.

"You are named Onion and you are Syrup," she said. "Hello, Syrup, yes, that is a nice hairdo. Where did you get that ugly dress?"

She ate the cereal left in the box by the bedside. She fed some to Onion and Syrup. After a while she tried the eyelid trick on me. "Are you home?"—lifting a lid and peering under. "Mommy?"

"Ow, honey," I said. When I turned my face up to her she saw the bruise.

"Poor *thing*, Mommy!" Hallie said. "Poor thing." She reached tenderly to touch my cheek but I held her hand away. "Did you fall down?" she asked.

"Yes," I said. "But I'm okay."

"Good; then, get up," she said brightly. "I'm a little hungry."

So I had to get up. It was around eleven and it was Saturday. Marcy would not be coming.

"Daddy?" Hallie said, downstairs. "Where's Dad?"

"Maybe hiding," I said.

She looked in all the rooms.

"Not here, Mom. Find him. You find him."

It was a good idea, I thought. Hallie and Onion and Syrup and I would get in the car and go down the Expressway past Quogue and Sag Harbor and the Hamptons, Bridge and West and South, all the way to Montauk where I'd find Milo. Hallie would be the bait, because who could resist her? I would put her out in the open, hide in the blind, and then when Milo came to scoop her up, I would leap out and tackle him with my net and tell him: *It will be fine. It will all work out. Listen to me. Here's what happened.* I would bring him back in my teeth, limp but alive.

I took some very strong painkillers. Codeine or Valium, or maybe both. I drank coffee. We got in the car and drove two hours straight.

But Milo wasn't there. There was no sign of him. No car in the driveway. The house was shuttered and locked, musty and dark inside.

"Daddy?" Hallie called. She waited and looked at me, shaking her head. "Not here," she said, forlorn.

...

Milo always said, if you find yourself lost, stay put. People will come looking for you; search parties will set out. If you are roaming around they won't be able to find you. Milo had taught me all kinds of things he knew about survival in the wild, about edible bark and berries. You should hollow out a cave in the snow for warmth, save your energy, send out distress signals at regular intervals. So Hallie and I would stay put for as long as we had to.

Surely Milo was on his way. He'd be here any minute.

Daddy, Hallie would say, when we heard his wheels on the gravel.

Hey, I would say, and he would see me over the top of her head.

Music would be swelling, violins, and we would embrace, murmuring all our regret and tender apology; and when we had explained ourselves in few words, we would smile at each other, smile down at our little girl, each of us taking one of her tiny, perfect hands, and walk down the beach, our backs to the camera, waves licking our bare feet, an American family with our pant legs rolled up like the pant legs of the Kennedys, walking until we were out of sight, leaving deep footprints behind us in the sand. Except Milo didn't come.

30.

Darryl would know where Milo was. All Sunday afternoon I tried to reach him, leaving messages at his various numbers in New York and L.A. *Hello Darryl it's me Charlotte, would you please call me please when you get this? Tell Milo to call me.* Finally, after Hallie was in bed and my drinking was solidly under way, I tried all the possible numbers for Milo and Darryl again, but no one answered. Then, around eleven that night, the phone rang.

"Pink!" said Darryl. "I got your message. What's up?"

"Where's Milo?" *My name is not Pink.*

"Milo Milo Milo," he said. "He was just here."

"Which is where?"

"New York City." *New York Citay.* Like he was doing his Stevie Wonder imitation.

"Where in New York?"

"My hotel, of course. We had things to discuss."

"He said he was coming here."

"But he didn't."

"He said he'd be here."

"But he's not."

"You tell him I need to talk to him."

"But he does not need to talk to you," Darryl said. "To twist a phrase of his, he don't need it *and* he don't want it."

"Darryl, you tell him," I said through my teeth.

"I can't tell that guy anything. I do tell him but he doesn't listen. Believe me, I tried. I tried to tell him about you."

"What about me?"

"Just that you would pull something," Darryl said. "Like you pulled with that project in Newark. Which—just so you know, since I know he'll never tell you—has hurt our friend Milo. To the bone. There is serious talk. *Serious.* Are you listening? of a boycott in the community. Have you got your radio on? Are you tuned in at all? Cade Blockade."

"Which means what?"

"Which means no more Cade soft drink ads. No more Rebel Fury toothpaste. No more Liquid Ore candies. No more gravy train. Sponsors are nervous. You know what I'm saying? Are you listening to me? You better quit that sniffling crying, Charlotte, because hey: You play, you pay, right? The snake will have whatever's in the belly of the frog. So listen—"

I was listening. The phone was attached to the wall with a wire. I was stuck listening to Darryl like a dog chained to a doghouse.

"You cannot be a black film actor in these United States of America without the faith of the black audience," Darryl said. "You cannot do it. If the people won't come to the show, you got no show! Like if a tree falls and there's no one to hear it, did it make a sound? You see what I'm getting at? Boycott equals Studio Untouchable. So the man Milo Robicheaux is hurt in the pocketbook. Right in the wallet. Where else he is hurt I do not know but I can guess, and he will find his medicine, rest assured."

"Please tell him to call me," I said.

"I don't think he's going to be calling you," Darryl said, and the way he said it was gentle, almost, his voice velvet. "I don't think so. I have talked to the man. Milo is over you, Pink. He is past you. Done."

My breathing was shaky in the silence then.

"Calm down, calm down," he said, listening to me.

"You tell me! You tell me where—"

"I am telling you! I am trying to tell you. Listen to me!" Darryl said. "For one time, you listen. Everyone has to go through their little ignorant phase, you know, before they get their education. He saw you. No, take that back. He saw hair and eyes. Looked just like the stuff in the magazine. Damn! It *was* the stuff in the magazine. You were. And snap! he had to try it, have it. So he had that ignorance but he's over it. He is educated and you educated him by speaking your truth, yes you did. He's a big boy now. He sees your true colors, such as they may be, and he knows which side his bread is buttered on."

"You put all that in his head!" I said. "You don't know anything about me. About him, either."

"And you do? Oh, that's good," Darryl said, laughing. "Look, Pink, calm down, because you must admit: You know that was it for you, too. Right? You had your own little questions. Listen to me now: You had. To check. It out. Our boy was your, how shall I say, your chocolate fantasy, right? Just you on your black booty quest. Am I right?"

"Don't talk to me like that!" I said.

Darryl was cracking himself up laughing now. "Barbie on a Black Booty Quest! Yessir."

"You can't talk like that to me!"

"Damn, Pink, that's how I talk! And you know it, too."

"I'll tell him what you said about him," I said. "That you said that to me."

"He knows!" Darryl crowed. "Damn, Pink! That's how I talk to him all day long! That's our saying about you! You should hear *him* do it, too. Whoo! The chocolate fantasy! It's a joke! *Was* a joke. But not now. Because when you come out and say: *Ooooh, we should blow up the black people's houses!*" Darryl made his voice girlish and stupid and white. " *'Cause, oooooooo, you know they're all rapists and welfare cheats and drug dealers!* Then it's not a joke."

"I did not say that!"

"You did."

"You put all that stuff in his head," I shouted at him. "It's your fault!"

"Ohhhhhhhohohho. My fault. Right. We have the words on tape. We saw you say them on TV. What's next, Charlotte? You gonna cry rape! You'd cry rape faster'n I could say Atticus Finch, wouldn't you? Cry murder! Like that Boston doctor who shot his wife and blamed it on a black man? Is that next?"

"What's next is you're fired, Darryl. I'll make him fire you."

"Ha."

"You'll be fired," I said. "Wait and see."

"Someone's gonna go," Darryl said, "but maybe not me." He sucked air through the space between his front teeth, a sound like lazy steam rising in a radiator.

"Fuck you."

"I don't think so," Darryl said. "Not me."

I hung up on him. So hard the phone broke, cracking the receiver and leaving a hollow bell sound lingering in the air while I sat with my heart walloping the cage of my chest.

So, Milo was somewhere in New York and he was not calling me. Even though Milo had hit me; even though he had not shown up here or called me to say where he was, I had believed he would calm down and come back and we would patch it up. I'm telling you I still did. I was Lois Lane, clinging to the skyscraper ledge, knuckles raw, reaching for the outstretched hand. Maybe if that hand appeared, I thought, we could crawl in off the parapet and be happy, despite the cracked things that had happened, that we had said. I touched the bruise on my cheek and stood up with my hand to my face, and went up the stairs to bed, leaving all the lights on, carrying my face like that.

The next day, Monday afternoon, we heard wheels on the gravel outside.

"Daddy!" Hallie said, and started running.

But it was not him. It was a car I did not recognize. A small blue one with a woman at the wheel.

Bobbie.

She climbed out of the car and shook the long drive off herself. She was smiling, holding her arms out wide. "Charlotte!" she said. "Hey, Hallie girl!"

Hallie hid behind my legs. I picked her up and and ran over to Bobbie and let her fold us up in her arms. "Bobbie," I said into her neck. "What have I done?"

"Now wait," she said, pulling back and inspecting me. "Hang on." I saw her notice my bruised face, professional concern in her eyes.

"A door," I said. "I—"

But she stopped me with a finger on her lips. *Does she know?* "Shhh," she said. She opened the trunk of her car and Hallie squirmed to follow her, peeking in on tiptoe.

"Presents!" Hallie said.

Bobbie laughed. "Presents indeed! You'll never guess what. Not that it's quite visible," she said cryptically. Then she pushed her jacket aside and swayed her back so I could see the swell of her belly. She was beaming and at least five months' pregnant.

"Bobbie!" I said. I was dumbfounded and so happy my eyes welled up. "Oh, it's wonderful!"

"I think so," she said. "Marcus does."

"Oh, it's such good news."

"Not according to everyone."

"According to me."

"Not Milo," Bobbie said, and looked at me gently. "I talked to him, you know." She touched my hand briefly, as if to say it would be okay.

"Where is Milo?" I asked her, too quickly. "Do you know?"

"Milo is skiing," Bobbie said. "He's gone skiing," as if he had just gone to the cleaners to pick up some shirts. "Help me with this stuff." She handed me a bag, and we went inside to sit at the big table looking out over the dunes. Hallie clamored for attention, and in between her demands, Bobbie told me that she had had a long talk with Milo. He had told her he was going to Wyoming to ski with Winks.

"My brother," Bobbie said, "thinks better when he's going fast."

"Did he tell you what I did?"

"Yes," she said, and looked at me steadily. "What happened?"

"Oh." I winced, avoiding her. "Not yet. I'm not— What about you?"

Bobbie leaned back in her chair with her hands on her belly. "Look at that," she said proudly, showing off the hard ball of baby stretching out her spandex shirt. "Isn't that beautiful?"

It was. I told her so, glad for the distraction.

"Due in August," she said. "We're thrilled, Marcus and I. Not Hattie and Milton. Yet. At least not about the unwed part of it. And Milo *really* isn't. He's mad at me for not telling him till now, for being irresponsible, not being married. Especially not being married. And, well—he's mad at me."

"He's mad at me, too," I said.

"I know," she said, her eyes on the bruise again.

"I bumped into a door," I said again to see if she believed me. I couldn't tell how much Bobbie really knew. Surely Milo would not tell his sister he hit me. Still, I imagined she was using her laser-beam eyeballs to see through my skin to the lies tangled in my entrails, the way she saw through nervous teenage girls who appeared every day in her office. "I just—" and started crying again.

"Well, don't, okay, honey?" She sighed. "Don't do that. Say why. Say how it happened."

Which? I thought. *Bumping into the door? Or what I said on TV? The part where I goaded Milo before he hit me? Or just the hitting? What does she know?* I stood stalling and stammering while Bobbie continued her steady doctor's office gaze, waiting.

"It was because I was flustered," I said finally. I explained about the shoot in Newark, the explosion. Did she know about that? She did, she said, Milo told her. Well, I said, you don't know how upsetting it was. The crowd, the falling building. I wasn't prepared for it. The reporter flustered me. I was rattled by that man who yelled at us. *Why are you here? Why don't you stick the camera in your own face?*

"I was upset because I thought he was *right!*" I said to Bobbie. "We shouldn't have been there. He was right."

"Apparently he was." Bobbie sniffed.

"I wasn't thinking," I said, halting and stammering. "I was distracted and trying to please so I said what everyone else had been saying. The mayor."

"Ah," she said.

"I'm sorry," I said. "I wish I had never—"

She was studying my face as I talked. "And why exactly are you sorry?" she asked.

"For saying what I said. For being stupid."

"Oh. You think you're stupid."

"Yes."

"Okay. You're stupid. It was stupid."

"I know."

"It was *naïve,*" she said, looking exasperated. "It was lazy. Ignorant. Thoughtless. I'm not saying I don't *blame* you, because I do, but I'm also saying, it's not surprising."

So she had been expecting it, too. What did that mean? Did it mean I could never be trusted? That I was hopeless?

"There were other people there!" I said desperately. "Not just me! The mayor was there. They said the same thing! Same as I did. And that woman who pushed the detonator button, she was a former resident. She said *good riddance*. Nobody paid any attention to any of them. If there hadn't been models there nobody would've cared that they were blowing up those houses."

"Maybe not."

"And if I wasn't married to Milo."

"There you go," she said. "See? Not stupid. Smart. Smart Charlotte."

"No," I said sadly. "Sorry Charlotte. Stupid Charlotte."

"Oh, stop it, please," Bobbie said angrily. She got up and looked out the window at the water. "Sorry's not all that helpful after the first time you say it, right? Stop being sorry and do something about it. Do something useful. If being a fashion model in front of a housing project gets attention to the problem, then go do that! Stand in front of a crack house or a welfare office or a prison. Something. Whatever. You're the one with the magazine, right? It's up to you."

"I'm just a model," I said. "I—"

"Fine. You and Milo both. I said the same thing to him and I always have. But no! He's just an athlete. You're just a model. Fine. You were made for each other." She wheeled away from the window and saw how her words stung me. "I said that to him and now he won't speak to me, either." She tried to smile but you could tell she didn't feel like it.

Hallie was watching us warily from where she played on the floor. "Go to the beach?" she said hopefully.

"Good idea," said Bobbie. "The beach." She waited out on the sunny steps while I got a jacket on Hallie and found buckets and shovels and the beach blanket. We walked out over the dunes. I sat down on the blanket but Bobbie took Hallie's hand and left me there. The two of them walked along, picking up jingle shells, orange ones the color of cantaloupes. The blue April sky surrounded them so they looked like cutouts, and the lettuce-leaf edge of the waves rushed at their feet. Hallie twirled and skipped and when she fell, Bobbie helped her up, brushing sand off her knees. I wondered what they were saying. What Bobbie was thinking. After twenty minutes, they came skipping back. Bobbie was calm again, amused by Hallie.

"Look," Hallie said, "crab bodies." She showed me a bucket of dead spider crabs, like broken prehistoric toys in pink plastic.

"Lovely," I said, hugging her.

"They'll live in my room," she said with a certain deliberate charm, roguish like her father's.

"Doesn't she look like Milo?" I said to Bobbie wistfully.

"Yeah," Bobbie said. "Same rascal face."

We walked quietly along the sand for a while, me thinking about Milo's rascal face. Enraged.

"What else did Milo say?" I asked warily.

"Well," Bobbie said, "he's a little wigged out right now."

"Me, too."

"Listen, I didn't mean to yell at you," she said. "I'm just so sick of how I have to constantly be the nursemaid and explain."

"I'm sorry."

She glared at me for saying it. "What I meant is: You're not alone. Milo is right up there with you, Charlotte, cruising at his hot-air altitude with his fame and his friends and his money. He was due for some of this. I was afraid of it."

I did not know what she meant but I wanted her to keep talking. "Darryl said—"

"Darryl." She snorted. "I don't like the sound of that guy."

"Why?"

She didn't answer for a while. "We talked about Darryl," she said. "Maybe he uses Milo, too."

"He said Milo—" I could hardly say it. "He said Milo's gone. He said he's not going to be calling."

Bobbie shook her head. "That wasn't my impression," she said. "Look, Milo is smart. He'll figure it out. I hope so, anyway."

"I hope so, too."

"But you should be prepared," she said. "It might take a while. A long time. And you will have to hang in there, because it might be . . . *unpleasant*." She saw me wince at that word. It was medical. "Look," she said, putting a hand on my arm, "my brother loves you. I believe this because I know him. He comes from a family where you stick things out, you get married if you're a parent, you don't give up, you're honorable in good faith, you keep your promises. That's what Robicheauxs are like, mostly. He loves you," she said. "I've seen it. I'm pretty sure of it."

I wished I was sure; wished on stars, or anything that resembled stars:

car headlights and neon signs, the tiny red battery light on the smoke alarm above the bed. I wished Bobbie was right. I wished Milo would come back. *My brother loves you.* For days after she left I held on to her words, winding them tightly around my dread like Catholics hold rosary beads wound in their fingers.

31.

I never did tell Bobbie that Milo hit me. Maybe she knew from Milo. Maybe she guessed. Maybe she didn't ask because she was waiting for me to say something. But I never did. Not to her. The only person I told was Claire.

It took me five days; five days of Milo not arriving and not calling; five days of me and Hallie digging to China, going stir-crazy at the beach. But finally, fortified by drinking, I called Claire. I told her everything about the Bombshell shoot and Newark. I skipped what happened next: the shouting and the way he floored me. It was too shameful. Instead I told her I was alone there on the far end of Long Island and everyone on the radio was still talking about me as if I were toxic.

Claire just listened.

When I appeared to be finished she cleared her throat. "First of all," she said, "I haven't heard anything about it. Nothing about Newark or you, or Milo. It's not on my radio stations, so it's fringe. Number two: I have been in buildings like that. And guess what? It's *true*: Those projects *are* just festering wretched breeding grounds for bad guys of every description. So don't beat yourself too hard for saying they should be blown up. Just don't."

I felt she was wrong but her words were oddly comforting to me.

"Nuke them all, as far as I'm concerned," she said. "Don't feel bad." She was about to launch into more of her speech when I stopped her.

"Milo hit me," I said, trying the words out.

"He *what*?"

"He . . . hit me."

"He *hit* you?" She was just shocked. I should have known. She was up and pacing around. I could picture her. "I can't believe it," she said. "I'll *kill* him. I can't believe he would do that! Jesus. He *hit* you?"

"Yes," I whispered.

"Oh," she said, softly now. "Your face? Oh no, honey, your face."

"It's okay, it's just . . . a bruise."

"Just a bruise," she said. She was writing something; I heard the pen scratching. "What else are you not telling me? Have you called the cops?"

"No," I said. "No. Listen, it was . . . my fault."

"Don't say that!" she said. "That's classic. Do you hear yourself? *He* hit *you*. You can't blame yourself. You need a therapist. Maybe the cops—"

"No," I said. "It's nothing. It's not a police thing. Believe me. Look, I wish I hadn't said anything. I wish I hadn't told you."

"No, you have to," she said. "Be careful, Charlotte. I see this all the time."

"Yeah, but I was just—*asking* for it."

"Stop saying that, please, it's scary," Claire said. "I know you care about him, but this kind of thing doesn't get better. It's a downward spiral. I'm worried about you, Charlotte."

"Claire," I said, "I fucked up, is what happened and he got mad at me." I told her it was really nothing, that Milo and I were both drunk and that it wasn't that bad. "You know how I get, Claire, how I just go off and say *whatever*." I wished I hadn't told her. It was shameful. She was blowing it out of proportion with her prosecutor's eye and her loyal concern. It made me mad at her, if you want to know the truth. I didn't want to hear her theories. I wanted her to say it was a fluke, that she knew Milo, this wasn't the kind of thing he would do. It would blow over, he would be back, he loved me and would forgive me. But she didn't say what I wanted to hear, so I didn't listen.

The phone rang every day out on Montauk but it was never Milo. It was Claire, checking on me, or Bobbie. It was my agent, my booker, or Lucy, or Kevin. I apologized but they were all furious. Especially Kevin. "Your husband's people are harassing me! They are suing me! What is going on, Charlotte? Tell me the meaning of this!"

This was all the Robicheaux money, the entire investment stake pulled suddenly out of *Edge*. This was the Newark pictures—whichever ones included me, which was nearly all of them—completely tied up in a legal dispute by Milo's people.

"Unusable. Completely out of the question for the next issue, if ever, thank you very much," Kevin said.

"I'm so sorry," I said sadly. "Kevin?"

"Just go back to L.A.!" he shouted at me, and hung up.

I would go back. Everyone said I should. Claire. Bobbie. My sister. Nobody in L.A. ever heard of *Newark*, that's what Claire said. Nobody in L.A. had any memory. They could care less. Maybe she was right. So after my face was healed and clear, after three weeks of waiting for Milo to call or pull in the driveway, I headed for the airport.

My keys shook, standing on the doorstep. I don't know what I was expecting. Him to be there? Us to start over? "In, in in," Hallie said, pushing. I opened the door and the place spread out before us, full of sunlight, the bold full kind that blasts straight off the ocean. It smelled clean. It looked like someone's lovely home, with draperies and lots of green plants, and carpets vacuumed in perfect stripes, like a newly mown outfield. There was that sculpture in the entryway, a large, polished piece of granite, a sort of human form curled into an egg, that we bought—Milo and I—in San Francisco, just before Hallie was born. There was her little wicker chair over by the window; there was her carved rocking horse.

Our house. We had only been gone a short time, but it seemed to belong to other people now, not us. Hallie ran inside. "Where's Daddy?" she said.

There he is. On the answering machine.

Hello. It's me. I'm still in Wyoming. Roaming in Wyoming. Ha ha. Hi, Hallie honey. I'll be home on the fourteenth. Which is soon. Okay? I'll see you then.

His voice came sixth, after the message from the security company saying the alarm had gone off, that a neighbor had checked, and everything seemed to be fine, *Please call us at your convenience;* followed by a child's garbled voice asking *Please can Hallie come over;* then my sister saying *It's Mom's birthday coming up;* then my agent with *Some questions regarding this* Edge *thing;* then someone hanging up; then Milo. Followed by someone hanging up again; my hairdresser from Beverly Hills; Marcy, saying she'd be back to work the next day; another hang up. There were ten messages.

I played number six again.

Hello. It's me. Roaming in Wyoming. Ha ha...home on the fourteenth.

Well, I would be out on the fourteenth. It was two weeks away and I'd be somewhere else. Anywhere. Milo would see that I wasn't sitting around pining, not Charlotte. I was that girl with spine, not some invertebrate paramecium on the couch sipping my drink at three o'clock in the afternoon, desperate and wrecked, waiting for my far-flung husband with Hallie nestled in the curve of my lap, the television on and the *Bugs Bunny* theme song finishing up right at that moment.

Which is exactly what happened, I am not kidding.

I had time to wonder if that was a car door slamming. I had time to sit up and then lie back down thinking *No. Anyway, it's the thirteenth, not the fourteenth.*

"Hey," he said, so quietly it scared me.

His hair was longer, or something. He looked different. Wild, or nervous, or maybe not so clean-shaven as usual. He had on a navy stretch shirt, short sleeved, with USA on the turtleneck. He had his mirrored sunglasses on and was just taking them off.

"Daddy!" Hallie ran to him and leapt up into his arms.

"Hey, pigeon," he said, and kissed her and kissed her.

She held his head in her small arms so his face was squashed up awkwardly, but still he was looking at me. He was holding her and saying "Hey, babycakes, hey, I missed you," and he was looking at me.

Milo, I said.

Yeah, he said.

It was excruciating, really, that moment.

I stood up and walked toward him. Both of us said small nothings, talking through Hallie. *Daddy's home! He's back!* checking each other. *What was that?* I thought. *There in that look?* Some tightness in the way he was breathing, some sidelong avoiding of my eyes. I wondered if he might be ready to hit me again, or kiss.

Both of us knew that we were not really going to talk about it, but that it would be decided now, today, any minute, that second. We would stay together or we would not. I did not know where he had been or what made him come back, but I was thinking: If I could only get my hands on his shoulders, and then, if it seemed okay, if I could just run my hands along the hourglass of his arms, then I would know.

He smiled at me bleakly.

I smiled back, looked away.

"How was Wyoming?" I said.

"Fine."

"Did you ski?"

"Yep."

"See Winks?"

"Yep."

"How's he?"

"Winks's good. Fuckin' lunatic."

"You thirsty?"

"Sure."

I moved past Milo toward the kitchen, a lump in my throat like an egg.

"Hey," he said, and held me by the arm.

"What?"

He pulled me in, turned me hard, and pushed my head down on his shoulder, the palm of his hand to the back of my head. He held me there by his collarbone. It surprised me, the sudden way he did it and the familiar smell of Milo in the hollow by his shoulder.

"Hey," he said again softly, so the egg in my throat cracked and broke. We stood in the wide hallway, its walls hung with a hundred photographs. I was crying and Milo was saying *Shh*, while Hallie circled around our legs, chirping *Pick me up*, and all the photographs—of us and our parents and sisters and brothers, of newborn Hallie and the guys from the ski team, of Darryl and Claire, and of everybody we have ever known—stared at us from their frames, like witnesses.

"So here we are in the hallway," Milo said finally.

"Yeah," I said, not crying now.

"What do you think?" he asked.

"It's nice here?" I said.

"Let's just stay then."

"Right where we are."

"In the hallway."

"We'll stay put."

Hollow out a cave in the snow.

"Up," Hallie said.

We sat down on the wide runner of carpet, and Hallie climbed into our laps, delighted, patting our faces and honking Milo's nose so he had to say *beep* every time she did it, which forced us to laugh despite everything. We couldn't help it. *Beep.*

"You did not give me my space powers," she said to him. "For a long time, not even any."

"You're right!" he said. He took her hand and put kisses in it, made some space noises, closed her fingers around them. "There you go."

Solemn Hallie kept her hand closed, put it in the pocket of her jumper. "I'm keeping them in here," she said.

"Okay," said Milo, smiling.

So I held my hand out, too, palm up, asking for something, some small kiss like Hallie's. Or maybe offering something.

Milo hesitated. Some hitch was there again, in the way he looked or didn't look. It was that way he had, of parking his gaze just to the side, or just above. I used to believe when he did this that there was something about me Milo did not want to see. But now I have come to understand that this shift of his eyes was really him hiding something. Something about himself he didn't wish to reveal.

My hand rested in the air, open in front of him. Milo took it, finally, holding it like a fortune-teller, tracing the lines of the palm with his fingertip. Then he put his mouth right down on it, so his lips left a warm impression, on the heart line and head line and life line, and I clenched my fist on whatever that foretold and stowed it away down the deep V of my shirt. Milo's mouth cocked up in a smile. "Do that again," he said. I held my hand out and he kissed it again, wickedly, so I smiled now, too, and stowed that kiss away with the other one.

We waited till Hallie was asleep.

Milo was sitting on the terrace in the back, quiet, watching the waves rolling in, greasy in the moonlight. There was no wind. I sat next to him and pulled my legs up under my skirt, laid my head on my knees. Then I began. I tried.

"You know... what I said..."

He watched me trying to get the words into sentences, trying to get the building to stand upright again, reconfigure all the pieces of rubble, like film running backward.

"There's... no way..." I said, "to explain."

"I don't want to talk about it," he said.

"But I wanted—"

He shook his head.

"To say—"

"Say nothing."

"I'm sorry. That's what I wanted to say."

"Okay," he said. "I'm sorry, too." He said it with the thumb side of his fist to his mouth, as if he were punching himself. "I'm sorry, too."

At first I thought he meant he was sorry I had done what I did, said what I said. But then I thought maybe *he* was apologizing. For hitting me. For leaving me and Hallie for five weeks alone.

He *was* sorry. I could see it, but he never said for what.

Later I knew for what. For betrayal. For where he had just been. For who he had kissed, the bed he had slept in, the words he had spoken; I can just imagine them, each flash of it like hitting me again. Sorry. Yeah, sure, he was sorry.

But for us that night, apology mixed with hurt, plus anger, plus guilt, was highly combustible, volatile. The fusion of these in Milo and me caused such a violent reconciliation, forgiveness like a sport, like blood wrestling. One minute we were sitting quietly outside, watching the helium moon rise higher, lost in our thoughts, feeling the wind pick up and loosen the tops of the trees; and the next minute our fingers were tangled and our wrists cocked back, pulling hard against each other. On that tension alone we rose to our feet, kissing, stumbling inside, banging into furniture, cursing, spilling glasses over, laughing, toppling down in the living room, rolling around. We burned our skin on the carpet. All the sounds we made were against our will, wild cries and gusts of words through teeth. I cut my tongue where he bit me. Milo's shoulder bled where I scratched him. We were up all night.

. . .

But of course, in the morning, the beast of what happened was still there, curled by our hearth, still begging under the table waiting to be fed on scraps of suspicion and doubt or, if we could possibly manage it, caged and tamed and housebroken.

We sat with coffee outside, watching Hallie running in the garden, trying to catch butterflies. Her hair flew out behind her and caught the sun so it shone down her back, black and bright. She was a butterfly herself, flitting around the lawn with a small net that she smashed wildly down, always missing. Each time she swiped, she would stop and check to see if we were paying attention. Look! she kept saying, and we would have to say Yes! or Oh! or anything to prove we noticed.

"Milo?" I said, out of the blue.

"Hmm."

"Darryl said—"

"What?"

I hadn't meant to speak, but now that I had started, words kept leaking out, as if I were a broken faucet. "He said I had a sick interest in you," I said, "and you had a sick interest in me, and that's all it ever was."

"Well, that's just Darryl," Milo said carefully, sipping his coffee.

"Is that just you?" I asked him.

Here there was a pause. "I don't know."

"Why not?"

"How do you know something like that?" he asked.

"Like what?"

"Like what's a sick interest."

"*I* know," I said.

"What do you know?"

"That it's not sick," I said. "Mine in you, I mean."

"Why not?"

"It's healthy," I said. "See?"

He looked at me and allowed a smile. "Yeah," he said. Then, after a minute: "What else did Darryl say?" He asked me this idly, not as if there was something in particular Darryl might have said, some beans he might have spilled. "What else did he say?"

"Nothing."

Inside the phone was ringing. It was a Saturday morning, and if things went as they usually did, the phone would be ringing all the time now, with people calling to invite us places, for tennis, to parties on their boats, to charity balls and dinners and weekends somewhere exotic. I was looking forward to things going as they usually did. I was hoping for some frivolity and tennis, maybe some flashbulbs and some starlight and some dance music to be coming along soon.

"Hello?" I said. No one spoke. "Hello? Hello?"

Whoever it was hung up. I went back out and Milo asked Who was that? and I told him No one. "They hung up," I said.

"Hmm," he said.

"We had a lot of those, on the machine," I said. "And more just in the last couple of days, two a day, sometimes." I also told him about the message from the security company, that the alarm had gone off while we were away.

He sat forward abruptly. "Are you saying somebody broke in here?"

"They just said the alarm went off."

"Why?"

"I don't know."

"What was it?"

"Apparently nothing."

"What happened?"

"They said it was fine."

"Did they check?"

"Don't yell at me."

"I'm not yelling. I'm trying to get you to realize."

"They said they checked."

"Who checked?"

"That a neighbor checked. Mrs. Deraney."

"They sent the neighbor? That's all? A neighbor?"

"They said to call them."

"You bet I'll call," he said.

At the time I did not wonder who it was that called and hung up, or whether anyone had tried to break into our house. Although I worried about things like that—intruders or deranged fans—mostly they seemed as unreal to me as cartoon bad guys. They were things that happened to other people. Also, Milo was home now, and I could see that he was worried about our safety, our family. Hallie got tired and as we talked she fell asleep on Milo's lap. Sitting there, I was happy; glad the subject was changed from what *had* happened to what was going to happen now: the future. Milo used the word *we*. *We'll get guard dogs. We'll hire a security guard. We'll have to have someone here when we're away.* But then the phone rang again and Milo's arms were full of sleeping Hallie, so I went in and picked it up.

"Hell-oh there, Miss Anne!" Of course it was Darryl.

"Hello," I said flatly.

"So he's back. Well, well."

"So," I said, "you were wrong."

"Was I, Pink?" Darryl said, so lightly. "Maybe so. Maybe so."

My skin prickled, hearing him. He was jovial. It just chilled me.

"May I speak with him?"

"Hang on," I said. "It's Darryl," I told Milo. My mouth was dry.

He slid Hallie gently onto a long chaise and took the phone back into the house. He winked as he went and I could see him talking, the phone clamped to his ear with his bare shoulder. It was a short conversation. He hung up and came back out and sat with me.

"What did he want?"

"Just meeting tomorrow with some money people for *Justice Warrior*." *Justice Warrior* was the next Cade movie. Cade Four.

"On a Sunday?"

"Yeah. Sorry."

"You just got back—"

"It'll take an hour. Two. It's just lunch."

"It's Sunday."

I didn't like the thought of it. Milo and Darryl. My ears burned already, at the thought of the jokes they would tell.

"I don't like Darryl anymore," I said.

Milo peered at me the way his father did sometimes over his glasses. *Explain*, said the look.

"I don't like him," I said. "He gives me the creeps."

"He's a pussycat."

"He hates me."

"He doesn't hate you. Don't be ridiculous."

"He's not good for you, Milo."

"Without him there would be no Cade."

"True," I said. "He calls me Pink."

"So? Should be used to it by now."

"He calls me Miss Anne." How pathetic my reasons seemed, aloud.

"That's how he talks. It's just a joke. He's yanking your chain."

"It's not a joke to me," I said.

"What is the matter with you? Calm down."

"He makes me nervous."

"What are you trying to say?" Milo narrowed his eyes at me in a warning way.

"When you were gone," I started, "he said you did not want to speak to me." Milo looked interested now, so I kept going. "He said you would not be calling me. He said you were over me, that it was over, that you said it was."

"I did not say that."

"I asked him to please tell you that I needed to talk to you," I said. "To get you a message."

"I did not get a message."

"Darryl said you didn't want to talk to me."

Milo looked away. "Did you get a message from me?" he asked.

"Bobbie told me that you were skiing," I said.

"I was skiing," Milo said. "Listen: Not from D.? No message?"

"Darryl just told me you never cared about me in the first place."

"I don't want to hear this," he said.

"He told me what you say about me. Your joke."

"I said I don't want to hear it."

"He said—"

"Stop it."

So I stopped.

But then Milo asked: "What joke?"

Should I tell him? It was funny, right? *Chocolate fantasy, black booty quest*. He asked me so I took a breath and told.

"Fuck him, the fucker," Milo said when he heard. "That was not my joke."

"Whose was it?"

"His."

"Did you laugh?" I asked him.

Milo thought about it but you could tell he didn't want to. "I don't know," he said wearily, almost as if he was admitting something. "I guess I laughed."

Of course he laughed. Because it was funny! *Barbie on a Black Booty Quest*. It was a riot. When I heard it I pictured Astronaut Barbie in some rocket ship, her stoned, starry eyes stuck open, having trouble with the control pedals because of her feet in lifetime stiletto position, questing and lusting through the cosmos with her pointy torpedo bosoms at the ready. I could care less if Milo laughed. It was funny as long as it wasn't true about me.

"Barbie on a quest—" I said. "Is that what you think about me?"

He took a long time to answer. "You know me," he said, shrugging and guilty. But then he said it again with a different inflection. "You know me."

"I do?" I asked, surprised. "Really?"

"As much as anyone," he said. "More, probably."

At the time I bought it; his words pleased me so much. The idea was a shiny bauble from Milo's lips, not even an answer to my question, distracting me. *I knew him.* I wanted to buy it so I did, without asking the price. How expensive it turned out to be—to think I knew him, or could. Because how can you know anyone, really? I don't care how many times you have slept with him or next to him, listening to him breathe or snore, dream or kick the covers. What did I *know*? That he liked sugared cereal for breakfast? That his waist is a 32 and his shirt collar is a 15? That when he was a boy he had his tonsils removed and was terrified of the doctor? I knew a long list of things about him. So what? The mother of the murderer says, *He was such a good boy.* The neighbors of the drug dealer say, *You would never believe that about her! She was an A student.* The wife of the playboy says, *He was home every night for dinner.*

Milo was quiet that afternoon. I was calmed down. Hallie woke and I was busy with her, making her lunch. Milo watched us from a kitchen stool and joined in the conversation a little, but he was distracted, restless, pianoing his fingers and nodding occasionally as if he were arguing something out with himself. What was it? Once I asked him and he smiled and brushed my hair with his hand. *Nothing*, he said. He picked up Hallie and sang to her. He rinsed the dishes, looking glassily out the window into the dark.

"What?" I asked.

"Nothing," he said.

He didn't sleep well, tossing and keeping me awake. The sheets were pulled to his side of the bed, tangled around him.

The next day he went to lunch with Darryl and when he came home, it was all over, just like that. "Darryl and I have decided to go our separate ways," he said, beaming in the front door, announcing his news. He seemed almost relieved, saying *Where's my girls?* Grabbing us up the way he did to people at parties. I smelled cigar smoke on him. It was in his hair and in his mouth. I tasted it when he kissed me.

"We just decided to part company for a while," he said.

I was shocked. I said I was.

"Welp," Milo said, explaining, "if you're not moving forward, you're standing still, right?"

"But Darryl was your friend."

"He is still my friend. He's just not my agent or my business partner."

"Did you tell him what I said?"

"I told him he makes my wife nervous, yeah."

"I wish you hadn't said that."

"Why?"

"Because he'll think—he won't know what I meant."

"He doesn't care what you meant. He thinks what he thinks."

"So what did he think?"

"He thought it was funny, that he makes you nervous. He thought it was hilarious."

"No," I said, "about you firing him."

"I didn't fire him. We came to an agreement. An amiable agreement."

"Which was what?"

"To dissolve our partnership. I'll buy him out. Pay him for his half."

"Just like that?"

"Yeah," Milo said.

"But why?"

"I thought you'd be happy. You're the one who wanted me to move on."

"I didn't say that."

"Well, not in so many words." Milo shrugged. "But listen: Sometimes you just need a new coach. One guy teaches you what he knows, then you go learn something new from somebody else. I learned a lot from Darryl. He got a lot out of me. We had a great run. Right now we're both on different courses, you know? It's not a big deal."

"How's he feel about it?"

"He wants to direct," Milo said, as if that explained it.

What took place I still don't know. They had lunch. They parted company. They were still friends, or so Milo claimed. I don't know what was said between them any more than I know whether they ate steak au poivre or Caesar salads. I don't know what agreement they had, or what Milo meant about paying Darryl, buying him out. I didn't ask questions such as: Did Milo have his own reasons for easing Darryl out of the picture? Would Darryl blame *me*? I tried not to think of it again, that lunch, those long bad weeks, until I had to. I was ready to forget all about Darryl and his names for me, his schemes for Milo, his theories about us; I was happy to forget what happened in Newark and that terrible night in our New York living room. I would just not think about it, ready to move on. Now, though, I sift these scenes obsessively, as if they were a sandpile where I'd lost my wedding ring, on the slim chance that it will turn up again, hard and glittery like a fact.

32.

Here is the part where we were happy for a while. Here is the part where Hallie learned to skip, and we all had to go around skipping to my lou my darling, singing that song because she liked it, and being lighthearted. Our hearts were so strangely light during those days, considering our bitter words, and the fact I had hurt Milo, and he had hit me and left me for five weeks. Now he was always hugging me and reaching for me in the night, kissing me languidly in the kitchen. *Why?* It breaks me to think about it now, the way he kissed me sometimes; as if he were privately sad about something. I thought it was tenderness. I thought he was sorry for hitting me, and had forgiven me. There was not one warning of the kind I had been raised to watch out for, some sign from Heaven, angels or plagues. Nothing like that. Just once in a while a distractedness. And Milo had always been like that, moody and pensive.

He got up in the early mornings with Hallie, and they took walks along the beach, skipping, of course. Hallie was so proud of herself because it is quite an accomplishment for a three-year-old to skip. She was astonishingly coordinated. She had a gymnast's body, with hard little muscles in her thin arms. She started to call Milo Daddy-boy. I don't know where she heard it or whether she made it up, but that was his name. Daddy-boy, Daddy-boy, all day. It was during this time that she took such a shine to him. He was about to start shooting Cade Four, *Justice Warrior*. He had a new power agent from the biggest agency in Hollywood. A white guy

named Roy DiCostanza. Roy had a chestnut-brown mustache and a sta-
ble of talent including everyone you ever heard of. Roy was going to take
Milo global. He was going to cross Milo over. Beyond Cade. That's what
he said. Milo was talking about new projects, about producing, about writing his own scripts. Every day he'd work out and go over his lines for
Justice Warrior, and the rest of the time, except for rehearsals, he'd play
with Hallie. At night we had conversations like this:

"Trevor."

"James."

"Jayson."

"Adrian."

"Adrian!?" he said. "Adrian? Adrian is a girl's name."

"Is not. Adrian Robicheaux. What? Don't make that face."

"Jake. Now that's a good goddamn name. Jake Robicheaux."

"Jake?"

"What's wrong with Jake?" he said.

"Sounds like some guy with a moonshine business."

"Well, what the hell then? What do you like?"

"Leland?" I said.

"That was my grandmother's name," he said. "Her maiden name."

I nodded.

"Leland Robicheaux." Milo was smiling now. "For a boy."

I could see he was pleased at the idea, that his mother would like it.

We saw Milo's parents in August that summer, when Bobbie had her
baby, a beautiful tiny acorn of a son named Marcus, after his father. We
flew east and I held him at the hospital, Brigham and Women's in Boston.
My nephew. He was not more than ten hours old, and I looked down at
his elfin face and his long fingers crinkled like pigeons' toes, feeling how
light and small he was, while his father and Bobbie beamed dopily around
the room at the whole Robicheaux assembly. Hallie was saying "A cousin!
A cousin!" Milton was looking proud and uncomfortable in the doorway.
Milo was next to me and Hattie was leaning over my shoulder, tears in
runways down her cheeks. All during the afternoon visiting hours that
day, tears were tracking down the women's faces, Bobbie's especially.

"I'm thirty-six years old," she said, "and I never thought I could be so whipped by love as this."

"What about me?" Marcus said, pouting and kissing her.

But Bobbie looked at me and we shook our heads and said, *This is different*, smiling at each other knowingly. We had been talking a lot, me and Bobbie, ever since she'd shown up in the driveway in my hour of need. Mostly we talked about babies and pregnancy and what to expect: the pain and the various swellings, the exhaustion and the euphoria. I sent her my books and all my maternity clothes. I gave her presents and advice.

"What's with this bra with the windows?" she said, calling me. "What's with the shelf on the top of this shirt?" She laughed when I said soon she would be a human restaurant.

Milo was disgusted with her for the longest time. "Can't believe she's going ahead with this," he kept saying. "They should get married."

"You should buy her a new house," I said.

"*He* oughta buy her a new house," he said. "Marcus should."

"Maybe he counsels prisoners for practically no money."

"What's that got to do with it? They should get married," he said.

"Why?" It made me happy that he put such a premium on matrimony.

"Because she's having a baby," he said. "Babies need fathers."

"Marcus *is* the father."

"Then he should marry her."

"Maybe they're working things out," I said.

"Having a baby is worked out enough," he said. "What about my parents?"

"They're already married."

He rolled his eyes. "They are none too pleased."

"It'll be fine. You'll talk to them and reassure them. And you'll buy Bobbie a big house somewhere nice," I said.

"I will?" he asked, looking dubious.

"Also, you'll set up a trust fund for that baby before it's born, so it can have a yacht and a governess and a pony."

"I will?" he asked.

"And then you will get your sister a private hospital room."

So he did. Milo talked to his parents, calmed them down, spent a lot of money, stopped harping on weddings. And because of that, there we all were, gathered in the private room with a view of Boston Harbor where Bobbie had little Marcus; where she took my hand and pulled me down to whisper in my ear, *Thank you, Charlotte, for bringing Milie around. I know you did. It means so much to us.*

Then she asked me, Would I be the baby's godmother?

I would be so honored, I said. And I was. I picked up my godson and, after a while, handed him to his Uncle Milo, who made faces at him, kissed him, said, "Hey, Mister Man."

Bobbie said, "So when's your boy coming?"

Milo dipped his head and smiled. He shrugged and looked embarrassed.

We were trying. All that fall we were working on it. We didn't care, girl or boy. We just wanted another one. Hallie was asking, demanding a baby. We said, We'll do our best. Not that we suffered, trying. I thought we were relaxed now and knew everything to expect, the drugs and the tests and the appointments. I waited and hoped. I tried not to think too much about it, tried not to drink too much or at all except in the evening, tried to be grateful for what I had. Just to be with Hallie and Milo. I couldn't work anymore. That was clear. Not after Newark. I tried not to care, told myself it was not important. I did care, actually, and I was still offered plenty of jobs, despite what happened with *Edge,* but I couldn't work. I was unable.

Every creature in the fashion kingdom knows that the Third Eye of self-consciousness is death to a model. If you have it, you can no longer create a fiction, an illusion. Your pictures come out goofy, ugly; they are all failure pictures—of you not passing muster, of you being embarrassed and shy. You must never, ever, mentally ask what the camera is thinking of you. You tell the camera what you are thinking; *you* create a *look* with your form, your face. But I could not do that anymore. It had started even before Newark, but after that it was worse. Terrible. As if I were a separate person judging myself. I had the Third Eye now, badly; not only modeling, which I quit, but all the time, every day. I watched myself from outside, as if my whole life were a bad shoot, as if all my smiles and gestures were poses. I couldn't move without thinking: *Is my face telling a story? Are my eyes the window of my soul? Is my skin my uniform?*

Walking down Rodeo Drive one day that fall, I caught myself at it. In the sidewalk traffic of tanned white people in sunglasses and tucked dewlaps and rhinoplastied noses, I passed a black woman holding the hand of a small white boy. I passed a black man in a suit, another holding a broom, an older woman who looked like Milo's mother. When I passed I smiled at them, very slightly, lifted my chin in a nod, looked them in the eye; the same subtle exchange I saw happen with Milo sometimes, that *same skin understanding*. Only I did not have the same skin. It was as if I wanted to tell them: *I have gotten hate mail! My daughter has brown skin! I know all about Emmett Till!* How stupid, really. The man with the broom ignored me, the woman with the little boy smiled absently, maybe she thought I was noticing the child. But the man in the suit and the older woman both looked back as if to say: *What the fuck are you looking at, staring like that at me?* If I could have answered, it would be to say: *I just wanted to show somehow: This is not my uniform.*

I needed a new leaf, a clean slate, a different drummer. Something. I did not need another picture of myself pouting on glossy newsprint. I did not need to spend three hours waxing my legs or being slathered with far-fetched facial masques made of lamb placenta or pond algae. Bobbie had said, *You can stay naïve or you can do something about it.* I heard her words in my head now, the way I hear my mother's. *It's up to you.*

But do what? What would I do now? I stewed about it and tried to think up some kind of job for a new, improved Charlotte. I read the papers every day and looked at ads, wondering what would I be good at? What about a résumé? Mine wouldn't say anything but that I could stand around like a human clothes hanger. But I wasn't looking back. I was looking forward. To Christmas, to Milo wrapping up Cade Four in February, to Hallie's fourth birthday party in March, to a spring vacation in Hawaii with Milo's parents and Bobbie and the two Marcuses. I looked forward to the days stretching out ahead of us, a new baby, someday, I hoped so; Hallie reading, children growing up, me and Milo growing old, corny and bittersweet, finding a gray hair at his temple and pulling it out.

In January, Milo went to Canada to shoot scenes for *Cade, Justice Warrior*. This was going to be his best movie, he said. *Cade Three, Truth to Power*, had been too talky, too preachy, a disappointment. This one was more in the original heroic action style, about Cade single-handedly liberating hundreds of prisoners from a secret American gulag in Saskatchewan—where Cade's own brother is held at forced labor, prospecting for Big Oil. Cade, "a restless seeker after justice," as the script said, infiltrates the gulag, organizes a revolt, and leads the good guys across the frozen tundra to freedom.

Many of the scenes required skiing—mostly cross-country, which Milo hated. *Too much work for not enough speed*, he said when he called me, which he did every night. Sometimes twice. He didn't mind the cold. What he minded was how small the location town was. How dark it got and how early. And being a thousand miles away from me and Hallie. He wanted to come home, he said.

But he could only get home here and there, weekends. He had to be away for weeks. Half of January and part of February. It was too cold for us to visit.

"What are you doing all these days without me?" he asked.

"Thinking up a Charlotte Sequel," I said. "Charlotte Two."

"Charlotte One was a good flick," he said, laughing. "But the sequel has all the marks of a classic. A thriller, right?"

"No," I said. "A classic family film." I said how much I liked being home with Hallie, driving her to nursery school and dance class. I was taking a dance class myself, also tennis. "When you get home, I'll ace you," I said. "Six-love in straight sets."

"Hmmm," Milo said, "I like the sound of that."

I didn't tell Milo about who called me one morning. Why should I tell him? He was far away on the frozen tundra, and why bring it up?

I was out by the pool with Marcy and Hallie, who had a little friend over. The girls were playing mermaids, and Marcy and I were lifeguarding, dangling our legs in the pool, when the phone rang.

"Charlotte?" It was a man. "Do you know who this is?"

"I know your voice," I said, curious and smiling.

"You do know it," the man said. "That's for sure."

"Jack? Jack Sutherland?"

"You got it," he said. "Hi there."

He sounded exactly the same. "Oh my God," I said, just so surprised to hear from him. "How are you? I can't believe it! After all this time." I made a polite surprised fuss.

"I'm here in Los Angeles," he said. "I've been in Japan mostly, all this time, as you know. But, guess what? I'm headed permanently back stateside now, so: I just had to call and tell you."

"I'm so glad you did." *But not really.*

"I ended up getting your number from your mother. You keep changing it!"

"That's life in Hollywood," I said. "Unfortunately."

"At first I tried you in New York, but your mom said you're spending more time in L.A. these days."

"True." I was wondering just what it was Mom had said.

"So I'd love to see you."

"I'd love to see you, too!" I was friendly and warm enough to him. Why wouldn't I be? We were grown up now and bygones were bygones.

"Great," he said. "I'll pick you up in what, half an hour?"

"Oh, Jack, today's not great. I'm—not feeling well." I wondered if Jack could hear the fibs in my voice. He offered to come over but I told him not today and he sounded concerned.

"Are you okay? Are you all right?"

"Sure," I said.

"Unfortunately I'm headed back to Japan tomorrow. Won't be back till April sometime."

"But you're coming back, moving back, right?"

"You bet," Jack said. "I'd've called sooner but, hey: took me a while to get everything set up here."

"So we'll have plenty of time then."

"Yes we will."

"Sorry about today."

"*Shimpai nai.* Don't worry. I'll call you probably in a coupla weeks. Depends on how long it takes me to wrap things up."

"Well, good luck," I said, and we hung up.

"So who was that on the phone?" Marcy asked idly.

I explained Jack was my college boyfriend and how we broke up. "Milo knew him, too," I said. "We all knew each other."

"Really?" Marcy was fascinated. She had confided to me that the reason she had moved out of our garage apartment a month before was because she was living with a boyfriend. "In my country we don't talk with boyfriends anymore after marriage. Husbands not happy about that."

"Oh, it was a long time ago. Jack just called for old times' sake." Marcy looked quite interested. "He was devastatingly handsome," I told her.

"Maybe you still like him?" she asked. "Maybe your stars say what it means, the call."

I wished suddenly I hadn't told her anything about Jack. You can't be too careful. I was trying to learn that lesson and yet here I was again. Indiscreet. I'm telling you I worried more about whether I had said too much than I ever worried about Jack tracking me down. I told myself that talking to Marcy didn't matter. She would not say anything to Milo or anyone. And what if she did? What if she sold this old-boyfriend phone call as some *tidbit* for the tabloids? Who could find fault? Old friends called up and why not? The past resolved itself just by being past, didn't it? Jack was an okay guy, I thought. We'd go have a drink next time he was in town.

Darryl called, too, the week after that. I hadn't heard his voice for months. It was very businesslike now, very matter-of-fact. "Just tell him to call me," Darryl said. "Say it's about Mrs. Curtis."

"Okay," I said. I was polite. "Who's Mrs. Curtis?"

"Why don't you ask him?" Darryl said.

I waited for him to elaborate but he didn't. "Okay then, I will," I said, and hung up.

When Milo called that night, I gave him the message. "Darryl says for you to call him, and to tell you it's about Mrs. Curtis."

"Oh," Milo said. A long silence came from the phone.

"Milo?"

"Yeah," he said. "I'll call him." His voice was quiet.

"Something bad?"

"No, no," he said quickly. "Some fan, I think. One of those charity requests. She has some charity she wants me for, or something."

"Oh," I said. I was sure it was Darryl that was making Milo uneasy. I thought he felt guilty about firing his friend but didn't want to bring it up. I paid no attention to the name Mrs. Curtis. "How is Darryl, anyway?" I asked.

"Okay," Milo said. "Not great."

"Why?" I asked him. "What's the matter?"

Milo paused. "His business is off, he says. He says he's got no A-list clients right now and that the big studios won't go near his projects without somebody big."

"Don't worry, Milo, don't," I said. He sounded worried.

"Maybe he blames me," Milo said.

Something in his voice. I don't know. It did something chemical to my nerves, made a weakness in the muscles. "Milo? Are you okay?" I said.

"Yeah, yeah, yeah, just tired. Be glad to be done with this, come home."

"Hallie is pining for you."

He asked me to tell about her. I turned my light off and lay there, telling him how Hallie found my lipstick and painted her face with it, and all her dolls. How she took all my shoes out of the closet and walked around in them, teetering precariously and posing. *Really, Milo, like she's on the catwalk, it's scary.* How she liked to sing a song I taught her called "Dance to Your Daddy My Little Baby"... because it had the words *You shall have a fishy in a little dishy, you shall have a fishy when your daddy comes home*... how she thought he was really going to bring her a fish. When I ran out of stories I just held the phone, half asleep, murmured, "There's a good smell of you on the pillow here, Milo."

He said nothing. I heard him swallow. "Aww, God," he said, and let his breath out.

"What?"

"Nothing. Never mind," he said softly. "I'll see you Wednesday."

We had a tender reunion when he came home, more than usual. He was so glad to see us, see Hallie. He did bring her a fish, a live goldfish in a glass bowl, and she was so delighted. She named the fish Dishy and sang the song for Milo in her clear little voice. We all danced around the living room singing it, Milo holding Hallie, his arms around us. I felt safe. I was blessed and lucky.

You shall have an apple, you shall have a plum, you shall have a rattle when your daddy comes home.

"I missed you," Milo said, up late into the night.

"Nahh," I teased him. "You don't care. You didn't miss me. You'd be fine without me."

"Stop," he said. "Don't say that." And I thought then how sweet he was, with a film of tears in his eyes, smiling. Now, though, I think those tears were there because he knew a secret, like he had a terminal illness or three months to live, or I did.

Hallie turned four in the middle of March. We had a party outdoors with festoons of paper streaming from the trees, little lanterns along the drive, with a strolling clown and a magician who kept pulling things out of the children's pockets, out of their ears and their sleeves. The cake was in the shape of a rainbow, but very muddy-looking, because Hallie had frosted it herself. After the cake, a pony named Pie went up and down with kids on her broad back, suffering their petting, their little hands gripping her mane. Milo gave rides, too. He invented crab rides and towel rides and elevator rides and upside-down pineapple rides. The kids liked him more than the pony. The party lasted until well into the evening, when all the half-drunk parents carried their limp, exhausted children to their waiting cars and went home. Milo's friend Diego, from the *Cade* crew, filmed it all on good-quality stock and promised to edit it into a movie with a soundtrack, as a present to Hallie. Diego is selling it now, that footage, for a lot of money. Some shots have already aired: me and Milo lighting the cake, singing, the birthday candles casting an unholy light on the underbellies of our smiling faces.

We went to Hawaii in the beginning of April. On my dresser now is a picture of all of us taken on the beach there. Hallie, Milo and me, Milton and Hattie, Bobbie and Marcus and their little son. Our eyes are so clear, like gems, from the sun and the reflected water. We look fake. Like we were hired for an advertisement. We are all smiling, especially me. I like that picture of me. I like the way I'm smiling in it. My face looks, I don't know, nice. As if I am a nice person with little smile lines at the corners of my eyes. I was feeling happy.

Just before that picture was taken, Hattie had surprised me. She was sitting in a beach chair, wearing a flowered bathing suit with a flared skirt, watching me and Milo play shark with Hallie and little Marcus. He was in the waves splashing, his diaper so swollen with seawater he could hardly move. Bobbie was taking pictures. Milo and I scooted along low in the water humming *Jaws* music, scooping Hallie and Marcus up in our arms and pretending to gobble them up. Hallie screamed and the baby laughed. After a while I came and sat next to Hattie, drying off, and was surprised to suddenly find her hand on my shoulder. "I'm so glad I was wrong about you, Charlotte," she said.

"Wrong about what?" I asked.

"Milo's happy," she said.

"Thank you," I said, and hugged her. I was soaking wet but she hugged me back. "I hope you're right."

She wasn't right, of course. The happy part ended about two weeks after we got back. Or maybe it had ended way before that, but without the words *The End* coming up on the screen to confirm it. Looking now at that Hawaii picture is like looking at photographs of people who have died, been hit by a bus or something, so that you think idiotically: *They were so happy then, and now they're dead*. Milo and Charlotte. I remember the smell of coconut on our skin, the taste of pineapple and rum in his mouth. He is smiling down at me in the picture and his arm is around me, Hallie between us. It seems made up but it wasn't. It happened. It was not even long ago. Just weeks ago. His arm is around me. Right after it was taken everybody went back to their own apartments. We put our salty sleeping little girl down for a nap and closed her door behind us. In our own bed, we lay stretched out with the room stippled by sun and shadows, the loud waves rolling in so close to our window they seemed to be all around us. *We're on an island*, we said, and our whispers and murmurs and little cries were smoothed over, swept up into the hush of loud water and wind and breath.

33.

It was a Wednesday. I remember because Wednesday is a garbage night in Malibu. Milo put the cans out. We could have hired a guy to put it out by the street, but Milo never seemed to mind doing it. It was just a quiet night. We did the dishes instead of leaving them for the maid. He took the garbage out and came back to the kitchen where I stood at the counter, a sponge in my hand.

"Charlotte?" he said after a while, watching me.

"Umm?" absently.

He came and took the sponge from me, placed it down on the counter. He looked me in the eyes, took my hand. "Come here," he said. "My darling, we have to talk." He led me, and with a lurch of terror I saw that dread and sorrow and apology were mingling in his eyes.

I didn't know what he was going to say to me but right away I was mentally flattening myself down on the floor, going stiff, dragging back, skidding my heels, resisting. *No, I'm not coming.* But he pulled me into the living room, to the sofa by the glass doors. He slid them open. Smells from the sea came in, the sound of a siren somewhere. He sat me down. He was gentle.

"I have something to say to you," he said. He swallowed. I remembered he had not eaten much at dinner, had said little. My own dinner was haunting me now already. "I thought I would never have to tell you this. I wanted never to have to say any of it," he said.

"Then don't."

"If I don't tell you someone else will. I have to tell you. I have no choice." He closed his eyes and started.

"Listen: I will not lie to you. I will always tell you the truth even if it's a terrible truth. Promise to believe me. Promise, Charlotte."

"No," I said. As if refusing could protect me.

"Somebody is trying to extort money from me," he began grimly. "She's trying to blackmail me into giving her money. The way she's doing this is to say that her child is my child."

My mouth opened but no words were in it. I bent my head, pressing hard against it as if to keep his words from exploding out the top of my skull. *Her child is my child.*

"That call you told me about. Mrs. Curtis. It was about—"

It was about how you can't ever know anyone.

"—Geneva Johnson. Maybe you remember who she is, from the foundation, from the grant we first gave out. That dancer."

I stared at him, not crying or even blinking. *That dancer.*

He kept talking, plodding on, avoiding my eyes.

"Althea Curtis is her mother. They've been threatening to expose me as the father of this kid if I don't pay the daughter a half a million dollars now and something like six million over the next three years."

The father of this kid.

"I have to tell you this. Because—I have to go to the police. It's extortion. They're threatening— They say if I don't pay— They'll go to the press with it." He smiled ruefully, as if he hoped I might laugh at the ludicrousness of it. "She has a son," he continued. "She claims it is my son. I'm telling you now, Charlotte, that it's not."

I imagine that if you fell out of a plane there would be the same howl of wind and sick free-fall feeling I had listening to him, knowing the hard ground was seconds away, what he would say next.

"You are not answering the question," I said, ill and tumbling.

"Which question?"

But I wouldn't ask it, knowing the answer as well as he knew the question. *She has a son.*

"I did sleep with her," he said finally. "I'm sorry." His voice hitched and his face contorted, but he set his jaw and kept talking. "Just one time. That time. Right after. I'm sorry. I wish it had never, Jesus. Charlotte, what you said that day . . . It just made me— If you had never—" He shifted, as if recoiling again from me, remembering. "I was supposed to be in Wyoming but I stayed in New York part of that time."

Roaming in Wyoming. That phrase came back to get me now with its jaunty lie, the treacherous angle of its hat over glittering eyes, pushing me down into some slough of terror, forcing me to ask *What is happening? What is he telling me?*

"In our apartment?" I said.

He closed his eyes, shook his head. He couldn't look at me. Couldn't say it.

On Mercer Street. With that girl, the yellow smiley-face necklace. She'd be grown now, into a dancer, long neck, long legs, long arms.

"No," he said, "not there—"

"Don't tell me!"

"It was one time," Milo said. "That time. It meant nothing. It was— when the building, when you said— When they were saying those things about me. Because of what you said. And then you were...so drunk. Later—when I..."

When you hit me.

"When...I left. And went out. That's when it happened."

I stood up trembling, got away from him, anywhere. Just away. I couldn't talk or listen, stumbling through rooms.

"It was a long time ago," he said, following. "It's over."

He's over you, said Darryl. *He is past you. Done.*

"It was...it just..." He was behind me, talking.

"Why? Why?"

"I'm trying to tell you. I'm trying to get through telling you."

"I hate you." I was crying so much. "God damn you!"

"It's not mine," Milo said. "He's too old to be mine."

It's a boy. The way he said it. *He's too old.* As if he knew him, had held him, that baby boy, knew all about him, his name, his first tooth.

"Go away from me," I said. "Go to hell. I don't want to talk to you."

He doesn't want to talk to you, is what Darryl said: He knows which side his bread is buttered on, he is hurt but he will find his medicine, rest assured, someone's gonna go but maybe not me.

"Charlotte, it's a six-month-old baby—"

I got up and ran to the car. I revved it, with Milo standing in the driveway, saying my name, saying don't leave. His hands were up, gesturing, describing broken shapes in the air. Don't, he said helplessly. Let me explain. I backed out and drove. Who knows where. Up into the hills, winding past canyons, on roads without streetlights, just headlights sweeping past eucalyptus trees, over the hills and back down, trying to stop my mind's eye. The two of them, I knew just how he looked, knew his face, but with her. I was demented with it, exiting off the highway in Santa Monica, finding Venice Beach, careening down to the strand, tormented with Milo's voice. *She says it's my child.* I was braking, crying, nearly crashing, head down on the wheel, remembering *That look. The day he came back, there in his eyes. It was guilt. He was fresh from her, shifting his gaze. Guilty.*

How was skiing?

Fine.

See Winks?

Yeah. Guy's a lunatic.

I was crying so hard I was ill, wracked, holding on to the steering wheel as if it could comfort me. *Milo milo milo.* His name was a nonsense word, meaningful now as speaking in tongues.

Oh how I love you, I had said.

And oh how I love you, he had said back.

None of it meant anything now. It was all tainted, all a lie. Whatever he said. Betrayal remakes your whole life, so that the past is not what you thought it was, never can be again.

Him in the arms of her. Her soft brown arms.

He said it was nothing, meant nothing; when clear as these tears it meant something, everything. She had whatever I did not, could not give. Something he'd always wanted, wondered about, had to have. *A soul mate, so to speak.* With her surely he felt some ease, some relief, some kindred empathy, that he could never find with me, no matter what, and worst of all was the scalding thought that I deserved it. His affair. I couldn't blame him, not after what I said, how I betrayed him first. To think it was my own fault. That killed me.

The ghost of Charlotte got out of the car and walked down some Venice Beach street, blinking, crying but trying to see, to find the bar, with some name like Deadeye Dick's or Popeye's, something like that, with *eye* in it.

I went in and sat on a stool. The bartender didn't talk, just poured shots of tequila and watched me get drunk right away. Three in a row. I rested and then had some more. I wasn't counting. The jukebox played "Little Deuce Coupe." It was a surfer bar but mostly for retired surfers. Grayish-blond guys with meaty stomachs hanging over their cutoffs sat in the back playing darts. The women had leathery skin and their hair hung in stiff bleached hanks of blond. They smoked. One guy—you could see where his cheekbones had been, how blue his eyes still were—came and sat next to me and said Buy you a drink? I said Okay. He put his hand on my knee when he talked. I don't remember his name but his knuckles were puffed and the flesh grew up around his wedding ring. I don't know exactly how long I stayed, or how I got out of there. Somehow I got out and got in the car, drove home.

Milo found me at four in the morning passed out in the front seat, the car in the driveway with the engine still running, headlights on. When he couldn't get me to walk, he carried me in and put me to bed. I fought him. I vomited on him. I saw the mess: his shirt and the towel he cleaned it with. He told me all this later, the next day, but I wouldn't look at him when he said it.

"You were passed out."

I wish I were still.

"You threw up. On me."

Good.

He sat on the side of the bed. I couldn't look at him. My head hurt, a sharp pain with every heartbeat. The bed sloped in a valley where he sat.

"I'll take care of it," he said. "I promise."

I looked away.

"It will go away."

My lips were pressed hard together to keep them from wobbling.

"Charlotte. You know I—"

"Stop," I said. "Shut up."

"It'll go away," he said again.

"It can't go away," I said. "It's a child."

"It's not mine. I had to tell you."

Every word he said was like something pelting me. I flinched and put my hands over my face.

"It's not true," he said. "First of all."

"What? That you didn't do it?"

"No," he said, swallowed. "That part is."

"For three years," I said. "Since you gave her that check."

"No!" he said. "I told you."

"I don't believe anything anymore. Nothing you say."

"It didn't happen then."

"Didn't happen when?"

"At that party, or whenever. The awards, with the picture."

"Stop." I remembered the picture. That handshake.

"I met her but it was nothing but formalities. It was—"

"Stop talking."

He is lying. He remembers her even from the party. He was thinking of her, even back at the party, talking to her, not talking to me. She was shy. She ducked her head and looked at him from under her lashes and said he was an influence. She was tall and lovely. She had those teeth with braces. He talked to her and let me go off alone. He shook her hand and gave her the check and remembers there's a picture.

I had my face to the wall. He tried to turn it toward him but I wrenched my chin out of his hand. He talked to the side of my head. "Charlotte. I had to tell you last night. They've been calling. It's a swindle. They're about to go to the newspapers. Her and the mother. It was just...it was that once. Please. The whole thing—just happened. You had said what you said on TV and there was all that stuff on the radio. Darryl was...He egged me on. He had her number and he called her." Milo stopped. He was looking at the carpet between his feet. His bare feet.

He's lying. He called her. It was his idea.

"It wasn't my idea," he said. "It got out of hand. One thing led to another." He was so uncomfortable, forcing himself to come clean, as if that were the honorable thing to do. He talked on as if he could convince me of something. But what? That it didn't matter?

I wanted to believe him. It was just the once. Could you forgive once?

"Charlotte. Sometimes, you know how the women, the way they throw themselves—" He stopped again. "It got out of hand."

"It got out of hand," I whispered. "And right into bed. Now there's a baby." I was crying, strangling the word *baby* so it died in my throat. "Go away," I said. "I'll never forgive you."

"I'm sorry," Milo said, breaks in his voice. "You know how ... what you mean to me ..."

"No," I said, "I don't."

I made him leave and went in the shower. The water drilled holes in my head. It was scalding but I didn't care. I got out and looked for myself in the mirror in a room full of steam. I wasn't there. No one was. Just a ghost. A steam-colored ghost.

34.

Thursday afternoon I woke up shaky and ill, and was worse when I came downstairs and saw that Milo was gone. Hallie napped on the couch while Marcy read one of her zodiac books.

"Sorry you are not feeling well," she said.

Meaning I'm sorry your husband has cheated on you. I was sure she knew everything, that it was aligned there in my star chart all along. Soon everyone would know. The papers, the TV, our parents, Bobbie. In the kitchen I washed down aspirin with coffee, then shut myself up in the den, to avoid Hallie waking, Marcy chirping to her. But there on the desk, the small red light on the answering machine was blinking. Probably tabloids calling, I thought, or so-called reporters. The blinking filled me with dread.

"Char-lotte," said Claire's voice on the machine. "Three o'clock, right? That would be *today*, okay? Don't forget, ya birdbrain." I sat woodenly while she left kisses and the number of her hotel, remembering that she and Tim were in town for some conference and I was supposed to take her shopping. *Shopping?* I thought. I couldn't. I would call her and make something up, go back to bed.

There were other messages, people talking as if life just went plodding on. Hallie's teacher. Our travel agent. Jack Sutherland. "Hey, Charlotte," he said. "So I just got back. Call me." I wrote his number down next to Claire's. Maybe I would call him, maybe not; who knew what I would do now? Anything was possible now, any rash act. My handwriting was spidery, like someone else held the pen.

Next to the answering machine was the mail Marcy had brought in and piled up, special offers and bills addressed to Mr. & Mrs. M. Robicheaux, all in a stack by our wedding picture in a silver frame, as if nothing had changed. It was all appalling now, the wedding picture, the mail. But I opened it and read it, numbly, even the cancer appeals and the one with the picture of the starving child whose every bone was visible. *You must cope, Charlotte. Cope.* I tried to focus on the facts. On what I knew so far. *What if it was only the one time? What if Milo's telling the truth, it's not his?* I leafed mindlessly through the pages of catalogues and magazines as if they might help me. *What if I could forgive him? I can never forgive him. Perhaps I have to. Perhaps I am to blame.* There was a large white envelope. It had my name on it with no return address, postmarked New York. I opened it up and fished out a plain sheet of paper with a single typed line.

Perhaps this will convince him was all it said.

Behind the paper was a photograph, enlarged and printed on thick stock, that stole my breath right there, looking at it, with a feeling like plate glass breaking at the top of my head and shattering down through the veins.

It was a picture of Milo and her. Geneva Johnson. It's night. It's in a restaurant or a bar because you can see glassware and candles with flames in the shape of white tears and a floral arrangement washed out by a flashbulb in the foreground. She is wearing a white strapless dress that scallops over the bosom like a dress Marilyn Monroe might have worn with underwire. Her hair is braided simply back off her face in rows and caught up at the crown of her head. Milo's eyes are closed in the picture. The lashes of the eye nearest the camera make a fringe on his cheek that is so familiar, vaguely feminine. His hand rests on the flesh of her upper arm, hers likewise with him. Their lips touch.

I turned it over with a cry escaping me and saw there was writing on the back of the photograph: February '89, SOB's. Not Son of a Bitch as you'd expect or might reasonably say aloud, but Sounds of Brazil, a place I know in New York. A place we go. We have danced samba and salsa there, Milo and I. We had a play fight once with limes there, throwing them and missing, and once he put miniature umbrellas from a tropical drink in my hair. We have stayed there late into the night. It is near our place on Mercer Street, within walking distance. Last winter was February '89, the winter before the building blew up, the winter we were sometimes in New York and sometimes in L.A., and the winter Milo was in Park City skiing, supposedly. February '89 was the last winter the Hughes Homes in Newark were standing with the wind blowing through their broken windows, two months before they were blasted to rubble, before I said what I said, before the One Time it was supposed to have happened. The chronology alone was enough to make me insane, but I knew that if a baby was six months old now in April 1990—born in November, I counted on my fingers—February '89 would be right about the time it would have taken root. February. Months before just the once.

Could I forgive once? Yes, perhaps.

But not a lie. Not love. Not a son.

I stood up, trying not to sink down. The picture lay facedown on the desk, and I pushed the pile of mail over it, like hiding a stain. I was weak from seeing it. It is one thing to *imagine*, but to *see*, to have a photograph: I would never get it out of my mind now, their lips frozen, touching for all time by candlelight. My legs gave way, thinking of it, and I lay back down on the recliner. On the cold leather I could smell the faint spice of Milo's hair lingering terribly. Just a moment ago, I thought, I was about ready to forgive the *once*, coming around to believe what he said, *It was a one-time thing*. But now here was this picture, *February '89*, months before just the once, laughing at me.

Maybe this will convince him.

Well, I didn't know about Milo, but surely that photograph convinced me. I couldn't stay here, trapped in the den with it and a pair of his sandals kicked off under the couch, empty, shaped like his feet. I concentrated on getting out of the chair, finding my jacket, pocketing my car keys. I told Marcy I was going out and climbed in my car. I would find Claire. She would know what to do.

I pulled up in front of her hotel a little after three o'clock. Claire was standing there checking her watch and straightening her skirt, looking for me in the passing traffic. Watching her for a moment, it struck me, how long I had known her, how long she had been my friend. I didn't know how I would tell her, say what I had to say: *Milo has this child with some-one else.* I nearly drove away, afraid of uttering the words, but she saw me and waved. Her face lit in a smile.

"Hey!" she said. She ran toward me and opened the passenger door; climbing in, she saw my face. "Oh my God," she said. "What?"

I shook my head. I had trouble talking. "You drive. I can't drive." I slid over and she ran around and got in the other side. "Just get on the highway," I said. "Just get as far away out of here as possible."

"Oh, Jesus," she said. "Are you frightened of somebody? Are you hurt?"

I shook my head no.

We drove up the Pacific Coast Highway in silence, with Claire worried and reaching to touch my arm now and then. Her questions and what I had to say were riding like fat passengers in the front seat between us. After about twenty minutes I said, "Okay. Okay. Here." I told her to pull off by a scenic overlook pretty far north of Malibu.

"Okay," I said. "I'll just say it."

I had a hard time getting through it. Claire had to keep saying "Just slow down. Just take your time." She didn't ask me anything yet, about the picture or the timing or where Milo was. Her face was so focused, lis-tening, and there was no judgment on it, not of me. But sometimes, such as when I said *He says it's not his,* she looked furious.

"I'm having trouble," I said, my eyes raw, "knowing what to believe."

"I'm not having that trouble at all," Claire said. "There's a picture."

I winced.

"You might as well get drunk and celebrate now," she said, "because the sooner you praise the fact that you are free from someone who would do this to you, the sooner you will feel better."

"I will never feel better."

"Take it from me," she said.

I took it. What else there was to take I didn't know. At least for the time being I would take what advice and solace I could from Claire. She knew how it felt.

"Sweetie," Claire said quietly, "this is not a man you want to hang on to."

"But I do," I said mournfully.

"This is a man who has another child."

I winced again.

"He has hit you in the face," she said gently. "I haven't forgotten, you know. And while I respect what seems to be your wish not to speak of it, I am not surprised now to hear about this latest so-called development. I see it all the time."

"But—he says it's not his."

"Awww, sweetie," Claire said sadly. "You have a *picture*. With a date."

"But who sent it?" I asked her.

"Are you defending him?" She was shaking her head. She started the car's engine and backed up out of the rest area. "We need to drown your sorrows. Come with me."

We went back to Claire's hotel and sat in the bar and ordered rounds of whatever we could think up, and continued in the hotel restaurant for dinner.

"You'll move on. You'll be glad," Claire said. "I was, after Carl."

"No," I said, "I won't."

"But, Charlotte, face it, you and Milo are just so different. It's at the heart of all your problems, don't you think? All your fights. You're just so different."

Yes, he has two children and I have one, I thought. I didn't want to ask Claire what about us was so different. I was tired of what I thought she thought. I drank and listened to her various prescriptions and coping techniques with a detached feeling, as if I was watching a slow movie, waiting for it to be over so I could go home.

"You should *not* go home tonight," Claire announced. "It would be a mistake. Stay here. Get a room."

"Milo will think I'm with some other man," I said.

"Well, we don't want him to think that," Claire said.

Yes we do. The idea interested me. "Yes we do," I said.

"No! That's insane," Claire said. "You need to be very, very careful."

"Claire," I said, "it's just Milo. We just have to talk."

"When a man hits you—" She was on a prosecutorial roll.

"But—that's not the point," I interrupted. *He has another child.*

Claire leveled a look at me. "Charlotte," she said, "you know you'll need to leave him, don't you?"

I stared at the glasses on the table, glassy myself.

"You will have to begin facing it," she said. "The sooner the better."

"I think I should go home."

"You stay with me tonight," Claire said. She began developing an elaborate plan, which involved canceling her flight the next day at six in morning. Tim would go back to New York without her and we would get Hallie. All of us could stay in the hotel until I was "stabilized." That was her word. "I can stay through the weekend at least," she said. "Till you figure this out."

"It's okay," I said. "You go back with Tim in the morning."

"But I can't just abandon you in this situation."

"It's not what you think," I said. "I have to go home."

Claire looked very skeptical and worried. "I think you're making a mistake," she said. But she knew me well enough not to try talking me out of it. Later she said she wished she had. She was so sorry. But she never would have changed my mind. I was going home. I was not really thinking about the scene once I left her. I just concentrated on operating the heavy machinery of my arms and legs, getting up from the table, walking Claire to the hotel elevator. I said good-bye to her and left, wobbling drunk past a trash can where I threw out all my teary Kleenex, and also my promise to take a taxi, and all of Claire's ideas about leaving Milo, moving on. *She's wrong*, I thought. *I just have to face it*, going home.

When I got there, the cathode blue flicker of the television lit the windows at the side of the house. Milo would be watching the game. I didn't want to start, didn't want to go in, to say what I found. That picture was smoldering in there, kissing inside my home, singing foreign music from the nightclub Sounds of Brazil; it was lying in wait there on the desk, whispering huskily, teasing me. *I will just go get it*, I thought, *Carry it out to the beach and leave it on the rocks for whoever finds me floating, like a note explaining why.* But just as I came around the side yard and crossed the flagstones, Milo yelled. "Agggghhh!!" A bellow. It startled me and I stopped. The sneaker squeaks and the crowd roar of the basketball game filtered through the screens into the night air. Slowly I went to the window of the den off the terrace and looked in, watched Milo through the glass.

Magic with the rebound over to—oh, now it's a Phoenix ball—

"Goddammit, Magic!" I heard Milo say. "Get with the game!"

The Lakers were playing the semifinals. How could Milo be interested in it? A game. How could he be? I watched through the window. He was in his chair. The phone rang and I watched him pick it up. He spoke several times into the receiver: *Hello? hello? Who is this?* He cursed and hung up, annoyed.

It was like he was inside a diorama. I stepped right up close to the glass but not so any light fell on me. He couldn't see me. He was unguarded in the way his face furrowed and relief crossed it; so unfailingly attractive to me. Hairline cracks had begun to appear at the corners of his eyes, which gave him a look of kindness. He was thirty-four years old, and his body was taut and muscular as ever. His calves were ropy and hard; the blades of his shoulders were sharp in his back. His habits were so familiar and dear to me, the way he curled the tip of his tongue over his lip, thinking, the jiggling of his leg. His feet were bare, and his toes gripped the carpet, long and fine-boned, *Like little spaghettis*, his mother said, *Milo's toes*. The sight of his feet hurt me. As I watched him I realized I could never fix my feelings for him; and it felt at that moment like I loved him despite anything, his betrayal and his lies.

Phoenix driving toward the net, only thirty seconds left on the clock in the first quarter. Magic up to block the shot. Foul!

"Goddamm it, Earvin!" Milo yelled. "Shit!" He lowered his head to his hands. His team was losing. He was grief-stricken over a game. He was cursing now, talking to the television. He had more passion and sorrow in him about the orange ball lofting up and falling through a net than anything having to do with us. I went inside, looking for a fight now, the real fight, about proof and love and what was going to happen to us.

"Charlotte? That you?"

"Were you expecting someone else?"

"It's late," he said. "I was worried."

"Why, that your team would lose?"

"No," Milo said. "About you."

"About whether I'd stay out long enough for you to watch the whole game in peace?"

"Charlotte, please."

"Charlotte, please," I mimicked him, making my voice low.

"Stop."

"Stop."

"Stop. That's it! I've had it!"

"You've had it! You!" I said.

"Don't mock me!" His teeth grit.

"What about me? What about me?"

"What about you?" he said. "I apologized! I'm sorry! Please. What more can I do?"

"Stop lying is what."

"I told you I wouldn't lie to you," he said. "I am not lying."

"Then what's this then?" I walked over to the desk and fished out the picture and the typed page along with the envelope, and handed them over. He took these from me, puzzled, and I turned to the window, the way you would turn your back on someone undressing. I heard the rustle of the paper and the way his breath fell out of his mouth.

"Oh," he said. "Well."

I looked at him now. He was standing with the picture still in his hand. His eyes were cast up to the ceiling, then at me, then over to the side, full of something, shining, trying to speak. "It's...I told you," he said. "Where did—who gave you this? How—"

"Turn it," I said. "Look on the back."

He did and his face creased, taking in the writing, the date, the meaning of it. *Caught,* I thought. He shook his head. "No," he said, "that's not right, this was that time, this *was* the time, this is not—"

On the television the Lakers missed their free throw and I saw Milo checking the game from the corner of his eye.

"How can you watch this?!" I screamed. "How can you?"

He looked panicky at me, caught with his eyes not on me, the photo in his hands fluttering because he saw I was holding that wedding portrait of us in its silver frame and my arm was cocked back to throw it like a rock at him.

"No, Charlotte," he said, holding his hands up.

I threw it. I hurled the picture at his head and it hit his hand and broke.

"God damn you!" he said. He was bleeding where the glass cut him.

I ran then. I stumbled through the house, drunk and out of my mind, when I saw he was chasing me. "Don't you throw that at me!" he was shouting. "Don't you fucking throw anything!"

"Leave me alone!" I was screaming, the two of us running in and out of our house, through the front and then around the back like a cartoon chase.

"Listen to me," he shouted. "It's a mistake."

"Shut up!"

"It's not the right—!"

"Leave me alone!"

God knows what Hallie heard, from upstairs, or the neighbors. Surely they heard me slamming all the doors in Milo's face, locking the one in front, heard him pounding, "Goddammit, Charlotte, open the door!" He kicked and banged, rang the bell, rapping with his knuckles, hammering the brass knocker, engraved with R for Robicheaux. Milo locked out of his own house.

"Let me in! Goddammit! You hear me? Open up!"

Right back to where we began so many years ago, with Milo at my door, me behind it, face pressed to the wood. Only now I was yelling "No! No, get out of here!" And he was out there kicking, hurling himself, bellowing, shouting that it was not the right date, that it was not his handwriting anyway, where did I get that fucking picture? saying Listen to me! But I hated him too much to listen. I was sure whatever he had to say was lies. I never did know whose handwriting or how the picture got there, who sent it. I never did hear his side. Maybe I should have listened that night, when he was pounding the door and roaring. I could see his face through the glass panes at the sides of the entry; saw him seething. He was trying to get to me, make me see it his way.

I set the alarm and went upstairs, dizzy, into Hallie's dark room. I bent over her, laid my cheek against her head, her heart. I rested next to her. But there was something unbearable about the softness of her hair, the flowery smell of it like some inarticulate longing, so that I had to cover her and leave. I went out onto the terrace off our bedroom and stayed bunkered in a chair, awake all night, gazing out across the trees to the black water out there, to the safe peace of the dark sea, the dark sky. After a while, I heard footsteps and crashes downstairs. Milo had gotten in somehow, breaking something. I heard him disarming the alarm, punching numbers on a keypad. The phone rang and I knew it was the security people calling, asking for the code. "Ice," Milo would tell them, the password we picked. "All is well."

Then it was quiet. I listened, frightened of our fight. He did not come up. I wanted him to. I'm telling you I still wished he was right there with me. I tensed for him to come, expecting him, and dreading it: How he would say my name, whispering at the door. *Charlotte?* He did not come, though. I sat breathing around the stones and bricks in my chest, and watched the clouds thin out. A shaving of moon appeared. It lit a white path across the glossy black water, one that seemed to stretch beyond the reach of my eye, far away to China, to Japan and Australia, spreading out like a white burn on filmstrip, fading away with the sunrise, the bluing of the morning sky. And out of that blue, Jack called.

35.

Maybe I slept an hour. I woke and it was Friday now, early. Hallie was in my bed with me, bouncing and whispering *I won't wake you up so you won't be mad so I'm whispering*. When I got down the stairs with her there was a message on the machine from Marcy: Did I remember her doctor's appointment was today? She was taking the day off. Did I remember that? No, not that, but everything else: that bad dream that was not a dream. Milo was nowhere to be found, but the broken glass from the broken wedding picture had been swept away, I noticed.

All day I let Hallie have whatever she wanted: television, sharp scissors, glitter glue, candy. I couldn't speak much, and when I did my voice seemed as if it were coming from a long way off, somewhere down in Central Charlotte, buried and faint. Hallie kept me functioning with her demands. Glitter glue stained her in patches, so that when the late-afternoon sun came through the kitchen window she caught the light and was dazzling, my dazzling daughter. I had a glass of wine to numb the effect of her beauty, another one to dull the heartbreaking surroundings of our house, our possessions and furniture turning cold now.

Around five o'clock Milo pulled into the driveway. Hallie rushed him, and I kept my distance. He looked at me warily, expectantly, but I stayed away, hating him but also wishing he would come over and say *What's the matter?* so that I could turn and put my head on his shoulder and say *It was a nightmare.* But he went upstairs without a word.

I was feeding Hallie dinner when the phone rang.

She was singing *Little Rabbit Foo Foo hopping through the forest, scooping up the field mice and bop them on the head* ... jumping one of her french fries around the table like a rabbit and trying to scoop up peas but of course the plate slipped so ketchup splattered me and I began to cry. Green peas were bounding all over the place, rolling across the floor as I swabbed it with a dishtowel.

"Sorry, Mommy," Hallie said, and began to eat her french fries directly off the table.

"Use your fork," I said.

"I'm pretending I have no hands," she said.

"Honey, please."

"If you have no hands," she said importantly, "you have to scratch your nose like this." She scratched her nose on the edge of the table and this time her cup fell on the floor with a crash.

"I told you!" I screamed at her.

"Mommy!" Now we were both crying.

"Goddammit!" I threw the wadded, sodden towel at the sink, where it landed and broke a wineglass.

The phone rang.

"What?" I shouted into the receiver. There was silence, which was strangely calming. "Hello? Hello?"

"Hey, Kitten!"

It was the equivalent, for me, of the arrival of the man on the steed. Just when you need him. Spurs jingling, hair streaming back, standards waving in a fair wind. Just in the nick of time.

"Hi, Charlotte?" said his voice. "You know it's me, right?"

"Jack Sutherland!"

Milo came into the kitchen exactly then. His timing was perfect. I was amazed at how quickly I swallowed and got the tears out of my voice, the anger. The flush on my face was useful. I tucked my hair behind my ears, flirted right into the phone.

"Ja-ack," I said tenderly. "How was your trip?"

Jack wasn't quite settled yet, he said, but he wanted to see me. He wanted to get together. I made arrangements to meet him the next night. I did it loudly, in a way that Milo could hear, and when I had said good-bye to him, fondly, several times, and hung up, I went back to the table where Milo was trying to clean up the broken plate. "It's so wonderful to hear from Jack," I said. "He sounds wonderful. He's moving back here, you know."

Milo said nothing, and I threw caution to the wind, held it out like a handful of sand and blew it all over the floor with the peas and the ketchup. *I'll say what I want, who cares?* It was a relief.

"After all these years," I said. "His voice is exactly the same."

Milo ignored me. Hallie was using a french fry as a lipstick, painting her mouth with ketchup.

"I know you always hated Jack," I said, "but really. You're turning white with anger, Milo."

"Fuck you," he said.

"Daddy!" Hallie said. "Bad word."

"Hallie," I said, "let's go watch something," and when I came back from parking her in front of the television so that she would not be scarred for life by having to watch her parents disintegrate in front of her, Milo was seething.

"He's been calling here, hasn't he, Charlotte?" he said abruptly.

"No, he hasn't."

"You're lying," he shot back at me. "I heard that message from him yesterday. Don't think I didn't hear it."

"Don't start, Milo," I said.

"He's the one who hangs up whenever I answer, right?"

"No."

"How long has he been calling you?"

"He hasn't," I said, but it wasn't quite the truth.

"I don't believe you," Milo said.

We regarded each other so coldly. There was half a smile of triumph on my lips, and I know he saw it. His eyes were shot through with red and he looked wrecked. *Good,* I thought. *A taste of his own medicine.*

"Maybe it's someone calling *you*," I said. "Maybe it's her."

"She has no reason to call, believe me," he said.

"Believing you is a little bit hard for me right now," I said.

"It's not my kid," he said, the words in his teeth. "It's not."

I wished for him to be right. I still did. I wished to reach across the kitchen, hold on to him and see what happened. But the word *kid* was stopping me, crawling along between us in its diaper.

"If you're lying to me?" I said. "If that's a lie, Milo. If that's your son—
I'll..." I didn't know what to say, what to threaten. *I'll die.*

"You have to believe me."

"If you lied?" I said. "I'll take Hallie."

He stayed quite still when I said that.

"I will, Milo." I was so bold now. "And I'll get her, too. You know I
will."

I'm not proud I said it, of what I was insinuating. "I'll win," I said.

He roared and picked up his drink and threw it. It smashed in the sink
and sent shrapnel of glass splintering onto the counter. "This! is not! happening!" he said. "Not!"

We had it out then. We were throwing anything we could at the other,
old sentences and misunderstandings, wounded feelings going back years.
You said. No I didn't. Yes you did. All of our hurled words were landing
on each other, piercing and bruising. It was the cornered fight of the
wounded married. It was that fight about love. About fear and hurt and
truth. The same old fight couples have. Only with race smashing and
breaking like an extra set of dishes around all our grievances. Is this about
us? Or is it about It? Skin and History.

Milo was yelling for me to listen. I was yelling at him to shut up. He
was yelling it wasn't his! and I was shouting, What is that then, that picture? What is that date? Who sent it here? He did not know, he did not
know, he did not know! He did not know whose handwriting, he did not
know who took it, he was trying to find out! Liar! I shouted.

And then we saw Hallie in the doorway. I don't know how long she
stood there, watching us, listening. We saw her framed there and we both
stopped. It was so quiet, with her looking up at us, her face a question
mark.

"Oh, Hallie," I said.

"I'm going," Milo said.

I heard the front door slamming, his car starting in the driveway.

"Dad's mad," Hallie said. She said it a few times, pleased and distracted
by the rhyme, as I was distracted by how pleased I was. At his anger. I
wanted him to be jealous, to see how it felt. We were stalemated, and I
know now, where that word comes from, the old crusts of our married
mistrust too hard and moldy to chew.

I don't believe you.

I don't believe you, either.

That night I went to bed with a feeling that I would get even with Milo somehow and that I had already started.

It was foolish. I should not have gone. I should not have talked to Jack. I wish I hadn't. But if you were there, at the moment, you would have seen how unreasonably happy I was, to have some strike I could make against Milo. The idea of it got me through the night, when Milo was there just briefly, long enough to sleep in the spare room; it got me through the morning and afternoon of the next day, Saturday—the day it happened.

Milo was gone early that day, after seeing me for just a moment in the kitchen. He came in from the guest room when I was pouring coffee. We did not speak. It was the last time I saw him. That I remember. We were alone in the morning light, but still the room was full of shadowy people: Jack was there, grinning, and so was Geneva Johnson, dancing around; that baby was babbling under our feet, while Darryl serenely watched from a comfortable chair in the corner. I stirred sugar in my cup and kept my mind's eye on the word "Jack." Milo was so stony, looking at me, knowing I was going out and he couldn't stop me. *A taste of your own medicine*, I thought.

In the evening I took a long bath. I dried my hair and perfumed myself and marshaled all my wands and sable brushes and sharpened pencils. I wanted to be stunning. I wanted to be a bombshell on nonstop legs. The dress I picked was black and backless with a high halter neck that fastened in a band around the throat. With it I wore the wide, hammered-silver collar Milo gave me for Christmas with a matching wrist cuff, big silver hoops for my ears. As I fastened the clasp and brushed my hair, I thought about Jack, what he would think of me now, never having seen me, I remembered, in anything but jeans, the prairie-girl fashions we wore then. He would have adventures to tell me. Perhaps he'd married, had pictures in his wallet. But maybe not.

Milo was still out when I left so I wrote him a note. "Meeting Jack at Spago 6p. Home by 9. Dinner?—C." To spite him. Or to invite him. As if I were inviting him. Maybe I was.

I arrived early and arranged myself at a table in the bar, crossed my legs. I saw Jack coming before he saw me, and let my hair hang down in a curtain over one side of my face. As he reached the table, just as he got there, I turned to him.

"Jack."

It was terrible what I did. How I softly looked up from under my hair, said his name, stood and put my arms around him right there, let myself rest against him. Terrible the hushed murmur of his name I let escape. *Jack*. How odd it was, the familiar feel of him, his hands on the bare skin of my back. The same smell of Jack.

"Charlotte," he said, and I could see by his struck, brimming smile that he had been waiting for just this greeting between us, was relieved by it. He looked down at me. I saw a leathery quality to his skin that had not been there before, but he was the same. His hair was long and still blond as mine, pulled back in a ponytail. He had that easy, crooked grin and a looseness in his limbs, sitting down slouched, stretching his legs out alongside the table.

"You guys are brother and sister, right?" said the waitress, handing us our drinks. "You are, right?"

"Who's older, then?" I said, eyes sideways at Jack, and laughing.

"Oh, golly," said the waitress. "He is?"

"You're right," I said. "Older and wiser."

"Your parents must have a really good gene pool," the waitress said.

"Yeah! Pool's great," said Jack. "Fabulous. Just a little incest in the family, is all." And he leaned over the table suddenly and kissed me on the lips.

"Jack!" I said, startled, but smiling and laughing anyway, my hand to my mouth.

"Incest is best!" Jack said, with a mischievous eye on the waitress, who retreated like a crab back to the sea. He raised his flute of champagne and said, "Charlotte Halsey: to you." He drank while gazing at me over the rim. "I could just drink *you* in," he said. "As beautiful as ever. More."

I smiled and raised my glass to him. "Thank you, Jack." We sat for a charged minute. "Tell me about yourself," I said. "Catch me up."

"All right then," he said, and took a deep breath. "You heard about the bogus so-called accident that ended my racing career."

I arranged a polite hospital-visitor look on my face.

"I'm sure you know about it, or think you know totally about it, more like," he said. "But this is not the time to try that case, you know?"

"No," I agreed.

"Anyway," Jack said, "I had major consequences of that injury for a long time. Dizziness. Memory problems. Balance."

"Poor Jack," I said.

"No. No. Not poor Jack." His hand was up as if to stop traffic. "I'm fine now. Number one, I'm a philosophical kind of dude. If something is meant to be it's meant to be. Que sera sera. Can't be helped. *Shikata ga nai, ne?* as the *nihonjin* say. Things happen for a purpose. I accept that."

"You have a really good attitude," I said.

"Well, yeah, but, Charlotte, you helped. To accept it. I am patient. To everything there is a season, right?" He gave me a meaningful look.

"Right," I said, puzzled.

He told me that he had gone back to Cabot College after his injury, finished up there and then moved to Japan, where he lived for thirteen years. He ran a ski school in Nagano, but was moving back now, he decided, after all those years abroad. "Had a premonition. Time to come home," he said. "Turned out to be right."

"You haven't been back in all that time?"

"I checked in periodically. Visited. Just to see." He looked at me. "*Eetto ne, boku wa sukebei na hito desu yo, honto ni.*"

"God, Jack, you're amazingly fluent, aren't you?" I had no idea what he said, but his personality changed as he said it, his face and voice did, something guttural in it. "You're practically Japanese."

"No way! Not this American boy. Never could be. An American? No way. Can't be Japanese unless you are Japanese. Even a Korean. If you're born there? Doesn't matter. Still a *gaijin*."

"What do you mean by that?" I asked him.

"A foreigner. *Gaijin.* Japanese believe they're the most superior race on Earth." He was incredulous, shaking his head, eyebrows arching. "It's like part of their religion. Can you believe it?"

"Huh." I kept my thoughts to myself.

"Anyway," he said, "I ran *Jacku-san no Ski Schooru* up in Nagano."

"That's great. You must have just loved it."

"Love is a funny thing, Charlotte, isn't it?"

"I'll say," I said, under my breath, but I saw my words were not lost on Jack. He smiled as if he understood just what I meant.

"Japan," he said. "Some of it I loved. Food's great. Mountains are cool.

But, hey: no place like home." He looked meaningfully at me and then quoted that Byrds' version of Ecclesiastes again. "To every thing there is a season," he said. "And a time for every purpose? Right?"

"Yeah," I said. We sat with our empty champagne flutes. Jack asked the waitress to bring another bottle to our table.

"Celebrating?" the waitress asked warily.

"Long lost love," Jack said, melodramatically putting his hand on his heart. I smiled, but awkwardly. "Take your glass, like this," he said, and showed me how to hold it resting on the open palm of my hand, while he poured. He explained the custom in Japan is for table companions to pour for each other. "Now you," he said, and watched me fill his glass. "You do that well. Grace is like the most important quality for a woman in Japan, did you know that?"

"Really? And what else did you learn about women in Japan?" I asked, in a teasing sisterly way.

"A little bit," he said, winking. "Of course...a little knowledge is a dangerous thing." He raised his glass. "So here's a toast to you, Charlotte." I raised my glass to his. "*Campai!*" he said.

"Yes," I said. "Definitely," and drank. "Whatever that means."

"About the same as 'ow, ow, ow, ow.'" Jack laughed, and snorted like the ski team used to do. The sound of it must have stirred some kind of nostalgia on my face, because Jack looked softly at me and brushed the back of my hand with his fingertips. I didn't move my hand away but turned my palm to his.

How pale Jack was, pallid to me. The color of his fingernails did not stand apart from the color of his hands. His sweetcorn–colored hair had coarsened at the temples. I was conscious of inspecting him. I was conscious of my engagement ring turned under, how it clicked against my glass when I picked it up, gleaming weakly through the bubbles.

"So how are you?" Jack asked me. "Charlotte."

"You know, I married Milo. Milo Robicheaux."

"Yeah," he said softly. "Of course I know."

"And we have a daughter."

"Aeggh," he said, shaking his head, blinking.

"What?"

"Can't believe it," he said. "It just makes, it makes me—ah." He sighed.

"Never mind. It's not the time, not the time." He shuddered. "You're here, here we are. Right now."

"And I'm, I used to be a fashion model, for a while—"

"Of course. Know all about it." He smiled. "Followed your whole career."

"Jack," I said. "Really?"

"Yeah, of course, really. Saw all the series you did, the cosmetic campaign, those ads you did for what's his name, the designer? I'm like, so proud of you. I'm reading along, some magazine, turn the page: There you are, Miss Apparition." He mimed himself reading, glimpsing a picture, doing a double take. "Me, a million miles away, and yet bingo: There you are. Your face. As if it was some kind of secret message for me, or something."

"That's very flattering," I said.

"No, no, no," he said. "Not flattery." He smiled at me for the longest time, then he asked, "How's your mom?"

"Fine."

"She's a great lady, your mother. As you know, I've called her, now and then, over the years," Jack said, "starting when you left school and nobody knew where to find you. You just dropped out."

"She did say once you called," I said, "but I—"

"I always have remembered what she told me," Jack said. "She said: Nobody knows the future, right? And one day maybe Charlotte will need a shoulder to cry on."

"She did? She said that?" I asked him.

"Well, I know that—" He stopped. "She mentioned you had had some hard times," Jack said. "I spoke to her last spring, I guess it was."

Which would have been during all those days, weeks, that Milo was gone. *Roaming in Wyoming*. Not that I ever told my mother. The only one in my family that ever knew things like that about me was Diana. My mother would have heard about it from her. Milo's absence.

"So, I know how it can be," Jack continued. "Lonely days, hard times. And I just thought I'd give you a call."

And since it was true, what he said, *lonely days, hard times*, when I looked back at him my eyes were full of tears.

He reached across the table and laced his fingers with mine.

"Charlotte," Jack said, "don't now. Hey." Tears spilled down my cheeks. I had not remembered Jack as a comforting man. But he stroked my hand gently, saying "It's okay now, everything will be okay.

"I can't imagine what it's been like for you," he said. "All this time."

"Oh," I said. "Just all kinds of people over the years who don't want me and Milo together, you can guess how it would be."

"Yeah," Jack said, "I can."

He seemed about to tell me what he meant, but just then the waitress arrived to say our table was ready, the one by the window. It surprised me, since I had not planned on dinner. I had said I would go home for dinner. In my note I said I'd go home, and suddenly I wanted to. "I'm not terribly hungry, Jack," I said, after a moment. "I don't think I could eat."

"You never did eat," he said.

"I do. Now. But— I can't."

"Come on then," he said. "We're outta here."

"I should get back."

"It's early. Let's go."

"Where?"

"Let's just—" He winked. "Let's go."

He pulled my hand so I had to stand up. My napkin fell on the floor. He put his arm around my neck and fished around in his wallet, grinned at me like a bad boy, and threw two one-hundred-dollar bills on the table. His arm drifted down to my waist as we walked toward the door, and I did not remove it.

"Wait," Jack said, halfway, "I'm forgetting something." He went back to our table, plucked the dripping bottle of champagne from its ice bucket, and carried it out of there.

Outside, it was just dusk. There was a breeze and I shivered. As we walked toward the parking lot, Jack took off his jacket and put it around my shoulders, along with his arm. My hair blew across my eyes and I tossed my head, turned to the wind to free it. Jack pulled me to him suddenly, lifted the hair off my face, and was left holding a single strand of it in his fingers, threading out loose in the wind. He put it to his mouth and drew it across his lips. He watched me, smiling. "Remember?" he said.

Oh Jesus. "Yeah," I said weakly. "Oh. That's right." *Burlington Airport.*

"That was really something, Charlotte," he said, laughing. "Wild. I couldn't believe you did that! Never shoulda done that. Whoo! You were something else. Wild." He was shaking his head and seemed happy, amused at the nostalgic fact of himself out with me. "C'mon, we'll go in my car."

"Where are we going?" I asked.

He winked again, pulling me along through the parking lot. "Let's go for a drive, a little champagne tour."

"Jack, I don't know," I said in a small, kitten-mew voice that was alarming to me: how quickly I could be what other people wanted me to be. How now I was Meek Charlotte.

"What do you mean, you don't know?" he asked.

He stopped and faced me. I gazed over his shoulder to avoid looking at him, his klieg-light eyes searching me. In the middle distance I saw cars pulling up in front of the restaurant, a couple arriving, the doorman smoking, looking at his watch, the palm leaves streaming in the wind, Milo's car. It looked like Milo's, over Jack's shoulder. *His red car.* It was far across the lot, but under the halogen streetlight blaze it was unmistakably his, with the U.S. Ski Team decal in the back window, and I knew he must be around somewhere. *You practically invited him, after all, Charlotte, didn't you? Wanted him here, right?*

Jack was looking at me. "Charlotte," he said, and put one finger under my chin and lifted my face up.

Milo, are you watching?

Jack's fingernail hooked gently in the soft throb of flesh under my chin and his eyes searched me out, beckoning my face close to his.

See, Milo? Are you watching? I hope you are, because you'll see how it feels, see I can do this, too. Here I go. Kiss Jack Sutherland, your old enemy. Watch. I've done this kind of thing many a time for the cameras, that's all it is, lip to lip with the boy model in the surf, or rolling on sheets, like you, like you, Milo. So why not? why not?

Why not. Because it was awful, kissing Jack; felt like starving but having to eat food that was off, like drinking medicine that curdles you, like being swallowed. I remembered Jack now, how he kissed, how he practically vacuums the tongue from your mouth, how he doesn't stop, doesn't open his eyes, doesn't check to notice mine are open. I was looking around, seeing cars like sleeping animals in rows under the lights, the blur of traffic passing, seeing Milo.

Was that Milo? There by the restaurant.

Lips turning like doorknobs, Jack's hands wandering.

Was that him? Somebody at a distance stepping out into the light, off the curb, then retreating behind the building. A man, a lean dark man in a light linen sport jacket. Him. Close your eyes, Charlotte. Close them. You think you see him everywhere, you always have, always do. You think you see Milo.

I looked again, lips detaching, over the high shoulder of Jack Sutherland. "Hey."

It was. It was Milo, I had no doubt.

"Jack."

He pulled away from me and opened his eyes. "God, Charlotte, you're still so beautiful," he said. "It kills me, how beautiful you are."

"Jack."

He saw I was terrified.

"What is it?"

"Milo," I said, "I think he, he—"

"What?"

"He's, I think, he—" *He saw me kissing you.*

"Here?" he asked me.

"Maybe, I don't know," I said. But I did know. I saw him. "I think I see his car."

"Whoa!" Jack said. "Come on." He took my elbow and steered me fast to a dark-blue Jeep. He opened the door and pushed me down into the front seat in one fast motion. "Don't worry, don't worry," he kept saying, as if this were some kind of movie adventure for him. He handed me the champagne bottle and got behind the wheel, but backing out, he braked and turned to me. He was so cavalier, the way he looked, with his crooked smile. "To hell with it," he said. "It's gonna be fine." And with that wild impulsiveness of his he kissed me again across the front seat, and I confess I didn't stop him again, would stop him *later*, not now, not while there was a chance Milo would see, look through the windshield at my arms around Jack's neck. *I want him to see*, my fingers lacing his hair, pulling it loose from the band around it, gathering it up in my hands and pulling him to me, sinking down in the seat, my head against the window glass and Jack's long straw hair thick around my face. *Watch*, I thought.

"Drive," I said giddily, after enough time. I knew, I was sure, as we pulled away, that Milo had seen, that he had watched us go, and of course would be imagining where we were headed, me and Jack. And I felt better already, driving away. *We're even now*, I thought, and although we were not, exactly, it was enough for me, that Milo had seen.

Jack drove fast. "I think you'd better take me back home," I said.

"Hang on," he said, smiling. "I have something to show you."

When Jack finally stopped the car we were pulled up to the Beverly Hills Hotel. He got out and gave his keys to the valet but came around to hold the door for me himself. We walked up the walk and inside, his hand on the back of my neck. I turned toward the Polo Lounge, where I had been often.

"No," Jack said, "this way." He steered me to the elevator.

He's staying here, he's taking me up to his room.

"Jack, I don't think I should come to your room."

"Come aaahhnn. I got somethin' to show ya," Jack said, drawling, persuading. He took my hand. "A souvenir." For just a moment he seemed so earnest, there by the elevator, with his rock 'n' roll hair, pulling me the way Hallie does sometimes. He was a grown man and he had had his own lonely days, I thought. His old dreams had not come true, it seemed, and he had not dreamed new ones.

"I can't, Jack."

"Come on, come on," he said, winking, ribbing me. "You'll laugh. Don't worry." He was smiling again in that cocksure way he had, as if he had never had a cloudy day in his life, as if there were no situation too dire for Jack Sutherland. He pulled me and I went.

"Okay," I said. "But I can only stay a minute. I— My daughter."

Panic bloomed briefly on Jack's face. "Yeah, but you have to see this," he said, and we rode up to the second floor and walked down the corridor with Jack grinning. He put his key card in the lock and the door clicked open. "Don't worry, don't worry, Miss Proper," he said, "you can wait out here in the hallway." So I did, standing out there. Jack went in and crossed to the dresser, looking for something. Inside, I could see an enormous bed turned down, with two gold-wrapped chocolates and a scripted goodnight card on the pillow. Pairs of sneakers were lined up neatly by the closet. It was spare and temporary, I thought, maybe a little sad.

"Here," he said, coming back to me in the hall. He had a worn envelope in his hand. My schoolgirl writing looped across the front of it in faded ink. *Jack Sutherland, Cabot College Station.*

"I saved it," he said, handing it to me. "Of course."

Curious, I unfolded a blue-lined piece of notebook paper, and was shocked to see what it was, how long Jack had held on to it.

> March 22, 1975
> Dear Jack,
> Hi. It's me, your "Kitten." I'm so confused.

The letter was embarrassing and it made me sorry for the mixed-up girl I was. It tried every way not to say what it was saying, which was Good-bye. It said: *This isn't good-bye, okay? It's just to say till we meet again.* The letter was afraid to speak its own mind, afraid of its own decisions. *Remember that poster that hangs in my dorm, with the picture of the butterfly on it?* I quoted the poster and also Ecclesiastes, the Byrds' song: *To everything there is a season...* It was dopey, and mostly creepy, what I did. *Jack, it's too soon. Too much too soon.* I got to the end, where a hand-drawn butterfly hovered in yellow hi-liter. The *love* had a heart shape in place of the O.

Jack was watching me read it. "Come," he said.

"I—"

He pulled me in, sat me on the bed. *I owe it to him,* I thought. *Just a conversation.* Finishing something unfinished. I was not afraid of Jack, only wrung out and sorry for all the havoc I seemed to have left in my wake wherever I went. Maybe, I thought, you could fix your old mistakes. By listening. By paying attention. I listened while Jack described receiving the letter on a spring day, coming back to school from the Albany hospital where he'd recovered from his concussion, the smell of the lilacs outside Chisholm Hall, students passing him and slapping his palm, glad to see him. He had a sense, he said, that I would be coming across the quadrangle, and he had pictured how he would pick me up and carry me to his room.

"And then I read this," he continued, "and it was like, God." His lips twitched.

Is he about to cry? I wondered, but then he winked. *No, I was wrong,* I thought.

"At first I tried to find you," he said, and explained that nobody—not my parents, the school—had any idea where I was. "Then, just when you turned up in New York, and I called, your friend Claire said you'd left again."

"Yeah, Jack, I—"

"So all I had was this letter," Jack said. "And you know, this will sound crazy, but suddenly, the whole butterfly thing you wrote made sense to me. That's you! *Flighty!*" he said, tapping his temple. "Here one minute, gone the next. The more I read it, the more I saw what you meant. And you know? I agreed with you. It wasn't the right time. We were too young.

"In Japan, I studied t'ai chi and also kendo," he said. "I learned patience. I learned that you wait. You wait and wait for a time that's right, and then when it's time? You make your move." He smiled, then leaned in and kissed me.

I kissed back. Not for long, but I did. It's not like I wasn't weak or tempted. You know, I almost shut my eyes and let him. I nearly did. Tempted to just sink under the spell of someone murmuring my name, someone longing for me. But I couldn't. I pushed Jack away.

"I'm married," I said, "I'm married to Milo. We have a daughter. Her name is Hallie. We—" *We have our troubles, big troubles, oh, God, get me out of here.* I stood up and headed to the door.

"Charlotte."

"I have to go home." My hand was on the doorknob.

"No, you don't." His eyes crinkled warmly as he stood up and came over to lean against the wall next to me. "I wish you wouldn't. You're beautiful as ever," he said. "When can I see you again?"

"Never."

Something compelled me to say that, finally one honest word, one truth. I had led him on. I could see that. He was deluded. Not that I was any picnic of sanity, either. I had only a few crumbs of sober judgment left, but I could see I had to tell him right there.

"Never?" Disbelief was filling his eyes.

"We can't, Jack—I'm married." As if it mattered, to be married.

"Not for long, that's what I hear."

"From who? Who tells you?"

"Rumors, gossip, grapevine." He shrugged. "I know."

"It's not true," I said.

"You can't be happy with him," Jack said. "Let's be honest."

I opened the door sadly. "I'm sorry," I said.

"Charlotte, stay!" Suddenly Jack's face showed an instant of havoc that was familiar to me, from years ago. He stopped me, but with his hand lightly on my wrist now, smiling slowly. "Let me tell you something," he said easily. "These things never work out. I've always known it. He was always evil, that guy, Robicheaux, an evil ego. *And* a cheater. He is bound to show you his true colors sooner or later. If he hasn't already. It's only a matter of time. I assumed you'd had enough by now. So, sorry if this is too fast for you, but—"

"I have to go home to my family," I said, and pulled the door open, walked down the hall.

"Hey! Listen," Jack called. He was walking right behind me, loping casually with a little chuckle in his voice. "Tell me one thing. Did he ever give you the real story? Or did he just tell you anything to get into your drawers?"

"Stop, Jack, please," I said.

Jack shrugged. "Don't get the wrong idea, Charlotte, I just want you to see how he *stole* you. You saw his medals. His money. Which he got by pushing me out of the way, by the way. Boom!" Jack said the last word so loudly I jumped. "Did he tell you?"

"Jack—"

"Blinded you, didn't it, that medal, huh? To the fact that you should not be with him."

I could hear the soft machinery of the elevator starting. *Hurry hurry.*

"I'm sorry, Jack," I said. "It was all a long time ago."

He stood shaking his head with a rueful smile, watching me. "He *has* been cheating on you, though, hasn't he?" His voice was quiet and knowing.

"What would you know?" I said. "You don't know anything about us!"

"Maybe I'm just guessing," he said serenely. "But I'm right."

The elevator arrived and I got on it without speaking. Jack gallantly held the doors apart, as if doing me a favor. They bucked against his arm. "You know, Halsey," he said with a big grin, "you're gonna change your mind about seeing me again. I know you are. Because I'm *right* about you two, that it's not working out. Easy to predict as sunrise, sunset. Trust me. See how long before he cats out on you again, if he hasn't already."

His words crawled on my skin. "Just shut up!" I said.

"You'll be sorry, Charlotte," he said, shaking his head, still smiling.

"I *am* sorry," I said, close to tears.

We heard a door opening abruptly down the hall and a man with a briefcase hurried toward us, glancing at his watch. Hold that, he said. Jack stared hard at me, glanced at the man, who now got in the elevator car and stood nervously to one side, waiting for Jack to let go of the doors.

"I am not giving up," Jack said, cheerful as a game-show host. He winked at the briefcase man and said, "Never give up on a good woman, right, pal?" The man nodded uneasily.

"You want something, you gotta go for it. Right?"

"Right," I said. "I really should leave."

Jack waved. "Good night, Kitten," he said, and blew me a kiss, as the elevator coughed and closed, shutting him out. It carried me down, and through the doors I heard him whistling.

36.

I got a taxi to pick up my car at the restaurant and drove home. It was around nine by then, I think. No Milo. Marcy did not know where he was. "Maybe he called you," she said helpfully. "The phone is ringing a lot just now." I said good night to her and as I went upstairs to check Hallie, the phone rang.

"Hello, Charlotte? It's me. It's Jack."

I hung up and the phone rang again. "Charlotte? It's me. It's Jack."

"Don't call here," I said. "Don't call me." I hung up.

But the ringing did not stop.

It was all a mess. Where Milo was, when he would be back, how much he had seen, how it would start, how he would explain himself, and I would, where it would go: I didn't know. Nothing—no scene I could try out ended up in happily ever after. Still, I couldn't help feeling a little game hope, because Milo *saw*. This thought gave me a certain kind of strength and made me curiously hopeful for a while. I couldn't help believing he would be home for supper, that we would have it out, the whole truth of his philandering and his betrayal, and then somehow it would go away, the way Milo said it would. Which is what I wanted. I'm telling you I still did, still doggedly expected *normal life*, waiting for some phoenix of happiness to rise up, our family on the fire-forged back of it, the flames below. Even now I think of it. If it were possible. Even now.

I went in the kitchen to make dinner, to keep drinking, to listen to the phone ring. Jack saying Hello? Hello? Pick up! into the machine, drowning him out with Linda Ronstadt and Kate Bush and Tracy Chapman. All that sad music of women blaring out in the heart of the Malibu Colony. The words to those songs are the last ones I might ever sing, *I'm goin' back some day, come what may, to Blue Bayou,* cutting the chicken into cubes, threading it on skewers, expecting Milo any minute, pouring chardonnay into the marinade, into my glass, into the salad dressing, down my throat.

He didn't come and he didn't come. The clock hands advanced. The phone stopped ringing. It was past eleven. I turned the TV on and off. I erased all Jack's messages. I turned out the lights and lit candles everywhere. The coals in the backyard grill blazed and banked and then went out. The candles burned down and dripped on the table, making little wax rivers that I gathered up and shaped into cubes, balls, birds, burning my fingers. I called various numbers, Claire and Bobbie, but hung up when someone answered. I thought of Jack. That's how cracked I was. Of calling him back, inviting him over. Milo wasn't coming. He had seen me kissing another. Well, it served him right. Now he had a movie in his head, of me and Jack, the way I did, of him and her. Which is what I wanted, but—he wouldn't come back now. Milo was a proud man, and it was a low sordid thing I had done. Like he had done. He wouldn't come back. I hadn't thought of that, only of getting even. He and Darryl were off somewhere. He was with some woman and her soft Swiss name, her rugged mountains. He wasn't coming home for dinner. It was over. Finished. *He's not about you anymore.* No more Milo. He was gone. *What would I say to Hallie? How would I explain? Hallie, sweetie, Daddy and I...we...* I was deeply sad. Weeping. Okay, desperate, trembling by the time I found the bottle and opened the childproof cap and selected a handful of pills, two Valiums and some Percodans Milo had left over from surgery. Not too many. Just enough for pretend euphoria to kick in. Maybe if Milo came home after all, I thought, I would vomit on him again.

The lullabye of the waves and the wine and the Valium was making me sleepy out on the back terrace, lying in my chaise. I had my blanket and my glass for companions, but the porch lights were bothering me, too bright, giving me a headache. I lurched up and turned them off, lay back down, looking up, looking for constellations, consolation. The house was dead dark, but the sky wasn't. It was the color of dirty paper, lit by the glare from the city, beyond the palms. *Not moon light, city light. Light pollution. That's called light pollution,* I was thinking, rambling and inane now. There were no stars out that I could see. *What will children wish on?* I was wondering. *What will I wish on, for that matter?* I lay there listening to the waves, made a wish on something that turned out to be an airplane. *Let Milo come home.*

At some point, I called Claire.

"Hello!" I said. "It's me."

"Charlotte, are you okay?" She was groggy. "It's three in the morning."

"Not here it isn't," I said. "What time it is depends on where you are." That seemed completely profound, to me.

"You're totally wasted, aren't you?" she said.

"Yes, dahhling," I told her, in a Russian accent. "We've had a r-r-r-eversal of r-r-r-roles, you and I."

"Are you okay?"

"If my husband comes home," I said.

"I knew I should've stayed with you," she said. "Never should've left. I tried to call you earlier to check in. A couple of times."

"I was out," I said.

"How's it going, then? I'm worried about you."

"Great!" I said brightly. "I got even with him." I would not cry. I refused. "I gave him a taste of his own medicine." Ice rattled in my glass and I chewed a piece of it, changing the subject. "How is your perfect husband? He's home, of course, unlike other husbands. How is he? Faithful Tim."

"He was asleep," said Claire, "but since he's not asleep now, he's pissed." I was disturbing them. I imagined Claire in her New York bed, with Tim. Her short hair would be poking up the way it did when she'd slept on it. Her mascara would be grainy under her eyes.

"I'm sorry to wake you," I said.

"What do you mean, you got even with him?" she asked.

"I went out," I said importantly.

"With a male?"

"Yes!" I said.

"Oh, boy," Claire said.

"No, not a boy. A *man*. You will never guess who."

"Paul Newman."

"Jack."

"Jack? Nicholson?"

"No, idiot. Sutherland."

"Oh, God, Charlotte, you didn't."

"Yes, I did."

"But you told me he went back to Japan."

"Nope. Tonight he went back to the Beverly Hills Hotel."

"Oh, Jesus," Claire said slowly, leaping to conclusions. "You had better not trumpet that around. Not to Milo, especially."

"Oh, he knows!" I said. "I flaunted it right in his face. It's fine. It serves him bloody right."

I could hear Claire breathing. She was getting out of bed, I could tell, walking around with the phone. I lay on my long chair and listened to her three thousand miles away.

"Charlotte," Claire said, "he knows where you were tonight?"

"Oh, yeah. And that's not all," I said. "He saw us."

"That's bad. That's really bad, Charlotte."

"Hey, what's that?" I whispered. There was a rustling in the bushes. "Something's here." I listened. "Just an animal. Maybe a snake." *Maybe a person.* I wondered if I forgot to close the front door after Marcy left. Did I?

"Charlotte, this is serious," Claire said. "You're making me nervous."

"The snake will have whatever's in the belly of the frog," I said. "Did you know that?"

"Jesus," said Claire. "Have you taken something, Charlotte?"

A light went on, inside the house. The front hall light. *Maybe I forgot to lock the door, too,* I thought. *Or maybe it's Milo! Of course it is.*

"It's him," I said, with melodrama. "He's home. The man of the house. I'm saved."

"You're really wasted. Don't— What are you going to do now?"

"Fuck if I know," I said. I was slurring and witless. The den light went out and the living room light went on. I couldn't see inside from where I was, around the corner, through the leaves. I could hear Claire whispering to Tim. Then the light inside went out again altogether. Maybe Milo was leaving. He had just been retrieving something, his possessions, and now he'd be gone again, without a word to me. He was leaving. *Bye, Milo.*

I sat up on the chair and I was scared. Also determined. *Get your glass, Charlotte. Get yourself together.* "I am going in now to face the music," I said to Claire. "Hup two three four."

"Right now?"

"Yup," I said. "That's what I'm going to do."

"No, listen. Wait," she said. "You're liable to fuck it up, you know that?"

"Tccch. Thanks."

"You know how you get, watch what you say—"

"Watch what *you* say, Claire," I said. "It's not what you think. Just because he's— I know what you think." I was angry with her now, too.

"Charlotte, you know I don't think that. Come off it. Look—"

I hung up.

It was dark inside the house. The sunporch was dark and also the living room adjoining it. I think I could hear the opening of drawers in the kitchen. "Milo?" I whispered. I pictured him. He would blink when he saw me. His eyes would be tired; we would smile sadly and sit down and we would figure it out. *No.* He would glare. Flames would come from his eyes and steam out of his ears and I would set my jaw against him, sharpening my words, and we would start. We would have it out, the whole truth, and then decide. *So you saw me, so what?* I would say, scathing, *serves you right. Now you know how it feels.* I would say whatever I damn well pleased, primed for it.

"Milo?" I assumed it was him.

There was no answer. "Milo?" I turned the corner into the kitchen.

It happened then.

He tackled me and choked me. His fingers were on my neck. He throttled me so viciously the larynx smashed, the hard cartilage crushed against my heavy necklace and his hands. He smashed a wine bottle down on the granite edge of the counter, leaving him holding the jagged neck of it. He brandished it at me and cut me with it, my neck and hands. Blood was all over the kitchen. By the oven, by the sink, spattered on the cabinets, on the tablecloth. He cut my bare arms where I held them in front of my face. I fought him and fended him off and he cut my hands. He sliced a flap of skin off the tip of my middle finger so they had to sew it back on.

I don't remember any of it. Nothing. It's what I'm told.

He floored me. I do remember that, only that. The feeling of the breath forced out, the weight of someone, and the rage but not whose.

I came around the corner. Who I saw, what he was doing, what we said, how it started I don't remember.

A neighbor heard arguing but she said she often heard arguing.

Claire says she called me back, maybe fifteen minutes after I hung up on her, and when the line answered then went dead, she did what she did. Called the cops.

Things, fragments of it are vivid.

Hallie's plaster handprint on the wall. For some reason I remember a flash of its nursery school colors hanging by the refrigerator. I saw it from the floor. Just that. I remember looking up and seeing it. *Hallie.*

I know but can't know.

I was tackled on the floor, grappling. Sharp pains bit my back, from rolling on glass. Or was I told that. I remember the smell of wine and wetness, blood on my clothes, my hands. Pain like teeth in my neck. I remember trying to get up. Getting up and falling. I got out, outside. I must have. He chased me, grabbing my hair, my dress, was he? I say *he* but don't know who. I was falling again. I saw headlights on the road, turning in. Were they? I do remember headlights. *Help me.* I ran, I must have. They found me outside on the porch.

I can't tell you. The pills have that effect, alcohol does. I have had alcoholic amnesia before, blackouts. *Or should I say whiteouts?* I have no useful memory of what happened. Trauma has that effect, also, wiping out details the way light obscures stars, so we don't recall the specifics of violence or pain, the moments leading up to catastrophe. I don't. I remember *squat*, as Milo would say. Blank blank blank. I know music was on. I know what I was wearing. I can picture just how I looked.

37.

Right now the California sun is shining idiotically outside my window. The late-afternoon sky is blue as you'd expect. The sea is also blue, and bland, and perfectly calm except at the shoreline, where the waves are hurling themselves hysterically. I am up here in our room, seeming to look out but not really seeing the real estate dream where I live, the spectacular ocean views, the bluff falling to the beach, the white peel of sand curling away toward the big city. I have been here all day, just crying, without being able to stop. It's been more or less like this for the four days I have been home. Before that I was in the hospital for five weeks, nearly dying, but then, not dying.

Downstairs, in the rooms and wings of the house, I hear Hallie playing and crying, singing and running. I hear my mother calling her, the way she called me when I was little, drawing out the syllables of her name. *Haaaa-leeeee.* Hallie's name, her noises, are like electric shocks to all the dead nerve ends of my interior wiring, cattle-prodding me to get up. But I can't. I can walk around but I can't make myself go to her. The first day I came home from the hospital she stared at my neck, reached to touch the bandage, to inspect with her fingers. "It will get better if you kiss it," she said, and puckered her lips toward me.

Don't! I mouthed the word and pushed her hands off, held her away, and went back to my bed. I heard her crying. Marcy soothing her. I can't explain. How could I?

All I can manage is sitting still and listening. I hear the faint occasional horn of a car out on the road. I hear the wind and the relentless hush of waves from the shore. Inside, the faucet drip from the bathroom is too loud. I hear carpeted footsteps, someone approaching, the doorknob complains a little when it's turned, and somebody—my mother, Claire, the doctor, a therapist, twice that detective—comes in to check on me, asks, *Do you want anything? How are you feeling? Do you remember anything after that? Do you remember any unusual cars parked in the neighborhood? Can you begin to work through the anger?* It requires incredible will and concentration to answer, to shrug or nod or move my lips, my pencil. This morning my mother came in. "Would you like to get dressed?" she asked. I didn't move or look at her. She thought I might like to get dressed. She had something for me.

She has been here since it happened. She was at the hospital. My father and both the boys, my brothers, apparently came. My sister, too. They all went back home when it seemed I would not die. I have no real idea of how much time passed, from the night—that night—how much time till I began to be conscious of what was happening around me, the doctors and nurses, floral deliveries, injections and IV drips and the sound of the television, my mother crying softly as the doves outside the window in the morning. I woke thinking it was doves, and there she was, her head down next to me on the bed. I moved my hand to her hair and thought to say *Mommy*, but no sound came out. Her hair was brittle to the touch. She turned and saw me and stood up. She leaned over me and pressed her face against me so I felt her cheek was wet. "Darling," she whispered.

Now she stays here and helps Marcy, tries to help me. This morning she brought me one of Hallie's flowery rainbow drawings with a prayer on it. *The Lord is my Rock and my Fortress and my Deliverer*, it said, but in Mom's writing. She laid the drawing on the table next to my chair. "For you," she said. I looked at it and thought that in another life I would've wondered, Why would I need a rock? What was the Lord delivering? But now I didn't care what she was teaching my daughter about the Baby Cheese. I cared about holding still. I cared about swallowing without choking. I cared about the jagged cuts stitched together all along my neck, the itching of the new raw skin.

My mother crossed the room, opening the curtains, the windows. She got a hairbrush and brushed my hair. The spikes of the bristles felt good and painful on my scalp. She finished and kissed the crown of my head and then hesitated, as if deciding something. She put her hand in the pocket of the apron she wore and pulled out an envelope.

"This came," she said, "just now"and put it down, grimly.

The sight of it got me right away. His handwriting and my name *Charlotte H. Robicheaux* across the front of it. It made me nauseous to see it. I began weeping quietly again, and I have not really stopped, not yet today.

Dear Charlotte.

They arrested Milo. They found him leaning over me on the porch. My blood was all over him. On his hands and face. His clothing. He resisted arrest. He punched a cop. He fought with them and was acting deranged, the police said. He was drunk. They beat him but he kept shouting *That's my wife,* and fighting to get at me, they said, raging to get me. He's in jail now. The judge denied bail because he was considered a danger to me. Not to mention a flight risk.

"You don't need to worry about him coming back and hurting you," Detective Phelps said, putting his hand on my arm. "He's locked up."

The police terrify me. They scare me with their navy blue questions and the silver badges of their likely scenarios and their evidence. When the detectives come to ask about that night I pull the blankets up around me. I have been naked or mostly naked in front of entire rooms of photographers and people staring at me, and never minded, and yet with these detectives, in my hospital nightgown, or home in my robe and slippers, it's as if I were completely nude, or hairless. It's not a feeling of having something to hide, but of wanting to hide. That I have no cover. The police saved me, saved my life, but now they watch me. For days they waited outside my hospital room, but I was in no shape for them, as I was sedated with a tracheostomy tube in my neck. When they were finally allowed in, I could sort of sit. They asked for all the details and I told them I didn't remember. I hardly moved my face, just mouthed the words, wrote them. *I remember nothing.* I could hardly look at them. They kept saying *Try.* I tried but I couldn't think of anything that happened.

They came to my house, just after I was released from the hospital. In all the rooms they picked things up, handled photographs, the trophies on the bookcase. Milo's medals. "Mind if I use your bathroom, Mrs.

Robicheaux?" Phelps asked, and when I shrugged, he went up the stairs! I know he was rummaging in the medicine cabinet. He was reading prescriptions and opening plastic bottles and sniffing their contents. He was bloodhounding through the rooms, with his camcorder eyeballs and wiretap eardrums. It's as if they suspect me, as if I have done something wrong.

Perhaps I have.

I have left parts out. Big parts. The fact that I was kissing Jack. That Milo saw. *What did Milo see?* Claire asked me. But I'm not sure if what he saw is a good thing for anyone to know, or not. Knowing would just confirm what everyone thinks about us anyway. They would picture the parking lot, me and Jack, with Milo in the shadows, and they'd think: *The trashy white slut, and the jungle jealousies and appetites of her black husband.* They would. And then the rabid newspapers would have it along with their pictures of my husband and his Other Woman. The police would have their motive. *He savagely attacked her in a jealous rage.* The investigative reporters would find Jack and point their TV cameras at that restaurant, Spago, their lurid lights illuminating, what? A parking lot.

It's nobody's business. It's private.

Claire says I have to tell them. She flew back here from New York right away. When she came in my hospital room and saw me finally awake, the state of me, she said, "It looks like you've been a little too intimate with a helicopter." I smiled for the first time, I think. She sat down on the bed and hugged me. "I love you, Charlotte," she whispered. "If it weren't for you I would have jumped off a bridge a long time ago."

It set me off again, crying. I love Claire. She has been with me the whole time, flying back and forth, advising me. I'd be lost without her. I would have died. She is the one who called the police that night from New York, who gave the address, saved my life. She provided a description, told them it was my husband. They came and found him there leaning over me. They arrested him right away, due to the blood on him, Claire's description. The fact that he hit a cop.

On the news, I saw the cop they said Milo hit. Officer something Paladino. His eye was swollen purple, with black dried cuts scabbing in the flesh. He turned his face to show the camera, and you could see a splotch of bright red on the white of it, blood in his eye. *Good for you, Milo,* I thought fleetingly. *Good,* but then began to cry again.

Because I am not sure it was Milo who did this to me. And I am not sure it wasn't.

Most of what I know comes from television.

In the hospital the private nurses left it on so they had something to watch when they gave the meds, suctioned the trake tube. They thought I was out of it, heavily sedated, and half the time I was. They went out in the hall and chatted and left the TV on, perhaps thinking it would entertain me in my stupor. *That's his wife?* I heard one of the staff nurses say. Half the time they didn't know what I heard, or what I saw.

I saw the whole downfall story. I saw footage of Milo being led away from the scene. There's the bloody front porch, red stains on the steps. The big bush of ornamental grass by our driveway looks pale in the nightwash of the camera lights. Milo's face is washed out, too, bruised and smeared with gleaming dark streaks. His lip is cut and his light shirt has red splotches. He has a hangdog head. He looks like someone else. His hands are behind him, cuffed, and police are holding him by the elbows as he walks. He is limping. Then an officer pushes down on him like he is bobbing a ball underwater, pushes to get him into the backseat of the patrol car. Milo looks back at the camera, and in that moment, his eyes *are* wild, they *are* deranged. He jerks his head to get the cop's hand off him. He tosses and wings his elbows up behind him to get them away. He's trying to see something, get to someone. *To me,* I thought, when I saw it, *to be with me.* He tries to turn back. *Hallie.* He looks bloody and dangerous, unless you know him. If you know him, he looks scared. Young. His eyeballs stand out, white and crazed, and that's of course where they freeze the frame, every time. From that, they go straight to footage from one of the *Cade* movies, to stills of Milo as a blue-blazered sports reporter, and then all the way back to the footage of his 1976 medal, that moment I remember so well, of him lifted up and carried on the shoulders of his teammates, and snow coming down like fairy dust all around.

They cut from his victory to *his wife, Charlotte Halsey,* modeling something, with my milky smile, and my hair glaring. They cut from me to our daughter, from her to the mistress. There she is. Geneva. The Dancer. She is long-necked and dressed in white, some *Swan Lake* costume, and her arms make an oval frame for her graceful head. Then up pops Bobby Armstrong on the screen: dark suit, red tie, hair gray-wolf gray at the temples. Milo's lawyer.

Here is what Armstrong says. What he claims. This is the defense:

"Mr. Robicheaux came home and found his wife gravely wounded. He attempted to administer mouth-to-mouth resuscitation. When the police arrived, Officers Paladino, Cruz, and Stoddard did not stop to ask questions but beat Mr. Robicheaux. Brutally. Severely. And he defended himself. The police did not follow proper procedures. They have no evidence against our client, and his right to bail has been denied illegally. We demand his immediate release. That's all we have to say at this time, except that Mr. Robicheaux loves his wife, loves his daughter, and expects to be reunited with them when this tragic matter is resolved."

I know Bobby Armstrong. He's a friend of Darryl's. Darryl calls him "Bo-bo." He specializes in rights. Not civil rights, but foreign rights, serial rights, licensing of products, like the Cade doll. He's an entertainment lawyer, balding, with the beginnings of jowls. I've met him several times, at parties. He and Darryl were friendly. Never more than now, with the two of them out there saying the same thing: "My client is not guilty."

Darryl said that on TV. There he was talking to a bank of microphones, "Darryl Haynes, Robicheaux's Agent" supered under his face while he talked:

Milo Robicheaux and I went out on the evening of April 20, the night of this hideous crime. We had dinner, as we have many times over the years. We had a few drinks. We left and went home somewhere around twelve-thirty. Milo Robicheaux is not just my client, he's my friend—

Well, a couple of things got me right there. The word *client.* The word *agent.* Because I had been operating under the idea that Darryl was no longer employed by Milo. Now here he was, saying *client.*

And there he was, being Milo's alibi.

We talked that night about his wife, Charlotte, Darryl said. *He told me his concern that she has a severe alcohol and drug problem, and career problems due to what I like to call the fascism of the fashion business. Due to her age, and whatnot. Age discrimination. She was suicidally depressed. My friend Milo was trying to get his wife professional help. We are all now praying for her recovery, and for Milo Robicheaux's release from his wrongful imprisonment.*

As usual, Darryl is full of shit. As if I would choke myself and slash myself. The fascism of fashion. As if that were what depressed me.

Moreover, Darryl is not praying for my speedy recovery. He sent flowers. "Thinking of you," said the printed note from the florist. *Thinking what?* I said to him in my head. *Thinking it serves me right? Thinking you wish the job had been done properly?*

The flowers were carnations, all pink.

"Who do you believe?" goes Darryl's big ad. It's a double-page spread in the *L.A. Times. Who do you believe? Who do you trust?* As usual, Darryl is asking the right questions. And as usual he answers, too. He says: *When white folks say justice, what they mean is "just us."*

Who do I believe? Who do I trust? Bobbie. She wrote to me.

Dear Charlotte,

Words cannot begin to convey all our worry about you and what has happened. We are praying for you and for Milo of course, and little Hallie. My heart is breaking for you all. Please, Charlotte if you can, do not believe what they say. You know down deep what is true. You must have faith in your own heart. Please, for Hallie's sake especially, be strong. I will come and see you if you ask me, but under the circumstances I will wait for you to send word, as I tried phoning and was told you were not receiving any visitors. Understandably, perhaps, Mom and Dad are too overwhelmed right now to come. They have been to see Milo and are doing as well as can be expected. We would do anything to support you both and help you recover. I know with all that has happened you must be sorely put—as we are, too—to believe or have faith. But if you can, for all our sakes. For Hallie's.

Love Bobbie.

But Bobbie, you do not know. I would like to have your faith, any faith. I would like to know in my heart. But the more I know the harder faith is to have. For example, Bobbie, if you knew that your brother saw me kissing Jack; if you knew that was not a door I walked into; if you knew that he lied about a woman and she says he has a son. There is a picture of them kissing, and now this latest one in the newspaper! the one Hallie saw, of the two of them, emerging from a restaurant, it says, in New York, but not when.

She has written me a letter, too, that woman emerging from a restaurant. I gave it to Detective Phelps. Why it would matter, I don't know; but they asked. I cooperated. Such a nice letter, beautiful penmanship. *Please accept my apologies for any part I may have unwittingly played in this tragedy. Sincerely, Geneva Johnson.* As I said, unwittingly is the word I question. Also apologies. Also Sincerely.

Do you know I don't care about any of that? Not about the clues and the picture, who took it, or who sent it, or what time it was when he left the restaurant. I don't care about anything at all except Hallie and whether it was him. Or not. I just want to know.

And I don't know.

If I knew, if I had the truth, then I would...what would I do? I would get up. I would get on with things. I would make plans. If yes, then *A*. If no, then *B*. If *this*, then *that*. It would help. Save me from this paralysis, this room with this bed and chair, this ignorance.

"The system works," is what Claire says. "They didn't arrest him for no reason. You'll just have to let the system work." Yesterday she was up here with me by the window, reading magazines. She seemed to have given up trying to talk to me, and I knew that soon she would have to go back to New York. I sat, afraid of moving, of dislodging clots of tears. I stared in a trance at nothing, but she was suddenly looking at me so hard I had to close my eyes.

"Was it him?" she asked me then.

I looked at her as if she'd hit me.

"Was it him?" she asked again, and then a third time. "Was it Milo?"

I don't know! I got my own pen and wrote this down so angrily it tore the paper, mouthing the words.

I can't remember! I thought it was him in the house but I'm not sure!

"But you said you had had so many arguments," she reminded me, almost as if she was trying to talk me into it. "You told me you fought constantly. Do you remember an argument that night?"

No. I shook my head.

Claire was the one who told the police Milo hit me. They used her statement at the bail hearing.

"Charlotte," she said, after a long time, "something like eighty percent of all murders and attempted murders are crimes of passion." Her voice with me now was gentle and narcotic. "These things are crimes of passion. It's just a sad true thing." For a moment, I thought she meant that the passion itself was the crime. Charlotte and Milo as a crime.

...

Milo's handwriting on the envelope slants hard to the right as if it is lean-ing into a strong wind. *Charlotte H. Robicheaux*, it says, *29149 Cliffside Road, Malibu, California*. I imagine him writing my name, and I wonder what he was thinking, if he pictured my face while he wrote.

When my mother put it down next to me this morning she announced, "One of his legal people delivered it. With instructions to give it to you." The sight of it, just the envelope, set me off. I've been reeling and crying, jagged for the day.

"I knew it," my mother said, tightly. "I knew this would happen. I should never have." And moved to take it back.

No. I shook my hand at her and shooed her away, backhanding the air with my wrists flapping, the way you wave off flies. My poor mother. I should like to tell her *Sorry*. That I love her. But I don't have the strength for it.

Everything now is basic. Yes or No. Stay or Go. Him or not him.

She left and the letter shook in my hands.

I held it against my face. I don't know what I was expecting. For it to smell of him. For it to kiss me? Hurt me? I was afraid of it, what it might say, what it might not. When I opened it and took out the paper my hands were trembling. I couldn't look. Couldn't read for the longest time. The lines of his writing blurred across the page.

Dear Charlotte. Dear Charlotte. Dear Charlotte.

I hear Hallie out on the back lawn. She has a playmate, a little girl with flyaway hair. I see them twirling till they are dizzy. They fall down laugh-ing, looking up at the trees, then get up and do it again.

The world is spinning all the time, Milo told Hallie, just a few weeks ago, was it? *If you want to see it move, you have to twirl yourself around, too, like this.* And then he spun with her, their arms spread out like wings, turning in circles till they tumbled to the grass side by side.

Dad, she said, *I see it. It's whirling.*

It frightened her at first, until something he said made her laugh and she did it again. She did it constantly, as she is doing now, she and her small friend giddily twirling toward the front of the house, where cameras are lurking. I want to get up, call them back, shout *Stop!* Save her, if only from those cameras. Their high-powered lenses are everywhere, day and night, up in the hills, hungry for footage. Of anything. Of our shrubs and driveway gravel. Our toolshed. Those dizzy children. Various channels and tabloids have hired helicopters to get aerials of the house. I've heard them hovering overhead. They will milk anything. One lingering shot of Hallie's overturned bicycle by the driveway has aired frequently, a zoom in to the wheel, spinning in the wind. As if it stands for something. Perhaps it does.

"Tell them everything," Claire said.

I have been trying to think it out: What I would say, what I would write. What the police would do if I told them.

Officer, you see, I was kissing my old boyfriend Jack in the parking lot, just in a crazy way to get even with Milo, because Milo—

Don't say why. Don't write why or you'll cry.

Milo saw us. In the car. I think he saw us kissing and leaving together. This was—just that night. Just hours before.

They would be taking this down, following the Jealous Husband line of inquiry. It would provide a motive, fit with their theory, make sense of the senseless, the cuts in my neck.

Detective, see, my old boyfriend, this man Jack Sutherland, had been calling me, asking that I see him. I told him never to contact me again. He was angry about that. Once he nearly choked me. Once he threw a ski pole at me. Where is he? Do you know?

There has been nothing from Jack since I hung up on him that night. No more calls, no notes or word. He was calling me that night. Calling and calling. But then, at a certain point (when?), he stopped. Gave up, I assumed. What did he do then? Where did he go? Where is he now?

"This is absolutely a crime of passion, of rage," Claire said so gently yesterday. "It happens with a man who has a terror of losing. Someone controlling and possessive, a man who is used to winning, to getting what he wants."

I listened.

"Like your husband," she said. "Am I wrong?"

So it was only yesterday that I told Claire about Jack. I wrote it out, the part about the kissing and the letter he saved insanely for fifteen years and the flashes of havoc on his face. I told her what Milo probably saw. Her eyes got solemn and sober and she nodded her head as if she could see right away what I meant by my question.

The police, I wrote. *Who would they believe?*

"Still," she said, "you have to tell them."

If I told, the police would find Jack and see how charming he is. He would buy them beers. He would wink and backslap and say: *Hey, guys, it was just a kiss good night, for old times' sake. Charlotte was a slam hound anyway. Always was. And if her husband was watching, it was just some sick thing he was into. He always was a violent man.*

Claire looked at me so hard. Her eyes went right through me. "I know what you're thinking," she said, full of pity. "Charlotte—oh honey—for him to come back. That can't happen. Just get it out of your head. Unless of course you remember—" she stopped. "You know that the human mind forgets what it can't bear to know, don't you?"

I nodded. I was just wooden. She hugged me a long time and left. Last night she went back East. I tore up all the notes I wrote her and flushed them down the toilet.

Claire is right. I will tell them, the detectives. Soon. I have to, don't I?

In dreams I can speak. I sing, in my dreams, me and Hallie in the car belting *John Jacob Jingleheimer Schmidt! That's my name too! Whenever we go out, people always shout! There goes John Jacob Jingleheimer Schmidt!* We do it at the tops of our lungs, Hallie just shouts "Schmidt!" and then we do it all over again. I sing in my dreams, and talk.

It's possible I will speak again, my doctor said. "Some of the nerves to the voice box, Charlotte, were severed, so, you have some paralysis." As she talked, Dr. Hovnanian lifted her chin and pointed to places on her own crepey neck. "After your larynx heals completely, we'll see." My larynx, the voice box, was smashed. The ambulance crew cut a hole so I could breathe, right in the hollow between my clavicles. *The speed bump,* Milo always called that hollow, running his finger across the bones in the dark, *Slowly...now...watch the speed bump.*

"Try to whisper if you can," Dr. Hovnanian says, "I think you should be able to." I try but no sound comes out, only wisps of air. It's exhausting and it hurts. It's futile. I can't do it. I just can't.

"Not to worry," Dr. Hovnanian says. "Give it time." She has set me up with speech pathologists already. She has an upbeat attitude. "The glass missed all the important veins!" she said. "The carotids and the jugular, so, you're extremely lucky."

I'm a lucky duck.

I was lucky that night I got choked and cut in the throat. Lucky to have that high-necked dress on, yes indeed. Lucky about that silver necklace, the jagged break in the bottle. They found shards of it everywhere— in the kitchen, on Milo's shoes, stuck to my dress. But the neck of it and the shoulders, the part that stabbed me, was crushed too completely for any fingerprints, ground to bits on the kitchen floor.

Hallie's laugh peals out and up to my window. Hearing it, watching her skip, you'd never know her family was a shambles. But in the night she cries. She has been waking up and calling for me, for her daddy. I rest in the day and save my breath for Hallie, all my words made of air.

Last night in the dark I went to her. She couldn't see my scars in the dark, couldn't see my eyes, couldn't see what a sliding, raw, cracked egg of a mother she has.

Mommy! she said, holding on.

Hallie girl. I couldn't sing but I could make my breath say words.

She was shaking. She held on to me crying.

Everything will be all right, I whispered, desperate. *You'll see. I prom-ise.* I would promise anything, moons and planets, stars for her. *A fishy in a little dish.* I said it with just the barest husk of sound. And she knew. What I meant. What I was saying.

Daddy, she said.

Yes, I told her. *It will be all right.* How could I not say that? I had to.

Milo's letter rests in my lap, weightless as fire, burning holes of questions right down through my skin. *Dear Charlotte.* I am holding still. A bird's caw startles me so I jump. I don't feel safe. There is nowhere to go to be safe. I lift my hand to my throat and feel it. I am ugly.

People tell me to let it go, as if it were just a decision about whether to put your sick old dog to sleep. My mother, Claire, my sister, they say: *Put that night behind you, it's in the past. Heal up by moving on. It's over.* That's not possible or even true. It's still happening, and will be happening now forever. Trauma gets passed down through families along with the silver and the china, heirloom trauma, just as the mauling of her mother and the jailing of her father are being passed down to Hallie right now.

It's important for her to feel safe, for her routines to continue, the doctors all say. *You must be strong for her sake. And of course, as she's ready, you must tell her as much of the truth as she needs to know.*

But how will I tell her this truth, if I don't know it myself?

I need to know for myself.

What I remember and don't remember is now druggily mixed up with what I've been told. What I feel, what I know, what I wish, what really happened, are all hopelessly pickled in my thinking. You can try to be truthful. Good luck. Anyone who's ever been photographed knows you can't fix reality. A photograph is just a version of truth, just some photographer's version. You see what you want to see.

For me, truth has always been in the eye of the beholder.

Milo, though, says it's in the eye of the beheld.

I have read his letter so many times now.

Dear Charlotte,

I would not hurt you. I would not do this. You have to believe me. Please come here. If there were some other way to convey what is in my heart to say to you, I would do it. But a letter is not adequate. They tell me you cannot speak on the phone. If you will come here you will know. You will see the truth. I know you will. You have to. Please. It's all I ask, that you look me in the eye.

Love, Milo

I don't know. I don't know if I can see him.

What I wish is that we were blind. I wish I was. This is a child's wish, but still. I'd rather it had been my eyes poked out. I don't want to see his orange prison jumpsuit. I don't want to see any shackles or locks, barbed wire or bars. I don't want to see his eyes fill up with tears. Or not. And I do not want him to see me, with red snakes of scars around my neck and arms. I don't want him to see I am not what I once was, or was made out to be. Not kissed by the sun, as they wrote about me once.

I'm frightened to see him.

Frightened I'll fall for him all over again.

And where will I be then?

Behind a glass wall. I have seen these in the movies, a glass wall with phones attached, for speaking to your loved one when you are separated by the law. *Hello, Charlotte,* he will say. I will not be able to speak, but will put my hand up to the glass, and he will put his hand up, matching palms misting on the glass.

For your own protection, they will tell me.

Why, then, knowing he is there, do I not feel safe?

Even here I do not feel safe. I feel exposed as bone in a wound. I am here in my house with doctors and I do not feel well; I am here with servants and I do not feel rich; I am here with the glittering blue sea below my windows, and I do not feel surrounded by beauty. Only by longing, longing, longing. For something to lift us right up out of here, an eagle ride like the ones I imagined in church with my sister and brothers, singing out in our pressed clothes and white ribbons, *He will raise you up on eagle's wings, hold you in the palm of his hand;* knowing all the words and the rules; having them be true and right. *We shall not all sleep, but we shall all be changed in a moment, in the twinkling of an eye.*

If only we could be saved like that, in a twinkling, with the trumpets and the band playing, the tickets free, the wand waving and the flags fluttering; all the colors new.

But we can't. That's not how it happens.

So I will go see him. I have to. I've decided now. It's up to me. Whatever happens, *him* or *not him,* to tell Hallie as much of the truth as she needs to know, to find it for her. Just to find out. So I will get up out of this chair. I will brush my hair and put on earrings. I will go see Milo.

The truth will set me free, as they used to teach in Sunday school.

If you come here you will know. It's all I ask, that you look me in the eye. So I will. Right in the eye. What I find there, lies or my own reflection, will finish us off or set us free. When I see him then I'll know. The true truth. It's in the eye of the beheld. What happens is up to me. *Him,* or *please, not him.* It's in the palm of my hand. I'm holding it there, a wish like a bird, a dove or an eagle, a prayer for a phoenix flying; for a girl, running across the grass, twirling in the sun; for me singing to her at nightfall; for her father hurtling down the mountain, racing across the snow and the ice and the danger toward home, where he will come through the door beaming, his eyes lit by the sight of me, and scoop us up, our arms ringing around, all of us whirling and hurtling onward, me and Milo and our children, on and on, forever and ever. Amen.

Acknowledgments

First grateful thanks must go to Roberta Baker and Amy Wilentz, for their many wise and patient readings of these pages. Others whose insight, encouragement and experiences have helped me are Benita Watford and Bob Raleigh, Khairah Klein, Diane McWhorter, Bobbie Smith, Barbara Jones, and Sally Cook. For excellent baby-sitting I am beholden to Teresa Mason, Victoria Pisos, and Rita Grant. For their expertise, I am grateful to Tia Powell, Jim Wilentz, Dr. James Thomas, Camilo Vergara, and Robert Lipsyte. The books that helped me are too numerous to mention, but I am especially grateful for *Black on White*, edited by David Roediger, *Beyond the Whiteness of Whiteness*, by Jane Lazarre, *Thirteen Ways of Looking at a Black Man*, by Henry Louis Gates, Jr., and a book about the US Ski Team, *Right on the Edge of Crazy*, by Mike Wilson. Many many thanks to my amazing agent Wendy Weil. My patient, exacting editors, Susan Kamil and Carla Riccio, have my respect and heartfelt gratitude. For my beloved parents, Joan and Jim Manning, thank you is all but inadequate, having to cover as it does my lifetime of love and gratitude to both, for everything. To Jim and Rob, Melissa and Kim, Wendy and Mike, Pat and Rich, my appreciation for all your support. And finally, endless thanks and love to my children, Carey, Oliver, and Eliza, and especially to my husband, Carey, for sustaining me.

About the Author

KATE MANNING is a former journalist and television producer. She lives in New York City.